An excerpt from *Falling for the Enemy* by Katherine Garbera

"There is so much I've missed..."

"What if I helped you out?" Kit suggested.

"With driving?" Rory asked, because it was the safest thing to suggest.

"And other things," he said. "I have to be honest with you. I want you."

He wanted her.

She swallowed and felt her eyes widen and then realized that she had no idea what to do next. "I...I..."

"You don't have to say anything. Do you want to spend more time with me?"

She nodded.

"Do I make you nervous?"

She shook her head. "You should. You're a stranger and a man... I am not sure why you don't."

"Well, I'm glad to hear that. What if we date? We can take things at your pace. I'll teach you to drive and whatever else you have on your list," he suggested. His voice was that low rumbly tone...and it made her feel like she was back in his arms.

An excerpt from *Stranded with the Runaway Bride* by Yvonne Lindsay

"You have to admit, you weren't the most welcoming..."

"Well, it's not every recluse's dream to have a mud-spattered and soaking-wet bride arrive on his doorstep."

Georgia sighed, making Sawyer regret his choice of words.

"But," he continued. "It hasn't turned out too badly, right?"

"No, it hasn't—so far."

That twinkle in her eyes was back and he felt something lighten in his chest.

All the way along the trail, Sawyer felt as though there was an itch deep inside him. Something he couldn't quite put a finger on. He knew it had to do with Georgia, and it wasn't until they reached the cabin and she bent to unlace her boots that he realized what it was.

Lust. Good, honest, pure lust. He hadn't wanted anything like he wanted her right now.

She was one hell of a woman...and he wanted to unwrap her like a gift.

KATHERINE GARBERA
&
YVONNE LINDSAY

FALLING FOR THE ENEMY
&
STRANDED WITH THE
RUNAWAY BRIDE

HARLEQUIN
DESIRE

Recycling programs
for this product may
not exist in your area.

ISBN-13: 978-1-335-45792-9

Falling for the Enemy & Stranded with the Runaway Bride

Copyright © 2023 by Harlequin Enterprises ULC

Falling for the Enemy
Copyright © 2023 by Katherine Garbera

Stranded with the Runaway Bride
Copyright © 2023 by Dolce Vita Trust

For questions and comments about the quality of this book, please contact us at CustomerService@Harlequin.com.

Harlequin Enterprises ULC
22 Adelaide St. West, 41st Floor
Toronto, Ontario M5H 4E3, Canada
www.Harlequin.com

Printed in U.S.A.

CONTENTS

FALLING FOR THE ENEMY 9
Katherine Garbera

STRANDED WITH THE RUNAWAY BRIDE 233
Yvonne Lindsay

Katherine Garbera is the *USA TODAY* bestselling author of more than 120 books. She lives in the Midlands of the UK with her husband, but in her heart she'll always be a Florida girl who loves sunshine and beaches. Her books are known for their sizzling sensuality and emotional punch. Visit her on the web at katherinegarbera.com and on Instagram, Twitter and Facebook.

Books by Katherine Garbera

Harlequin Desire

The Gilbert Curse

One Night Wager
It's Only Fake 'Til Midnight
Falling for the Enemy

Texas Cattleman's Club: Diamonds & Dating Apps

Matched by Mistake

The Image Project

Billionaire Makeover
The Billionaire Plan
Billionaire Fake Out

Visit the Author Profile page
at Harlequin.com for more titles.

You can also find Katherine Garbera on Facebook, along with other Harlequin Desire authors, at Facebook.com/HarlequinDesireAuthors!

Dear Reader,

It's bittersweet to be writing this particular letter to you. This is the last Harlequin Desire novel that I will be writing and the last book in the Gilbert Curse series. Some of the very first books I read as a thirteen-year-old were Harlequin Desire novels by Elizabeth Lowell, Joan Hohl, Stephanie James, Joan Johnston and Peggy Moreland. I loved this line from the moment I picked up my first one in the used bookstore.

I was addicted to the strong heroes and the feisty heroines who were more than their match. Their love stories were so deeply emotional and shaped in me the kind of relationship I wanted as an adult. I was never willing to settle for a man who couldn't be everything that those heroes had been. Loving, supportive, sexy and willing to bend and meet the heroines halfway.

I am so happy that I've been able to write seventy titles for Harlequin Desire and I loved every one of them. Thank you so much for reading my books and enabling me to keep telling stories that embodied so much of what I learned to love about romance as a teenager.

I'm pretty excited that Rory Gilbert's story is my last one. She was such a fun heroine to write. My first attempt at a *Sleeping Beauty*–inspired story. I love how fierce and brave she is and wish I could face the world with that kind of courage every day—I do sometimes, but not always.

Kit was great too. A man conflicted by his past and what he's always been told and truly believes and this woman who has knocked him off-kilter.

Thank you for reading the Gilbert Curse series and all of my series since my first book, *The Bachelor Next Door*. I have truly loved sharing this ride with you.

Happy reading,

Katherine

FALLING FOR THE ENEMY

Katherine Garbera

To my Harlequin Desire friends who have made the journey so much fun, especially Karen Booth, Joanne Rock, Joss Wood and Reese Ryan. Our monthly chats are the best and I'm lucky to call you all my friends.

To all of the authors who wrote for Harlequin Desire—for the great reads, inspiring characters and stories that lingered long after I closed the books.

One

The Gilbert sister was the key.

Somehow when Kit Palmer referred to his teenage crush, the woman whose life had been ruined by his older brother and a family grudge, it was easier to pretend she was a stranger. Like there was distance between them despite their tragic connections.

If he was brutally honest with himself, he knew that there was no putting distance between Aurora Gilbert and himself. When she, her brother and her cousin moved to Gilbert Manor and he saw her for the first time, he'd fallen.

Hard.

It hadn't mattered to his eight-year-old self that he and his family lived in the old factory houses on the outskirts of Gilbert Corners or that his father was the shift manager at the old factory. As a child he hadn't seen that they were in any way different, and at that summer party where all the kids from Gilbert Manufacturing families played together, he'd found himself alone with Rory for the first time.

She'd been brave and fearless, and when the older kids, including his brother, had walked across the river that surrounded Gilbert Manor and flowed through the town, Kit had hesitated. He didn't know how to swim and didn't want to be left behind but… Rory had held out her hand to him. Taken his palm in hers and said, "We can do this together."

And they had. And in that moment, his life had changed.

Which was why he was referring to her as Dash's sister and not his childhood heroine. She was the key to reckoning with his past. As long as she was a Gilbert, nothing else could matter.

Kit's family hadn't stayed in the factory houses for long. His father and his brother were ambitious and started moving up in Gilbert Manufacturing, until old Lance Gilbert promised Kit's brother, Declan Orr, the position of CEO of Gilbert Manufacturing. Finally, they had arrived and would be a force to be reckoned with in Gilbert Corners.

But the car crash had changed all of that. The factory had closed down, and in his grief his father had bought up shares in Gilbert Manufacturing, mortgaging their house and selling assets to take over the company and the position that had been promised to Declan. Something that Dash Gilbert had gotten wind of and had used to lure his father deeper into debt until all that was left of their assets was the deed to that crappy, run-down factory-provided duplex.

Now as he sat in front of the house that held too many mixed memories, watching as his new neighbor Rory Gilbert moved in, he couldn't help but think that he might finally have everything he needed to destroy Dash Gilbert, cure the bad karma that the Gilberts had passed on to his family and at long last get over the woman who was at the heart of his plan.

There was a rap on his car window and he turned, surprised to see Rory Gilbert standing there. Her hair had darkened over the years from that white blond she'd had as a child to a dark honey-blond. She had a heart-shaped face and pretty blue eyes. Her mouth was full, her nose delicate and she quirked her head to the side as she waited for him to open the window. He turned off the car and got out.

"Can I help you?"

"Yes, that's what I hired you for," she said.

Hired him. "I think you've got the wrong guy. I'm not a mover."

"Oh, I know that," she murmured. Her voice was as he remembered, light and lilting, sweetly melodic. "But you are here for the thing that I hired you for, right?"

He had absolutely no idea what she was talking about, but before he could tell her so, her brother, Dash, walked out of the house with a sour look on his face.

Rory looped her arm through his. "Just pretend we're old friends and don't mention what you are really doing here. I hate lies but I can't take another minute of having my older brother and cousin telling me I am too fragile to do anything."

Her touch on his arm was electric and sent through him a pulse of awareness that he tamped down. He had no idea what Rory was up to, but if it meant irritating Dash then Kit was all in.

"Sure. My name is Kit, by the way."

"Kit. Great. Just follow my lead," she said.

He intended to do just that. He had been trying for years to come up with a plan to find something to use as leverage against Dash Gilbert, and he had known in his gut that the sister was the perfect ammunition, but nothing had come of it. Rory had been in a coma, and after his engagement had been broken almost eight years earlier, Dash had become a recluse.

"Dash, you heading off?"

"Not yet. Who's this?"

"This is one of my old friends, Kit," she told him. "Kit, this overbearing dude is my brother, Dash."

Kit hadn't met Dash Gilbert before. He'd been eighteen on the night of the ball that had culminated in the car crash that had taken his brother's life. He held his hand out to the man that Kit had wanted to destroy for the last ten years. However, when their eyes met, instead of the pure evil he'd expected to find, he saw an easy smile and a semi-exasperated look.

"I'm not overbearing," Dash said. "Well, not too much. This one thinks that six months from waking up from a coma she can climb Everest."

"Not Everest yet," Rory replied.

"Then what?"

"Well, I'd settle for being on my own and trying all the things I missed in the last ten years."

Dash stiffened. "I agreed to you living here but the other stuff—"

"Too late," Rory said. "That's why Kit's here."

"Why *am* I here?"

"To help me experience all the things I missed in the last ten years," Rory explained.

"The hell he is," Dash said.

Rory wasn't going to argue with her brother in front of Kit. He wasn't at all what she was expecting but she'd hired him from a website that had offered discreet help for anyone experiencing extreme anxiety or problems leaving their home. Everything from the everyday stress of ordering a coffee to sex. Rory wasn't sure what she'd need, so had checked all the boxes. Frankly, after ten years in a coma, there was so much she didn't know. Like, did Lizzie and Gordo stay together? But also stuff like social media. The solutions, according to what she'd read, were designed to push her out of her comfort zone.

And she needed that.

As much as she'd been saying she wanted Dash and her cousin Conrad—who was like another older brother—to stop treating her like she was made of spun glass, a part of her had no idea how to do it.

Ten years in a coma had been hard to recover from. Physically, she was still stretching her limits and trying to regain her strength. If she overdid it and was on her feet for too long she had to use a cane. But those physical limitations were somehow easier than the mental ones. Rory had found it too easy to stay holed away in her suite of rooms at Gilbert Manor, with the staff eager to cater to her every need. She had started to really live in what she couldn't help but think of as her cushy tower. And, in many ways, she knew that she'd let herself fall into a second coma of sorts.

But *no more*. She'd used some of her inheritance to buy this half of the duplex and was determined to fix it up and make it into something that was hers. And as part of her grand plan, she'd hired Kit. But he was a bit more handsome than she'd been expecting. Okay, more than a bit. He had dark black hair that he wore short and spiky on top, and he had a light dusting of stubble that made him look stern until he smiled. A sigh escaped her as she continued to drink him in. He had a full, firm-looking mouth, which indicated that kissing him wasn't going to be a problem.

In fact, she couldn't help wondering what his mouth would feel like on hers, which stirred feelings that a twenty-eight-year-old woman should be able to handle. But while that might be her actual age, mentally she still felt like she was eighteen. Rory hadn't been sexually active before the accident, so she had a lot to catch up on.

So she'd hired Kit.

He was going to teach her everything she needed

to know about modern dating and help her get over her fears of being touched. He was going to just help her do those things she was afraid of doing. Like going into Lulu's crowded coffee shop and ordering a coffee. Or going into the city to eat at Conrad's exclusive kitchen.

She'd tried to do it on her own, and knowing she'd see her cousin had gotten her out the door. But then she'd frozen. Part of it was the walking stick she still had to use. It was hard not to feel like everyone was staring at her. Which in Gilbert Corners was a very real fear since she was a Gilbert and everyone was aware she'd been in a coma for ten years.

She knew that fear had dominated her for too long, so when Dash made it clear he did not approve of her plans with Kit, Rory felt her hackles go up.

Pulling her arm from Kit's, she squared her shoulders and faced off with her brother. "Dash, I know, in your eyes, I'm still that little sister who was sleeping for too long. So I get that you want to protect me, but you are slowly smothering me. I need someone who will help me embrace all of the things that I'm a little bit scared to try but that I know I have to do."

"And you think this guy is the one?" Dash asked stiffly.

"I do," Rory assured him. "He's not a stranger. As I said, we're friends."

She glanced back at Kit. His mouth was a firm line and when their eyes met for a moment, she wasn't sure what she read in his gaze. But then he gave her a nod and a wink.

He turned to her brother. "I give you my word that I will not let any harm come to her," he promised.

"That's not necessary," Rory said. If she'd learned anything from Elle and Indy, her soon-to-be sister/cousin-in-law, it was that women didn't need a man to back them up. Rory was doing this for *herself.* That said, it was nice to have Kit along for those panicked moments she knew would come. Case in point…she'd already had an anxiety attack as she'd entered the house that she planned to make over.

As a coping mechanism, she'd stood there, doing box breathing and then singing that one song that always cheered her up. "Island in the Sun" by Weezer. She'd just sung it over and over until she'd heard the moving truck outside. Then she shoved her anxiety into a box, like her therapist had said to, flashed a smile and met the movers.

She hoped that doing stuff with Kit, living in this house on her own, finding her voice and strength again would slowly start to feel normal. That maybe she'd be able to face her fears and not worry about crying or shaking or having to sing "Island in the Sun" over and over again.

"Fine. But I'll be keeping tabs on both of you," Dash warned. "And, Kit, I'll need your full name."

"No, you won't!" Rory protested. "He has nothing to do with you."

Dash gave Kit a tight smile as he took Rory's arm in a firm but gentle grip. "Will you excuse us for a moment?"

He didn't wait for Kit to answer but just led Rory out of Kit's earshot. "You're a Gilbert and a very wealthy woman," he whispered. "It's irresponsible for you to spend time with someone we don't know. Just let me have him checked out."

"No. Dash, I mean it. You know I wanted to move across the country so I'd be forced to stand on my own. However, I stayed here in Gilbert Corners because I love you and I want us to be the family I remember. But you have to let me do this my way."

It would be easy to give in to Dash's demands and stay locked up inside Gilbert Manor for the rest of her life. She'd have a nice, safe life, one where everyone took care of her, but Rory was beginning to realize she wanted more.

When she'd first awoken from her coma, she'd felt eighteen, scared and unsure. But over the last few months, she'd started to realize she wanted to be a twenty-eight-year-old woman. Not that frightened, protected girl.

"I hate this," Dash bit out.

She hugged her older brother, knowing that as much as he might not want to let her do this on her own, he was going to.

"Thank you."

He just sort of grunted and hugged her back, and when he walked away, past Kit, he said something to the other man that Rory couldn't hear. Then he got into his car and drove away.

And she was left with this stranger whom she was counting on to help her find herself.

* * *

Kit smiled at Rory as her brother walked past him, pausing to warn Kit that if he hurt Rory he'd come after him, and then left.

Now what? He had no idea what exactly the person that Rory had hired was meant to do, and as much as he had wanted to use her to ruin Dash, it felt wrong now. Rory's smile sort of melted away as soon as her brother was gone and he heard her muttering what sounded like a Weezer song under her breath. And in that moment, he realized that using Rory wasn't going to be something he could do.

For one thing, despite the bad history between their families, he still liked her. For a second, he wanted to help her rebuild her strength and transform back into that brave, fearless girl she'd once been…

Kit blew out a frustrated breath. It seemed like every time he was ready to wreak vengeance down on the Gilberts for what they'd done, there was some sort of universal intervention showing him that they had already wrecked themselves.

"Hey, it's okay," he said, walking over to her. She had one arm wrapped around her own waist, and the song sounded almost manic at the speed she was singing it at.

He put his arm around her, slowly recognizing that she was having an anxiety attack, having seen his own mother in a similar state more than once. Rory didn't seem to feel his touch and he pulled her close into the curve of his body. She closed her eyes and he drew her even tighter against him, ignoring his own reaction to her nearness. He started talking in a low, calm tone.

"We are on a tropical island, the sand under our feet is powdery soft and so white it almost seems like no one else has ever habited this place before. The sun on our skin is warm and soothing, not too hot. Your hand is in mine and when you look up, you see the blue waves washing gently on the shore. The breeze wraps around us, and as you exhale in one long breath, the stress gradually seeps away."

He stopped talking as her breathing started to slow and she stopped singing. He wasn't sure if she still needed him to talk her through this or not.

But she lifted her head and opened her eyes. Her blue eyes were bright and clear, but in his mind he knew they still had clouds in them. He had thought she was the key to Dash's undoing but she might be the key for him, the key to closure on the past and the anger and revenge he'd always wanted but had never been able to commit to.

He knew revenge was what his family needed and he'd always been the soft brother. The one who'd been more like their mom. Losing his brother and then watching his father's slow descent into alcoholism had changed Kit. Or had forced him to stop being the son that had never measured up in his father's eyes.

He just wasn't the type of man his father and brother had been. He had legally changed his name after Dash had ruined them and he'd chosen Palmer.

He couldn't use someone else to get what he wanted; he knew that now.

"You okay?" he asked quietly.

"No, but I'm *better*. Thank you," she whispered. "I don't know if this is what you signed up for, but I have a feeling there are going to be a lot more moments like it."

"That's fine," he assured her. "But I have to tell you, I'm not the person you hired."

Her eyes widened. "You're not?"

"No. But I think we can help each other, which is why I showed up here today," he said. Throwing out revenge meant nothing if he continued to lie to her. He couldn't let her think she'd hired him. That was deceit at its worst.

"Well...the person I hired was a stranger, which I thought would make it easier than someone who knows me and my entire family history."

"I can see why you'd want that." His conscience pricked at him, but he decided not to reveal that they'd known each other in the past, or that his brother had been involved in the car crash that had put her into a coma. If he did, he knew she'd shut him out. Rightly so? He had no idea.

"The movers are almost done here and I am supposed to be trying to leave the house more," she said, then hesitated, suddenly looking very nervous.

"Why don't we go to Java and get a coffee and talk?" she asked, the words running together in a rush. "But... Hang on a second. If you aren't the guy I hired, why *are* you here?"

"I am moving into the cottage next to yours," he said. Which was the partial truth. He had planned to move back into his childhood home. The home that had symbolized the last time he'd been happy. He might have had ulterior motives for returning to it, but now that he'd crossed paths with Rory Gilbert again, he knew that his plans were changing and he hoped that he'd be able to figure out what was next.

"You are? Well, then, we're neighbors. That's good," she said, scrunching her forehead in thought. "So... coffee?"

"Yes, we can have coffee if you like. What did you mean by you're *supposed* to go out?"

"I... I was in a coma for ten years—so tragic, right?" She tried to laugh it off, but her discomfort was obvious. "Anyway, I've been out of it for six months but have found myself unable to actually start living again. I mean at first I needed to recover my strength physically, but as you just saw... I'm not at my best," she said.

"I saw nothing of the sort. You handled yourself beautifully, standing up to your brother and championing your cause. Then when it was over you just needed some recovery time."

She let out a long, slow breath and nodded over at him, the smallest smile playing around her full mouth.

"I think I'm going to like having you as a neighbor, Kit," she said.

"I think I will like being neighbors, too."

They agreed to meet at two that afternoon for coffee, and as he watched her walk back to the movers, an uneasy feeling settled in his chest. He knew that he was going to have to tell her who he was, but at this point in time, he knew it wouldn't help her. Of course, it wouldn't help him either.

Two

Indy Belmont was Rory's soon to be cousin-in-law. But she was also instrumental in revitalizing Gilbert Corners. She'd moved to this town about two years ago and brought her popular show *Hometown, Home Again*, which aired on the Home Living TV network, here to film. She'd started with Indy's Treasures, her bookshop on Main Street, and had slowly been working to get other projects off the ground.

When Rory had decided she had to leave Gilbert Manor, Indy and Elle had been her biggest supporters. And it had been Indy who had suggested possibly buying one of the Victorian-era duplexes and redoing it to help Rory adjust to being back in the world.

So, because she had a lot of love and respect for Indy, as soon as the movers left and she was alone in her new home, she was tempted to call her. She needed advice about Kit.

Kit.

He had the dreamiest brown eyes and she couldn't stop fantasizing about how his thick dark hair would feel beneath her fingers. She remembered when he'd wrapped his arms around her and helped calm her down with the soothing, deep timbre of his voice. His body had felt solid against hers…and she hadn't panicked.

She'd been so afraid she would when a man held her because the last memory she had of the night of the car crash was being forcibly kissed and held against the wall by Declan Orr, the man who had died in the car crash that had left her in a coma.

But in Kit's arms she hadn't felt scared. Maybe it had been his voice or the woodsy scent of his aftershave. Or perhaps it was the solid beating of his heart, which she had heard under her cheek. Whatever the reason…she couldn't stop thinking about him.

She was a bit bummed that he wasn't from the agency she'd hired, because the person they were sending was supposed to help her figure out how to kiss and have sex. All of her knowledge of that stuff had been a few brief make-out sessions in high school and then that one sexual attack that had scared her.

What was she going to do? Maybe this entire plan to meet Kit for coffee and talk to him again was a mistake.

But Elle, who was also her doctor, had said that mistakes were bound to happen. And that Rory would learn from them and become stronger by making them. Also, what was the worst that could happen?

That was what Conrad said to her every time they talked. Her cousin had been in the same car accident as Rory, and recovered, though it had left him badly scarred. He had confessed that it had taken him years to feel anything close to normal and he liked to do things that scared him. His advice to her was to go for anything that wouldn't land her back in the hospital.

So, what was the worst that could happen if she met Kit?

He might not show up. Fair enough and that would be fine. But, on the flip side, he might come through for her and prove to be that kind of man who could be an ally. Also fine.

And if he *did* show up, they might hit it off and then she'd want to kiss him and… Her mind whirled with the possibilities. She'd be in his arms again and this time their lips would meet. And that would be more than fine. She figured she had to have a first *real* kiss… Why not Kit?

Though he might not want to be her first-time guy.

It would not be the end of the world if that happened, but she wondered if she'd have the courage to ask someone else. But she was also supposed to be doing things that scared her, so in this case she was going to do it.

Rory got dressed, taking her time. She had a long,

jagged scar on her leg. Things were different now, and she was trying to come to terms with the body she'd woken up in. So of course the scars were to be expected. But they just made her feel less like herself. The Rory she remembered had long, slim legs. These were flabby with cellulite on her thighs that Indy had reassured her everyone had.

Rory stood in front of the mirror in the wrap dress with the skirt that ended at the top of her knees. She saw the imperfections but shook her head, pushing those thoughts firmly out of her mind. She couldn't hate the flaws, because they made her who she was, and if Kit did…then he wasn't the man she was hoping he'd be.

She grabbed her purse, put on her sunglasses and blew herself a kiss in the mirror before opening the front door and stepping outside.

This was it. Her new life started today and she was going to seize every opportunity that came to her.

No more hiding in her bed and being afraid of the outside world.

Kit slid his car into a spot in the public parking lot near the park that was across the street from the train station. Behind the park were the shops on Main Street. He had contemplated not coming to meet Rory. But the truth was he *had* to.

Whatever fantasy he'd entertained about her over the years had paled compared to what he felt when he'd held her. It was sexual, but more than that. He'd never allowed himself to think of the future or to really have a permanent relationship with anyone because he'd been so focused on vengeance. But one moment with Rory and now he was questioning it? Was it just the remembered childhood feelings of friendship or something more?

He couldn't deny he was excited just being with her. His phone pinged and he glanced down to see it was a text from his aunt Mal. Mal was his father's sister. The two of them were all that was left of the family and they had been working together to restore their fortunes—which they had—even though Dash Gilbert hadn't left them much to rebuild with.

Did you find the sister?

Kit thumbs-upped her question. He wasn't sure what else to say. He really didn't have any news for her. And he certainly wasn't going to text Aunt Mal that he'd changed his mind about using Rory. He sucked in a breath. And was he even sure that he had?

Yes.

Kit and Aunt Mal had reformed the company using his middle name Palmer into Palmer Industries and they were thriving. It was only as Gilbert Corners was being revitalized and new industry was coming back to the town that he and his aunt had thought about what the Gilbert family had taken from them once again. They were interested in buying into the old factory that Declan had been meant to run before his death, and wanted to put in their own manufacturing plant there.

But they both knew that they were going to have to be careful about how they approached the deal. Hence him coming to town to figure out how to get some leverage with Dash Gilbert.

His aunt texted again.

Call me when you're leaving GC.

He replied: I might be a while. I'm having a look around town for potential investment properties.

The girl won't work?

Not sure yet.

Aunt Mal ended the conversation with Talk later. He pocketed his phone. Mal was his last living blood relative. Although he had distant cousins, he wasn't close to any of them. He and Mal had had each other's back for longer than Kit could remember. As much as he wanted to think that he could figure out something that would benefit both him and his aunt, while hurting the Gilbert family in the process, nothing in his past dealings with them had proven fruitful to that end.

He knew that part of his reluctance to involve Rory in his plans was that he didn't want to use Rory the way that the Gilbert family had used his brother. Yet wouldn't that be the perfect revenge?

Sitting in his car, waiting and watching the town that was somehow cheerier than he could remember from his childhood, just served to remind him of all that he had lost. Sure, Rory hadn't really been responsible for those actions, but she was a part of the family. She had, according to his father, led his brother on and then accused him of misreading her advances and had him thrown out of the party after Conrad had punched him.

Kit shook his head. When he'd seen her earlier, he'd been catapulted back to his childhood and the innocent girl Rory had been before she'd grown into a Gilbert woman. He had to remember that.

He saw her walking toward the coffee shop with her cane and got out of his car. His breath caught in his chest as her long blond hair, stirred by the wind, flew around her face and shoulders. She tipped her head back toward the breeze, a smile playing around her lips. As he glanced at the scoop-necked dress she wore and noticed the gentle curves of her breasts, he remembered how she'd felt in his arms.

Now that she wasn't in distress, he recalled how perfectly she'd fit against him. Her head on his chest and her arms wound tight around him. He remembered the floral scent of her hair and the way she'd exhaled softly, the warmth of her breath brushing against his neck and stirring him.

He wanted her.

She was his enemy's sister.

She was also his long-lost crush.

Kit shoved a hand through his hair and exhaled a frustrated breath. She was *complicated* and, honestly, he knew the smart thing to do would be to turn around and leave and let Aunt Mal come back and figure out a way to use her to get to Dash.

But she noticed him, lifted her hand and waved at him, and it was too late to resort to plan B. So instead, he found himself locking his car and heading across the green, well-manicured park toward her. As he got closer, he realized that everyone was watching her and then began noticing her watching him.

Rory had said she was trying to find her way back to living outside the mansion and he could see the struggle it would be for her. Again he wanted to help her. Wanted to be the hero that she'd been to him when they'd been children. But could he really be that for her, and was she truly deserving of it?

He sighed. All he knew for sure was that he had to come clean and tell her his name. He didn't want to deceive her the way her family had his brother. He needed to know that when he and Aunt Mal were finally in a position of power over the Gilbert family, they could be satisfied that they had done it aboveboard.

Which meant no sneaking and deceiving the way that Lance Gilbert had been with them. And while he suspected that earlier he might have been swayed by lust and nostalgia, he couldn't afford to be now. It was time to remember who was responsible for all of the destruction that had happened the night of the ball.

Kit smiled at her as he got closer. "If I knew you were walking to town, I would have joined you."

Yeah, so now she had to tell him she didn't drive.

But she could be vague as to the reason why. She didn't have to say that she still freaked out a bit every time she was in a car. That being around people made her uneasy.

On the other hand, the ability to be outside and walk was something… *Magical* wasn't quite the right word because she'd worked damned hard at physical therapy to get to this point, but it did feel special to be able to walk.

She sort of smiled and then realized that Kit was awaiting her response.

"Oh, that's okay. I don't drive yet," she said.

"You don't?"

"Yeah, you know I was in a coma forever."

"I guess I'd forgotten that," he said with a sheepish look that was way too charming. In high school she would have flirted back but it had been ten years since she'd talked to a man who wasn't related to her or a medical professional, and she was so rusty.

"So outside or inside?" he asked.

"I'd prefer to be outside if you don't mind…"

"I don't. Why don't you grab a table and I'll go and get our drinks?" he suggested.

She asked him to get her an iced coffee of the day. And then went to find a table away from the others in the shade. As she sat down, her phone buzzed and she took it out. It was in her group chat with Indy and Rory. Indy had a good view of the coffee shop from her bookstore.

Indy: Who's the hottie?

Rory: Kit. He's my new neighbor.

Elle: I've got a patient in five. But I want all the details. Drinks at Indy's shop tonight?

Rory thumbs-upped the message and then put her phone away. She didn't have any good girl friends that she remembered from before the accident, and Indy and Elle had welcomed her as if she were their sister. The more her memories had returned, the more she realized that she hadn't had any friends in the town of Gilbert Corners. That her grandfather had deliberately kept her and Dash and Conrad apart from the townspeople.

She didn't like the fact that she'd been so easily led by his selfish desires. But she did remember that they had all been a little bit afraid of him.

"The coffee of the day was a strawberry white mocha," he said.

"Great. I haven't tried that before. But Lulu hired a new barista who has been experimenting and I haven't been disappointed yet."

He flashed a grin. "Good to hear. I followed your lead and got the same."

They both took a sip. Rory closed her eyes as the icy, sweet and fruity coffee slid over her tongue. She liked it. It was cold and delicious; she took another sip of it before opening her eyes to find Kit staring at her.

Oh.

The look in his eyes was intense and unlike anything she'd noticed before. His lips were parted and his pupils dilated, and there was a slight flush to his skin.

"Do you like it?"

"Mmm-hmm," he said. "So tell me about the person you thought I was."

"Yeah, about that. It turns out that the person canceled but I hadn't received the message. I'm sorry for putting you on the spot like that."

"I didn't mind," he said, taking another sip. "But you haven't said what you hired them for."

She turned the paper straw in her cup, staring down at her drink instead of at Kit. "I hired someone to help me get caught up on…um…life."

He leaned back in his chair and crossed his arms over his chest, drawing the fabric of his black button-down shirt taut across his chest. She stared at the muscles, which she could see for longer than she knew she should. "Like what?"

Kissing, she thought. She wanted to kiss him but she knew she'd be awkward at it and she guessed he probably wasn't going to be up for her fumbling around and figuring that out.

"Driving?" he asked when she didn't say anything.

"Yes and other things," she said. "Pretty much everything. I was eighteen when I went into the coma, so a lot of stuff that I should have picked up in the last ten years I didn't. I just don't want to wait for life to start. I need a jump start and I thought hiring someone to help would be the answer."

"But they backed out?"

"Yes. Or Dash found out and fired them," she said,

her lips twitching. "He didn't think it was a good idea. That's why I said you were a friend."

"Well, if it helps, I did meet you when we were kids briefly."

"Did you?"

"Yes, at a summer party at Gilbert Manor."

"I can't recall too many details of the past, but I do remember the parties were always fun in the summer," she said. How dumb was that, right! She couldn't help feeling frustrated by the fact that she couldn't remember a party that her family threw. Rory knew they'd had a bunch of them and there were photo albums in the library that showed them, but she never looked at them after she realized they weren't triggering any memories.

"They were," he said, reaching out and brushing his finger against the back of her hand where it lay curled on the table. "What else do you need to learn?"

Fear was right there waiting to wrap itself around her and make her retreat, but instead she turned her hand under Kit's, slid her fingers through his and a shiver went through her entire body. "Everything."

He leaned in closer. There was something electric in the way their eyes met. God, he was cute. She loved the dark stubble on his cheeks and his thick eyelashes. The scent of his aftershave was subtle. She took a deep breath, inhaling it all in. He rested his elbow on the table as their eyes met and something that felt almost magical seemed to pass between them. *"Everything?"*

She nodded. "There is so much I've missed."

"What if I helped you out?"

"With driving?" she asked, because it was the safest thing to suggest at this moment.

"And other things," he said, in a lower timbre. It sent a quiver throughout her entire body. Her lips felt dry and she licked them. His eyes tracked the movement of her tongue and his mouth sort of opened. Was he flirting with her?

"What kinds of other things?"

Ugh. The words just popped out and her tone... that was her flirting tone. Did she want him to flirt back with her?

"I have to be honest with you, I want you."

He *wanted* her.

She swallowed. So yes. He definitely wanted her to flirt with him, too. Her eyes widened and then she realized that she had no idea what to do next. "I... I..."

He squeezed her hand. "Do you want to spend more time with me, Rory?"

She nodded.

"Do I make you nervous?"

She shook her head. "You should. You're a stranger and a man... I am not sure why you don't."

"Well, I'm glad to hear that. What if we date? We can take things at your pace. I'll teach you to drive and whatever else you have on your list," he suggested. He spoke in that low, rumbly tone that resonated through her body and made her feel like she was back in his arms.

"Do you want to do that?" she whispered.

"One thing about me, I don't say things I don't mean."

Wow. Well, okay, then. That kind of honesty was what she was looking for. She was tired of people who were nice to her because of her condition and Kit was offering her a chance to have everything she'd been dreaming of with a real guy. Not the faceless lover who sometimes showed up in her dreams.

"Duly noted. Oh, and one thing about me? I'm trying to say yes to everything."

"So then we'll start dating, Rory Gilbert."

Dating. OMG. Was that still a thing? She didn't know, but apparently it was for her. A wave of giddiness swept through her. She was going to go out on *dates* with Kit and get to bask in his dreamy eyes, thick eyelashes and that kissable mouth of his.

"Yes, we will, Kit…" she said, then paused. "I don't know your last name."

Three

What *was* his last name? He had decided not to lie, and if he told her the truth there was a chance she wouldn't connect him with his brother. But then again, he wasn't sure. Something as small as a name could spark her memory. "Palmer. Kit Palmer," he said.

Liar.

But he still wasn't sure what part, if any, Rory had played in his brother's destruction that night.

"Palmer. I like it. So your family is from around here?" she asked.

He exhaled, releasing the tension that had been roiling through him. "We were for a bit. When the factory closed, we moved," he told her. "I was in college on the West Coast so didn't get to say goodbye."

"What did you study?"

"Business management."

She frowned.

"I'm a CEO, so it's served me well."

She shook her head and took a sip of her coffee. "It's just so *practical*."

She made it sound like it was the most boring job in the world. And honestly, she wasn't wrong. But he'd made the choice he had to in order to help his family survive. It wasn't exactly a dream job but he hadn't had her financial power to fall back on.

"Not all of us were born into the Gilbert family," he reminded her.

"Fair enough. I wasn't even thinking of that. I'm sorry," she said.

She sounded contrite and when she looked away from him, he realized he'd made her anxious again.

"What's worrying you?"

"Not trying to make excuses, but I haven't had a lot of conversations with anyone not related to me since I came out of the coma. Sorry to use that for my reason for everything but I truly didn't mean for that to come out—"

"Stop," he said, taking her hand in his and rubbing his thumb against the inside of her wrist. "It's okay. I think I'm a little bit sensitive when it comes to my past."

"You are? Why? You seem like someone who's got everything together."

"I have insecurities just like everyone else," he admitted.

She turned her hand in his, lacing her fingers

through his, and a bolt of pure desire went through him. Their hands fit so well together, almost like he knew their bodies would. He wasn't sure what he expected Dash Gilbert's sister to be like but it certainly wasn't Rory. She was charming, shy and flirty but in an understated and almost innocent way. Made sense given she'd been in a coma for ten years.

A tendril had come free and curled against her cheek. There was something about this woman that stirred him to the core. And for a moment, he forgot she was a Gilbert and just enjoyed the thrill of being turned on. He shifted his legs as he started to get hard and looked instead into her eyes.

"Of course you do," she said. "One of the things my therapist told me was that just because I felt like I'm being held together with yarn doesn't mean everyone else has a solid foundation. Sorry again."

Kit lifted her hand and brought it to his mouth because he wanted to touch her and this might be the only time he could and not want more. Brushing his lips against the back of her hand, he rasped, "Apology accepted, and going forward you have nothing more to apologize for."

She shivered a little as his lips had grazed the back of her hand and then licked her lips and gave him that innocent smile of hers. The one he was sure she had no idea affected him as deeply as it did. But he knew he had to get his head back in the game. He had to stop looking at Rory and just seeing her as a woman he wanted. He had to—what? For the first time that he could remember, he wanted someone for himself.

Wrong woman, dumbass.

"You don't have to apologize either," she said.

Kit nodded. "So your list. I have about two hours free this afternoon. Is there something small we could tackle?"

She took another sip of her iced coffee, closing her eyes as she did so. "Hmm. This drink is so good," she said before pausing, as if this was the biggest question of her life. "Not really. Today was meant to be a get-to-know-each-other day. What do you suggest? Whatever you propose, I'm pretty sure I haven't done it."

"I haven't been back here for a while. Should we walk through the shops on Main Street?"

"No. I've done that. But what if instead of the shops, we go toward the path by the river?" Her eyes lit up. "I heard there are some wild blackberries growing down there. Maybe we can pick some and I'll make you a pie."

A pie? It was the last thing he expected of an heiress. But it suited Rory. It was almost too easy to picture her picking berries and making a pie. He had to admit that was another thing that made him want to kiss her.

"All right. Have you seen any?" he asked.

"No. I haven't had anyone willing to walk down the path with me. It's sort of steep and 'rough' according to Dash, but the truth is he thinks I should be carried everywhere."

He laughed at the way she'd put air quotes around *rough*. He couldn't say no to helping her with this goal of hers, especially since it would annoy her brother. But he knew they'd have to be careful.

They finished their coffees and headed toward the river. Today it was flowing steadily, looking serene and picturesque. Now that the train station and surrounding shops had been renovated and cleaned up, the town was starting to come to life again. He noticed that a camera crew was set up across the street.

He knew from his own research that they were from the Home Living TV network. Indy Belmont—Conrad Gilbert's fiancée—was filming a makeover show where she redid buildings in this town.

The paved road ended near the bridge and then a steep path led down to a dirt walkway that ran alongside the river. He looked at the trail and then back at Rory. The last thing he wanted was for her to hurt herself. "Someone should put a handrail in here."

"I'll mention it to Dash."

"Or you could go to the town council and tell them yourself," he suggested. She was too connected to Dash and if he was going to spend time with her, he wanted to see her standing on her own.

She nodded. "You're right. I'll do it."

Rory hadn't realized how much she needed someone like Kit until he pointed out that she could go to the town council herself. She had been thinking of the actual things Dash was forbidding her to do when she'd moved out. But she hadn't really contemplated taking a starring role in her own life.

She liked the idea of it but she knew that when it

was time to show up and present her ideas, she was going to be nervous. But she didn't need to dwell on that just yet. For the moment she looked down at the slope and wondered how she was going to navigate it.

"Any suggestions for how I can do this?" she asked Kit. "My left leg is weaker than my right."

"Wait here while I see just how steep this is to walk down."

She watched with more than a little envy at the nimble way he went down the slope. He took his time, though, looking for rough patches and checking the sturdiness of the dirt path. When he got to the bottom, he took a few steps in both directions and then came back and returned to her side.

"Okay. The way down, I think you should put your hand on my shoulder and I'll lead the way. We will go slowly and you will be in charge of the pace. When we get to the bottom, the river path is level and has been edged with pavers, so it's clear someone has been maintaining that part. But getting back up might be harder."

Rory had already been thinking about that. She'd noticed the deep, almost lunge-like movement of Kit's legs as he'd come back up the path, and she wasn't sure she could do that. When she did lunges at her physical therapy sessions, she'd only managed two on each side and then her thighs started quivering.

"Do you cross that bridge when we get to it?"

"We can. But be prepared for me to do a lot more assisting. Is that something you're okay with?" he asked.

She had made so many strides in walking and getting around on her own, but she'd known from the beginning that when she tried more strenuous activities there would be times when she'd have to rely on someone else to help her.

It frustrated her because she wanted to be able to do things for herself. But she had no shame in asking for help. Conrad had been the one to make her feel normal about it. He told her that after his post-accident surgeries he'd had to ask for assistance with everything. With that one thought, her big, six-foot-five-inch, muscle-y cousin had made her realize that she was going to recover, too. But only if she asked for help and respected her limitations.

"Yes. Are *you* okay with it?" she asked. If he wasn't, then no matter how hot he was she was going to have to end this before it really had a chance to get started.

He tucked a strand of her hair behind her ear and smiled at her. "I am. I like being your knight-errant."

She smiled at him. "Knight Kit. I like it, but I don't want to be a damsel in distress."

"You won't be. Ready?"

She took a deep breath. Then closed her eyes for just a second and looked up at the sky before glancing back at Kit. His dark brown gaze was steady and patient. He wasn't going to rush her. She also felt like he wouldn't judge her if she suddenly said no. But this was her year of *yes*.

She nodded.

"Okay, so something I have learned is that the first step is always the hardest," he said.

"Why do you think that is?"

"Because you don't know what it's going to be like."

She put her hand on his shoulder. He was strong, solid, and she felt the strength in him. He looked over his shoulder and winked at her. "You've got this."

She licked her lips and nodded. She did have this. And if she didn't, she'd come back tomorrow and try again. Hopefully with Kit, she couldn't help but think.

"Ready?

"Yes."

He moved slowly as he'd promised, and with her hand on his shoulder for balance, she found her footing without too much problem. In fact, it felt at times he was going too slow, but she knew that caution was needed. She realized about halfway down that she was holding her breath and reminded herself to breathe.

When they got to the bottom, she felt like she was going to cry. She blinked a bunch of times, keeping the tears in, but did take out her phone and snap a picture of the path she'd come down.

"Want me to take your picture next to it?" he asked.

"Yes, that would be nice." She handed him her phone. "I'm trying to document all my firsts so I can look back on it on the bad days."

"Good idea."

He watched her for a minute and then lifted the camera phone. She wondered what he saw through the viewfinder. Kit made her feel different, more like a woman than a sister or a patient. Which, let's face it, was totally a good thing.

But the butterflies in her stomach as he moved around trying to find the right angle…she wasn't sure what they meant. Of course, she liked him and he *had* said he wanted her…so now she couldn't help watching him and wanting him, too. Wanting to feel his arms around her and his mouth on hers.

He moved toward the river to get a good position of her and the trail, and she looked up at where she'd come from and felt like screaming for joy. But it came out as a little yelp as she turned and smiled at Kit.

He snapped her picture and then came over and put his arm around her shoulder, careful not to pull her off balance, and took a selfie of the two of them.

Then he turned his head and looked down at her. Their eyes met and something passed between them. Something electric.

She had no idea what she'd do if he lowered his head and kissed her. She knew she'd kissed boys before. Rory had never let being an heiress get in the way of living the life she wanted. But she had also been sexually attacked just before she went into her coma, which made her hesitate. All the thoughts she'd been having about his mouth and his body. Suddenly, she wasn't sure she was ready for a kiss.

What if she kissed like a high schooler instead of a woman? What if she totally sucked at it because it had been a long time since she'd locked lips with anyone? What if…and this was the scariest thought of them all, what if his kiss made her remember the man who attacked her and she freaked?

She chewed her lower lip…just watching him.

Waiting to see what would happened next. But then Kit cleared his throat and handed her phone back to her.

"Where are these blackberries I've heard so much about?"

"That way," she said, pointing toward the left.

She took her time putting her phone away, trying to calm the disappointment that was coursing through her. She wanted to kiss him. Had almost given in to the impulse but had stopped herself. One thing at a time.

But thinking about Kit and his firm mouth that was smiling at her as he waited for her to start walking toward the blackberries was a distraction. The best kind of distraction. Her body was alive in a way that it hadn't been despite all the months she'd been out of her coma. Those butterflies were back in her stomach and they made her feel warm and fuzzy all over.

It was like how she'd felt when she'd walked for the first time without the Zimmer frame or how it had felt when she'd eaten ice cream and realized how much she loved it.

But this time it was Kit giving her all the feels. Making her hum and vibe to something that she didn't really understand but she craved more of.

There was still so much that she hadn't realized she'd been missing until this moment.

Until Kit.

Nothing was going according to plan, and he knew that when he got home Aunt Mal was going to expect a report. But he realized he wasn't going to share this with her. This afternoon had made him feel like… well, in a way he hadn't in a very long time.

Kit was experiencing something with Rory that he hadn't with anyone else before.

He needed time to reassess and figure out how he was going forward…but not now. A small smile flickered on his lips as he watched Rory. She'd taken a folded cloth bag from the crossbody she'd been carrying and they'd put the blackberries in it as they picked them. Then she brushed one on the skirt of her long dress before putting it in her mouth and closing her eyes.

"Perfect. Sweet but with just a tiny bit of tartness. Try one," she said, brushing another one on her skirt and holding it up to him.

Her fingers grazed his lips as she put the berry in his mouth. He stood stock-still, willing his body not to react to her closeness, but it took every ounce of his control and he didn't entirely succeed. He chewed the berry while looking at Rory and noticed her blush when he winked at her and said, "Tart and sweet just like you."

She turned away slowly and they continued picking berries. "I can't remember, but Dash and Con said we used to do this on our property when we were growing up."

"Is that why you wanted to do it again?"

"It is. But when I asked to go recently, Dash said no."

"Does he say no a lot?"

"He does. But the truth is it was just him alone for

so long after the accident, and I don't think he's sure how to handle both myself and Con being healthy and functioning." Rory collected more berries, her silence filling in the blanks of Dash's and Conrad's lingering guilt.

"What happened to Con?" he asked. He had heard a brief report from his aunt that there were injuries, but Aunt Mal had only known that Rory was in a coma.

"He was thrown from the car because he wasn't wearing his seat belt and he broke every bone in his body and was covered in cuts from the glass. Apparently, it took multiple surgeries and then months of recovery."

Kit turned away. Slightly shocked to hear how badly injured Conrad had been. Why hadn't he ever been told about that? Kit had come back for Declan's funeral and then flown back to Berkeley to withdraw. By the time he'd returned, his father had started drinking heavily and had been living with Aunt Mal. Dash and his grandfather Lance had crushed all of his family's prospects.

"I never knew the Beast had gone through anything like that," Kit said, referring to Conrad by his celebrity chef name.

"He's better now. In fact he said I should pick blackberries, but then he and Dash got into it and I dropped it," she said.

"Why?"

"Because I don't like to see them fight. We're all

each other has. Plus I knew I was moving out and I'd eventually go on my own."

A shot of fear went through him at the thought of her trying to come down here on her own. "Promise me you won't come down here alone until there is a handrail."

"I won't. That's why I have you, Kit."

Hearing her say she had him made him feel… *fuck*. He wasn't sure he could do this. He was in some sort of muddy water here with her. Since the moment she'd looped her arm through his and said, "Pretend we're old friends," he'd been spinning out of control. He'd been pretending to make up some plan on the fly but he had to face facts right now that the was lying to himself.

He was totally at Rory's mercy. Hard as he tried to fight it, he was enchanted by her and he couldn't allow himself to fall for her. She couldn't be his weakness.

He had to get back on track.

"You mentioned making a pie. Have you made one before?"

"Maybe before the accident. But Conrad recently showed me how to make a crust that wasn't too complicated, but then Indy showed me a refrigerated one I could buy. So I have two in my fridge. I had been planning to pick blackberries this week."

"Why did you say you weren't sure when I asked at the coffee shop?"

She chewed her lower lip for a moment. "I thought you might not want to. But then when you said something so tame as walk down Main Street I realized that if I didn't start saying what I wanted I'd never get it."

"Yeah, took me a while to learn that one as well. But with me, Rory, you don't have to hedge. Whatever you want, if it's in my power to help you with doing it, I will."

She turned and put a handful of berries into the canvas bag and then tipped her head to the side, looking over at him. "Anything?"

"Anything." He was pretty sure that even at her wildest, there wasn't anything she'd request that he wouldn't want to do. "Well, nothing illegal."

She giggled at that but then got serious again. "What about dangerous?"

"More dangerous than coming down here?"

She nodded slowly.

"Definitely."

"Good. I want to see you push yourself," he said. "I love watching the joy on your face. It's like...well, you come alive when you try something new. I love that I get to experience that with you."

He expected her to ask him for this dangerous thing but she simply shook her head and turned back to her canvas bag. They finished picking the berries and went back to the path. He stood behind her this time, putting his hands lightly on her waist to steady her as she climbed up. She was moving slowly and her legs started shaking at one point, so he was tempted to offer to carry her.

But when he started to, she glared at him. "I want to do this on my own."

"No rush."

But he was still worried for her. She took about four steps and then had to rest. He was beginning to see Dash's side of things. Rory seemed to not want to acknowledge her limitations. But when they finally got to the top and she smiled at him, he realized it was worth it.

She hugged him, pulling him close and pressing her body against his. He held her in his arms, desperately wanting to claim a kiss, but knowing that he needed to figure out a few more things before he did that.

Four

That almost kiss lingered in her mind for the next few days. She wasn't able to forget about it or how it had made her feel. What she felt around Kit was a sharp contrast to the feelings she could recall from that night ten years ago. She remembered flashes of moments from the night of the crash. When Declan—the man she'd been dancing with all night—had pushed for more than a few kisses in the upstairs hallway. She'd ripped her gown and he was in the process of clawing at her panties and trying to tear them off when she screamed.

Luckily for Rory, both Dash and Conrad had heard her. Conrad had gotten to them first. Rory wasn't sure of all the details of that moment. She'd heard Conrad yelling and punching her date. She'd sort of cowered there against the wall, trying to hold the bodice of her dress together over her breasts.

Dash had arrived and offered her his jacket and then things got fuzzy. The next thing she remembered was her grandfather admonishing her, Dash and Conrad to conduct themselves with more decorum and Conrad telling Grandfather to fuck off. Then they'd gotten in the car and…nothing.

Those memories were still so vague. She wished she couldn't remember her date's name or his face but she remembered it all. And as she stood in the kitchen waiting for her blackberry pie to bake, she wondered if the details she forgot, the details about why her date did what he did, were important. If unlocking that information would bring her closer to healing.

She knew there must be more to the story than she remembered, and if she was being completely honest with herself, she knew that she didn't want to linger in that memory. In a way she wished the events of that night had never come back to her.

It was sort of annoying to think that she had to relearn so many things but that one thing she wanted to forget wouldn't go away.

Her phone pinged. She still wasn't used to her cell phone. Everything was on there. Adjusting to technology was an entirely different challenge. She picked it up and saw she had a text from Dash asking for more details of her "friend." She sent him the angry face emoji as a response. Though she wasn't really angry.

She could appreciate that he loved her and worried about her. But her therapist had pointed out that unless she put some boundaries in place where Dash was concerned, Rory might never be able to stand on her own.

He texted back a thumbs-up.

She looked around the kitchen. Conrad had been over to look at it and recommended the appliances that Rory had purchased and installed before moving in. But the rest of it was in okay shape—dated and in need of work, but okay. The linoleum on the floors was faded and torn in a few places. The cabinets had been white originally but had faded to a dusty, dirty version of it.

The mansion she'd grown up in had been perfect. Everything was kept pristine by the housekeeping staff and the kitchens had been renovated every three years so they were always current and modern. But it had been the sort of perfection found in showrooms or magazines rather than a home, which was what she wanted her place to feel like.

Every room that she made over in her house was deliberate and she made choices that appealed to her, not because it was a room worthy of the Gilbert name.

Indy had helped Rory set up an inspiration board for the kitchen, and between Indy and Lulu they had indicated the projects that they thought someone with Rory's nonexistent DIY skills could master. Lulu and Indy were best friends and had a TV show they did together.

She decided to bake the pie before she started on the first project. Her legs still ached from the climb up the embankment after they'd picked blackberries. It had been raining for the last day and a half, so Rory had been inside.

Partially because of the weather and partially because there were times when the outside world felt too big and too much for her. Her phone pinged again and she glanced down, ready with the girl-with-her-hands-up emoji for Dash, but her heart skipped a beat when she saw the message was from Kit.

Sorry I had to run the other day. I'm back in town. What's next on your adventure agenda?

Glad you're back. I'm about to take the blackberry pie out of the oven. Next up is removing the doors from my kitchen cabinets. So adventurous...

For a slice of pie I'll be your helper.

She grinned as she typed, Done.

On my way, came his reply.

She couldn't help that giddy feeling in her stomach as she went to the hall mirror and checked to make sure her hair wasn't too messy. Rory sighed. She looked...well, like her. She hadn't been out in the sun, not that that would have made a difference since she'd always been extremely pale. She'd pulled her hair back into a ponytail when she'd been baking, because as Conrad had succinctly told her, no one liked hair in their food.

She wore a pair of skinny jeans and a Hello Kitty T-shirt as she went to open the door. All the design pictures she'd seen of these long, wooden-floored hallways had area rugs on them, but Rory wasn't ready for that yet. She had a hard time walking on surfaces as they changed so she'd kept the hardwood.

Her doorbell rang. She felt another swell of excitement in her stomach as she undid the dead bolt and stepped back to open the door.

Kit stood there, his dark hair damp from the rain. He had on a leather jacket, black jeans and a tentative smile.

"I'm all wet. Sorry I should have grabbed an umbrella."

"That's okay," she said, gesturing for him to come inside.

"I don't want to ruin the wood," he protested.

"You won't. There are some towels in the powder room if you want to dry off and the kitchen is in the back. Join me when you're done," she said.

Rory linked her hands together and turned away to keep from touching him. She wished she'd stroked his face when they'd been so close the other day, but she hadn't. Now with the rainwater on his face, his thick eyelashes had stuck together and he looked starkly masculine with that water dripping off him. She'd wanted to put her hands on his face and kiss him.

Feel that strong mouth against hers.

But she wasn't sure what *he* wanted. Maybe that was why the memories of the past had been swirling around in her mind. She would never want to force herself on anyone.

After two days away from Rory he'd told himself he could come back, do the recon he and Aunt Mal needed and keep his perspective. When his brother was killed in the car accident, their family had lost everything. Lance Gilbert was no help and Dash was even worse, punishing their family while they were still grieving the loss of his brother.

Aunt Mal had been the one to keep them together as his father turned to drinking, and Kit, who had switched colleges and was still going to night school, tried to get up to speed on starting their own business. Returning from Berkeley had been a sort of wake-up call and he'd gone from frat boy to the one everyone relied on in what felt like a heartbeat.

The days away had sort of helped to clear his head. There was no way Rory could be as...enchanting as she'd seemed. And he knew that there wasn't another person on the planet that he'd describe that way.

But Rory had left him with that impression. He'd almost convinced himself that he'd been wrong until she'd opened the door to her cozy cottage on this cold, fall day. She'd smiled at him like she was happy to see him and invited him into her home that smelled of vanilla and blackberries.

She'd been so chill, not like women he'd dated

in the past would have been after two days of total radio silence.

But of course he wasn't dating Rory. Was he? He'd come back for more Gilbert family secrets. That was all.

Except he knew that wasn't the truth. He hadn't been able to stop thinking about how she'd felt in his arms. Hadn't been able to talk himself into staying away from Rory Gilbert. Or Gilbert Corners. Hadn't been able to stop regretting that he hadn't just leaned down and kissed her after they'd picked those blackberries.

So here he was in her powder room, staring at himself in the mirror after having toweled off most of the water, trying to convince himself that he was cool with letting go of his need for revenge if it meant hurting her.

And the thing was, he didn't buy it.

Lying was such a slippery path. He could justify going after Gilbert International—after all Lance Gilbert had made promises to Declan that he'd reneged on when he'd sold the factory. He knew there had been a big fight at the winter ball between his brother, Dash, Conrad and Lance. But the details… well, no one on his side of the family knew them. But Aunt Mal and Kit assumed it had to do with the closing of the factory. Declan had been a hothead and there was no doubt the loss of the factory would have set him off. Had their brother tried to stand up for the family? Or had anger dominated him that night, making him do something rash? They'd never been able to get any answers and Kit feared they'd never know the truth. It had died with his brother in the accident.

What a mess.

He opened the door to the powder room, left his boots near the door and put his leather jacket on a hook before heading toward the kitchen. Stopping in the doorway, he realized that Rory was singing along to "Helena" by My Chemical Romance.

When she tipped her head back and screamed, *"What's the worst that I could say,"* he realized that whatever lies he might have been trying to convince himself with were just that. He wanted this woman. He wasn't here for any other reason than that she was enchanting him.

Kit shook his head and started to sing along with her. He had already decided he wouldn't do anything to harm Rory and he was going to have to trust himself not to. Because he couldn't walk away from her. And he wasn't going to pretend otherwise.

Her eyes flew open and she gave him a huge smile. "You know this song?"

"Love the band," he said, offering her his hand and pulling her into his arms.

She leaned into him for a second, and he felt her hands flutter against his chest as she looked up at him. Their eyes met and everything masculine in him went into overdrive. There wasn't a part of her that he didn't want to claim.

He skimmed his gaze down her face, over her pert nose to the pink of her cheeks to that sweet mouth that he had spent way too many hours thinking about. Kit started to lean down, not wanting her to feel pressured in anyway, and she came up on her tiptoes, her eyes closing. He felt the brush of her breath against his lips just as his brushed hers.

Suddenly, the kitchen alarm went off and she jumped, her feet slipping on the hardwood floor. He steadied her and stepped back as she muttered about the pie. She walked slowly to the oven, opening it.

The scent of freshly baked pie filled the kitchen, but honestly it was the scent of her perfume that lingered for him. He watched her as she bent over to retrieve the pie, then had to turn away after noticing how curvaceous her hips were.

"Done," she said.

"Looks good." Those were the only words he could force out as his mind was busy thinking of how he would love to have his hands on her waist and his body pressed up against her and this wasn't the time to indulge in such carnal thoughts.

But his needs had always been more savage than he wanted to admit. And with Rory he knew he needed to be more of a gentleman than he'd ever been before.

She just stood there in awkward silence after she'd placed the pie on a trivet, and he knew he should say something to make her feel at ease. But what? Forcing down the lust that was clawing at his self-control, he turned to the windows, saw the water dripping down from the rain. It had changed to a light, steady drizzle.

"It's been so long since I've been in the rain," she

said, almost under her breath. "Before I used to like walking in it."

Just those words calmed the beast in him. *Before.* She was a woman recovering from something that took more strength than he'd ever understand.

"Would you like to walk in it with me now?"

Rory was mentally cursing herself for not staying in Kit's arms. She almost had that kiss she'd been aching for. But once the timer had gone off, she'd gotten nervous. Begun having second thoughts. She had wondered at first if he simply wasn't attracted to her, not enough to go at her pace. She knew that those feelings weren't always a two-way street. But now, after seeing the look in his eyes before she'd pulled away, she was pretty sure he was.

However, there was no denying that Kit was a hard man to read. It might be that she was simply out of practice because she hadn't been around people who weren't either related to her or hired to help with her medical needs. Also Kit treated her like she was...well just Rory. Not a Gilbert from Gilbert Corners or the tragic heiress. With him she was just herself. And even though he was indecipherable, she wanted to kiss him, so now she was second-guessing every-dang-thing she did with him.

"Rory?"

"Hmm?" She couldn't take her eyes off his mouth. His lips were full but not overly so; his mouth looked like it would be firm against hers, and from that one brief brush she'd had of his lips, it had been.

"Do you have shoes?" he asked.

She forced her gaze away from his mouth. "Yes, but...um... Okay, so the thing is, Dash is afraid I'll fall because the ground is slippery and I think I should mention that Hank, my PT guy, also said I should be cautious."

"What does that have to do with shoes?" he asked. "I know you have to take things slow. But we made it up and down that embankment. Do you trust me?"

She did.

It seemed to her that Kit might be the only man in the world to see her for who she was. Hank saw the muscles that had atrophied and needed exercise and routine to regain stamina. Dash and Conrad envisioned her as the broken girl who'd lain in a bed for ten years. But Kit... She wanted to believe he saw Rory. The woman whom she *wanted* to be.

"I do have shoes," she murmured, "but sometimes I'm steadier in bare feet."

"Let me take a look at the backyard and we can go stand out there if you like?"

"And walk?"

"Yes, walk. But not too far," he promised. "Your brother would definitely kill me if anything happened to you."

She laughed at that. "Are you afraid of him?"

"No. I'm sort of afraid for you. I don't want to see you get hurt even though I know you need to try new things."

"Ah, thank you. I was joking," she said, at his fierce denial. "I forget you're not really from around here. But everyone sort of holds my family in this odd way in town. Like the livelihood of the town is somehow tied to us. Anyway, that's what I meant. Plus there's the curse thing."

"What curse?"

Darn! Why had she brought the curse up? "Well, everyone thinks that the Gilberts have been cursed since Grandfather closed the factory. That was the night we were in the accident and then the economy in the town started to fail. But then Conrad came back and I woke up from my coma and Dash is living here again..."

"So the curse is broken?" he asked.

"I'm not sure there ever was one, but I was out of it for a while...and missing walking in the rain," she said.

"Let's fix that." He smiled gently. "Let me check the yard. I'll be back."

Kit toed off his socks and then opened the back door and stepped out onto the concrete pad that had recently been poured. She'd hired a crew that Indy had recommended to clean the debris from the backyard. The bushes and flowers were all overgrown but the grass had been recently mowed.

She watched as Kit took his time walking around the yard, checking the ground for stability before he turned back to her. The rain was soaking his T-shirt, making it cling to his shoulders and his chest. She felt that pulse go through her entire body, to her feminine core, and she stood there watching and wanting him.

Rory knew she was playing a dangerous game because she wasn't entirely sure if she could be brave enough to take what she wanted. To follow through on what she now realized she wasn't sure could walk away from.

"Ready?"

She hesitated as she stared at his hand held out toward her.

"It's up to you," he said.

It *was* up to her. She could stay in the kitchen, looking out at the world or she could take Kit's hand…

She did it, put her palm in his and he wrapped his fingers around her hand, holding it securely as she took a step out of the house. She stood there as the rain fell on her. It was colder than she remembered rain being. She tipped her face up and felt it falling on her cheeks and her hair.

Emotions roiled through her and she felt like she wanted to scream with them, but knew that wasn't okay so instead a grunt sort of erupted from her.

"You okay?"

She nodded and then looked over at Kit. "Better than okay."

"Ready to walk or are you good here?" he asked.

"Walk, please."

"The ground is pretty firm closest to the center of the yard. So we can walk out and then turn and come back."

She held his hand as they stepped off the concrete, and the first touch of the wet grass under her foot tickled a little. Spreading her toes out, she felt the sprigs between them. She stood there for a long minute, just happy that she could feel her toes and happy with her body.

The body that she'd been resenting more than a little because it was taking so long to recover and do what she wanted it to. But right now she was so glad to be standing in the rain with the grass under her feet and Kit at her side.

Five

"So when I decided to buy this property, Dash was—"

"Can we not talk about your brother?" he interrupted her. "Sorry if that sounded rude, but it seems he dominates your life. What about this property attracted you?"

He wished he had a plan to separate Rory from Dash in his mind. He didn't want her to have any part of his revenge for his brother. But he was realistic enough to know that might not be possible. Also, when he was with her, he wanted to throw off the heavy mantle of expectation that Aunt Mal had placed on him.

The rain was soft and a little cold, forcing him to be present, and he was enjoying their slow walk in her yard. Kit normally just put his head down in the rain and rushed to get out of it, but there could be no rushing with Rory. And if he were honest, he didn't want to.

She was enjoying this. Her steps on the grass were gentle and almost gliding. She tipped her head back repeatedly, her face turned up to the rain, and he had the feeling that this was something she had desperately missed.

"Sorry about that."

"You don't have to apologize," he assured her. "I like you more than your brother."

"I'm glad," she said, leaning toward him again.

He was struggling with that lip-lock they'd almost shared and really trying to keep some distance between them. Not because he'd changed his mind about wanting to kiss her, but she'd pulled back to get her pie from the oven. It could have waited. She'd chosen to move away. And he was going to respect that.

"So, about this place…? It's not exactly where I picture a Gilbert of Gilbert Corners living."

"Well, that's what I was going for. I wanted a place where I could figure out who I am," she confided. "I want to make it my own, so I talked to my financial advisor and he found this place."

"Is Dash your financial advisor?" he asked.

"No. My inheritance comes from my maternal side. So Dash oversaw it while I was in the coma but he didn't merge them."

"Why not?"

"He knew I'd wake up," she said. "At least that is what he told me."

He believed that Dash loved his sister, but Kit had always thought it was a guilty conscience that drove the other man. Now he was getting a glimpse that it might be more nuanced than all of that. "So you're happy here?"

"Yes, I am. My family wanted me to stay close and I agreed if they backed off. I have a home in northern California but haven't been there in years."

She started laughing after she said that. "I mean even before the accident."

They reached the point where he thought they should turn, and he halted for a second, looking around the overgrown brambles and flower bushes that lined the fence on the left and the right. This place also seemed special. Like it was hidden and, though neglected, it didn't have the abandoned feel that some of the other parts of Gilbert Corners had.

"I like it."

"Me, too," she said, then gave him a questioning look. "Why are we stopping?"

"This is as far as we go. Time to go back toward the house," he said.

"Can we stand here for a minute?"

"Of course," he said.

She moved so that they faced each other and their eyes met. His mind sort of stopped working as he watched a drop of rain roll down her forehead to her nose and then it hung there on the tip. He reached up to touch it and he felt the shiver go through her.

Every molecule of his body craved her. Kit wanted to feel her mouth under his as the rain was falling around them. He needed to know the taste of her on his tongue so he could understand her more fully.

He turned so that he wouldn't give in to his desire and his bare foot slipped on the wet grass. Acting on instinct, he tried to pull his arm from Rory so he didn't drag her down with him. But instead she put both of her arms around him, using her body to steady him.

She was pressed against him, her head tipped back and laughing and he shut off his mind to all the why-nots that he'd been dwelling on and kissed her.

Her laughter and joy flowed into him as their lips met. She opened her mouth under his and he felt the tentative brush of her tongue over his. He found his footing and made sure it was solid as he put his arm around her waist and lifted her more fully against him. Their wet clothing wasn't much of a barrier and he felt the fullness of her breasts against his chest.

His erection stirred. He wanted her with every fiber of his being, but he knew it had been ten years since she'd kissed anyone. His conscience demanded that he let her set the pace. Yet it was all he could do to keep his hand on the side of her face gentle. To just touch her with the lightest of caresses instead of pushing his fingers into her thick, rain-drenched hair and tilting her head so he could deepen the kiss the way his body demanded.

Then she sucked his tongue into her mouth and shifted against him. He felt the pebbled hardness of her nipples against his chest and savored the way her hips rubbed against his erection as she held tightly onto him.

He rubbed his tongue back over hers, tasting the sweetness that was Rory. This passion that was unfolding between the two of them felt like magic as he held her in the rain, taking his time with this first kiss and getting more turned on than he had been in a long time.

Kissing Kit was even better than walking in the rain. Another first for her. He tasted of coffee and mint. His tongue rubbed against hers, stirring to life feelings that she hadn't thought about in ages. He held her gently but solidly.

The joy she'd felt at being able to steady him had easily bled back into desire and this embrace was doing things to her that she hadn't anticipated. Her entire body was awash in sensation and her skin felt almost too sensitive. His hand against the side of her face was warm against the chill from the rain and she wanted to feel his big, strong palm moving down her body.

She couldn't remember ever having had a lover, but there was so much of that time before the crash and coma that she still couldn't remember.

He lifted his head, looking down at her with that fierce gaze of his. Her breath hitched because she wasn't exactly sure what she should say.

"I…"

"Rory? Where are you?" Dash called from inside the house.

"Out here."

"Out where?" her brother asked.

"I think we should start making our way back," Kit whispered in her ear.

"I suppose so. I'm getting cold but a part of me wants to stay here since I know it will tick Dash off."

She saw a smile tease the corners of his lips. "I can appreciate that but we don't want you to catch a cold, which will only prove he was right."

"True."

"Good God, Rory! What are you doing? And you, Kit, should know better than to—"

"Enough of that," Rory said sharply. "We are perfectly safe. Now either come join us in the rain or go sit in the kitchen and wait for us."

Kit didn't say anything but she felt the tension in his body as they walked slowly back toward the house. She was surprised when Dash stepped outside and stood there in the rain that was even lighter now, barely falling.

"Why are you doing this?"

"I haven't felt the rain in years."

Dash nodded and his face softened as he tipped his head to the side. "When you were little we used to dance in the rain, do you remember?"

He walked over to them and they all stopped. She didn't recall that and couldn't imagine Dash ever doing that. "You're making that up."

"No. Mom loved it. Sometimes she'd even entice Dad to join us."

Rory turned to her brother and saw that usual mix of love and concern but also something else. Maybe a hint of sadness. She barely remembered her parents as she'd only been six when they died in a plane crash; but Dash had more memories. "I wish I could remember them."

"Me, too, ladybug," he said, then he looked past her to Kit. "Thank you for helping Rory with this."

"No problem," Kit said. "That's what I'm here for."

"Is it? I thought you were an old friend."

"He is. He meant that's what friends are for. He's helping me with all the things I can't remember doing and all the things I want to," Rory explained.

"Like what things?"

"All the things," she said again. She wasn't going to mention kissing because, to be fair, she wouldn't have kissed a life coach. Or would she? Her life was full of extraordinary surprises. Maybe she would have kissed anyone who was attractive and spent this much time with her.

If Rory was honest, she was sure it was only Kit whom she wanted to kiss. But then again, she hadn't really been around a lot of other men that weren't related to her, since coming out of the coma. There was Hank, of course, but he was married and also was always forcing her to do exercises that hurt. She glanced back over at Kit.

Wanting something didn't mean she'd get it. She

also had to be careful with her emotions. She had no real idea of the woman she'd been before but this woman she was today wanted connections. Wanted friends of her own, and after that kiss, a lover to call her own. She wanted it to be Kit, but was she just forming an attachment to him because he was the first hot guy she'd been around?

"Are you okay?" Kit asked.

"Yes," she said. "The pie should be cooled down enough for us to have some now."

"I'm looking forward to trying it," he said.

"It looks delicious. What kind is it?" Dash asked as they walked back to the cement pad outside her back door. She noticed he'd put a towel down on the floor when they came back in.

They all sat down in the doorway one at a time and dried their feet. Rory went first and once she was in the house went to the linen cabinet and grabbed bigger towels for Dash and Kit.

They took them and toweled off in the doorway. "I'm going to go and change quickly," she said. "Will you two be okay?"

"Of course. It will give us a chance to get to know one another," Dash said.

"Don't be…"

"What?" her brother asked.

"You," she responded with a grin. "Be nice."

"I can't be anyone other than myself," he told her.

She looked over at Kit and he just winked at her, which she assumed meant he'd be fine. She just didn't want Dash to say anything that would make

Kit leave her. Then she realized how silly that was. Kit wasn't the kind of man to do anything he didn't want to do.

Kit hadn't been in the same room as Dash Gilbert since he'd been a boy, long before his family had started working their way up the corporate ladder at the factory and long before the night when his brother had died. In his mind he'd spent so many years hating Dash because he was the face of the company that was to blame for his family's hardships.

But this man didn't *look* evil.

"Thank you," he said as they both finished toweling off and moved into the kitchen. "I know that Rory needs this kind of activity but I can't get past my fear that she's going to fall and be back in the hospital."

There was no doubting Dash's sincerity. "She's capable of more than you realize."

"No doubt. Want some coffee?" Dash asked, deftly changing the subject.

"Sure," Kit said.

Dash moved around the kitchen, clearly familiar with the layout and where everything was, and started making coffee with the single-use pot that was on the counter. "So, what is it you do exactly?"

"I run my family's business," he replied. "You?"

Dash arched one eyebrow at him. "I run my family's business. Seems weird that we haven't met before. I know I'm not supposed to pry, but I don't remember you and Rory being friends."

"Fair enough. I think I'd have to say we were more acquaintances than friends," Kit said. "But we always enjoyed each other's company."

"You did? Are you from GC?"

"I lived her for a while in elementary school and then we moved away when the factory closed," Kit told him.

Dash sighed. "So many families did. I'm not sure what my grandfather was thinking… Well, he was concerned with the financial bottom line, but the impact on the town was definitely worse than he had anticipated."

"It was."

Kit didn't want to talk about the closing of the factory with Dash. His time with Rory made him want to find a way to make peace with Dash but he wasn't prepared to be chill about it with the other man.

"Milk or sugar?"

"Milk," Kit said. It felt odd to feel this angry and have a mundane conversation about coffee at the same time.

"I hope your family wasn't too greatly impacted, though I guess you did okay since you are running your own business now," Dash said.

"We are. It wasn't easy at first but I think the move forced us to find something of our own," Kit said. He remembered finishing college remotely so he could save money and live with Aunt Mal while his father drank himself to death mourning his eldest son. Not good times at all. But they had shaped him into the man he was today.

Kit realized he needed this conversation with Dash to remind himself of why he'd come back to Gilbert Corners. It was one thing to say he was enchanted by Rory, but the truth was, he was a man who lived in the real world. And revenge through business was what had kept him going in the last ten years.

There was a big part of him that was afraid he was nothing without revenge. His entire adult life had been shaped by Declan's death and the fallout from it. The boy-man he'd been was a distant memory. He'd stopped dreaming of his future and focused only on taking down Dash Gilbert. Until he met Rory. She was the first one to make him lift his head up and see that there might be something other than getting back at the Gilberts.

"Glad to hear that things are going well for you. So where'd Rory get the blackberries, do you know? I'm hoping it was the grocery store."

"It wasn't," Kit replied. "I helped her down to the path by the river in town and we picked them."

Dash cursed under his breath. "Honestly, she's going to be the death of me. How'd she do?"

Kit looked over at the other man who leaned against the counter sipping his black coffee. "Good. It took a lot of effort to get back up the path and there were times I thought she might ask me to carry her but she didn't. She just gritted her teeth and kept on going."

"She's stubborn."

"Are you boys talking about me?" Rory asked as she came into the kitchen. Turning toward her, Kit noticed she was using her cane and she'd changed into a pair of leggings and long sweater. She'd braided her hair and it hung over one shoulder.

"We are," Kit confirmed.

"And?" Rory asked, giving Dash a pointed look.

"And nothing. I'm glad I didn't know you were climbing down to the river until *after* you were safely back in your house. Want some coffee?"

"Yes, please," she said.

She walked over to get down plates. Dash set her coffee on the table across from where Kit sat and then went back to get napkins and forks. It was interesting to watch them working together and Kit realized that he missed this—losing his brother had taken that one person whom he'd had so many shared memories with. The person who remembered the family they had been. And as Dash and Rory talked about pies of the past and their father's obsession with them, he realized this was one more thing that Dash had taken from him.

But this was tempered by the fact that he and Declan had never really been close. They might not have had this kind of close connection even if his brother had lived. In fact, Kit knew they wouldn't have, because Kit had planned to stay on the West Coast and live his life out there.

"What do you think?" Rory asked as he took a bite of the pie.

The taste of the warm, sweet blackberries with just a hint of tartness and the buttery crust was delicious. He opened his eyes, looking over at her, remembering the taste of her as he'd kissed her as well. "Delicious."

She blushed.

"I'm glad you like it."

"I think I might be addicted to it," he confessed.

"It's pretty good," Dash chimed in. "In fact, I think it might be better than Con's…but don't tell him I said so."

Rory glanced at her brother and then immediately back to Kit. It was as though she'd forgotten he was there.

"I am definitely going to tell him," she said with a wicked grin.

Six

Rory sat next to Dash, enjoying her brother in a way that she hadn't in a really long time. Moving out had been scary—she wasn't going to pretend that sleeping at night was easy all alone in this shabby house—but she knew it was the right move.

"I'd better be heading off," Kit said.

She looked over at him, realizing that something had changed since their kiss and Dash arriving. Reaching for her cane, she stood when Kit did. "I'll walk you out."

Her leg was feeling the stress from being on her feet so much. But also she'd braced herself hard when she'd steadied Kit earlier. Something that Hank had taught her to do when she felt unsteady, but it always had repercussions.

"You don't have to," Kit protested.

"I do." She wanted to say goodbye to him in private, and also she knew if she sat with her leg like this it would just hurt more. Moving always made her feel better.

"Okay," he said. He put his mug and plate on the counter near the sink and she followed him to the front door, realizing as he sat on the floor to put his boots back on that she needed to get a bench.

"Sorry my brother arrived when he did," she told him candidly.

"Me, too. But I can see that his concern comes from a good place."

"Yeah, it does. Even though it feels suffocating sometimes. So...about the kiss..." she murmured as he stood back up and reached for his leather jacket.

He tipped his head to the side, watching her and waiting.

"I don't want to make assumptions and I'm not good at guessing what other people are feeling. So did you like it?"

Kit smiled at her and moved toward her, stopping when there was just a few inches between them. He leaned in closer, their eyes met and her heart started beating just a little bit faster with excitement.

"I did. I want to do it again. But your bro is here, so..."

"Good. I liked it, too," she said.

"I know," he said, brushing his mouth over hers. Then he lifted his head, winked at her and waved goodbye as he walked out the door.

She stood there, watching him leave. He didn't look back and his steps were sure and steady on the wet pavement. Something she knew he probably didn't have to worry about. But she worried for him.

Oh.

She was starting to care for him. There were butterflies in her stomach and her heart felt full when she thought about the kiss he'd just given her. It had been short and sweet and set off fires in her body. He waved once more as he drove by and she closed the door, carefully turning to walk back toward the kitchen.

Dash stood at the end of the hallway.

"You like this guy?"

"Kit. I like *Kit.*"

"Yeah, Kit. Your old friend, except you don't have any old friends," he said.

"I'm sure I had friends, Dash, don't be a dick."

"I'm not being a dick," he said. "Or if I am…it's just because I'm concerned about you."

"Well, thanks, but I'm a big girl. I can handle myself."

"I know that, Rory, but it's hard for me to stop being your big brother." He sighed. "Honestly, there are times when I can't really believe that you are out of that hospital bed."

"Dash," she said, going over to her brother and hugging him with her free arm. "I'm okay now."

"Yeah."

But she knew that as hard as it was for her to make up for a decade that she'd lost, it must've been equally as hard for her brother to watch her missing out on life. He was the one who had to sit in a chair next to her bed and wonder if she'd ever wake up.

"You know I love you but I can't let you boss me around," she said at last.

"Life would be so much easier if everyone would just let me do that," he deadpanned.

"It's not just me?"

"No. Elle and Conrad are on that list, too," he admitted.

Of course they were. Dash wasn't ever going to stop watching over the people he loved. Even though she, Elle and Con didn't need his protection, Dash couldn't help himself. She linked her free arm through his and turned him back toward the kitchen. "You like independent people."

"I guess I do," he said. "So, about Kit…"

"No, we're not going to do this. I like him. I think he likes me. And I'm going to just see where it goes. You know my therapist said to try new things."

"She also told me to butt out of your life," Dash said gruffly.

"And you didn't fire her?"

"Ha. As if I could. You made it clear she worked for you," Dash reminded her. "Which I'm glad you did. Seeing you in the rain today was something special."

"I felt so alive." As she murmured the words, Rory realized that it wasn't just the rain that had made her feel that way, but also Kit's kiss.

"That's all I want for you," Dash confessed. Then

he looked at his watch. "I didn't just come over to butt into your life. Conrad wants to start Sunday dinners at the Manor. You can bring a friend. Sunday at two."

"You had to come here to tell me?"

He shot her an unapologetic look. "Yes. I didn't want to just get a thumbs-up emoji. I wanted to see how you were doing."

She gave him a thumbs-up, which made him laugh. She started laughing, too.

Dash helped her take off the doors to the kitchen cabinets before he left and as she worked on cleaning and refinishing them that afternoon she realized that she was slowly figuring out who Rory Gilbert was.

Aunt Mal's house was in an older, established neighborhood on the suburbs of Boston. She'd bought it with the profits they'd made in their first big year. It was one of the McMansions that were all the rage back in the early 2000s and Aunt Mal had decorated it with her flair for midcentury design.

It was sleek and modern-looking in that sort of old-century way. Her housekeeper, Castor, opened the door when Kit arrived.

He hadn't planned on visiting his aunt today, but after seeing Rory and Dash together he had realized there were pieces to the Gilbert family puzzle that he didn't have. Something about them didn't add up the way he'd expected. And if anyone knew what had happened the night of the party, it would be his aunt.

"I wasn't expecting you today. Did you find something we can use?" Aunt Mal asked as he was shown into her sitting room. She was tall, thin and always wore her straight black hair pulled back into a tight bun at the back of her neck. She favored caftans in the summer but in the fall went all in on long, flowing skirts and sweaters with feathers on them. Today's outfit was a deep purple skirt with a black sweater.

She was seated on one of the tufted settees that she used in most of the rooms in this house. They were pretty small and when he sat on them he felt too big. The walls were lined with bookshelves and there was a mahogany desk that sat in front of the picture window overlooking the side yard.

"I'm not sure yet. I was able to spend time with both Rory and Dash today. And I have a few questions."

She arched a brow. "Like what? Did they say something about Declan or your father?"

"Nothing like that. It's just… Aunt Mal, what exactly happened the night of the ball?" he asked. "Some of the stuff they mentioned didn't really add up."

"Of course it didn't," she said, getting to her feet and walking over to him in a cloud of Estée Lauder perfume. "They are liars. We know this."

Liars. Except that Rory wasn't. In fact, if he had to place money on her being anything, it would be bluntly honest. Dash…well, he was a harder read. After a decade of watching his every move in the business world, Kit had thought he'd known the other man, but the truth was a bit more convoluted. There was so much to Dash that he hadn't known.

Ever since Conrad had returned to Gilbert Corners, he'd noticed a change in how Dash was running the company. And after Rory had woken from her coma there had been more changes. More focus on the communities and people. More giving back.

The man he'd met today had been sincere in a way that didn't surprise Kit that much, as Dash was known in the business world for being ruthless but fair. What had kind of thrown him was the humble love he had for his sister. It was painting a different picture of Dash in his personal relationships. Which was the type of relationship his brother and father would have had with Lance Gilbert.

So had they read Lance wrong or was Dash different? Though Kit remembered very clearly Aunt Mal calling him, crying as she informed him that Dash had been driving the car that had killed his brother.

"Do you know what happened at the party?" he repeated.

"I don't. Your father just said that the Gilbert heirs started a fight with Declan, and Lance was furious," Aunt Mal said. "Did they tell you more?"

"No. I didn't ask and I haven't told them I'm related to Declan." Kit was doing this for his brother and his intention had always been to avenge his death in the car crash. But it had been easier before he'd met Dash in person. They'd competed in some business deals and Kit had won a few, but this was different.

Dash was a loving and caring man with Rory. Which was more shocking than Kit had expected it to be. He remembered his father had been the same demanding man at work and at home. It was hard to reconcile Dash as two different men. But the Dash he'd met wasn't a cruel or vindictive man around his sister. He was loving.

"What's going on with you?" Aunt Mal asked suspiciously. "Is it the girl?"

"Nothing is going on with me. You know I like to have all the facts before I make a move. It feels like there is more to the incident between Declan and the Gilbert heirs than we know," Kit told her. "I need more information."

"I'll see what I can find," Aunt Mal said with a sincerity that Kit didn't doubt. The two of them had tried to piece together the truth. But his father… might have been an unreliable source of information since he'd been drunk most of the time. "Are you staying for dinner?"

"Actually, I'd love to take *you* out to dinner," he said.

She smiled. "That's my boy. Shall we say the Club at seven?"

"Perfect. I'm going to go back to the office until then. If you dig up anything else on that night, let me know."

"I will. But really I'm not sure what else we need." She shrugged. "We know that there was a fight at the Manor and that the cousins all piled into a car that crashed into your brother's car—killing him and injuring most of them. Except for Dash, who ruined your father and left us with nothing."

His Aunt Mal's summation wasn't wrong. All of that had happened that night, and Kit had been left picking up the pieces.

Rory had decided she wasn't going to worry about kissing Kit; she found herself sitting in her bed two nights later doing just that. She wondered if she should hire someone to teach her to kiss better. At the time it had felt sort of natural and she'd thought she was doing it right, but Kit hadn't called or texted since he'd left.

Of course, she knew *she* could text him.

Indy and Elle had wanted to know more about Kit but Rory hadn't really known what to say. Had she been the kind of woman who liked to talk about her feelings before? Who knew? She definitely wasn't that type of woman now.

But she did want to talk to Kit.

She was hesitating… The question was why. Why?

Then, after mulling it over, the truth finally dawned on her. She was *scared*. Fear had wormed its way into her mind and her heart. She was thinking of all the reasons why Kit hadn't reached out to her and she had to wonder if maybe he felt the same way.

Not about kissing her. He had been a really good kisser, so that wouldn't be a fear. Maybe he was afraid she didn't want to hear from him again.

She picked up her phone and saw the picture of the blackberry pie she'd taken and then the picture of her and Kit that he'd snapped when they'd picked the berries. Using her fingers, she zoomed in on the photo on Kit's face. She looked into his eyes and tried to see what he felt.

As if that had ever worked.

She was going to text him. She had heard via Indy that there was a Goth night coming up at the speak-easy next week. That sounded like fun and like something she hadn't done, so she was definitely going. She was going to text him before she lost her nerve.

Rory: Hey. You up?

Kit: Hey. I am.

Rory: So...there's a speakeasy in GC and they have a Goth Night coming up next week. Want to go with me?

Kit: Yes. But I don't want to wait until next week to see you. And I totally spaced on helping you with your cabinets. Can I stop by tomorrow?

Rory: That's cool. I refinished them and started re-hanging the doors. But could use your help with a ride to the hardware store.

Kit: I'll bring my truck.

Rory: You have a truck?

Kit: I do. I use it when I'm feeling macho.

Rory: laughing emoji

Kit: Uh-oh.

Rory: What?

Kit: You don't think I'm macho.

Rory: Is that important?

Kit: Nah. Was just being silly. So, what have you been up to?

Rory: Pt. Hank was impressed I'd made it up the embankment. And oh, I talked to the town council and they are adding ramps and railings to the pathway by the river.

Instead of texting back he video-called her.

Rory answered the call, smiling when she noticed that Kit was sitting on a couch wearing a faded T-shirt and jeans. He had some scruff on his jaw, which made him look more devilishly handsome than she had expected.

"Hope you don't mind," he said. "I just wanted to see you. Sorry I was radio silent. I've been out of town on business."

"That's fine. I know you have a life," she told him. "What do you do?"

"I run a global conglomerate."

"Ah, corporate gibberish."

"Ha ha. It just means I oversee a company that owns lots of smaller ones. The global bit means we have companies all over the world."

Rory smiled, liking the deep timbre of his voice. She asked him more questions and he relaxed as he talked about what he did. Sighing, she sank deeper into the pillows on her bed. She hadn't thought that just hearing someone's voice could make her feel alive. Maybe because a voice was the one thing that had pulled her from her coma, but there was something about Kit's voice that made her feel tingly all over.

"But that part is boring," he said.

She hadn't been paying attention to his words so had no idea what he'd said. "Not it's not."

"Trust me, no one wants to hear about the accounting department." Then he turned the conversation toward her. "Do you have a job?"

She shook her head. "I am intending to get one but I can't really stand for a long period."

She realized how lucky she was not to have to work or rely on anyone to support herself. "I'm also fixing up the house. Indy offered to have her crew film me but I'm not ready for that."

"I didn't mean to put you on the spot. I know you're a Gilbert."

"Yeah, right now I'm concentrating on getting healthy," she admitted. But at some point she hoped she'd be healthy enough to have a job. "I have no idea what I'd be good at when I do start looking for work. Maybe you should tell me about accounting."

He smiled. "It's working with numbers and spread-sheets all day."

She made a face. Numbers were always a jumble in her head, and having to go to an office every day made that seem even more like torture. She was still trying to figure out what she wanted to do but she knew it wasn't that.

"Exactly. I think you'd be good with people," he said.

"That's a thought. I guess I better add that to my list," she said.

"Speaking of that list, what's next?"

"Driving."

"Do you have your learner's permit?" he asked.

"Yes. I took the written test a few months ago. But Dash doesn't drive after his accident and Conrad… he said he doesn't have the patience to teach anyone."

"Are you just doing it because he said no?"

At first maybe that had been part of the reason she'd wanted to learn to drive, but the truth was more complicated. "I need to be able to do things for my-self, you know?"

"I do. I'll give you your first lesson tomorrow," he said. "I should let you go. Good night, Rory."

"Good night, Kit," she said.

Seven

Rory pushed her doubts about Kit aside as she got ready the next morning for her driving lessons. Elle had been busy at the hospital. She worked with long-term trauma patients, like Rory had been, but she was also the on-call brain trauma specialist. However, last night…Rory could have used a girlfriend to talk her off the worry ledge that she'd managed to find herself on.

Looking at herself in the mirror as she plaited her hair into one long braid that fell over her left shoulder, she tried to be objective. She looked like a woman, which always surprised her when she caught a glimpse of herself. She still felt like that eighteen-year-old girl she'd been when she went into the coma.

It was odd to see that her face had matured into her mom's features.

Rory glanced at the photo of her parents that she'd stuck on the corner of her vanity. She had so few real memories of them because she'd only been six when they died. Dash had kept them alive for her by telling her stories. But their faces had faded. And when she thought of her parents it was simply in this pose from the picture.

It was odd to see her mother's face staring back at her from the mirror. She wished she'd somehow absorbed her mother's strength and confidence from back then, too. But she hadn't.

She wanted more with Kit physically than the arousing kisses they'd shared. But she wasn't sure how to tell him. And frankly, TV, movies and books weren't helping. It would be really great if there was an article about what to do when you went into a coma as a girl and woke up a woman. With tips on flirting and updates on what guys liked ten years later.

Which was part of the problem. Rory didn't want to change herself to make herself into something Kit wanted. And she knew, deep down, that he would not want that for her either. She put her head in her hands, smiling as she remembered the way he'd looked on his couch the night before. He'd been all relaxed and scruffy and cuddly but still undeniably sexy. She'd wanted to be snuggled up beside him, making out.

Except she hadn't really ever made out with a man

before. Well, there had been that one time the summer before the accident when she'd kissed one of Con's college friends on the deck of the yacht while the sun set. So romantic...until he'd told her he thought he'd had too much to drink and turned and vomited over the side of the boat.

Everything she'd done with Kit was way more romantic than that. But she still wasn't sure of herself as woman.

She went to the group text chat she had with Elle and Indy.

Rory: Help! I need to know more about sex.

Elle: Is Kit pressuring you?

Rory: I wish. I'm just so inexperienced and don't want to be.

Indy: I've got some books, come by the shop.

Her phone started ringing with a video call in the group. She answered and saw Elle sitting in her office at work and a moment later Indy answered from behind the counter in her bookstore.

"Sorry, thought this would be easier," Elle said. "So what is it you're unsure about?"

Rory shrugged and took a deep breath and told them both about the kiss she'd had with Kit and how he'd semi-ghosted her after Dash had arrived.

"Sounds like Dash was being overprotective," Elle said. "I'll talk to him about that."

Rory laughed. "No, it was fine. He and I are figuring that part out. Last night Kit called and we talked. He said he'd been busy with work but I have to wonder if he knows I'm not very experienced and is turned off by that."

Indy shook her head. "You're never going to know that unless you ask him. But if he called and apologized, I think you can believe him."

"I do, too," Elle said. "He could have just never contacted you again."

"I hadn't thought of that." Even though Kit had bought the condo next door, it seemed he was away on business so frequently that it would be easy for him to ignore her. "So…" She trailed off. She wasn't sure how to put into words what she really wanted to know. Then she suddenly decided to just ask these two women who were her sisters of the heart. "Should I really tell him I don't have any experience?"

"I'd just see how it plays out," Indy suggested. "I had a date push me too far and really struggled with intimacy, and I was obviously not going to tell Con but it sort of just came out after we kissed. It felt natural and just…well, Con got it and he was great."

Rory smiled to herself. Her cousin Con had changed from the boy she'd known, and she really liked the man he'd become. She also thought he and Indy were perfect for each other, so hearing that they'd had some struggles helped her. "It's easy to look at y'all and think that you got together without any big issues."

"Everyone has issues," Elle said. "If Kit is the right guy, you'll know. Rory…"

"Yes?"

Elle hesitated. "Do you have any more memories of what happened the night of the ball?"

Though Rory recalled being attacked by her date that night, Elle had confirmed she hadn't been raped. Even though he hadn't gone further, knowing that someone had tried to hurt her and force her was still difficult to process.

"No. None. And it's totally different with Kit. I want him to want me."

"Good," Elle said. "I'm sure he does. Is he seeing you again?"

"He's coming by later to teach me how to drive."

"I think it's safe to assume he likes you. Teaching someone to drive isn't an easy thing," Indy remarked. "My mom used to yell at me every time I drove with her."

"That's nothing like Kit," Rory said.

"Good."

The doorbell rang and she smiled at the girls. "That's probably Kit. Talk later."

"Yes. If you need us, text," Indy said.

Rory disconnected the call and then stood. Looking at herself in the mirror, seeing not only her mom now, but also herself. She just had to get used to so much more than this body and she knew she was getting there one step at a time.

* * *

Kit wasn't any closer to figuring out what the hell he was going to do about Dash Gilbert. No matter how many times he reminded himself that Rory wasn't really part of the Gilbert family that he hated, he knew he didn't hate Dash anymore either. Meeting him the other day, talking to him had confused the issue even further.

A smart man would stay the fuck away from Gilbert Corners. And Kit had always been praised for his intelligence, which he knew would end the minute someone put the pieces together about his identity/past. He was back.

He couldn't stay away from her. There was a white-hot attraction between the two of them and his guy brain was saying just hook up and then that would go away and he could move on. Get back to just coming to Gilbert Corners to plot Dash's downfall.

But despite what he was currently doing, he was smarter than that. The draw to Rory wasn't just sex. If it was, Kit wouldn't be here ready to give her driving lessons. He was here because he couldn't stay away.

It didn't matter that he knew it would be smarter and easier to take down Dash Gilbert if Kit had nothing to do with Rory. But that wasn't happening.

It was a clear, cool, crisp autumn day. The leaves were changing and fell as he walked up toward Rory's house. She'd put two large terracotta planters blooming with mums on either side of the walkway that led to her front door. The door had been painted since he'd last visited and had a large autumn-themed wreath on it with something hanging in the center. When he got closer he noticed that it was Jack and Sally from Tim Burton's *Nightmare Before Christmas.*

He rang the doorbell and stood there. Maybe this time when he saw her he'd be able to friend-zone her and let go of wanting to take her into his arms, kiss her and not stop until they were both naked and he was balls deep inside her.

He got hard just imagining that and shifted his legs, adjusting his erection before the door opened.

"Hi," she said.

His cock twitched and he had to look away from her to just try to get himself under control. But he couldn't get that warm, welcoming smile of hers out of his mind. The way her lips were curved, he knew what they felt like under his. He missed the taste of her.

How was he going to spend any time next to her in the close confines of the car and keep his hands to himself?

"Hi," he said back. He noticed she wore a black-and-white striped shirt tucked into a black flounced mini skirt, striped tights and a pair of flats. She looked cute and Halloweeny and he was trying to be chill.

But his chill was gone. He was completely swept away by the sight of her long, sexy legs in that fetching getup and then she smiled at him again and he was a goner.

There was no pretending that he didn't want more

than a friendship with her. It didn't matter that she was the sister of his enemy.

"Want to come in for a minute?" she asked.

Yes. *Hell yes*. He wanted to come into her house, take her into his arms, ravish her until she became soft and pliant in his arms and then… "I'm not sure that's the best idea."

"Why not?" she asked, reaching for a leather jacket on the hook and shrugging into it.

The action pulled the fabric taut across her full breasts and Kit wasn't sure how much more his body could handle.

"Because I want you, Rory," he growled. "You invited me here as a friend and teacher, and I know you're not ready for horny me to be all over you."

"Oh! Well, I want you, too. I'm not sure, okay, well…" She was sort of rambling. "I've never had sex. I mean, I made out once and the night of the ball my date was…well, he was forceful and tore my dress but no actual—"

"Stop. You don't have to tell me all of that," he said. He ached for her as she was telling him this story. And it confused him. *A lot*. Because that wasn't any part of the story he'd heard about the ball from his aunt. But then his brother had died before any of them spoke to him. Had Dec attacked Rory?

He had no idea how his brother had been with women. Kit did know that his brother had been angry after learning the factory was being closed. Declan had often gotten physical with Kit when they'd been younger and arguing about something, but Kit had always thought that was just a sibling thing. He opened his eyes and looked at her, saw that she'd kind of shrunken into herself, and realized she needed to know that they were okay.

He opened his arms. "That doesn't matter. You and I will figure ourselves out."

She stepped into them and he hugged her close. He held her carefully as his mind was now spinning with questions that he was pretty sure he'd never get any satisfaction from, but he knew he had to find out what had actually happened the night that his brother died and Rory went into a coma.

She shifted back. "It's okay if—"

He put his fingers over her lips, not sure he could handle anything else she had to say right now. "No more talking for now. Let's go for a drive and just spend the day together. I'm not going to pressure you into anything."

"Oh, Kit, I know that. I just don't want you to be disappointed in me. In how I drive or how I kiss."

"Woman, your kisses are the best. Don't ever doubt that," he said.

Nodding, she locked her door and they headed to his car. He got behind the wheel and they drove out of Gilbert Corners together, over that bridge where the accident had happened, and once again he couldn't help wondering what had happened that night.

It had changed so many lives, even Kit's, and he hadn't been in town. But it had put him on a path toward this moment, driving him to questions that he knew he had to have answered.

* * *

They got on the interstate, which wasn't busy this time of the day. The leaves on the trees on both sides of the road were changing. Rory didn't remember particularly liking fall before, but now she did.

"Where are we going?"

"Oh, sorry, I went into autopilot and was heading back to Boston," he said.

"Was it me talking about sex…?"

"Yes. But please stop. I need a minute to think about something other than what you feel like in my arms," he said, his voice growing a bit husky on the last part.

"How about we get off at the next exit and find a spot that's not busy and you can help me drive?" she asked. "That's not sexy."

He signaled to exit the interstate. "Everything about you is."

She blushed, glad to hear him say that. "I was fishing."

"I know," he said, a wry grin flickering on his lips.

As he exited the interstate, she noticed there was a co-op off to the side advertising fresh cider, apples and doughnuts. Kit pulled into the parking lot and parked away from the other cars. He turned off the engine and put his arm along the back of her seat as he faced her. "I don't mind you fishing."

"That's one of many things I like about you, Kit," she admitted. She couldn't remember dating before the coma. She had an idea that she'd probably been afraid to admit things back then. But having missed a decade of her life, she wasn't going to let fear keep her from the things she wanted.

And she wanted Kit.

"What else do you like?" he asked.

She undid her seat belt and reached over to put her hand on his thigh. She did envy him his healthy body but knew hers was getting there. She squeezed his leg. "That you keep showing up despite the fact that I coerced you into it."

"You didn't force me to do anything I didn't want to," he said, his hand idly playing with a strand of hair that had escaped her braid.

She and Kit noticed people coming out of the store. "We can try letting you drive here," he suggested. "Or we can go into the shop."

"Do you like apple cider?" she asked him.

"I do. You?"

"I'm not entirely sure. I think so. I know I've never tried apple cider doughnuts."

"Let's go," he said. "Afterward, I'll give you a chance to drive my car."

He came around to her side of the car and offered her his hand to get out. Which she took. She left her walking stick in the car because her legs weren't tired and with Kit by her side... She stopped herself. She was supposed to be getting stronger on her own.

And she was.

But she also realized she didn't want to be on her own all the time. She craved this kind of interaction. Perhaps he did as well? And while she wasn't sure what he was struggling with, it was obvious he had some things going on, too. She wasn't so self-absorbed that she'd missed that.

"Do you mind if I have to hold your arm while we're walking around? Or I can bring my walking stick…"

"I don't mind," he said. "I'm sorry about earlier. I just feel bad that someone hurt you."

"It's not your fault," she assured him. "But I don't want to talk about it. I just wanted you to know what you were getting into with me. I hate lying."

Elle and Dash had faked being married to help Rory's recovery but when she'd found out the truth, she'd realized she couldn't tolerate lies. It wasn't that she thought they'd done it for a vicious reason, it was simply that she didn't want to have to look at the people closest to her and have to watch her back.

"I'm not a fan of liars either," he confided. "But sometimes white lies are necessary."

"I don't see how."

"To save hurt feelings or sometimes when it's not your secret to tell," Kit said.

He'd given this a lot of thought, she realized. Should that concern her? "If I asked you for the truth, would you be honest?"

He took a deep breath and then tipped his head as he looked down at her. "I would."

"Then that's all that matters," she said. Both Dash and Con had done things they regretted, so she knew how difficult it could be to revisit the past when Kit may have been a different man. But all that mattered was that she trusted him now.

He led the way into the shop, which smelled of fresh apples and cinnamon. They had a café in the back and Kit bought them apple cider doughnuts and hot apple cider. When they were done with their snack, he showed her how to drive and let her try driving around the parking lot.

Her legs didn't give her any trouble, and though she'd only gone twenty miles per hour, she couldn't help feeling triumphant when she parked the car and looked over at him.

"Knew you could do it!" he said.

Flushed with success, she leaned over, taking the kiss she'd wanted since she'd opened the door and seen him standing on her front porch. Whatever else she was unsure of in her life, Kit wasn't it.

Eight

Kit dropped Rory off at her place and she invited him in.

"Sure. Do you need help with any projects?"

"Always. How's your house coming along, by the way?"

"It's in pretty good shape. I hired a company to redo most of it before I moved in. Want to see it?" he asked.

The house hadn't ever been meant to be his permanent home. It was his base in Gilbert Corners so he could get the jump on Dash when it came to buying up property and figuring out what the Gilbert family was up to. Which right now made him feel slightly icky and his stomach to roil. The closer he got to Rory and her family, and the more he learned

about his own, revenge seemed like overkill. He'd
dedicated his life to avenging something that might
have been a lie told by his father.

"I'd love to," she said. "I'm curious to know more
about you."

"Like what?" he murmured as he parked in the
driveway and turned toward her.

"Well, when we video-chatted, your couch looked
so cozy. Gilbert Manor is always decorated for show
and I want my place have a more homey feel, but I'm
not sure how to create that. Maybe your place will
give me some ideas."

"Ah, my place is sort of a bachelor pad. I don't
think you're going to find any inspiration here," he
said.

He got out and opened her door for her, offering
her his hand as she got out of the car. "You never
know…"

"Actually," he said as he led the way up to his front
door, "I'm thinking about getting some of the flower-
pots like you have. To pretty the place up."

His house had been completely brought up to code
and modernized, like Rory's had on the outside, and
it stood out among the other places that hadn't been
redone yet. Kit had purchased three more on this
street and was in the process of developing them
with an eye toward offering affordable housing to his
workers once he found a large enough property on
which to build Palmer Industries' newest work hub.

His front door had been painted black and was a
nice contrast to the brick stonework on the outside

of the row house. The accents had originally been more Victorian but Kit favored wrought iron, which gave the place more of a contemporary feel.

He opened the door, gesturing for Rory to step inside. "There's a rug, so be careful."

"Thanks," she said with a smile. She stepped inside and then stopped after he followed her in and closed the door.

She shrugged out of her coat and handed it to him and then looked down at her booted feet. "Want me to take my shoes off?"

"It's up to you. I have a cleaning service and they are due to come in tomorrow."

He opened the coat closet and hung both of theirs up. Turning to find she'd sat down on the wooden bench to remove her flats, he sat down next to her with the intent of doing the same, but she put her hand on his thigh again and leaned into him.

Her breast brushed the side of his arm, sending a wave of want through him. He felt the warmth of her breath on his cheek, the smell of apple cider and then her silky soft hand against his jaw as she turned his face toward hers and kissed him.

He had told himself he needed more answers to the past before he let this thing with her go any further, but he was so tired of denying himself. He wanted her. More than he'd wanted anything in a long time, except revenge.

He slipped his arm around her waist and drew her close to him as the kiss deepened. She tilted her head to the side, her tongue sliding over his. God, she tasted so good.

Like everything he'd ever wanted.

Which jarred him because all he'd wanted for so long was to see Dash Gilbert fall. That once-clear dream was blurred. Now all he could see and think about was Rory, and this kiss sharpened the need in him that hadn't been far from the surface all day.

Stop thinking, he ordered himself.

He lifted her onto his lap, she wrapped both arms around his shoulders and he pushed his tongue deeper into her mouth as he slid his hand under the hem of her skirt, just lightly caressing the tops of her thighs. Her fingers were still on his jaw but her little finger was rubbing his neck right below his ear. Making him harden under her hip.

She shifted, her legs parting as he caressed her thighs. He lifted his head, looking down at her gorgeous face. Her eyes were half-closed, her lips parted and swollen from their kisses and there was a flush to her skin. He used his other hand to touch her lips and she kissed his finger before he drew it down her neck. She shivered delicately in his arms and shifted on his lap.

As she arched her back, his gaze fell to her breasts. He lifted one hand to touch her but knew if he did, this would go beyond a few heated kisses.

She took his hand, putting it on her breast.

"Don't stop now," she murmured.

Her words stirred something in him. He wanted her with a fierceness that he was fighting so hard to keep in check, not wanting to scare her. But when their lips met, he couldn't resist plunging his tongue deep into her mouth. Tasting her again, but also trying to tame her. Trying to find some way to overcome the need and want she was pulling so effortlessly from him.

He still had no idea what he was going to do to resolve his own conflicted emotions about the entire Gilbert family. But as Rory writhed in his arms, making him crazy with desire, he realized she was becoming more important than the past.

Spending the afternoon with Kit had been fun but she knew she wanted more. Her life at times felt like she moved through it in a fog. Talking to Elle and Indy helped her to mold herself into the woman she was trying to become, but the truth was, she spent a lot of time dreaming about life instead of *living* it.

When Kit had sat down next to her on the bench in his front hallway, she'd started to think of what she wanted him to do and realized that she couldn't wait for that. She'd spent too long waiting. So she'd kissed him.

And it was…wow. Not at all what she'd expected but so much more. Her entire body felt alive in a way that she hadn't ever experienced before. She loved the feel of his jaw under her fingers. Loved the slight stubble under his skin and how it felt when she rubbed her finger against it.

The skin on his neck was soft and his lips were firm and felt so good when she'd kissed him. And the way his tongue had rubbed against her made her wet and her breasts felt full and sort of achy.

When he'd stopped, she was sure that he was going to slow things down. She didn't know why, maybe he thought that was what she wanted. But she didn't. Her life was already going entirely too slowly. She wanted him, and unless he told her he didn't want her, too, she wasn't ready to get off his lap.

She felt the ridge of his erection under her hips and his hand on her thigh kept creeping higher and higher. She parted her legs as his tongue thrust into her mouth. She'd been binge-reading her favorite romance novels and she knew what she wanted to happen next: his hands on her naked skin.

But of course she had tights on, not that that seemed to stop Kit. His big hand glided over her thighs around to her butt and she felt his fingers flex as he cupped her and shifted her around on his lap.

She moved to straddle him and her thighs started shaking. They were still so weak at times. He lifted his head. His left hand still under her skirt, his other hand fondling her breast. "You okay? Still into this?"

"Yes. I just can't sit like this on you," she whispered.

"How's this?" he asked as he moved her back to the position she was in before. Sitting sideways on his lap.

It was better, but she briefly hated that weakness in her body. She looked down at her legs, feeling upset with the fact that she still wasn't strong, but there was no time to dwell on that. Kit's hand was back on her thigh, moving up again as his mouth was on hers again.

Winding her arms around his shoulders, she held on to him as his hands moved over her body. She felt like she was on fire and that momentary quivering from trying to use muscles that hadn't been used for too long was gone. In its place were a million little fires that were being started by Kit.

His hand under her shirt slowly moved around to her back, unhooking her bra and then rubbing between her shoulder blades as he brought her more fully into contact with him. He lifted his mouth from hers and she felt his kisses on her neck and then her shirt was up, the cool air in the foyer brushing over her heated skin.

She looked down at his hand on her ribs moving up toward her breast. Full and curvy, she liked the way it felt beneath his touch. Her nipple was hard and got harder as he swiped his finger over it. She wriggled on his lap, her hip rubbing against the ridge of his erection.

He lowered his mouth and licked her nipple, sending an arc of electricity through her body and a pulse of moisture between her legs. She shifted her legs against his hand. Feeling the roughness of his jeans beneath her and his fingers between her legs. Stroking her as his mouth feasted on her breast.

Surrounded by Kit, she had her hands in his hair, felt his hard-on beneath her as his fingers were rubbing against her, driving her higher and higher. Everything in her body was driving toward something, toward a mind-blowing climax, and then she was shuddering and shaking in his arms as it washed over her. Nearly delirious with desire, she pulled his mouth from her breast and began kissing him. Sucking his tongue into her mouth as her body kept spasming.

She felt wet between her legs but he kept stroking her. His erection under her hip had gotten bigger, harder. She wanted more. The orgasm he'd given her had been out of this world but she wanted his cock inside her.

He lifted her into his arms and stood, carrying her down the hall and placing her on a large leather sofa. He stood there for a minute, and she could see the outline of his erection against the front of his jeans.

"Do you want more or do you want me to stop?" he rasped.

"More," she said, her voice sounding foreign to her own ears, filled with need and demand.

"Good. Are you on the pill?" he asked.

"I am not," she said. She'd recently come out of a coma after all. Birth control hadn't been the first thing on her mind.

"Let me get a condom. I'll be right back."

She lay there watching him go for a moment. Her shirt bunched up under her breasts and then she sat up and took it off, tossing it aside. She removed her tights and her skirt and her underwear. For a minute she worried about her body: it had scars from surgeries, but not too many, and she really didn't have muscle tone.

But then Kit walked back in, and she noticed he'd also taken off his shirt. He looked down at her as he undid his pants and took his dick in his hand, rolling on the condom. "You are the most gorgeous woman I've ever seen."

Seeing Rory naked on his leather couch was making it hard for him to think about anything but being inside her. Her blond braid fell over her shoulder to her full breasts. She had her legs slightly parted and as he let his gaze move over her body he couldn't help noticing the signs that were still present from her accident.

There were faded scars around her knees, and on her left hip there was a jagged one that looked like it must have been rough. He had also felt the scar at the back of her scalp when he kissed her.

Feeling her so alive in his arms a few moments ago made him so damn grateful that she was here now. These emotions weren't easy to process and his dick said, *forget about that for now.* She was naked on his couch, waiting for him.

She'd pretty much told him she was a virgin and he wasn't sure he'd ever been with one. He hadn't had sex until college and his girlfriend at the time had been five years older than him. She'd been the one with the experience. Was there something different he needed to do? He wanted this first time for her to be exciting and one she'd never forget.

But then she opened her arms to him and he realized he was overthinking it. He knew there were unresolved things he needed to deal with, but those could wait. Right now he wanted to feel her silky limbs wrapped around his body and forget about everything except Rory.

Her deep blue eyes, sweet smile and the sexy sounds she made as she came, *that* was all he wanted more of. Kit wedged his knee between her legs and then settled onto the couch, carefully putting his body over hers. He used his torso to caress her, feeling the moistness at her center against his stomach as he slid up her body.

Her nipples were tiny points against his chest and then he settled his cock right between her thighs. He kept his full weight from her with his knees and his arms, which he braced on either side of her head.

Her hands were on him as soon as he was close enough. He shuddered at the feel of her palms sweeping up and down his back and then cupping his butt and drawing him closer to her. And when she arched her back, parting her thighs and rubbing herself against the ridge of his erection, he groaned.

Needing to be inside her now.

He shifted his hips, put the tip of his cock against the entrance of her body and stayed there. She lifted her head and their eyes met.

"Will it hurt?"

"I don't know," he said gruffly. "I've never been anyone's first before."

She shivered a little under him. And rearranged her legs again, wrapping them around his waist. "I'm glad."

"Me, too."

Then he brought his mouth down on hers, using his hands to cage her head between them as her tongue rubbed over his. He took his time with the kiss, building the passion in her so that when he entered her it would be more pleasure than pain.

She started moving against him, her body undulating under his and he repositioned his hips, taking his time before he drove himself deep into her body. He heard her gasp and her tongue sucked his deeper into her mouth.

She used her feet against his butt to push him deeper into her body as she arched underneath him. He pulled back and drove into her again and she moaned in response. After that, thinking became impossible. Instead, it was just the feel of Rory's body under his as she writhed under him and made these cries in the back of her throat that drove him higher and higher until everything in him exploded and he came inside her. But he wasn't through with her yet. He kept driving into her and felt her pussy tightening around him, milking him as he kept thrusting until he was empty.

Afterward, he rested his forehead against hers as he caught his breath. Her hands swept up and down his back and her legs were still around him as they clung together, basking in the moment. He rolled to his side and pulled her into the curve of his body, holding her there and looking down at her.

"You okay?"

"More than okay," she admitted. "I had no idea my body could feel like that… I don't think you can understand how much I've been frustrated by how hard it's been to relearn everything. But today…helps me believe it's all been worth it."

He shook his head and kissed the tip of her chin. "I'm glad. I love your body. You should be proud of the strength you've regained."

"I know," she said, wrinkling her nose. "But everyone else—"

"Isn't you. Which I'm very glad for," Kit insisted. "Be glad that you're not like everyone else."

She tipped her head to the side. "I hadn't thought of it that way. Just saw all the things I couldn't do or didn't know. But with you that doesn't seem to matter, Kit."

She put her hand on his jaw as she said that and the smile on her face went straight to that part of his soul that he thought had died the same night his brother had. It felt like caring and it scared him.

He had started something when he'd come here and thought about using her to get revenge against Dash. Begun something that was wicked—or maybe the real evil had started that night of the crash that had killed his brother and left Rory in a coma.

Kit had no idea what everything meant, but deep down in his gut he knew bringing down the Gilbert family was no longer the most important thing to him.

This woman was becoming that. But a Gilbert had cost his family once and he knew that if he was wrong about this, it would cost his family again.

Nine

Rory had a girls' night with Indy and Elle, the women who were engaged to Conrad and Dash, so Kit left her at Indy's bookstore. His mind was a mess. Normally focus was the one thing he fell back on, but not now. He drove back to Boston with one clear mission. He had to find out what exactly had happened the night of the ball.

Had his brother attacked Rory? Or had it been another man? He knew that Rory wasn't lying about what had happened to her. She had always been honest with him, and besides, lying wouldn't gain her anything since she didn't know he was related to Declan.

He didn't even allow himself to dwell on what had happened on his sofa or how much he wanted to keep her in his life. But the half-truths he'd told her when they'd been strangers loomed, and Kit knew he had to come clean. But he needed more facts before that happened.

He called his Aunt Mallory as he was driving.

"Hello, Rory. What's up?"

"Do you know if Declan went to the winter ball with Rory Gilbert?" he asked her. His aunt had been living in Boston back then but she'd talked to his father and brother weekly.

"I believe he did. Why are you inquiring?"

"Well, she remembers her date…" God, why was it so uncomfortable to say this out loud and to his aunt? He wasn't the one who'd been attacked, Rory was, and *she'd* been able to just say it. "Her date assaulted her and almost raped her. Could that be Declan?"

There was just silence and then he heard his aunt's ragged exhale. "I hope not."

That wasn't a no.

"Was he violent around women?"

"Not to my knowledge," she said. "But he and your father were very angry about the factory closing… So much so that your dad decided not to go to the party and I invited him up here for the evening," she said. "But I have no idea if Declan was the one to attack the Gilbert girl. Your father never said anything to me about it either, but you know what he was like after the accident."

Which told him nothing. His brother and father had been angry because the Gilberts went back on their word. And Kit hadn't ever gone out with his brother, so he didn't know how he had treated women. Plus there was a part of Kit that knew his father would have lied to protect Declan. But even if his sibling had been a gentleman to every other woman he dated, it didn't change anything. Anyone could commit assault.

If only the person in question wasn't his dead brother.

"Are you going to be home tonight?" Kit asked his aunt. "I want to look through some of dad's old papers."

"I'm playing bridge with my friends but I'll tell the housekeeper to let you in," she said. "Kit? Do you think the Gilberts have made up this story about Declan to make themselves feel better about him dying in the car crash?"

Kit didn't know what to think. "I'm not sure. I just want to see if Dad has anything in his belongings that I missed."

"That makes sense. I hope...well I hope Declan didn't do that to the girl," Aunt Mallory said quietly.

"Me, too."

He ended the call after saying goodbye. He wasn't sure that he would ever really know what had happened that night. But he still needed more information.

Rory deserved the truth from him. He couldn't just say, "Oh, hey, that guy who attacked you was my brother and sorry I didn't say it before." He needed to make sure he knew what had happened so he didn't hurt Rory. Knowing her the way he did, he knew that she was going to be upset that he had...lied. *You lied, dude.* There were no two ways about it. But he wasn't going to be the one to traumatize her again.

He was beginning to think he was going to have to come clean with both Rory and Dash. Dash might be the only one who could provide the answers he needed.

He called his office and checked in and then went to work for the rest of the day, not leaving to head to his aunt's house until almost eight. When he got there the housekeeper let him in and Kit went to what Aunt Mal called "the library," where she kept all of his father's journals and records.

Kit grabbed a beer from the fridge before he sat down at the large writing desk in the corner and started opening the files that had been stored in an old, ornate-looking, leather-covered wooden chest. He pulled out some journals and notebooks as well as a bunch of business records.

Flipping through the pages, he found a few notes in Dec's handwriting. He ran his finger over the writing. There were so many questions he had for his brother. He remembered playing in Gilbert Corners at the factory on Saturdays while their dad was working. Running up and down the stairs that led from the floor to his father's office.

Smiling when he thought of his father draping his arms over their shoulders and telling them one day they'd run the factory. Those had been good times—before his mom had gotten sick and died, before Dec had left for college and his father had started drinking.

He rubbed the back of his neck, not really sure he wanted to keep digging. Then he saw the Gilbert International logo on a letter. He pulled it out of the stack and saw it was addressed to both his father and brother.

Dear Will and Declan:

I'm sorry to lead with bad news but the factory in Gilbert Corners in no longer viable. We've been losing money there for months and many of the local workers we relied on are leaving the town. The decision has been made to close the factory effective December 31.

The jobs offered to you both to buy a controlling share of the factory and take over running it is no longer an option. I'd like to offer you both new roles at our offices in Boston. Your salaries will have a fifteen percent increase and we will cover the relocation costs.

I know this isn't the news you'd hoped to hear, but I think this will be a good opportunity for both of you.

Looking forward to seeing you at the winter gala.

Sincerely,
Lance Gilbert

Kit let the paper fall from his hands, leaning back in his chair and locking his fingers behind his head as he stared up at the ceiling. *What the actual fuck?* Did Aunt Mal know about this? Kit figured she didn't, as she'd been the one encouraging him to make the Gilberts pay.

But his father had. Why hadn't the old man ever mentioned this?

He still wasn't sure that his brother had done anything wrong the night of the gala. But this clearly showed that his father and brother knew they weren't going to buy and run the factory. More than that, they still would have had jobs even when the factory closed—their family wouldn't have been ruined like he'd been led to believe.

What else had his father been hiding?

Rory was having fun drinking white zinfandel and sitting in the cozy corner of Indy's Treasures. Elle was getting ready for her wedding to Dash. So she had been showing them pictures of potential wedding dresses. She had her mother's veil, which she intended to wear.

"Though Dash has seen that," Elle said.

"He has? How exactly?" Indy asked, picking up a pretzel bite that her friend Lulu had made and popping it in her mouth.

"On our first date I had gone to pick up my parents' stuff from my stepmom's house. It was in there and I put it on."

Rory had long gotten over her feelings of upset at Dash and Elle for lying to her about being married when she'd first gotten out of the coma. "I love this. So you guys were going on dates behind my back?"

Elle flushed. "Yes. I was trying to be professional and all and just help you get your memories back."

Rory shifted on the couch and hugged the other woman. "I know you were but there was something between the two of you. Something that I saw before you two did."

"Well, I'm glad you did," Elle said, hugging her back. "But enough about me. What's up with you and Kit?"

Rory tried not to flush when she thought about what it had been like to make love with him on his couch. She'd felt different since he'd left and she'd gone back home. Awake but in a different way than she'd been before.

"Wow. That good?" Indy asked with a soft smile. "I saw you two drive by the shop earlier today."

"He took me for a driving lesson," she said.

"Oh, is that all?" Indy teased. "I mean you're blushing pretty hard for someone who just learned how to steer and brake."

"Not just driving," she said. "I think I'm falling for him."

"Really?" Elle asked, her eyes widening.

Rory thought she heard a note of concern in her friend's voice. "Why? Is it too soon?"

"There's no clock on emotions," Indy said. "I mean with Con… I think I fell the first time I saw him on the promo for his show. I mean I got hot all over when he looked into the camera and the voiceover guy asked, '*Who is willing to challenge the beast*?'"

"Hot and bothered isn't falling," Elle pointed out. "Is it lust, Rory? You're not on the pill—"

"Elle, be my sister, not my doctor," Rory said. "And yes, it's lust but it's also so much more. He just sees me. Not someone who's been in a coma for ten years like Dash, Con and you two do. Or that freaky Gilbert girl like the town does. And through his eyes, I'm starting to see who I want to be."

"Sorry, Rory, just looking out for you. I'm glad he sees you. Just make sure you keep being Rory and not Kit's version of Rory," Elle murmured.

Rory smiled at Elle, knowing the other woman had her best interests at heart. "I will." She turned to Indy. "So how's Con…?"

Indy chewed her lower lip and then rolled her eyes. "A diva as always. Ever since we decided to share a studio and build it here in Gilbert Corners, I've been seeing another side to the man."

Rory let the conversation flow around her as the other women talked about the two men who'd always been so influential in her life. But she was only half listening. She knew that Elle was just being protective, sort of like Dash was, but the other woman had raised some concerns for her.

She knew she'd been struggling to find herself since she'd woken, and moving out on her own had been step one. If that escort/life coach she'd hired had shown up…would she even have met Kit? Had she poured herself into being what he wanted because she didn't want to be alone?

She hoped not. But how could she know for sure?

They chatted for a bit longer and then a push notification from the Gilbert Corners Chamber of Commerce came through announcing the clues for the speakeasy for that night. They were going Goth since Halloween was just around the corner and were having a My Chemical Romance tribute band.

They were one of her favorite bands, and after tonight's thoughts about being Rory or Kit's version of Rory, she wanted a chance to test herself. She messaged Kit to remind him about their upcoming date. He texted back that he couldn't wait.

Goth night sounded like just what he needed. All those angsty emotions he'd outgrown during his twenties were back swirling around inside. Kit pulled on his black jeans and old black biker boots, black tee and his favorite leather jacket. He put on kohl eyeliner that he'd picked up earlier and realized when he looked in the mirror that he missed this part of his life. Back before tragedy hit his family hard, leaving him with nothing but emptiness.

Aunt Mal tried, but his father and brother and he had been a tight threesome before Declan's death. She couldn't fill the gap that his drunk father and dead brother had left.

Pushing all of that back into the past, he locked his door and walked down to Rory's house. He was going to pretend he was just Kit and she was just Rory. She was the woman he'd made love to that very afternoon and he hoped to do it again soon. He wanted more with her and that had nothing to do with her being a Gilbert.

He knocked on her door, and when she opened it, his heartbeat pounded in his ears. She had on dark eyeliner, too. Her lips were bright red and she'd twisted her blond hair into two ponytails that she'd colored the ends of black. His eyes drifted over her appreciatively. She wore a pair of tight leather pants and a black see-through blouse with a black bra underneath.

He got hard just looking at her. He loved it. Loved the fact that everything between them felt new and fresh. None of the past obligation or responsibility he had to his family could get in his way. The more they connected, the more Kit treasured getting to know who Rory was without the Gilbert name.

She cocked her head to the side. "I like this side of you," she said.

"Same. Are you ready to go?" he asked.

"In a rush?"

"Not really, but I can't help noticing you put a bench in your hallway and now I'm thinking about what we can do there," he said with a smirk.

She flushed. "Maybe later if you play your cards right."

"Oh, I intend to," he assured her. He helped her get her black leather jacket on and then noticed she reached for her cane.

"Everything okay?" he asked. She hadn't used it earlier.

"Yeah, my thighs got a bit of a workout earlier and feel weak," she said. "Does it mess with my look?"

"Did I hurt you when we had sex?" he asked hoarsely. Dammit, he should have been more careful with her.

"No. I just don't use my legs that way usually," she said with a tinkling laugh. "We can practice and get them stronger. That's what my physical therapist always says when I try something new."

"I don't mind practicing. So where are we going?" he asked to distract himself of the images in his head of her naked underneath him.

"The speakeasy."

"I don't know what that is," he admitted.

She told him that the Main Street businesses had all gotten together with the Chamber of Commerce and helped fund and promote a pop-up bar that had been themed as a speakeasy. They sent out clues that took residents of Gilbert Corners around town, leading them to the bar.

"Sounds fun. GC didn't have anything like that when I lived here."

"No, they didn't. There's sort of a new energy to the town lately. Part of it is Indy and Lulu bringing their TV show here. For a while I think people were waiting for my family to come back and make things happen, but then decided they should just do it for themselves, sort of."

"Your family does have a lot of power here," he remarked. "But what do you mean *sort of*?"

"Well, Indy did break the curse when she got

Conrad to come back and do his show, so it was like a combo of new ideas, new people and old superstitions."

He liked what she was saying and how she saw the town. Rory clearly loved it here despite the difficulties her family had faced over the years. He almost let himself get distracted and start thinking of business and how he could bring Palmer Industries into it. But he wanted tonight as a date. Not as an opportunity.

And until he figured out more of what had happened the night his brother died, he didn't want to push forward with anything involving either Rory or Dash.

"So the speakeasy is doing a Goth night?" he asked, not sure how it fit in with the previous theming.

"Yeah. I guess because it's October and Halloween is just around the corner. Or maybe they wanted to try something new," she said. "The tribute band is My Chemical Romance."

"You like them?"

"Loved them. I mean as soon as I saw their name, 'Helena' started playing in my head. I hadn't thought of them since I woke up but there the song was," she said.

Kit took her hand in his as they talked about music and followed the clues.

He knew that he was going to have to face the past and figure out what to do next, but for tonight it was enough to be with Rory, singing "I'm Not Okay" at the top of his lungs on a semi-crowded dance floor.

Her body brushed against his and he held her close when she stumbled. He knew that no matter what he wanted, sooner or later he was going to have ask her more questions about the accident and tell her about his brother, but not tonight. Tonight was about letting go. Tonight was for them.

Ten

The Gilbert Corners Chili Cookoff wasn't something that Kit thought he'd find himself participating in. Especially not in a booth with the Gilberts. But he had to stop thinking of them as Gilberts. So instead he focused on being here with Rory and her family. A few weeks had passed since their night at the speakeasy.

Indy and Conrad were doing a special that would run on the network where they both had television shows. It was combining her town makeover idea and his quintessential cooking challenge. The differences in this show were that the challenge was just locals all cooking their favorite chili recipe—normally Con's show focused on a showdown between his professional persona "The Beast" and a solo challenger.

And then Indy and her makeover team, which included Lulu who ran the coffee shop, had undertaken the old Gilbert Civic Center space. Rory had worked with Indy's team on redoing the interior of the convention space and, after some thought, Kit and Palmer Industries had partnered with them as well. The civic center was one of the run-down properties that he'd purchased.

Rory had come to him about the needed updates so he'd immediately offered to make a donation through his company.

Aunt Mal hadn't been happy that he'd donated it back to the town but she'd liked the plaque on the side of the building that thanked them for the donation. She wanted more plaques around town that didn't have the Gilbert name on them.

The town wasn't beholden to the Gilbert family anymore. Which suited Kit. He still hadn't had a chance to talk to Dash and Con about the night of the accident and he hadn't brought up the man who'd attacked Rory. A part of him didn't want to know if it had been his brother.

Coward.

But the truth was, Declan had been the only positive male influence that Kit had had. His father's descent into alcoholism had soured the relationship between him and Kit. Something that Kit knew he'd never been able to forgive. His father should have stayed sober and helped Kit rebuild Orr Industries. Instead, at twenty-one, Kit felt like he had to start a new business, Palmer Industries, running a business in a field that had been dictated by ruthlessness and revenge. It had been what he'd believed was his dad's severance pay and Aunt Mal's savings that had given them the start they needed. And then…well, dumb luck. Aunt Mal said he had a head for business and maybe he did. They'd gone after smaller companies until they were established and then had targeted opportunities that Gilbert International showed interest in.

And slowly Kit had developed the skills and acumen needed to defeat Dash when it came to winning business deals and wooing clients. Not all the time, but often enough that he knew he could eventually bring the man down. But bringing him down was no longer the goal. Kit had come to realize that Dash wasn't a villain who'd taken away his family's opportunity. He was just a man. And he was Rory's brother.

"I have to talk on camera," Rory said, coming over to him. She had her long blond hair loose, hanging around her shoulders in a way that nicely framed her heart-shaped face. "What if I sound like an idiot?"

He took her hand in his and drew her away from the booth where Conrad's assistants were setting up the cooking area for their team. "You won't. You are too smart and you already rehearsed it for me this morning. You know what you're doing."

She chewed on her lower lip. "I know but it was easier talking to you."

"Do you want me to go and stand behind the cameraman? You can look at me when you're talking," he suggested. The more time he spent with Rory the harder it was to have any sense of perspective on any of the past. He was falling for her and it would be silly to pretend he wasn't. She'd also made him face the hard truth of his perceptions about the past with his father and brother.

Being around her made him feel alive for the first time since college. He wasn't constantly thinking about what the Gilberts had taken from him but instead felt like he was enjoying an unexpected gift.

She tipped her head to the side and gave him a soft smile that went straight to his groin and made him want to carry her from the hall and make passionate love to her.

"We are more." There was something flirty and sexy in the way she watched him.

He *knew* they were. And that made the secret he kept from her even worse. However, he didn't want to hurt her anymore than she'd already been hurt by his brother and the past. But was he just making excuses for himself? His greatest fear was that the longer he kept the truth from her the more betrayed she'd feel.

"We are. So I think even your therapist would say it's okay for me to be there for you when you speak on camera for the first time."

She nodded. "I can't believe I'm doing this."

"Why not?"

She shrugged and looked around the hall. The interior was modern and sleek and the walls were adorned with artwork and frescoes created by local artists and students from the high school. The civic center, which had previously held a large portrait of all of the Gilberts who'd served on the town council was now more of a town-focused place.

"It's just that until now most of my work has been quiet and small. I loved working on the interior of the building and doing the behind-the-scenes work. But this is me being in the spotlight." She stopped and then shook her head. "It's not like the people of Gilbert Corners haven't always talked about me, but I've always pretended I didn't know they were."

"This time you're controlling the narrative," he pointed out. "You're going to get up there and talk about the work you put into this space and how it's really part of the town and the people who live in Gilbert Corners. I think that's important and I also believe you're the only one who can do it."

"Oh, Kit, thank you," she said, throwing herself into his arms. He caught her and held her close, shutting his eyes and breathing in the scent and feel of her.

He wanted her. Not just right this moment but forever. He'd never thought of forever before. It scared him. He'd always known once he'd come to Gilbert Corners things would change but he hadn't realized how they would.

Rory was nervous and not just for the reasons she'd given Kit. This was her first project at the first paying job she'd had. She wanted the people of Gilbert Corners to like what she'd done to the civic center. Kit had asked her if she wanted to take her new renovating skills and apply them to the project.

She'd said yes as she had to everything new and risky since she'd moved out on her own. The work had been more fun than she'd realized. She could have done it for gratis but Kit had insisted. He'd have had to hire someone to oversee the project if she wasn't doing it. Which had made her even more determined to make sure the building exceeded his expectations.

She'd leaned heavily on Indy and Lulu at first, asking them for pointers when she'd run into things she'd never dealt with before. But as she stood next to Kit in the hall, watching not only the TV crew get set up but locals as well who were seeing it for the first time, she felt a sense of pride as she overheard comments about how good the renovation looked.

For once, people were talking about her not because she was one of those cursed Gilberts but because of the work she'd done. She turned to Kit.

"Thank you for giving me this chance."

"You're welcome. I knew you could do it," he said proudly.

But she hadn't shared his confidence.

That wasn't something she was sure she would ever say to anyone but her therapist. But the truth was she'd had a massive anxiety attack after she'd signed the contract with Palmer Industries. She'd sat on her couch and listed all the reasons why she was going to fail and had to do box breathing to just calm herself down long enough to see.

But then she'd looked around her house at all the projects she'd done there and that had helped. And as Kit had said earlier today, she hadn't had to do it on her own.

Kit held her hand and stood next to her in his typical all black. Today he wore black jeans, a long-sleeved black button-down shirt and that thick leather belt that drew her eyes to his hips.

She felt a zing of sexual awareness go through her. Totally not what she should be thinking about at the moment. But when she was close to Kit it was hard not to.

The more time they spent together, the more she was starting to get used to him in her life.

Was that good?

He was the first boyfriend she'd had as an adult. Surely, she should date around before finding someone she wanted to spend the rest of her life with. And she *did* want a partner in life. She'd seen with Conrad and Dash how finding someone they loved and shared their life with had enhanced them. Made them seem more fulfilled.

She wanted that.

Was she just seeing in Kit what she wanted to see?

Her heartbeat sped up and a few doubts crept into the good endorphins that she always experienced when she was with him.

"What is it?" he asked, looking concerned. "You know, if you don't want to be on camera you don't have to do it."

She smiled and that knot in the pit of her stomach

started to relax. Kit always thought of her first. She knew that was important. Or at least it was to her. "I know. I'll be okay. Thanks for coming over here with me."

"Rory, if it's possible, I'll always be here for you."

Oh! Why did he have to say things like that in the middle of a crowded room? She kissed him, long and deep, and then pulled back before it went too far. "Thank you."

He flashed a grin that made everything feminine in her melt into a puddle of want and need. She didn't know if she was going to be able to wait until the chili fest was over to be alone with him.

She flushed, thinking about making love in the back hallway of the civic center. She knew just the spot that would give them the privacy they needed.

"How much longer until you need me?" she asked the director.

"About ten minutes. You can go and I'll text you when we're ready."

"Great," she said before turning to Kit. "Come with me."

Rory took his hand and led him out of the main hall of the civic center and up the back stairs to the small room that had been used as a projection room back in the day. She'd remodeled it into a private meeting space.

She closed and locked the door behind them after she'd led him inside.

"Uh, Ms. Gilbert…what are you doing?"

She winked. "I was thinking there's one thing that I need."

"And that's…?"

Kit. She needed Kit. She was being flirty and playful with him but deep in her soul she knew she needed him.

It might not be wise to fall for the first man she dated but she knew she was. She was totally vibing on Kit. Everything about him was ticking boxes and pushing buttons and in every way that mattered, he was just what she wanted.

She didn't know if she'd dreamed him up in her coma or how he'd dropped into her life…and she didn't care. She was just glad he was here now.

She pushed him back against the locked door, leaning into him and wrapping one thigh around his hip.

And from the look on his face he wanted her just as badly.

His eyes glinting with desire, he put his hands on her butt and drew her up into his body as his mouth came down on hers.

Kit was aware that Rory only had ten minutes until she had to be back downstairs. Hot and horny, all he wanted to was turn and bang her against the wall but he wasn't sure that would be satisfying for her. Though his mind was having a hard time staying in control.

Her mouth was on his neck, sucking at that one spot that seemed connected to his cock, which was only getting harder. She was rubbing herself against the ridge of his erection as her hands held his shoulders tightly.

"Rory…honey, we don't have time for this," he gritted out.

"I'm pretty sure we do. I mean last night you did it in five."

He groaned. He hadn't been able to resist her when she'd put on his T-shirt and danced around the living room, showing off her new strength. God, the more time he spent with her, the harder it was to keep from falling for her.

He looked into her pretty blue eyes and knew that it was time to stop pretending he thought he shouldn't fall for her. He'd already started. There was no going back and a part of him, deep down, knew he was looking for a way to have Rory and satisfy the need to even the odds with Dash Gilbert.

She put her hands around his neck and shifted so that her breasts brushed against his chest. He felt the hardness of her nipples through the silk blouse she wore. He lifted one hand, rubbing his finger over the tip.

Fuck.

He wanted her and she wanted him. Why was he hesitating?

The thought that he felt he didn't deserve Rory danced through his mind and he shoved it away. Not now. He'd deal with that later.

Right now his woman was in his arms, undulating against him and making him so hard he might come in his pants. Which would be a waste. He kissed her neck and then lower, undoing the top two buttons of her shirt until he could see the fabric of her black, lace bra and the upper curve of her breasts.

He groaned, knowing there was no way he was leaving this room without satisfying his woman. He turned them so that her back was against the wall. Putting one hand on the wall next to her head, he reached between them, shoving his hand up under her skirt. She wore tights and he pulled them down far enough that he could get his hands on her skin.

Damn.

Her skin was soft and as he pushed his hand closer to her pussy he felt the warmth of her. He cupped her and she tipped her head back against the wall, her breath coming in short gasps as he fingered her. She was so hot and so ready. He reached between them and undid his jeans, freeing his erection.

She'd started taking the pill so they didn't have to use a condom when they had sex. His mind was conscious of that as he shifted his hips until the tip of his cock was nestled against the heat of her center. Her hands were on his butt, urging him forward as he slipped inside.

He brought his mouth down on hers, plunging his tongue deep into her mouth as he filled her. She was always so tight when he first entered her and her pussy tightened around him as he drove into her again and again.

She sucked on his tongue, her nails digging into

his shoulders as he thrust faster, until she tore her mouth from his and moaned his name.

He drove into her harder until everything inside him tightened and he came in her in a long, heady rush.

Afterward, he braced his arm against the wall, holding himself up until he was empty. He rested his forehead against hers and she smiled up at him.

He shifted back from her, tucking his dick back into his pants and then doing up his jeans. "Why are you smiling like that?"

"Well, I had added *do it in a public place* to my list of things we should try," she replied. "But hadn't had a chance to mention it to you yet."

She pulled her tights up and rebuttoned her blouse and something deep inside him that had felt dead for too long sort of started to come back to life. His heart was racing and emotions that he didn't want to name swirled within him.

"*Do it?* Is that your sexy talk?" he teased, trying to keep things light when everything in him urged him to grab her and make her his. To take her away from Gilbert Corners and convince her that he was the only man for her. Now, before she learned who he really was.

She quirked a brow. "What do you call it?"

"Hooking up?"

"That's not really much better," she said.

Her phone pinged and she gave a nervous laugh. "I think I have to go."

"You're going to do great," he said again.

"Well, I'm not nervous about talking now."

"Are you still nervous in general?"

"Just hoping no one notices that hickey I gave you," she said with a wink as she unlocked the door.

Kit didn't mind if the entire world noticed. He was proud to be Rory's man. Grinning to himself, he followed her down the stairs. And as he predicted, despite what she feared when the cameras started rolling, she was a natural. She kept eye contact with him but her voice and attention were on the job she was doing.

His woman. He might not say the words out loud but his soul had claimed her and a part of him knew he was never letting her go.

Eleven

After that night at the speakeasy, Rory stopped worrying about being strong enough or perfect enough and just started to find her footing. They were seeing more of each other—Kit was working from home in Gilbert Corners, and spending most nights at her house in her bed, making love to her all night long.

Kit was awakening dreams in her that she hadn't given a chance to bloom. A part of her was afraid to accept them but that part got quieter and quieter the more time the two of them spent together.

They were having lunch at Lulu's and sitting at one of the outside tables on Wednesday. It was the kind of crisp autumn day that wasn't too chilly in the sun. They'd ordered the special, which was vegetarian chili and jalapeno corn bread. Kit was at the counter waiting for their order and Rory couldn't help staring at him, feeling warm inside.

He was her man.

"Hey, cuz. Mind if we join you?"

She glanced up to see Conrad and Indy standing near the table. She stood up to hug them both. "Not at all. Kit's grabbing our lunch and should be back in a moment. Do you want to drag that table over?"

Con complied and then gave Indy a squeeze before he went into the shop.

"It's odd that you two are free at lunchtime," Rory said, knowing that the two of them had been working on the studio they were building near the old Gilbert International Factory.

"Yeah, well, your cousin saw the two of you together and wants to 'get to know' Kit better," Indy said.

Uh-oh.

"Like how?"

"Like the third degree. He used his Beast's Lair glare on me when I said we should let you two alone." Indy huffed out a breath. "You know how he can be."

Actually she did. Both Conrad and her brother were so overprotective of her that at times it was downright smothering.

"I think he'll find that Kit is a great guy," Rory said.

"I have no doubt that he is, but Con isn't going to see it that easily," Indy predicted. "If he gets out of hand, I'll kick him under the table."

Rory laughed at that. Her cousin's fiancée was about a foot shorter than Conrad, who was six-foot-five-inches tall. He looked fierce, with the scars on his face and the tattoos that covered his body. But Rory knew that underneath all that he was a softy. "I hope it doesn't come to that."

"Whatever happens, happens," Indy said.

"You guys okay?"

"Yeah, I just… I'm used to always being in charge and Con is, too. Working together is both the best and the worst," she said. "Also Halloween is coming up, and that's when I was attacked, so I'm edgy, which is making Con edgy, too."

Rory knew that, like herself, Indy had been forcibly attacked by her date, and though it had happened years before, the scars remained for Indy. In a way Rory thought it felt like a blessing that she'd been in a coma. The incident with Declan was still so hazy. The night of the gala felt like a scary dream instead of a real memory.

"I'm thinking of having a Halloween party. Maybe having a new good memory will help," Rory said.

"That might work," Indy replied. "Also, I relish the idea of seeing Con in a costume."

That could be fun. And it would give her brother and cousin a chance to get to know Kit on a deeper level. "I'm going to as well."

She pulled out her phone and set up a new group text chat with Dash, Elle, Conrad, Indy, Kit and herself. She titled it Halloween Party.

This Saturday. Costume party at my place. 8 p.m. No excuses. Be there.

Indy's phone pinged and she smiled at Rory. "I'll be there."

She glanced up inside Lulu's and saw Kit pull his phone out and turn away from Conrad, who was standing next to him. Kit was tall next to Rory but not compared to Conrad and she noticed her cousin wasn't slouching, as he sometimes did, but stood at his full height.

Kit came back to the table with their tray and smiled tightly as he sat down next to her.

"Hi, Kit. I'm Indy. It's nice to meet you," Indy said.

"Nice to meet you, too," he replied as he placed a chili bowl in front of Rory and then one in front of himself.

Rory took the tray and secured it under her seat and then, noticing her cousin walking toward them with his tray, leaned over and kissed Kit. She took her time with the kiss and after a moment Kit did, too. Putting his hand on the side of her neck as he deepened the kiss.

He lifted his head just as Conrad arrived at their table and set his tray down forcefully. She looked over at Conrad.

"I'm glad you met my boyfriend, Kit."

"Yeah, me, too," Con grumbled. "So you're having a party?"

Rory almost smiled at the way Conrad said it. As much as he might not be sure of Kit, one of the things she loved about her cousin was that he was never going to be difficult unless the situation called for it.

"We are. I can't wait to see your costume," she told him.

"We're going to go as Beauty and the Beast," Indy chimed in.

Conrad looked over at her and she smiled at him and Rory saw her cousin's expression change into a look of pure love. Rory almost sighed. That was how she wanted Kit to look at her. Which floored her because she'd felt so flawed and like her life was still so much in flux that love wouldn't be right for her. But she knew that was what she wanted now.

"I guess I can wear my chef whites," Con murmured.

"Uh, no. A tux as you'll be the beauty and I'll be the beast," Indy said.

"Or we figure something else out," Conrad grumbled. "What about you two?"

Kit looked over at Rory. A couples' costume would be fun but he wasn't sure he had any good ideas. "Thoughts?"

Rory took a bite of her chili, he guessed to give herself time to think. She had her free hand on his leg and he was still turned on from the kiss she'd planted on him a few moments ago.

Working from Gilbert Corners had been a strategic move to give himself space from his aunt Mal and to try to piece together what had happened the night of winter gala.

But it had turned into something different. He'd practically given up his motive for revenge, spending more time with Rory with each passing day. It made him want to leave the past alone and start to think about a future.

The funny thing about revenge was that it never let you dream of anything other than someone else's downfall. It was a negative place to be for most of his adult life.

"Well, we could do classic monsters," Rory mused. "I've always liked Frankenstein and Bride of Frankenstein."

"Uh, not sure about that…"

"That's right, you don't like monster movies," she teased.

Kit didn't like being scared, so he'd been surprised when Rory had tried to get him to do a movie marathon of her favorite scary movies like *Halloween* and *Nightmare on Elm Street*.

"How about Rick and Evie from *The Mummy*?" Rory said.

He nodded. "You'll make a great Evie."

"And you a good Rick. Glad that's settled," Rory said.

"I think we should be Imhotep and Anck-su-namun," Indy murmured. "That would be fun and you'd be shirtless, which I always love."

"Not sure about that. We don't want Elle and Dash to feel left out," Con said. "We'll do Beauty and the Beast."

Kit couldn't really square the guy sitting across from him being sweet and tender with his fiancée to the man who'd glared and tried to intimidate him in the coffee shop. "So how'd you two meet?"

He felt like the more that Conrad talked to and about Indy the more he relaxed, and it wouldn't hurt to get to know him better. Conrad had been at the party the night of the crash and it might be easier to talk to him about that than Dash.

"I challenged him on his cooking show," Indy said.

"Who won?"

"The Michelin-starred chef," Conrad stated drily.

"But I also won because I got Con back here to break the curse."

Kit wasn't too sure the curse had been lifted. There was still too much unresolved with his family. No matter that the Gilberts might have been the cause of the curse on the town, he knew his family had a part in it, too.

Conrad leaned over and whispered something in Indy's ear, which made her blush and kiss him. Kit looked over at Rory, who watched the other couple and then turned to him and smiled. "They are so cute."

"Yeah, cute," Kit muttered.

The conversation changed to Gilbert Corners and he was surprised to learn that Conrad and Indy were doing a lot of work around town. He had heard of her television show and knew she'd been filming but hadn't realized that she was redoing more than homes.

"My company is developing property as well," Kit said. "I'm interested in getting the old factory space renovated."

Once he'd started helping with the civic center with Rory he'd realized there were more places and projects around Gilbert Corners that could use his expertise. He might have wanted to be the CEO of a global conglomerate but he was damned good at it. And he wanted…*needed*…to put some good into Gilbert Corners. Not just for Rory but also for himself and his deceased brother and father.

"We are, too," Conrad said. "So far we have used part of the space as a film studio for our shows and I'm working on a test/teaching kitchen in another part of the space. What does you company do?"

"We develop run-down areas with an eye not toward gentrification but toward making spaces that serve the community already living and working there. I know that sounds vague but it really depends on what each town needs. I've been looking around GC and I think we need shared office spaces so that we can encourage people to stay here instead of moving away for work."

Conrad finished his chili and leaned back in his chair, crossing his arms over his chest. "I agree. We don't have to bring everything here, but with the new hybrid working environment we need to have structure in place to make it doable. Dash and I have been working with the town council to bring the fiber and broadband up so it's the best available."

"That's a good start," Kit said.

"Yeah. We're meeting next week to go over the details and could use some more local partners. Want to join us?" Conrad asked.

"Yes, that would be great," Kit said.

As he answered, his pulse started racing. He knew this plan to collaborate with the Gilberts would be hard to explain to his board and to Aunt Mal. He'd been focused on trying to take business from Gilbert International for so long, and if he suddenly partnered with them...well, it would take some explaining. But this was something he couldn't say no to. He wanted to get to know these Gilbert men better, not just to answer his own questions but also for Rory. He wanted to find a way where he could tell her who he was and keep her in his life, and right now, it seemed this was the only viable way to move forward.

"Great. I'll text you the details," Conrad offered.

They finished their meal and said goodbye. Walking Rory back to her place, he noticed that she was quiet. "You okay?"

"Yes. Are you?"

He nodded but inside he wasn't sure. He wouldn't be until he found a way to keep Rory in his life.

It was the Saturday before Halloween and Rory was excited about hosting the get-together for her family and friends. Well, she and Kit were hosting. She'd told him to invite his friends along, too, but he'd told her that he didn't have many outside of work. Rory's house was coming along and Kit had started spending most evenings with her working on home improvement projects.

"Are you sure about this?" he asked, coming out

of her bedroom in the Rick costume that went with her Evie getup. She loved the slim-fitting shirt and the balloon-sleeve blouse she was wearing.

Kit looked dashing with the suspenders on, shirt open at the collar and his holster for his fake gun.

"Yes. We look good, don't we?"

"We do," he said, coming up behind her and putting his arms around her waist.

She looked at the two of them in the mirror and her heart beat a little bit faster. It was getting harder to deny she was falling for him. Not that she wanted to deny it. But she also wasn't sure where this was going in his mind.

"We never talk about your family," she remarked.

"I only have my aunt left. My parents and brother are dead," he said.

She turned in his arms, hugging him to her. "I'm sorry about that. I'd love to meet your aunt." She left it at that, knowing all too well how difficult it was to talk about grief.

He squeezed her close for a second and then dropped his arms and walked away to get the gun to go in his holster. "Yeah, we'll have to figure that out."

"Are you two close?" she asked because he sounded like he wasn't sure that he wanted them to meet.

"We are, actually," he said.

She almost let it go. But if she was going to let herself fall for him, then this wasn't the time to be timid. "So why don't you want me to meet her?"

He turned and the look on his face was…well,

more complicated than Rory had imagined it should be. She was introducing him to the people who were important to her so why was he reluctant to reciprocate? True, both Con and Dash had been forcefully trying to get to know him…but still.

"It's not that exactly," he said.

For the first time since they'd met she wasn't sure she believed him. She took a deep breath.

"I know my family is about to show up and we have a party to host, but what's the deal? Are you embarrassed by me in some way? Am I good enough for Gilbert Corners but not for—"

"Don't be ridiculous. You're perfect and a Gilbert, so when have you ever not been enough?"

She didn't like the sound of that. "I'm not a Gilbert with you, Kit. I'm Rory. And I've not been enough a lot lately."

"You're all I need," he said roughly as he came over and took her into his arms. "And regarding my aunt… It's not you. It's me."

"You? If you're close she must love you and want you to be happy," Rory insisted, trying to understand what he meant.

"She does. But…as you said, we don't have time to get into the details. But the night my brother died changed my family forever. My aunt and I united in our grief, trying to get the people responsible to pay for their actions."

"Oh, Kit, that sounds horrible. Like you've been carrying this for a long time. Is there anything I can do to help?" she asked.

"No, Rory."

"So your aunt doesn't want you to date?" she asked, still confused. His refusal of her help sounded harsh. Like she was the last person he'd want help from. Or was *she* the one confusing things?

"She doesn't care about my personal life. She just cares about our agenda," he said, a thread of pain in his voice.

She put her hand on his shoulder as he was about to turn away from her. "And what is her agenda?"

He took a deep breath and something in the air changed around them. She wondered what it was he was hiding. Because she suddenly realized he was.

"Revenge."

She shook her head. "That's not you, Kit. You're not someone who goes after people. I mean you helped me, a stranger, without even knowing my name."

There was no way she could reconcile in her mind what Kit was trying to say. Kit had been kind to her from the start. He'd been generous when she'd asked for his help in Gilbert Corners.

He was a man who didn't hesitate to offer aid. That was who he truly was. And hearing this…well, it filled in the gaps a little bit. The lonely man who seemed to carry the weight of the world on his shoulders would grapple with revenge.

"But I did know your name, Rory. I knew you from when we were children, remember?"

"Did you know it when I approached you?" she asked, having believed it was when she'd said her name that he'd connected it to who she was.

"I did."

"Oh. So…what are you trying to say?" she asked.

The doorbell rang. That was probably Dash and Elle. Her brother was always early.

"Go answer the door," he told her. "We can talk after everyone goes home."

She wasn't entirely sure she wanted to put this off, but she also didn't want to have this type of discussion while her brother waited outside.

"Okay. But I'm not going to let this go," she warned.

"I'm not either. It's time I told you everything," he said.

Everything? That sounded ominous to her. "Will we be okay after?"

He tried to smile but it felt sad to her. "I hope so."

But it didn't sound like he believed they would be. She went to answer the door, fake-smiling at her brother who was dressed as a patient and Elle who wore her surgery scrubs.

"We didn't have time to plan costumes so had to make do," Dash said sheepishly.

"You look great," she murmured, hugging her brother close and realizing that she was happy he was here. She had wanted independence and thought she could make a new life for herself with Kit in it, but suddenly nothing seemed sure.

"You okay?" he asked as Elle and Kit were talking.

"Yeah, I'm fine. Just realizing that life doesn't always go according to plan," she said. Which, honestly, she should have realized long before this. But the coma had warped things and made the last ten years seem like a long dream.

Kit had changed her, helping her to wake up and live. She was only now realizing that living meant dealing with good times as well as bad.

Twelve

Kit knew he'd fucked up when he'd let the conversation drift toward Aunt Mal and his tragic family history. But it was past time to talk to Rory about what had happened the night of the ball, and he knew it. As usual, his timing sucked.

"Con tells me you have some ideas for business here in GC," Dash said as he came over to him.

Rory was in the living room with Elle and Indy, getting her in-home speaker to use the playlist she'd created for the party. And Con was in the kitchen whipping up something that smelled really good.

"I do," he answered, not sure how much to elaborate. "My company, Palmer Industries, has been buying properties around town with an eye to making Gilbert

Corners a hub for people who want to live in a small
town yet work for bigger companies."

"Palmer Industries… I think you and I have gone
up for some of the same things recently."

"We have," Kit said. It seemed tonight was his
time of reckoning. He was done hiding and pretending.

"Nothing wrong with some friendly competition,
and if it helps GC I'm all for it," Dash confided. "And
if it's okay with you, I'm interested in seeing your
ideas. For so many years, it was just me trying to
come up with things… Well, honestly, I think I was
avoiding the town as much as I could."

Kit realized that Dash was treating him like a
friend in a way. Like someone his sister was dating.
He wanted to bc chill and just see where this went.
"Because of Rory?"

"Yeah, and Con and the accident. I don't know
how much you've heard about that night but there
was a huge car accident and another man died," Dash
said. "It was the worst night of my life."

Kit heard the pain in his voice. "What happened?"
he couldn't help but ask. To see if anything Dash
had to say would help him get the clarity he needed.

Con came over with a tray of baked brie bites.
"Try this." He gave Dash and Kit a curious look.
"What are you two talking about?"

"The night of the crash," Dash replied, taking one
and popping it in his mouth. "Fuck, it's hot."

"Let it cool down," Conrad admonished.

Kit took one and waited a moment before tasting

it. But his mind wasn't on food right now. He noticed Rory watching him across the room, and while the last time he'd been sort of cornered by Conrad she'd been sympathetic toward him, this time…she looked like she didn't know who he was.

He knew that she didn't. That he'd been lying from the moment she'd introduced herself and he was sick and tired of it. He wanted to just demand to know what happened that night ten years ago. To figure out why his brother was dead, what caused his father to slowly drink himself to death. He wanted to know why his aunt had said one thing but the notes he'd found in that antique wooden chest had shown something else. He wanted…he wanted Rory to look at him like he was a hero and not some villain.

"Why do you want to know about the crash?" Conrad asked him.

"For Rory," Kit said. "She has mentioned a few things… I just want to know more and I don't want to push her into talking about anything that makes her uncomfortable."

"I don't remember much of the crash. Dash walked away without a scratch. Safe to say he remembers the most. We can discuss it next week when we aren't around Rory," Con told him before turning to address his cousin. "Dash, did you tell her about the co-op I mentioned?"

"Not yet," he said. "For years Con wanted nothing to do with the business and now he's sending me proposals left and right."

"You said to get involved," Conrad said, and turned

to Kit. "He's a pain in the ass. But it was your idea, Kit, that got me thinking. We have a bunch of people with skills that are underutilized, like the Hammond sisters, who had run the kitchens at Gilbert Manor. They taught me to cook."

"I agree," Kit said, accepting the change of topic. "Can't wait to chat with you both more."

"Enough shop talk," Indy said, coming over to them. "It's time to get this party going. Give me those."

Indy grabbed the snack tray. "What do you have planned?"

Rory had set up a few games to play. Kit hadn't had a party like this before. It was so small and so intimate. While everyone was taking a seat and she handed out Post-it notes, he pulled her into the kitchen so they were alone.

"What's up?" she asked.

"I want this to be fun. There's just a lot of stuff in my life I haven't really ever talked about. But you are important to me," he blurted. He realized from her expression that it might not be what she was expecting from him, but still it had to be said. "I'm sorry for starting things before everyone got here. But the truth is… I'm nervous."

She looked up at him, then put her arms around him and hugged him close. "I'm nervous, too. Since you came into my life I've been just diving into things with you, trying to find someone to have in my life. I've been in a rush to know everything about you. And that's not fair to you."

He tipped her head back and looked down into her eyes, then kissed her long and slow. Everything felt better when she was in his arms. He needed to stop worrying and try to find the right words to say that would make her understand.

Because the truth was, there wasn't a way to explain what was between the two of them. He would do everything in his power to be the man she wanted.

"I think I want that, too," he confessed. "I'm not used to sharing things. I've always kept everything to myself."

She sighed. "And I'm trying to share it all."

"We're waiting, ladybug," Dash said, approaching them. "I'm glad you two are having a moment, but it's time for me to kick Con's ass."

"What exactly is this game?" Kit asked as Rory laughed at her brother.

"It's the Post-it note game. The category is favorite Disney villains." Rory explained the rules, which involved putting the name of a character on the Post-it and then putting it on the person to the left's forehead. A series of yes or no questions were allowed until someone guessed who they were.

Although Kit had never played it, he had a lot of fun, which wasn't surprising, but finding that Dash and Conrad were men that he probably wanted to be friends with was.

Somehow in his head it was okay for him to fall for Rory but actually liking Dash and Con…that was going to take a lot more time to get used to.

* * *

Rory watched Kit more carefully than she had before. It was one thing to tell herself she wanted to take risks and feel completely alive, but the reality was that at times it was still scary.

Her world was so small after she awoke from the coma and she was proud of herself for expanding her horizons and really going all in with Kit. But there was a lot she still didn't know about him—stuff that hadn't seemed to matter before but now did.

"Hey, kid, you okay?" Con asked as he was eliminated from a round of the game and came to help her in the kitchen, refilling drinks.

"Yeah. It's just… I didn't know how this night was going to go," she said. Then realized that might have sounded dumb. "I mean you know how Dash is and you were all big and scary the last time you met Kit."

Con laughed. "I tried to be. But your man held his own."

"I'm not sure he is."

"Your man?" Con asked.

She shrugged. Why had she mentioned that to him? It might be the rosé that she'd been drinking more of than usual tonight.

"What's up?"

"Nothing."

"Liar," he said gently. "I'm not going to pretend I have any advice for you but I will say this. Falling in love with Indy changed something inside me and I had no control over it. It was terrifying and I fought it with everything I had."

He grabbed three beers in one hand and Indy's glass of sauvignon blanc in the other.

"So everyone feels…out of control in relationships?" she asked her cousin.

"Just the ones that matter," he said with a wink. "Can you get those two?"

"Yes," she said, picking up her glass and Elle's.

They rejoined everyone else and as she sat down on the couch next to Kit she looked over at him. He put his hand on her thigh and gave her a squeeze, then their eyes met and he lifted one eyebrow. She just smiled and nodded.

Con's blunt talk had been what she needed to hear. He was the biggest, baddest-looking dude she knew. And if even he had been scared of love…well, it reassured her somehow.

"You brat," Elle said, turning to Dash. "Woody is not a villain."

Dash just shrugged and smiled. "He does pretty much plot to get rid of Buzz. I mean that's not heroic."

"You know that's not what I was thinking," she pointed out.

"Sorry you couldn't guess it, babe," Dash said, pulling her into his arms and kissing her.

"I think we should stop now before things get more intense," Indy said. "What other games do you have?"

"Monopoly. I saw it on the shelf," Dash replied.

"I'm not playing that with you," Rory said, shaking her head. "You're a dick when we play that."

"How about Uno or karaoke then?" Kit suggested.

"Ugh, I suck at singing," Con said.

"You're not supposed to be good at it," Elle pointed out. "Yeah, let's do karaoke!"

Everyone agreed and Kit came to help her get the microphones set up with her TV screen.

"This night is more fun than I thought it would be." Kit's voice was soft, wistful.

"Good. Why didn't you think it would be fun?" she asked him.

"I'm used to parties at my aunt's house. Lots of small talk and circulating waiters… This is, well, more homey."

She turned closer to him, looking into his intense brown eyes, searching for something that would reassure her about whatever it was he had to talk to her about later. "Homey is what we do best."

He quirked one brow at her. "The big parties at Gilbert Manor don't seem homey."

She nodded at that. "They aren't. But that's for show. That's for the town and the company. Nights like this when it's just the three of us…and now our partners. Those are the best."

He pulled her into his arms, his hands around her waist. "Am I your partner?" he asked gruffly.

She put her hand on his jaw. "I think so. I mean until—"

He kissed her to stop her from talking, which concerned her. The kiss was nice but she knew he'd done it to hush her.

When he lifted his head, he gave her a contrite look. "Sorry. I can't explain anything now. Being here with your family tonight has given me a glimpse of something that I didn't know I was missing."

His admission struck a chord in her. What kind of upbringing did he have? He'd told her about the tragedy and the things that had torn his family apart. But his aunt had surely provided for him… Yet maybe she was a bit like Rory's own grandfather had been. More concerned about image than about them.

"I'm glad to hear that," she said softly. "I was sort of pushing you to talk but I get that we can't now."

"I'm willing to look away for a few minutes but if you two are going to be making out, I'm not sure I can handle it," Dash interjected.

Everyone laughed and Rory couldn't help but blush because she knew that his comment was directed toward her and Kit. But her embarrassment faded as the group brought the mics over and song choices were made. Rory sat on the couch next to Dash as Elle and Kit sang "Rock Your Body" by *NSYNC.

"You were right to move out, ladybug," Dash murmured. "I was worried this would be too much, but I can see now that you're becoming your own woman."

She tipped her head against the back of the couch and looked over at her older brother. "Thanks. I know I was right."

"Brat."

"Seems to run in our family," she said with a laugh.

The party continued until almost midnight and Rory hadn't laughed that much in a long time. When everyone was gone and it was just her and Kit, she knew it was time for that talk she'd been thinking about all night.

But now that the time was here, she wasn't sure she was ready to face what was to come.

If finding the letter in his father's papers had started him questioning everything that his aunt and father had told him about Declan's accident, this evening had just muddled things even more.

Making it damn near impossible to keep the heat of hatred that he'd had for Dash Gilbert alive.

Because tonight, after watching him tease his fiancée, and duet with his sister and cousin, it was hard to keep that image of a man who was ruthless in his mind. Rory wasn't going to know what had happened during the car crash. Dash had said he didn't want to add to her trauma of that night, but next week when he spoke to Con and Dash, he'd learn more, hopefully.

But he was going to have to tell her who his brother was and try to find out more of what had happened at the winter gala, *before* the accident occurred.

"So…?" Rory was sitting in the big armchair catty-corner to the fireplace, with her legs curled up underneath her.

"I'm not sure where to start." That much was totally true. He'd made this into something bigger than he wanted it to be by his reactions earlier. And maybe if he'd been better prepared to let go of his vengeance he wouldn't have.

"Tell me about your family. I don't know anything about them," she said.

He moved to sit on the couch corner closest to her. Then glanced around the living room, seeing the work they'd done together to bring this room to life. This room could be a stepping stone to his future. If only he handled this right.

"You know my brother died, and then my dad turned to alcohol, which eventually led to his death." Starting with the easiest part of his past. Just facts. He tried to keep his emotions in check but it was hard.

"Yes, I do. I'm sorry about that. How old were you?"

"I was a freshman in college. I was on the West Coast when it happened. I flew back when my aunt called to let me know what happened," he said.

"I was a freshman, too, when everything happened to me," she told him. "It's funny that our lives were both changed at eighteen."

More like ironic. She didn't know it was the same accident that had shaped them. "Yeah."

That was all he could say to that. It was harder than he'd anticipated, going back to that time in his mind. The grief and anger and panic. All of those emotions had swamped him and it was only the fact that his father was always drunk that had kept Kit from turning to drink himself.

"So eventually it was just you and your aunt?" she probed carefully.

"Yes. I dropped out of Berkeley and moved back

to Boston. Our family business was shattered and I took night classes at a community college while working to try to save it."

He looked over at her. She watched him with so much pure emotion on her face that it made his insides hurt. She shouldn't be looking at him with compassion and empathy. Not now. Not when he'd taken what was left of his family company and reshaped it to go after hers.

He'd used those long days to form a plan with his aunt in their shared grief. One that would take everything from the Gilberts in return for what they'd lost.

"Kit, that's so..." She trailed off.

"What?"

"Sad. So sad." Turning toward him, she said softly, "You should have been enjoying college and making mistakes and finding yourself, and instead you had to come back and step into someone else's life."

Someone else's? "How do you figure?"

"Well, you didn't want to run your family company, did you? You had to because that's what your aunt and father needed you to do. You never had a chance to know if it was what you wanted."

He hadn't ever considered that before. At this point, ten years into running the company, he couldn't think of what else his life might have been. Until this moment, he'd just assumed that even if Dec had lived, he'd still be where he was.

But now he wasn't so sure.

"I guess so," he said.

"Did your aunt help you run it?" she asked.

"No. That's not her thing, really. She's good at socializing and finding the right connections. And I used those connections to build our business up from nothing," he explained.

"So you two are a team?"

"We are," he said. But he wasn't sure if they would continue to be. He knew there was no way Aunt Mal would accept Rory.

"So why haven't I met her?" she asked. "That's the thing I can't figure out. I know you're busy and that our relationship is new, but you and I...well, I think we have something real. Or am I just kidding myself?"

Thirteen

That was the thing about Rory, she never pulled any punches. Sitting in that chair cross-legged, watching him with those wide eyes of hers so full of emotion. He wanted to step up. Be the man she needed him to be. And fear made it so hard for him to just let go of the past.

"This is real for me, too," he said gruffly, the words torn from somewhere deep inside him.

"Okay. Then we can take the rest slow," she murmured. "I just needed to know you were on the same pages as I am. It's okay if you're not."

"I am, Rory. It's just family is complicated and my life…well, it's been on one path until you."

"Mine, too," she said.

"What path was that?"

"One where I thought the only way I could prove I was independent was to do everything by myself," she said softly, tipping her head to the side.

"And now you don't?"

She got up and walked over to him. "It's that I don't have to. I know I can do it on my own, but it's nicer with you."

He thought about that as she sat down on his lap, putting her arms around his shoulders. Life was so much fucking better with her in it. That was a given. But there had never been a time in his life where he'd put anything other than family first.

He wanted to come clean but he had to ask himself if that was more for his peace of mind than anything else. Dash and Con had been clear that Rory could recall parts of the night of the gala. The night his brother attacked her.

Would confessing he was Declan's brother make things worse for her? He didn't know.

And if he were being totally honest, tonight was one of the few times in his life when he'd felt this kind of comfort and peace from another person. He cared a lot about Rory and there was a big part of him that just wanted more happy memories before he admitted he was related to her worst nightmare.

Just a few more days to enjoy this budding relationship the two of them had stumbled into. A few more moments of being accepted for who he was, not what he could do for someone else.

He wrapped his arms around her waist, knowing he should follow her lead and let this conversation go.

But a part of him, the part that knew he'd lied to her about key things, wasn't sure that was the right path.

But then she shifted on his lap, pulling that long skirt of hers to her waist before straddling him.

He leaned back and looked up at her. She rested her hands on the back of the couch as she sat down on him. Her mouth found his in one of those deep, tongue-tangling, soul-jarring kisses that made thought impossible. All he felt was Rory draped over him. He was hot and hard with the aching sweetness that came only from being aroused by her.

He wanted more. Resting his hands on her hips, he found that she wasn't wearing any underwear and a red haze went over him. So he just cupped her butt, running her finger along the furrowed crack between her cheeks.

She shivered delicately in his arms and ground her hips down, her center rubbing against the ridge of his cock through the fabric of his pants. He groaned. He wanted her now.

"Are you okay like this? I love you on top of me and in a minute, I'm not going to be thinking about anything but how good you feel on my cock. So if we need to shift around…"

She bit the lobe of his ear and then whispered directly into it, her hot breath sending a shaft of heat through him. "I've been working to strengthen my thighs, so…we should be good."

He could barely contain himself as she pushed the suspenders down his arms and undid the buttons of his shirt. Her fingers were on his chest, her nails digging into his muscles as he was fumbling between them to free his erection.

She smiled with sensual delight as he scooted around on the couch underneath her until he was comfortable. Then he put his hands on her waist and lifted her until she was positioned so the tip of his dick was at the entrance of her pussy.

Rory braced her hands on his shoulders, which put her breasts right in front of his face. The buttons on the blouse she wore were strained by her position and he let go of her hips to undo the button that looked like it was about to pop open and then undid the rest of them as she slowly lowered herself on to him.

But the position was wrong and she got frustrated, so he shifted himself underneath her and then put his hands on her waist again, bringing her down on him. She moaned as he slid into her, and when he was fully inside, their eyes met and he knew he wasn't letting her go.

He didn't care what happened the night of the accident or who her brother was. Rory was *his*. Not just for tonight but forever.

She rode him, throwing her shoulders back and moving on him slowly at first but then picking up speed. He undid her bra and fondled her breasts underneath it as she gained momentum and then swung toward him with each of her thrusts. She moved faster and harder on him and he found her nipple, sucking it deep into his mouth.

He felt his own climax building and knew he needed more. Taking her hips in his hands, he held her to him as he thrust up into her with frenzied strokes until she cried out his name and he felt her body pulsing on his cock. He drove into her a few more times until he came in a long, hard rush. Emptying himself and cradling her to him as she collapsed against him. Her head on his shoulder, her breath brushing against his neck.

He held her to him, not letting anything but Rory into his mind at this moment.

Rory realized that she couldn't change what was going to happen between herself and Kit no matter how much worrying or planning she tried to do. The accident had been the kind of concrete proof that her life was on a path that she wasn't really choosing. But she could make the most of the journey.

Kit lifted her off his lap and sat her on the couch next to him about the time her thighs were beginning to shake. She looked down at her body, seeing the scars and the weakness but also feeling the strength. She'd changed in ways she'd never guessed she could and part of it was because of Kit.

He made her want to be whole—not perfect—just whole. That was a new way of thinking.

"Are you okay?" he asked tenderly.

"Yes. I think my thighs are going to feel it tomorrow," she said with a smile. Adjusting her skirt, she pulled it back down her legs, taking off her shirt and the unfastened the bra as well.

Kit stared at her breasts and then reached down to cup them. "You're so pretty."

She flushed. "Thank you. You are, too."

"Thanks. I don't know if anyone has said that before."

She laughed. No, she guessed they wouldn't have. Kit was pretty to her, but there was something rough and serious about him as well.

"I'm glad," she murmured as he lifted her into his arms and carried her into the bedroom. "Are you staying tonight?"

"Unless you don't want me to."

"I want you to."

He set her on her feet and she had to use him for balance when she took her skirt off. Her legs weren't as strong as they'd been earlier in the night and she was okay with that. For once the weakness had come from her actions. Not from the inaction of the coma.

In her mind that made a big difference. They got ready for bed not really talking. Her mind was buzzing with the excitement and affection that came from being in Kit's arms. She had no idea what he was thinking about.

But she felt she'd pushed him enough for the evening and let him be. When they were in bed and she was cuddled against his side, she felt his hands in her hair.

"I live in a big cookie-cutter mansion in a suburb of Boston. The house is the kind that I know my dad dreamed we'd live in before everything went to crap," he confided. "It's not very personal. I had an interior design firm decorate it for me, and when

I'm there I pretty much just sleep and sometimes eat standing up in the kitchen."

She turned her head up so she could see his profile. "That house doesn't really sound like it suits you."

"It doesn't? I guess I figured it's where a CEO should live," he said as he wrapped a strand of her hair around his finger.

"Kind of like me and Gilbert Manor," she told him. "I should have fit in there but I don't. Not anymore."

"I'm glad. I really like this version of Rory," he said.

"Me, too." She'd been volunteering and figuring out what she wanted her life to look like.

But Kit had a job and a house he didn't like. "What kind of home suits you? You said your place here isn't really you either."

He shrugged, which shifted her on his chest, her nose going into the light dusting of hair on it where the scent of his cologne lingered on his skin. She took a deep breath.

"I'm not sure. I like your place and the stuff we've been doing around here to make it into a home. But I'm not really into the antiques like you are," he said.

"Why not?"

He didn't answer her for a long moment and she wondered why.

"Just feels too fancy for me."

"Too fancy?" she asked. "You just said you are a CEO. You can have whatever you want. You've worked hard and you deserve it."

He let his breath out in one long exhale and then

moved around so that their eyes met. "I don't think that I do deserve it. I'm sort of on the path that I think my father wanted for my brother."

Her heart ached for Kit. She put her hands on either side of his face. "You've done them proud. It's time to start living for yourself."

"I'm not sure I know how," he admitted hoarsely.

There was a rawness to his tone that made her wanted to hug him tightly to her. "Well, as it turns out, I've got some experience in that. I can help you out."

"Would you do that?" he asked.

"Yes, I would. It's the least I could do for you, Kit, in return for all you've given me."

He kissed her then, pulling her fully under his body, and made love to her slowly and completely. She drifted to sleep afterward, and for once her sleep wasn't full of dreams of what she'd never had—they were dominated by Kit and their life in the future.

Kit left Rory sleeping and walked into town to Lulu's coffee shop to get some pastries and coffee for them both. He didn't let himself dwell too much on the fact that last night he'd made a decision for his future and he wasn't sure what his aunt was going to think of it.

But he *was* going to have to talk to her. And while he could use her busy social schedule as an excuse, the truth was that the moment he'd started sleeping with Rory, he should have let his aunt know that he wasn't as committed to their plan of ruining the Gilbert family as he'd been before.

There was a chill in the air as he walked back to Rory's place. It was early November and he couldn't help but feel that everything was coming together in his life. The accident that had taken his brother's life had been on December 12. Not too much longer until the eleven-year anniversary of his death. It was hard to think about a decade without Dec.

Last night was the first time he'd admitted to himself that he had been living the life that he thought that Dec would have wanted for himself. But they hadn't been close when Dec died, so Kit really had no idea what his brother had wanted.

Like Rory said, it was time to start living for himself.

He wasn't paying attention when he turned onto the street that he and Rory lived on but when he got to his house, he noticed his aunt's car in the drive. She got out when she saw him.

"Nephew," she said.

"Aunt Mal. I wasn't expecting you today," he said, going over and giving her a hug.

"I figured. You haven't been in Boston lately and you've been avoiding my texts. So I decided to come to you," she informed him.

"I'm glad. I'll let you into my house and then I have to go and give this coffee to my friend," he said.

"What friend?" she asked as he unlocked the door and motioned for her to go inside.

"Rory Gilbert."

Aunt Mal looked down her nose at him. "So you're still working that angle?"

"No. I'm not working her at all. I like her, Aunt Mal. Also, I have some questions about the Gilberts' involvement in our family's misfortune."

"Okay. Like what?" she asked.

"Well, for one thing, Dad and Dec were sent a letter telling them that the factory was closing and offering them work in Boston," Kit said. "That's different than what we were led to believe. Just makes me wonder what else we might have wrong."

She crossed her arms over her chest. "I see. Well, I guess we'll have to talk to the family."

"That's what I'm thinking. Get their side and see where there are discrepancies," he said.

"And you want to do all of this for the girl?"

He wasn't sure he liked the way his aunt referred to Rory. "She's a woman. And we've been dating. I like her, Aunt Mal. A lot."

His aunt stared at him for a long time before nodding slowly and then smiled. "It's about time you started dating seriously. I'd love to meet her."

Kit let out a breath he hadn't been aware he'd been holding. He'd been so afraid that Aunt Mal wouldn't want him to date Rory. But instead she was cool with it. How crazy was that? "I know she wants to meet you, too. Family is important to her."

"As it is to us," Aunt Mal reminded him. "We both only have each other. That poor woman was left in a coma and the cousin scarred. Seems to me that both of our families were impacted by that night and Dash's decisions."

They had been.

"Based on what we'd been told, I agree. It's why we started Palmer Industries," he said.

"It was. You were so determined to make things right."

The more Kit had gotten to know Dash the less he felt like the other man had made a rash decision to ruin his father, but then again he'd been in his early twenties that night. He might have done something out of temper instead of thinking it through.

"We were. I haven't told Rory that Dec was my brother or about our connection," he admitted to his aunt. He was anxious to go and get Rory so she could meet his aunt.

"Probably a smart decision for now," she said. "But what are you going to do? We can't pretend forever."

"No, we can't. I am planning to tell her everything soon. I have a meeting on Wednesday with Conrad and Dash and I'm going to ask them about the night of the ball. I told you that Rory was attacked by her date. I need to find out if it was Dec."

She narrowed her eyes. "Your brother was always honorable. I'm sure that the Gilbert men have it wrong."

He hoped so, but he didn't know either of them to lie. Not even old man Gilbert, who'd admittedly been arrogant and had closed the factory without much warning to the other townspeople, but still he hadn't lied.

The only lie that Kit knew of was the one his father had told him. And in truth he couldn't be certain his father hadn't been honest or if Kit had just interpreted what he'd said that way. There was a lot to sort out. But it was worth it if he meant he and Rory could be together.

He left his aunt at his house and walked down to Rory's place. She'd said she wanted to meet his family but he wasn't sure she'd be ready to do it this morning. Aunt Mal was a lot to take and he hadn't really done much to get Rory ready for her.

Fourteen

Kit's Aunt Mal wasn't at all what Rory had been expecting. She was so sleek and sophisticated, and Rory couldn't help but feel she wasn't measuring up in Aunt Mal's eyes. In fact there was something about the woman that reminded her of her grandfather.

The older man had strict rules about everything to do with keeping up the Gilbert image in a way that made it easier to understand Aunt Mal. Just pretending she was like Grandfather was the simplest way.

She wanted Kit's only close relative to like her, so when Kit was called out of town on business, she invited Mallory over for brunch. Rory and Kit had been growing closer and closer, so much so that Rory had also extended an offer for him and his aunt to join her family for Thanksgiving dinner at Gilbert Manor.

Conrad had been working on the menu for the last few weeks and Rory couldn't wait to see what her cousin came up with.

The doorbell rang and Rory walked to open it, realizing how far she'd come physically since she'd moved into the house. She still had to use her walking stick but not frequently and her physical therapist was moving her to a nonmedical gym for light workouts as her strength returned.

She opened the door to see it was a cloudy day and some snow flurries swirled around Mallory. Kit's aunt wore a fake fur leopard-print coat and a smart-looking pillbox-style hat over her slicked-back, black hair. Rory noticed that Mallory had on pointy-toed stiletto-heeled boots and for a minute she was tempted to apologize that she was only wearing her best black jeans and a silk pussy-bow blouse.

"Hello, Mallory. I'm so glad you could make it today," Rory said as she stepped back and gestured for the other woman to enter.

"Of course, darling. I wouldn't have missed the chance to have a little girl time with you," she replied. She undid her coat and handed it to Rory, who hung it in the coat closet while Mallory put her hat on the table near the door.

Soon they were seated at her kitchen table and chatting over the delicious quiche that Conrad had walked Rory through making, alongside a simple salad and mimosas. If ever there were an occasion when she needed some alcohol to keep the conversation going it was this one.

"Kit told me the two of you have been working on this place. It's quaint."

"Thanks," Rory said. "Kit's been a real help. He's really good at helping out but not taking over the job. It's been important for me to complete projects on my own as I regain my strength." Rory smiled at her guest, not bothered by the *quaint* label. She liked her house and when she looked around, she could see every part of it was filled with memories of her and Kit together.

"He is very good at that. When his brother was killed, Kit came home, determined to take over where Declan left off."

"*Declan?* I didn't realize that was his brother's name," Rory said. Declan Orr was the name of the man who'd been her date the night of the winter gala. The man who'd been drunk and angry and wouldn't stop when she had said she didn't want to have sex with him. She pushed her mimosa away and looked down at her plate.

Rory hadn't expected that name to be triggering. But it was. She noticed her hands were shaking and brought them together in her lap and laced them together.

"Are you okay, my dear?" Mallory asked. "I thought you knew that Kit was Declan Orr's brother."

Shocked, Rory could only stare at the other woman. What was she saying? "How? I thought his last name was Palmer."

She was trying to piece this together and honestly it was difficult to even figure out what his aunt was saying.

"Your brother ruined Orr Industries after the crash," Mallory said. "Just bought up all the shares and then dismantled it. Kit had no choice but to use his mother's maiden name and start a new company. He built it from the ground up."

Rory felt almost sick to her stomach hearing this.

"Kit told me his father drank too much, leading to his death and the need for Kit to take over the company," she said, not sure why Mallory was telling her all this and if what she was saying was even true.

"He did. After your brother took everything from him," Mallory pointed out. "I guess everyone has been keeping you in the dark."

Had they been? Dash could be ruthless—that was a given, but would he have ruined Kit's father just because Declan had attacked her? She had no idea and would need to talk to him. It was somehow easier to think of confronting Dash than talking to Kit.

Dash had been hurt and angry after the crash. She was glad he'd been her protector and had defended her while she'd been in the coma. And she also understood how her brother's mind worked.

But then there was Kit.

The Kit she knew who had lied to her. There was no two ways about that. He'd never mentioned that he was related to the man who had caused the accident that put her in a coma. Not even when she'd mentioned that a car accident had set both of them on this path.

The same accident. It was hard on him, too; his life had changed that night as well. She knew that and wanted to be sympathetic, but she was hurt. Then she remembered how hard it was for him to talk about the loss of his father and brother. Was there more to this than the other woman was making out? Could she even believe her over Dash?

"I'm sorry, Mallory…but I'm not buying this," she said.

"That's up to you, but it is the truth, my dear. Maybe you should ask your brother."

"I will," Rory responded tightly. Taking out her phone, she texted Dash, asking if he had time to see her.

He texted back that he was at Gilbert Manor and could be at her place in a few minutes.

"My brother is on his way."

Rory put her phone down. She wanted to call Kit. To demand he tell her if his aunt was telling the truth. Had he come into her life just to use her? She didn't dwell on the fact that she wasn't sure if she'd given him any information he could use to hurt Dash.

Instead, she just sat there waiting for her brother to arrive, trying to hold herself together. She'd wanted to be alive and to feel all the emotions. But in her mind she'd seen only the good and the happy side of falling in love. She'd never let herself even consider that love could hurt. Not like this.

Kit got halfway to Boston before realizing that the meeting wasn't urgent and he could go and join

Rory and his aunt for brunch after all. His aunt had been…well, *off* since he'd introduced her to Rory. Normally Aunt Mal stayed out of the day-to-day running of the company but lately she'd been in the office all the time and on the phone to Kit daily. He was afraid she thought that he was going to abandon her, which he'd never do.

It had been the two of them for so long that he understood where she was coming from. But after his discussion with Dash and Conrad at Rory's Halloween party, he was confident that his family's version of events was far from the full truth. He'd hoped to talk to the Gilbert men and get more information on what had happened that night, but because of Aunt Mal being in the office so much Kit hadn't had time.

But today he was determined to get this sorted out. Last night when Rory had been sleeping in his arms, Kit had finally admitted to himself that he loved her. He hadn't been sure what love would feel like or if he'd ever experience it, but that was definitely the vibe he was getting around Rory.

He wanted to be with her all the time and when he wasn't, all he did was think about her. He had to get the past history between their families settled so they could have a future together and that was all he was focused on.

Kit left the highway and drove toward Gilbert Corners. It was one of those cloudy autumn days that warned winter wasn't too far away. A light dusting of snow fell and gathered on the side of the road, painting the town in a soft white coat. Kit had so many complex feelings toward this town. He remembered the first time he'd met Rory when they were kids, the good times with his family until his mom got sick and died. Then the sadness when his brother was killed and they'd had to leave.

He'd never thought he would drive through Gilbert Corners and be thinking of it as his home. But he did. And he knew that was because of Rory.

His original intent of buying up property to keep Gilbert International from developing them had been just a move to block Dash. But now he saw those properties as an investment in the future. In a town where if things went well today, he and Rory would marry and raise a family.

He stopped his car to the side of the road as he approached the bridge where Dec had been killed. He wished that he could talk to his brother and find out if he had been the man to attack Rory. But he couldn't. He was almost afraid to ask Conrad and Dash because if they confirmed it, he would be broken.

He'd spent the last decade trying to avenge his brother's death. To make up for the wrong that had been done to their family by the Gilberts. But if it turned out that Dec's actions had been responsible, that Dec had assaulted the woman he now loved…he wasn't sure how he'd go on. How could he ask Rory to be his wife if his brother had done such horrible things to her that had led to both of their families being torn apart?

He rubbed the back of his neck, putting his head

against the steering wheel. To say he was conflicted was an understatement.

Sighing, he put the car back in gear and drove toward Rory's house. When he turned on their street he noticed Aunt Mal's car in her driveway but also Dash's. He parked his car in his own drive and hurried down the walk toward Rory's.

Why was Dash there? Had something happened to Rory? She'd decided to stop using her cane in the house. He knew she'd gotten much stronger, but the floors were hardwood and she had been wearing socks as the weather had turned cooler. Had she slipped?

He was in a panic as he raced up her drive and opened the door. Not even bothering to knock. But when he stepped into the hallway, he heard arguing and Rory's voice was the loudest of them all.

"I don't know what your brother told you, Mallory, but Declan was definitely the man who attacked me that night."

"And he paid with his life!" Mallory said. "Are you sure you weren't just overwrought with nerves? My nephew never had to force a girl—"

"Her dress was torn, exposing her breasts, and there were bruises and marks on her skin," Dash bit out the words coldly.

Kit raced down the hall and everyone turned toward him as he walked into the kitchen. Rory's eyes met his and he knew she was looking to see if he'd known these details. He hadn't. He was repulsed to hear the specifics of her brutal attack.

"Kit, I'm glad you're here. They are trying to make

the death of your brother his own fault," Aunt Mallory said. "As if his death meant nothing or was okay."

"I'm sure they aren't saying that," Kit said. "There's a lot of confusion about that night."

"*Is* there?" Rory asked, her tone steeled and sharp. "There is also come confusion about who you are. Is it Kit Palmer or Kit Orr?"

The fact that Mallory didn't like Dash had been obvious since the moment he'd walked into the kitchen. Dash had come over to Mallory; and Rory had for one brief moment seen a side to her brother that she'd never glimpsed before.

"Mallory Orr...you're Kit's aunt?" he asked. It had taken a few minutes to clarify, while Rory stood there in shock. She half listened to the two of them and realized that Mallory and Dash had met before. But Kit hadn't ever met her brother before this year.

As unrealistic as it was, she had hoped he'd be shocked by everything. But he wasn't. He had known about all of these connections. She wanted to ask if he knew his brother had attacked her. If he'd made love to her knowing that the man who'd caused the drama that night, which had led to the car accident that had stolen ten years of her life, was Declan.

But she didn't.

She *couldn't*.

Rory wanted to be alone when they talked. She needed to look into his eyes and hear what he had to say. Listen for the truth amid all the stories he'd told her since the moment they'd met.

God, she'd played right into his hands, hadn't she?

"Kit? I asked who you are," she said in a strangled tone.

She was struggling to hold herself together. Oh, how she wished she could be smart and cool the way that both Dash and Mallory were in this moment. But that was impossible. Kit seemed at a loss and there was a hint of sadness… Was there? Or was she just looking at him and seeing something her heart desperately wanted to?

"I'm legally Kit Palmer but I was born Orr. I had to change my name after you and Gilbert International destroyed what was left of Orr Industries. I couldn't get a business loan nor would anyone even talk to me about working with them." Kit's voice was totally flat and emotionless. Simply stating facts.

"See," Mallory huffed out. "You want to blame Declan for everything that happened but *you* ruined us."

"Declan ruined you," Dash said. "He behaved horribly when he was told he'd be given a job in Boston. He and your father didn't want that. They wanted to run the factory here. But economically it wasn't feasible."

Her brother elaborated on the business dynamics, but Rory didn't understand it or care. She couldn't stop looking at Kit. She'd heard what he said but the truth was so much more. He might have had to use a different name in business, but once he'd slept with her he should have told her.

"Rory?" Kit asked.

"I don't care about the business stuff. I hate that you lied to me. That you didn't one time tell me who you really were. Even after I told you what I went through," she said to Kit. Not even looking at Dash or Mallory because they hadn't hurt her the way that Kit had.

"I didn't want to hurt you again," he gritted out. "How would it benefit you to know I was related to the man who'd hurt you so deeply?"

"It wouldn't have, but you should have told me," she said. Dash came over and put his arm around her. "You should have been honest when you first got here."

"I couldn't. All my life I'd been told one version of the events of the night of the gala. The version we'd heard. Dash's actions I had seen firsthand, so that was the only part I knew for certain."

"What had you been told about the gala?" Dash asked.

"That my father and brother went there expecting to be announced as the new owners and head of the factory," Kit replied. "But instead your grandfather told them they were out and he was closing the factory."

Then he shoved his hand through his hair and shook his head. "But I now know that wasn't true. Going through my father's papers I found a letter from your grandfather with an offer for them to be transferred to the Boston offices and given generous salaries."

Kit turned toward his aunt. "At the time, I assumed

you were not aware of the letter. But now I'm not so sure." He narrowed his eyes at Mallory. "*Did* you know about the offer?"

She shrugged. "It wasn't what had been promised. They were meant to own the factory, not still work for Gilbert."

"Aunt Mal, we've made a similar offer to some of our workers in other situations," he reminded her, then turned back to Dash. "Given that, I wanted to ask you and Conrad about the gala itself and what had happened to Rory. I didn't know…we didn't know… that Dec had behaved that way."

"Are you sure he did what they are saying?" Mal asked Kit.

"Yes, Aunt Mal. Rory is telling the truth. Declan attacked her," he said.

"Then on behalf of our family, please accept our apology," Mallory said. She looked horrified as the details were being revealed.

Dash shoved his hands into his pockets, rocking back on his heels. "No one could have known about the assault but your brother. Your father had left earlier in the evening."

"What did happen? I have only snatches of clear memories," Rory said. "I don't mean just with Declan and me, but after that."

Mallory, Kit and Rory all turned toward Dash. Her brother took a deep breath. Rory wasn't entirely sure she was ready to hear about that night. Her memories of it were fragmented and Elle had suggested that it might be her mind's way of protecting her.

"Con got Dec first and yanked him off Rory. I arrived, pulling Con off him as Grandfather and a few other guests followed," Dash explained. "Grandfather was horrified at the spectacle and ordered us into the study. He demanded to know what happened. Dec suggested that Rory had led him on…and we had a fight. Grandfather wanted us to apologize and Rory and Declan to 'date' in public to make things look right. We refused and left."

Dash squeezed her tight as Rory was shaking and tears were rolling down her face. Images were jumbled together in her mind.

"Dec followed us, cursing the Gilberts. I'm not sure if he lost control of his car or rammed us, but he hit the back of my car as we were on the bridge. Both cars flipped and rolled. Con was thrown from ours as he wasn't wearing a seat belt. Rory was knocked unconscious. I got out as the emergency vehicles arrived. Your brother was mortally wounded."

Dash held her close as shudders wracked her body. Mallory and Kit looked at each other, their faces pale. "I think you two should leave," Rory said.

Fifteen

Kit didn't want to leave until he could talk to Rory, but the look on her face made it clear she wanted him gone. Aunt Mal turned on her heel, walking down the hall and out of Rory's house. Dash looked as cold and ruthless as Kit had always thought the other man to be.

Rory wouldn't meet his gaze, so Kit took a deep breath. "I'm sorry you had to find out this way."

"But not sorry you kept it from me?" Rory asked quietly.

"No. I didn't know you well. Or Dash, or anything about the Gilbert family except what Aunt Mal and I had been told and what I'd observed myself from being in the business world," Kit said, shoving his hands into the pockets of his pants and balling them into fists. "You were a stranger to me."

"I was," Rory admitted. "One who walked up to you and asked you to pretend to be someone else. But we stopped pretending the moment you started sleeping with me. I think you owed me the truth."

Dash's face tightened even more and Kit knew that this was a conversation he didn't want to have in front of Rory's brother. But he wasn't going to back down from this. Not now. "You're right. I went home and dug through all of my father's old paperwork and found that letter from your grandfather. It made me realize that not everything I took for fact was true. And when I heard about my brother... I believed you. I still do. But accepting that someone I loved could assault someone..."

Dash rubbed the back of his neck. "This is complicated and I don't think we're going to resolve it—"

"We're not," Rory interrupted him.

"Just let me finish this and then I'll leave. We hadn't been told any of that about what my brother did to you. When you told me your date—my brother— had attacked you... I had no idea what to do next. I stopped thinking of revenge and wanted answers. I knew I couldn't have a future with you until everything was cleared up. I wanted to know everything, to be sure I could talk to you about it without hurting you all over again."

Cleared up was such a small way to frame what Rory had been put through. What his brother's actions had put both of their families through. But at this moment it was all he had. His mind was a whirlpool of jumbled thoughts and there was too much to process right now.

"I agree," Dash said. "You and I need to talk about the business side of things, but this stuff with my sister…you are going to have to make it right. It's all I can do not to kick your ass for lying to her and using her."

"I didn't use her. I've never used you, Rory. I might not have told you everything, but I never deceived you," he said. "You were the first person who I was wholly myself with. But I am deeply sorry for hurting you."

He knew that there was nothing else to say right now. He didn't want to sound defensive and there was no other way to frame this in his mind. He turned and walked down the hallway, seeing the hardwood floors that he'd helped Rory stain and seal. This house had felt like a beginning.

But he'd known even at the time that a solid foundation couldn't be built on half-truths. It was one thing for him to try to convince them that he hadn't lied, but in his heart he knew he had.

He'd been afraid to tell her everything, afraid that once she knew who he truly was, she'd see all the darkest parts of his soul and he wouldn't be good enough for her.

His aunt was sitting in her car. She got out when he approached.

"About time you got here," she said. "We need to talk."

"I agree." They went into his house, and when

they were seated in the formal living room, he looked over at his aunt.

Some of the arrogance and pride that had always been so much a part of her was dimmed. She seemed smaller than she had earlier, which was exactly how he felt.

"I'm sorry I went behind your back. I was afraid you were forgetting our family and now... I know you weren't," Aunt Mal said. "That your brother would behave that way is unconscionable. I can never condone what Dash Gilbert did to us, but for the first time I think I can almost understand it."

"Thanks for apologizing. I could never forget you, Aunt Mal, never. You are the only one who has had my back for the last ten years. But you hurt Rory intentionally and that's going to take me time to forgive."

"I understand. I hope you can. You're all I have, too," she said brokenly.

For the first time, he saw her age. And that she was barely holding herself together.

"Did Dad know? I can't imagine that he did."

"I don't think so. He wasn't happy about the offer of jobs in Boston but he was preparing to move there and take the new job. When the job was rescinded, it destroyed him," Aunt Mal said. "It seemed like such a cruel move from the Gilberts after losing Dec."

Only knowing what the three of them had at the time, it had seemed that way. He was sad and angry about Declan. His father's drinking made so much more sense now.

"What's next?" Aunt Mal asked. "We've bought all this property in Gilbert Corners."

"I've been talking to local business owners. I think if we can work with the Gilberts, it might be the way forward. Take the tragedy of that night and turn it into a strength here for the town and our families."

"I'm sorry I betrayed you to Rory. If I'd known what Declan had done—" Aunt Mal broke off on a sob.

He went to sit next to her, hugging her. He wished she hadn't as well, but it was past time to come clean with Rory and Kit knew he had been too afraid to risk losing her to do it.

"Is there anything I can do to make up for this?" she asked hopefully.

"I'm not sure what you *could* do to fix it," Kit admitted after a long moment. He saw that she was sincere and contrite, and while he still wasn't ready to forgive her, he realized that it had been a scared woman who had gone to Gilbert Corners.

"Honestly? Me either," his aunt said.

He released a deep breath. "All I know for sure is that I am going to do everything I can to win Rory back."

"I'll apologize to her again," Aunt Mal said.

"I think it's going to take more than an apology."

"Just tell me what you need and I'll be there," she promised.

Rory felt numb in a way she hadn't since she'd first realized that Dash and Elle had been lying to her.

That had been months ago. She'd honestly thought there was nothing else from the past that could hurt her.

Oh, how wrong she'd been.

She'd had vague memories of what had happened the night of the gala but hearing Dash's abbreviated version had brought it all back. But now, despite the inner turmoil she was feeling, knowing she was safe and that her family had rallied around her, gave her strength. And the bad memories she had of Declan weren't as harsh as they might have been if she didn't have the distance of all the time she'd been in the coma.

Maybe her brain had been doing what it needed to in order to protect her.

"Are you okay?" Dash asked.

She looked up at her brother. "I have no idea. I'm not sure I really even know what okay feels like."

"What can I do?" he asked.

"Nothing. This is something I have to figure out on my own." She wanted to be angry with Kit and she was. He never should have lied to her about who he really was, but she could understand why he had at first. But the moment they'd talked about how car accidents had changed them… For the life of her she couldn't justify him staying silent.

"I hate this. I want to do something to fix this. I'm so sorry I had to bring up so much of what happened the night of the gala. Want me to call Elle or your therapist?" Dash asked.

Her big brother was doing his thing. Sweeping in

to protect her. But she wasn't all right and doubted she was going to be for a while. She did need to talk to someone but right now she just wanted to sit here and cry. To think about how she'd gone from feeling like she'd figured out her life and her future to being like this again.

It was almost the same way she'd felt when she'd woken from the coma...

"I think Kit was the man who was with me when I woke up," she said.

Dash narrowed his eyes and then nodded. "I think you're right. What was he doing in your room?"

"That's something else I'll have to ask him," she said.

"I feel like part of it is my fault," Dash said. "If I hadn't destroyed Orr Industries, then Kit wouldn't have retaliated."

"How is this your fault?"

"I was the one who went after Orr Industries. That was all me. Then when they tried to move on, I crushed their business."

"Dash."

"Yeah, I know how that sounds. I was angry and you were in a coma, they didn't know if Con was going to live... I wanted the Orr family to be destroyed."

She put her hand on her brother's wrist and squeezed it. She didn't know what to say. She couldn't justify his actions any more than she could Kit's. They had both reacted in anger to a horrible catastrophe. It would be easy to just say it had all been Declan's fault but she knew it was more nuanced.

"I'm sorry, ladybug, for my part in this."

"I know you are. I've never doubted that everything you've done for me over the years is based on love."

"That's true, but I shouldn't have done what I did to Kit's family. I'm going to try to make that right," he said. "Are you okay with that?"

She wrapped her arms around herself. For a minute, she wanted to say no. To strike out at Kit because he'd hurt her. But she'd seen the pain on his face when he'd apologized. He'd never set out to hurt her. That didn't mean she forgave him, but she couldn't condemn him either.

"Of course."

He blew out a breath. "Are you going to…"

"What?" she asked

"Take him back?"

"I'm not sure," Rory admitted. "I was just starting to feel like I'd found myself. And now I'm questioning things that I didn't before. Did I miss signs that Kit wasn't being truthful because I wanted to believe he was someone he wasn't?"

"I highly doubt that. He wasn't intentionally trying to fool any of us. We all like him. So aside from not telling us he was related to Declan, I can't fault him. He clearly had no idea his brother was capable of that shit. I kind of understand it."

She tipped her head back, closing her eyes. She could understand it, too. But he'd lied to her.

"That still doesn't make it right," Dash said. "But I get it."

"Me, too. I'm not sure where he and I will go from here."

"You'll figure it out. And if you decide you want that man, then you will make him yours," Dash said.

"I'm sorry, but do you mind leaving?" Rory said. "I think I just need to be alone and think things through."

Dash shook his head as he got to his feet. He leaned down and hugged her close. "I'm coming back for dinner and bringing everyone if that's okay."

"Sure. I guess you'll have to tell them what happened."

"No. That's up to you," he said. "I'll just say you need your family."

He wasn't wrong—she did need her family. After Dash left she looked around her house, the one that Kit had helped her renovate and make into her home. Rory saw him everywhere and in all the rooms. She sat on the couch where they'd made love after the Halloween party and felt tears burning her eyes.

She couldn't figure out what to do next, but in her heart she knew that without him even knowing what his brother had done to her, he'd helped heal that part of her.

The knock on his front door was loud, and when Kit walked down the hall to open it, he was not surprised to see Conrad Gilbert standing there. The other man stood on his doorstep in his chef whites, sleeves rolled back to expose his tattooed arms, glowering down at Kit.

Kit took a deep breath. "Are you here to talk or fight?"

"Talk," he said, but the word was bitten out from between his teeth.

"I guess you'd better come in, then," Kit replied, turning and walking down the hall to the kitchen, where he'd been sitting at the table, trying to make some kind of plan to fix the mess he'd made.

He heard the heavy sound of the other man's boots behind him. Conrad dragged out the chair across from Kit and sat down heavily. "So Dash said you're Declan Orr's brother."

"I am," Kit confirmed. "Did he tell you everything?"

"Yeah. That you guys didn't know what your brother had done to Rory and that Dash destroyed your father and your family financially," Conrad said. He rolled his head from side to side as if trying to relieve the tension. "Did he tell you I beat your brother pretty badly?"

"No. Just said you'd pulled him off Rory," Kit said, his own hands flexing. He had so much anger toward his brother and his despicable actions. There was no way to defend what Dec had done.

"Yeah, well, I probably would have killed him if Dash hadn't got us out of the mansion that night. I can't tell you what happened once we were in the car. But I wanted you to know my part."

"Thanks. If I'd been there, I would have done the same to my brother," Kit said. "I can't marry the image of his behavior with the brother I knew. He should never have done that."

"I agree," Conrad bit out. "Listen, I didn't know your brother at all before I pulled him off Rory. But you— I thought I had a handle on you since we'd met recently."

Kit didn't know what to say. Of course he hadn't been lying to them 24/7. "You do. The only thing I kept hidden was my family name."

"Yeah, see, that seems like a big thing. I get it, because I hated my grandfather and didn't want anything to do with him or my family name. He was a total dick. But you hurt Rory and I can't figure out why. What were you going to do, use her to hurt the Gilbert businesses?"

"No. It wasn't like that. I just needed to find a way to get closer to Dash, see if I could exploit something he'd reveal."

Conrad almost cracked a smile. "You suck at the revenge business."

"I know. It's not really my thing. But I wanted Dash to be held accountable for what he'd done to my family."

Conrad leaned back in his chair. "I think he was, in a way that you didn't realize. Watching Rory in that coma was a constant source of pain for him. And it took years for me to regain my strength and then I ghosted him… So believe me, his life wasn't all that great."

Kit's head hurt from thinking through all the other

ways he could have handled meeting Rory again. "From the outside I didn't see it that way."

"We never do," he said. "Fuck. I'm not sure what I was expecting when I came over here. It would be better if you were an asshole. Then I could punch you."

"Sorry."

"I'm not," Con said. "I texted Dash I was coming to see you, so he might show up, too. We never had a chance to talk about the business development in GC."

Kit had already talked to his board of directors and they were going to be doing some community outreach and using the property they owned toward that end. Aunt Mal planned to talk to the different charity boards she was on and get them involved, too. Dash did show up about thirty minutes later and Kit respected the fact that neither man said anything about Rory to him.

They talked about ways to make Gilbert Corners better, and after a few hours both men got up to leave. Dash lingered after Conrad had left.

"What are you going to do about Rory? I assume you're not walking away from her," Dash said.

"I'm not. I don't know if she can ever forgive me for lying to her, but I'm going to stay here and apologize as many times as I have to until she can believe me."

Sixteen

For the first few days after everything had happened with Kit, Rory sort of hid out at her house. She'd felt so exposed and raw. The fact that she'd allowed herself—as if her emotions had consulted with her!—to fall for him made her feel…dumb and sad and angry. She'd just sort of stopped going to physical therapy and sat on her couch.

Which worked until Indy and Elle showed up at her house. Rory hadn't showered and as she opened the door to find them standing there, she felt something snap to life inside her.

These two sisters of her heart took one look at her and both hugged her at the same time. And in that instant, the tears that she'd been fighting off and on for days finally fell. She cried as they held her, none of them saying a word. She didn't know how but suddenly the three of them were sitting on her large leather couch, which she had been contemplating donating since she couldn't stop thinking about making love with Kit on it.

"I guess you guys know it all," Rory said.

Despite Dash's plans to come to her house the night that she'd learned everything about Kit, Rory had put him off. She just didn't want to dissect everything. She needed time. But the more time she'd spent alone in her living room, the more she realized she had no idea how to move past this kind of betrayal.

"We do," Indy said gently. "Do you need to talk about it?"

Rory leaned back against the butter-soft cushions with a sigh. "I don't know. I'm so... God, I'm feeling too much. One person isn't meant to have all of these emotions at one time."

"Yes, you are. There's nothing wrong with feeling that much," Elle said. "You can be mad and still care about him. You can be hurt and not hate him."

"Thanks for saying that. I am just so confused. How could I have spent all that time with Kit and never once suspected he was lying?"

Indy shrugged, tipping her head to the side as she considered this. "Part of me thinks it's because Kit wasn't lying to you. Or he didn't think of it as lying."

Rory hadn't thought of that. "He definitely did at first. He knew I was Dash's sister..."

"So you think he's just a liar?" Elle asked. "Is it because he's Declan's brother you think he's like him?"

Rory chewed her lower lip between her teeth. "No. He's *nothing* like Declan was. Nothing. And I think he's been my white knight coming in the clutch when I needed him."

Elle leaned over to give her a one-armed hug. "So if Kit's not like his brother what does that mean?"

Rory looked down at her lap. She didn't know. All she knew for sure was that the man she'd fallen for hadn't used her. He'd been kind and almost selfless taking her to try things and helping her learn to live again. Was heartbreak the last lesson he had for her?

She realized she was struggling to believe that. And the white-hot anger and betrayal she'd felt when she'd learned who he was had started to cool. Now there was just hurt. And she knew it wasn't just hurt at his lie by omission, but hurt for *him*. Dash had behaved horribly to Kit's family, treating them like they were responsible for Declan's crime. She could understand and forgive Dash for that. So it followed she should be able to forgive Kit for harboring his own animosity toward Dash.

"I just don't know what to do," she said at last.

"Love is complicated… I'm assuming you love him. Otherwise none of this would matter. You'd be able to get pissed, give him the finger and move on."

"Yeah, I think it is. I mean, it's not like I always imagined love to be, because it's not perfect and it's messy. But I miss him. I'm still mad at him and I really hate that he lied to me, but I miss him."

"Love is like that," Elle said. "I understood why

Dash couldn't commit to me and it didn't make me fall out of love with him."

"I remember that," Rory said. Watching Dash work up the courage to open his heart had shown her a new side to her brother.

"So, what do you want to do?" Indy asked. "If you still love him, then how can we help?"

She smiled at the two of them. "You already have. I was sitting her going over the last time I saw him and feeling so stupid and betrayed. But talking to you two has helped me figure out that it's okay to still love him."

"Of course it is," Elle said.

Rory released another sigh. While she honestly wasn't sure how she was going to move past this, she knew she was going to have to talk to Kit. She wanted to know why he'd been at her bedside in the hospital and then see where they could go from here.

After Indy and Elle left, Rory took a shower, and as she sat at her vanity doing her hair, she asked herself if she wanted Kit back because she loved him, or if she was simply afraid to be on her own.

She thought of the last few days when she'd had no trouble being on her own and knew she didn't need a man in her life. She wanted Kit. Just Kit. Life with him was sweeter than anything she could have imagined. But he was going to have to promise to never lie to her again and…she was going to have to figure out if she could believe in him again.

Making up his mind to try to talk to Rory was one thing; actually feeling like he had any idea what to say to her was something else. But Kit didn't want any more time to go by. He'd been sitting in his house up the street from hers, just sort of waiting. He had hoped he'd see her walking by or even at Lulu's, where he'd gotten a dirty look from Lulu when he'd gone in with his laptop and sat at a table in the back hoping to catch a glimpse of Rory.

But she hadn't come in and he'd found that he wasn't as thick-skinned as he'd always thought he was. He'd never meant for anyone—certainly not Rory—to get hurt. Which was how he found himself in Boston at the cemetery, where both Declan and his father were laid to rest. He didn't know what he'd hoped for when he visited their graves but his heart was heavy.

He stooped low next to his father's headstone. It was simple, with just his name and the dates of his birth and death. Aunt Mal had added *Beloved husband, father and brother.* But Kit had never really felt the "beloved father" part. His emotions toward his dad were so tied up in resentment and disappointment at the role that Kit had been forced into.

But knowing what he did now, he was sorry he'd let those last years with his father slip away. As much as Kit hadn't really wanted to take on a leadership role in the family business, being CEO had suited him as nothing else had.

Swallowing a lump in his throat, he put his hand on his father's headstone.

He wanted one more talk with his dad. But that

wasn't possible. And really what would he say? *Sorry I was douchey at the end of your life?* Yeah, that wasn't much of a conversation starter. He just quietly apologized to his father, hoping his soul had moved on and maybe he knew that his son finally had let go of the bitterness that he'd been harboring all these years.

He finally stood up, putting his hands in his back pockets as he turned to the other headstone. This… he was dreading. He had so many complicated feelings toward Dec. His older brother. The guy who'd taught him to ride his bike, let him have his first underage sip of beer and had comforted him when their mother had died. No matter that he'd been killed in a car crash, Kit had still looked up to him.

But he couldn't…not anymore. Not after learning what he had done to Rory. He sighed, wanting to kick Dec's headstone but knew that would be useless. Instead, he crouched down and leaned in close as if somehow Dec's spirit was trapped in the headstone. "How could you do that? How could you be the kind of man who took your anger and disappointment out on a girl? That sweet, brave, remarkable girl. I don't pretend to understand any of your actions."

He shook his head as angry tears burned his eyes. "You were always my hero, Dec, not because you were perfect or anything like that. But because you were my brother and I thought you were better than what you became."

Kit stood up, realizing this wasn't going to bring

him closure. He was going to have to talk to Rory and hopefully find a way to ask for her forgiveness for Dec's actions. And then he was going to have to let go of this familial bond that he'd used as his guide all these years.

He wiped his eyes with his gloved hand and heard the sound of footsteps behind him. He turned to see Aunt Mal standing there in her fake fur coat and those ridiculously high-heeled boots she loved to wear.

"Thought I'd find you here."

"I'm surprised to be here. I don't know why I came," he said gruffly. Honestly, he didn't. He knew they were both still dead and had been for years. But at the same time he needed to talk to them. Needed to find some understanding and some peace.

"You always thought your father let you down and that if Dec had lived things would have been different," she said, coming up to him and looping her arm through his. "I think I did, too."

"I wish I'd been easier on Dad."

"I know you do," she said. "I feel the same. I hated that he was so weak and let addiction take control. I still sort of do. But Dec…"

"I can't forgive what he did," Kit blurted. "I'm not sure I'll ever be able to."

"I think we are both entitled to that," she said.

"I just always wanted to be like him," he said at last.

"You've never been like Declan or your father. You've always been the best parts of them. I know you think that they shaped the man you are today and in a way their deaths did, but you have always been a strong, honorable man."

"Except for our revenge plan," he added, but his aunt's words helped him more than he'd expected.

"We stink at revenge. Our big plan to buy up property, fix it up and then make sure that the town thrives so that the Gilberts know they aren't needed… I mean I'm pretty sure other people seeking vengeance would be embarrassed by us," she said ruefully.

He smiled and turned to hug her. "I love you, Aunt Mal."

"I love you, too, nephew."

Kit said goodbye to his aunt and headed back to Gilbert Corners, realizing that he'd done enough waiting. He needed to apologize and see if Rory could forgive him. He loved her and it was time to come clean about how he truly felt.

Kit texted to ask if he could come and see her. Rory responded yes. She had wanted to say more, but really in person would be better than text. She wanted to see his face when he answered her questions.

And she just wanted to see him.

Despite everything that happened between them, she'd finally admitted to herself she was in love with him. She wanted him to be in love with her, too, and she had already come up with too many different scenarios where he might say he cared for her when his feelings were motivated by guilt. He'd lied to her and she knew he felt bad about that. He'd apologized the last time she saw him.

But she hadn't spent ten years of life sleeping not to spend the rest of it wide-awake. So that meant taking risks. It was funny that she'd thought she'd been taking risks all this time, but until she'd admitted to loving Kit she knew she hadn't been.

She'd taken some chances but they'd always been with a safety net. And love was the biggest risk of all.

When the doorbell rang, her heart leaped into her throat, her pulse started racing and she shook her head. She had to calm down. This might be him just coming clean and clearing up the past. He might not be back here because he felt the same way about her as she did about him.

Ugh.

Rory stood at the front door, taking deep breaths and trying to rein in her emotions. She was so nervous and she hadn't been before. Well, other than that one day when she'd walked up to him and told him to pretend to be her friend. She'd been nervous then. The same man was making her feel that way again.

She couldn't help remembering how he'd smiled and gone along with her. And how that smile had made her feel—

"Rory?"

"Yeah, just need a minute," she yelled through the closed door.

"Take as long as you need."

She turned and rested her back against the wall.

That right there was why she knew she wanted to believe every word he said. He was always so calm and understanding. And finally something that she hadn't realized she'd been holding on to was set free.

In the pit of her stomach had been a knot of worry that Kit would be like Declan, now that she knew they were brothers. That stress and anger would make him react the way his brother had. Even though she'd always felt safe with him.

But this was the real Kit. This man who would stand on her doorstep all day waiting until she was ready. Until she was calm.

How could she *not* love this man?

She unlocked the door and opened it. A blast of cold air swept into her foyer and around her. Kit's hair was wet, making it curl around his face. His dark eyes seemed sadder and more serious than ever. He had stubble on his jaw, which just made her palms tingle from wanting to touch him.

Her arms ached to wrap around him and pull him close, but she didn't want to make a disastrous assumption. He might not be anything like his brother but that didn't mean he loved her.

Kit had come to Gilbert Corners and into her life for a very specific reason. She wasn't sure that falling in love with her had any part in his plans.

"Come in," she said after a minute, carefully stepping back and holding the door open for him. The need to touch him was so strong she wasn't sure she was going to be able to resist it. "Um, I guess we can go in the kitchen to talk…"

"Thank you." He shrugged out of his jacket but carried it with him down the short hallway to the table in her kitchen.

Rory hesitated as she saw him there, remembering the last time he'd been in her kitchen and how everything in her life had changed. She wasn't sure she was ready for another upheaval. As much as she wanted him in her life, she knew that she wanted him on her terms.

And she wasn't going to back down from them. She wanted Kit but he had to be honest. He had to be the man she thought he was.

Rory took another deep breath and realized that the panic she'd felt before she opened the door was gone. She was oddly calm. Squaring her shoulders, she sat down at the table, gesturing for him to sit across from her. "I know you have something to say but would you mind if I asked you something first?"

He shook his head. "Not at all."

"Were you in my room the day I woke from my coma?"

"Yes."

"Why?" she asked.

He leaned back in his chair and crossed his arms over his chest and then let them drop to his sides. "I came to talk to you. When I heard you were in a coma all these years and learned about the curse, I thought my actions were going to make a change. I told you that I was going to break the hold the Gilberts had on GC. But mostly I just talked to you about that first summer we met and how your kindness was the rea-

son I wanted GC to be prosperous again. Your kindness had helped me all those years ago, and I wanted
to pay it forward."

Seventeen

Kit was glad that he could finally tell Rory about being in her room the day she woke from her coma. He hadn't planned to stop by to see her but in a way he'd felt that she'd been another victim of Dash's. And he'd wanted her to know he was taking care of her brother for her.

He now knew different.

"Why didn't you say something sooner?" she asked after a few minutes.

It was hard for him to defend why he'd kept silent. Probably because his main focus had been on the big lie he was keeping. That he didn't trust her brother. That he wasn't sure how he could move forward with his plan and keep her safe. That once he realized the man who hurt her was his brother, he didn't want to make things worse.

"How could I? I had planned to keep my distance from you, but—"

"I came up to you and said just go along with me," she said. She put her arms on the table and leaned forward.

He couldn't help but remember his surprise in that moment. He still didn't know if it had been fate or luck or what. But whatever it had been was what he'd needed. It was almost as if everything had happened the way it had for a reason.

So he could find out the truth about their families' complex history and find a way to bring some closure to both of them.

He laced his hands together in his lap to keep from reaching out and touching her. He couldn't help it. It felt like it had been a lifetime since he'd held her. He missed her. So damn much. And seeing her now, she seemed tired but she also looked strong and healthy. He was proud of how much she'd changed since she'd moved into her home here.

"Yes. And then everything I had planned went out the window," he admitted a bit sheepishly.

"What was your plan exactly?" she asked.

"Well, funny you should ask. It was sort of a make Gilbert Corners awesome and then say 'see, Dash Gilbert, we don't need you.'"

She shook her head and smiled. He felt a *zing* all the way to his groin. She had the best smile.

"Great revenge plan, *not*," she deadpanned. "I can

understand why you wanted to get back at Dash and Gilbert International, so of course you couldn't tell me who you really were. But I'm struggling to be okay with the fact that you lied to me."

He reached for her hands then, taking them in his. "I'm sorry I did. I didn't know how to tell you who I was, and that was before I knew that Dec had hurt you. I can't forgive him for that. I don't know how you could ever accept me into your life knowing he's my brother."

She turned her hands under his and pulled them back, and the hope that had been growing in his heart stuttered to a stop. But of course he'd respect her wishes. He might have to spend the rest of his life in unrequited love with her but he wasn't going to be the second Orr man to take something from her that she didn't want to give.

"When I look at you, Kit, I see a man who is so different from Declan. That night is such a foggy memory that it doesn't have the power to hurt me. You are more real to me. I've never felt threatened by you. I've always felt safe," she admitted.

"I'm so glad to hear that. Can you ever forgive me for lying?" he asked.

She just looked over at him with her eyes wide and serious. He didn't know if words would be enough to convince her to believe him.

Kit got up and came around to her side of the table, dropping down on his knees next to her chair and taking her hands into his. He had always been afraid to admit how he felt, afraid to be vulnerable in a way that emotions always made him feel.

"I love you, Rory Gilbert, with my entire being. I know that it's going to take time for you to learn to trust me again. But I will do whatever I need to in order to make that happen."

She turned toward him but he stayed where he was. He needed her to hear this. He needed to tell her everything that was on his heart and mind.

"You might have asked me to help you take risks and learn to live again. But the truth is you were the one who taught me about living. You made me let go of the past and start to see myself—and the world— in a new light."

"Kit…"

She put her hands on his face and brought her mouth down to his. Her kiss was soft and tentative at first and he let her set the tone, but she tasted so good and he wanted her. With every cell in his body. He wanted her love, her happiness and her forgiveness.

He wanted this woman in his arms and in his life.

When she lifted her head, he waited for the rush of lust to pass so he could talk.

"I don't know if you can love me, but I am willing to wait as long as it takes until you do."

Kit stood up and looked down at her. He remembered the first time he'd taken her for a walk in the rain around her backyard. The first time he'd kissed her. His life had changed in that moment. He hadn't realized it then, because he had been too focused on trying to figure out how to keep Rory safe while bringing down Dash.

He should have known that there was no way he could hurt anyone she cared about. No way he could tear apart anything that mattered to her. She was the only thing that mattered to him. Her love and her happiness. He had to find a way to convince her of that.

She licked her lips and then stood up next to him. His heart was beating so loudly it was a pounding in his ears.

There was no doubting Kit's sincerity. She just had to trust herself to accept him. To say yes to this. And it felt riskier than anything else she'd ever done. He loved her. That almost made her more afraid.

He loved her.

She had to repeat it to herself because it was so hard to believe that he'd said the words. And how they made her feel. She stopped thinking about all of the bad energy that had been surrounding her family, and Kit's, since the night of the winter gala and the accident.

She stopped thinking about the fact that everyone thought there was a curse on her family and this town; and that the last person who anyone would have expected to break it were outsiders. But they had. Indy, Elle and now Kit had all done their part to bring love back into the lives of herself, Conrad and Dash. She knew that without love there could be no change.

Not for herself and not for Kit.

He'd dedicated his life to avenging his brother and father and when he'd realized he had the wrong idea, he'd changed. He'd started to question those long-held beliefs and he'd fallen in love with her.

But he was watching her and she remembered how she'd felt when she'd first learned he'd lied about who he was and why he'd come into her life. And as much as she'd wanted to lean into being angry and hurt and let that dominate her, she couldn't. Because she loved this man more than she'd known she could love another person.

"Rory?"

"Kit."

"Woman, you're *killing* me here. Did what I said mean anything to you?"

She put her hands on his face. She just liked touching him and holding him. "It meant everything."

She took a deep breath and leaned her forehead against his. "I love you, too."

The words, once they were said, weren't as scary as she'd thought they would be. "I'm not sure how we move forward from here. But I want to."

Kit lifted her off her feet and spun her around in his arms. She wrapped her legs around his waist, holding him tightly but letting her head fall back as she laughed. Love was flowing through her body, joy washing over her and making it impossible not to smile and laugh.

"We can figure it all out. As long as we love each other."

He set her down carefully. "When I came to Gilbert

Corners… I'm not going to lie—I had a lot of hate in my heart for your family and this town."

"I get it," she said. "Dash won't admit it but I think he felt the same way. Con definitely hated GC and he avoided it as much as he could."

"What about you?" he asked softly. "I never really asked how you feel about the town and everyone thinking your family was cursed."

"I was sleeping, wasn't I? So I didn't really know about the curse or the town. I think because I missed all of that and am here now, experiencing the rebirth of Gilbert Corners and my new family… Well, I like it here," she said. "I think that's because of you."

"Me?"

"Yes, from my first day here on my own, you were there with a smile and stories and a helping hand, even though I was a stranger."

"But you weren't," he said. "You were that sweet girl who smiled at me that long-ago summer day."

He put his arms around her, holding her close to him. This felt so good. So right. She leaned her head on his shoulder and found tears burning the backs of her eyes. She hadn't been sure she'd ever be in his arms again. And loving him the way she did, it hurt to think that she might have missed out on Kit.

"I missed you," she said quietly.

"I missed you, too," he admitted. "I thought about all the reasons you wouldn't want me back—and there were a lot. I thought about how I had used Dash's actions to rationalize trying to take him down. You'd be justified to do the same."

"I don't know if I'd agree to *justified*," she said, looking up at him and smiling.

"Well, I would. I treated you poorly—"

She put her fingers over his lips. "You never treated me poorly. I have spent a lot of time thinking about our relationship to date and I realized that other than not telling me you were Declan's brother, you were honest about everything else."

"I tried," he said. "Legally I did change my name, so that wasn't a lie."

"I'm glad. No more lies."

"No more lies," he agreed.

He lifted her into his arms once again, carrying her to the bedroom where he made love to her. Then he held her in his arms as they cuddled close and made plans for their future. And Rory realized that, like herself, Kit had been trapped for the last ten years in an almost choking vine of brambles. His life had been pushed down a path he hadn't chosen. But he'd made that path his own.

He'd woken her with a kiss in the hospital, but… "I rescued you."

"You did?"

"Yes. You were trapped behind the walls of half-truths and bitterness and you were doing your best to live your life. But then I came along and shook those walls and they started to crumble and made you look at the Gilberts and Gilbert Corners differently."

He rolled her underneath him, his mouth on hers, kissing her so deeply she almost forgot what she was saying. She was consumed by the feel of Kit's body against her. And she had to be grateful for her own body. The limbs that had been so weak not that long ago were now strong enough to wrap around him and hold him to her.

"You did rescue me by falling in love with me," he said. "I love you, Rory."

"I love you, too, Kit."

* * * * *

Award-winning author **Yvonne Lindsay** is a *USA TODAY* bestselling author of more than forty-five titles with over five million copies sold worldwide. Always having preferred the stories in her head to the real world, Yvonne balances her days crafting the stories of her heart or planting her nose firmly in someone else's book. You can reach Yvonne through her website, yvonnelindsay.com.

Books by Yvonne Lindsay

Harlequin Desire

Rags to Riches Reunion
Stranded with the Runaway Bride

Clashing Birthrights

Seducing the Lost Heir
Scandalizing the CEO
What Happens at Christmas...
One Night Consequence

Visit the Author Profile page
at Harlequin.com for more titles.

You can also Yvonne Lindsay on Facebook,
along with other Harlequin Desire authors,
at Facebook.com/HarlequinDesireAuthors!

Dear Reader,

I've always been fascinated by a runaway bride. What compels them to run? Why didn't they just stay and have a party anyway?

In *Stranded with the Runaway Bride*, Georgia is forced to face her groom's infidelity and she's adamant that she's not going to start her married life that way. She seeks refuge at her late grandfather's cabin, but she doesn't count on the cabin already being occupied.

Sawyer, an international photojournalist, was injured on his last commission and is taking time out from his harrowing career to reassess his life. The last thing he needs is a bedraggled bride turning up on his doorstep.

Can Georgia and Sawyer help one another heal from their hurts and losses? Read on to find out!

On a personal note, I just wanted to say what a privilege it's been to write for Harlequin Desire for the past eighteen years. I'm sorry to see the line end. To be a romance writer was always my dream job and I thank you, my readers, for all your wonderful support through my time with Harlequin. Follow me on Facebook for what's happening next: Facebook.com/yvonnelindsayauthor!

Best wishes and happy reading!

Yvonne Lindsay

STRANDED WITH THE
RUNAWAY BRIDE

Yvonne Lindsay

To Soraya Lane, thank you for being one of my biggest cheerleaders and for being such an amazing writing buddy. We have done millions of words together so far and I look forward to doing millions more!

One

Georgia stared at the phone in her hand barely able to draw a breath.

"No," she whimpered. "This can't be happening."

She plonked down on the bed in her hotel suite, the skirt of her wedding dress foaming around her in a sparkling cloud of tulle and diamantes. Downstairs, in the function room, chairs lined an aisle that was supposed to mark her last walk as a single woman in the gown that was everything she'd dreamed about ever since she was a little girl. The kind of dress that looked how being in love felt. But now those dreams were shattered, and all by something that was likely smaller than her little finger. She stared again at the phone screen, not wanting to recognize the outline of a baby in a sonogram posted on social media by a woman she'd never met before. It shouldn't have mattered. It *wouldn't* have mattered. Except the #baby-daddy in this post was the man she was supposed to marry in thirty minutes.

The door to the suite opened and Georgia's mom scurried in, all a'fluster.

"Nearly everyone is here, Georgia. Are you ready? Have you got everything you need? Been to the toilet? Oh my, I never thought we'd see this day."

It slowly seemed to dawn on Georgia's mom that not everything was sunshine and lollipops in the room.

"Georgia? Is everything okay?"

"No, Mom, everything is definitely not okay. There won't be a wedding," Georgia said solemnly.

She looked around the room. Aside from the garment bag her wedding dress had been packed in, the robe she'd worn this morning and her purse, everything else was packed in her suitcases and stowed in the back of her car, ready for her and Cliff to drive to the airport to catch a flight to the Cook Islands, where they were meant to start their new life together.

"Oh, Georgia, don't be silly. It's just nerves you're feeling now. Everyone goes through that."

"No, Mom. It's not nerves." She thrust her phone beneath her mom's nose.

Angela O'Connor squinted at the screen. "What's that? I can't make it out."

"It's a baby, Mom," Georgia said on a sigh.

"Well, that's a fine way to tell your mother you're pregnant. And on your wedding day? What were you thinking?"

Georgia would have laughed if she hadn't felt so wretched. "It's not mine, but it is Cliff's."

She waited for the penny to drop, watching her mother's face change from confusion to understanding, then to confusion again. "But how?"

"The usual way, I suppose. This picture shows a three-month fetus, and—" Georgia swiped the screen to the next picture in the announcement post. A picture of the baby's mother together with Cliff—his arms wrapped around her from behind and his hands resting on her lower belly—filled the screen. Georgia knew it was a recent photo because he was wearing a shirt she'd bought him only a few weeks ago. Things were all starting to make sense now. The broken dates, the hint of fragrance on his clothes sometimes that he'd explained away as fabric softener. Now this. The pair looked so picture-perfect it was hard to believe they weren't the ones supposed to be getting married today. "This picture shows Cliff with the baby's mom."

"Maybe they're just good friends?"

"Oh, I'd say they're good friends, all right," Georgia said with a pang of bitterness. "She refers to him as her baby daddy!"

"But it doesn't mean anything, right? The wedding can still go ahead."

"You think I should still marry Cliff?" Georgia shrieked, incredulous at her mother's suggestion.

"Of course. Honestly, Georgia, even if it is Cliff's baby, women are stepmoms to other people's children all the time. He's down there waiting for you.

I know he wants to marry *you*. And let's face it, it isn't as if you've had a line of men standing in front of you wanting to get married."

Georgia tried not to let her mother's statement hurt, but it did. The same way it always did when her size-zero parent took umbrage at the fact that her child was less than what she deemed perfect. Well, more—much more—to be precise.

"I'm aware of that," Georgia said carefully.

"Then what's the problem?"

Georgia stared at her mom a full thirty seconds before replying.

"You realize I said this is a three-month fetus, right?"

"Yes, so?"

"And you know that Cliff and I started going out six months ago and got engaged four months ago."

"Of course I know all that," her mom sniffed.

"He was unfaithful to me, Mom. He cheated on me, while we were engaged. That's a nonnegotiable for me. You should understand that, especially after what we went through with Dad. I won't put up with wondering every time he's late coming home from work or away on business if he's hooked up with some other woman. I can't trust him anymore. The wedding is off."

With that, Georgia stood and grabbed her purse. A short poke around inside and she snatched her car keys and headed for the door, a sea of tulle and sparkles billowing in her wake.

"But…what about all the people? What will they

think? And what about Cliff? Are you even going to tell him you're leaving?"

"You're worried about what people will think?"

"Well, no, not really," her mom sputtered, even though it was obvious to Georgia that was very much her primary concern.

Not the fact that her daughter's trust and love had been destroyed by infidelity. Not the fact that her heart was shattered and her self-esteem blown to the four corners of the earth. Georgia waited a few seconds more. Waiting for the hug of consolation she so desperately needed. The assurance that whatever happened, her mom would always love her. She waited in vain.

"I'll call Cliff from the car. Right now, I need to put as much distance between us as possible."

"Georgia, wait."

Georgia stopped to look at her mom again. Waiting for words of solace, of commiseration.

"Do you think we'll get our deposit back?"

"No, Mom, we won't get anything back. I've already made the final payment, so you all may as well have a party and enjoy the drama. Either that or donate the food to the nearest shelter. I leave it in your hands."

With that, she headed for the service elevator at the end of the corridor. Today was supposed to have been her denouement. She'd been the wedding coordinator here at the resort overlooking Puget Sound for five years now. Making people's wedding days the highlight of their lives was her jam. She took pride in everything she did, ensuring that no matter the budget, the resort's clients received a day so memorable that they couldn't wait to recommend her to all their unmarried friends. And as she'd organized her own wedding—right down to the last petal on the table arrangements—she'd been certain that everything would be perfect.

Cliff had swept her off her feet and into his arms so fast her head had still been spinning when he'd proposed. Overjoyed, she'd said yes, even if it meant she'd have to give up a job she loved as much as she loved chocolate and move to a Pacific Island nation she'd hardly heard of. She hadn't quite figured out what she'd do with herself while Cliff oversaw the construction of a new resort complex on the island of Rarotonga, but she'd been sure she'd figure something out. And now, she was stuck figuring out something else entirely. On the bright side, walking away would be easy. The lease on her apartment was canceled. Someone new had already been hired to take her job. She had nothing left here to stay for.

On the flip side, she also had nowhere to go. She made it out of the elevator and into the corridor that led to housekeeping, the laundry and the function room kitchen. There was a lot of clattering and chatter coming from behind that door as she swept past. The staff parking lot was on the other side of the double doors at the end of the corridor. Only another twenty or more steps to go. A door behind her opened and she heard footsteps on the polished concrete floor.

"Hey, excuse me, ma'am. This area is for staff only."

"I know," she yelled back.

"Georgia? Aren't you supposed to be getting married about now?"

"Not anymore," she said, her focus riveted on the door that was now only five steps away.

She reached it and pushed on the handles, bursting into the parking lot. A fine rain drifted on the air in typical Washington state fashion. She felt the product the hairdresser had coated her hair with grow sticky and heavy with the moisture. She ran-walked to her car as quickly as her voluminous princess line gown and long veil would allow and yanked open her car door.

Struggling to get into the driver's seat with sufficient room to see the dashboard and reach her gearshift around the poofiness of her dress made it painfully apparent she should have thought this through a bit more. But right now, all she wanted was to put as much distance between herself and her philandering groom as possible.

She put the car in gear and drove away, clearing the resort grounds in a few minutes and heading out onto the main road. As she drove, her eyes burned and her heart raced with the enormity of what she'd just done. She'd become that awful cliché she'd always worked her hardest to ensure her clients never became—a runaway bride. Tears blurred her vision and she found a spot to pull over as she finally gave in to the shock and, yes, the anger that had gripped her since she'd seen the sonogram.

In her purse, she heard her phone begin to vibrate. The incoming call hooked up to her car's Bluetooth and Cliff's name came up on the screen of her dash. It would be so tempting to simply ignore him, but he owed her an explanation. She accepted the call, but silently swore it would be the last darn thing she accepted from him, ever.

"Georgia? Where are you? Let me explain." Cliff's voice filled her car, laden with concern in that beautiful deep tone that was one of the many things she'd fallen in love with when she met him.

"I think your girlfriend's post says it all, don't you?" she answered, fighting to keep her voice civil.

"Ex."

"Ex what?" Georgia demanded.

"Ex-girlfriend. Shanna is my ex-girlfriend."

"Look, I don't care what or who she is. She's having your baby, right? Do you always sleep with your ex-girlfriends when you're engaged to marry someone else?"

"You're upset."

Georgia rolled her eyes. "You think? Yes, I'm upset. Finding out on our wedding day that you're about to become a father? Of course I'm upset. Just when were you going to tell me about this? Don't you think I had the right to know?"

"I couldn't tell you, I knew you'd overreact."

"Overreact? Seriously? You cheated on me."

"It didn't mean anything, honestly."

She was incredulous. "Well, Cliff," she bit out carefully, "it certainly means something to me. It means I cannot trust you. That's pretty important, don't you think?"

"Georgia. I love you. I want to marry you. Please, turn your car around and come back. We can still make this happen."

"No, Cliff. We can't. Our engagement is off, our wedding is off. Our future together is off. Enjoy your future with your ex, for your child's sake if not for anyone else."

She disconnected to the sound of his blustering voice echoing in her ears and closed her eyes. The *whoop-whoop* of a siren made her look up. A police cruiser had pulled up behind her, and the officer was now walking toward her car. Could today get any worse? She rolled down her window.

"Ma'am, are you aware this is a no-stopping zone?"

"Yes, I'm very sorry, Officer. I will be on my way now. I just needed to take a call."

He looked inside at her, taking in her apparel and what were probably streaks of makeup on her face from when she'd started crying.

"License and registration, please?"

She passed them over without another word.

The officer grunted and handed them back. "Everything seems to be in order. Are you going to a wedding, ma'am?"

"No, I'm leaving one."

"Are you okay?"

"Not right now, but I will be. Am I free to go?"

"Yes, you are. Drive safely."

Georgia put her window back up and took care

easing into traffic. The officer stood there watching her, no doubt wondering what the heck was going on. The fact that he, a complete stranger, had shown more concern for her well-being than her mom had wasn't lost on her. Mind you, she thought, catching a glimpse of herself in the rearview mirror, he probably was worried about whether she was even safe to drive in her state. She focused on the road ahead. The long, empty, lonely road.

"C'mon," she told herself. "You're better than this. You've survived disappointment before. You can do it again. Now, think. Where are you going to go?"

Grampy's cabin.

The idea came to her as if it was a lifeline in a raging torrent. Her mother's granddad had built a cabin near Olympic National Park back when he was a youngster. On his recent death, age one hundred, he'd left the cabin to her mom, who'd shuddered at the idea of heading out there and staying "in the wild." But Georgia knew it wasn't as wild as her mom made it out to be. Her great-grandparents had often taken her there during summer breaks. Yes, it only had one bedroom, but over the years Grampy had outfitted the place with every modern convenience known to man to give an off-the-grid luxury experience for anyone who stayed there.

That was what she needed. Peace, quiet and some quality alone time to reset herself and reimagine her life going forward. She steered her car to the nearest on-ramp for 99 and took the Edmonds turnoff, heading for the ferry terminal. Some of the tension that had gripped her body began to ease.

She stayed in the car on the ferry, and as soon as it docked she was on her way again. It was always better to have a plan. She was the queen of planning and felt completely ungrounded when she had an empty calendar. Planning was a form of control that was necessary to her well-being. She even had sub-lists on her lists of things to do. Her mom said she went too far; Cliff had merely been indulgent in a patronizing sort of way. Neither of them had understood that it was the one security she felt she had total control over.

Georgia thought back to her wedding planner's checklist, making a mental note to add "discovering the groom is a lying, cheating bastard" to her contingencies master plan going forward. Although, she fervently hoped no one she ever worked for had to face what she just had. And that was if she was even able to work in wedding planning again once the ignominy of her running away from her own wedding became common knowledge.

The drizzle that had been steady during her drive grew heavier the farther west she drove along Highway 101. Georgia groaned as visibility ahead worsened. Still, she'd been on the road from Kingston at least two hours, so the turnoff that would take her on the winding uphill road to Grampy's cabin couldn't be too far away. Tension built in her shoulders as she hunched forward, as if that would somehow make her visibility improve. There it was, the turnoff. Her car fishtailed a little as she stepped on her brakes a bit too hard, and her heart was pounding as she made the turn.

The bottom end of the road offered access to hikes in the area, but the top end was not for the public and was the only access to Grampy's cabin. As she got onto the private section of road, the paved road ended and she was forced to negotiate her way past several potholes and dips on the unpaved track before she reached the cabin. Georgia made a mental note that when the weather improved, it would definitely be time to get the road regraded. Even the small wooden bridge that spanned the creek felt more rickety than the last time she'd been here.

Her bones were definitely rattled by the time she neared the clearing that housed the cabin. Even in the rain, the place looked welcoming, or maybe it was just her sense of desperation that made it look that way. Warm light glowed from the windows and a curl of smoke drifted from the stone chimney at one end.

Hang on. Wait a minute. Light? Smoke? There shouldn't be any signs of life here. She drew her car to a halt, turned it off and peered at the house. One thing swiftly became apparent—the temperature here was a lot colder than back at the resort near Lynwood. Dressed in her sweetheart neckline strapless gown and without the car's heater running, she was feeling every drop in degrees. She couldn't stay here in the car wondering what was going on, she needed to get inside where it was warm.

It took only seconds for the rain to drench through

her veil and gown from the moment she left the car. Trudging through the rapidly deepening mud in her white satin, low-heeled wedding pumps, Georgia opened the trunk of her car and lifted out her suitcases. She tucked the smaller one under one arm and hefted the other two in her hands.

Aside from the household goods she'd put in storage, the rest of her worldly possessions were in these cases, including a wardrobe of resort wear suitable for a climate that, even though it was always windy, never strayed lower than sixty-nine degrees or higher than eighty-four. This was definitely not that climate. It was a good thing Grampy had always kept a selection of coats and boots in the wet room here, she thought as she made her way carefully up the wooden front stairs and onto the covered porch.

Georgia set the cases down on the deck and lifted her hand to the doorknob. Taking in a deep breath, she twisted it, pushed the door open…and promptly screamed.

Two

Sawyer Roberts's blood turned to ice at the sheer terror of the scream at his front door. He knew this was a remote area, but he didn't remember seeing banshees mentioned in the literature about this holiday rental. His eyes fixed on the apparition that framed the doorway, and he blinked hard. Nope, no change to the vision that stood there letting out all the warmth he'd so carefully coaxed from the wood fire in the living room. While he'd avoided weddings and all the trappings that came with them for his entire adult life, it seemed that somehow one had come to him.

There was no mistaking the tragic bridal effect of the woman standing in the doorway, with rivulets of rain and mascara tracking down her face and the lank wet strands of hair sticking to her cheeks. The puddle of water at her feet grew larger the longer she stood there, the fabric of her gown rimmed with mud and obviously sodden. In itself, the picture she presented was concerning, but what worried him most was the collection of luggage that surrounded her. Worse, she was now pulling it all inside the cabin and closing the door—with her inside.

"What do you think you're doing?" he demanded, stepping forward to block her path.

"I'm getting out of the rain. What does it look like I'm doing?" she snapped back. "And what do *you* think you're doing here? This is private property, you know. You're trespassing. You have five minutes to gather your things and leave."

The entitlement in her voice did nothing to distract Sawyer from the curves that were so enticingly displayed above the neckline of her gown. And to his chagrin, a spark of interest tugged deep and low in his gut. He quashed the sensation. This was not what he was here for and he had no doubt, judging by the expression on the face of the woman in front of him, it was not what she was here for either.

"Excuse me?" he asked.

"I think you heard me just fine. Four minutes and thirty seconds, buddy. Or I'm calling the police."

"I have a legal document saying I have sole and unfettered use of this cabin for thirty days. You, madam, are the trespasser here."

She snorted. "Madam? Seriously, who do you think you are?"

"The current lessee of this property, which means you need to leave, now," he insisted.

"Show me that document and I'll consider it," she said, equally insistent.

With a huff of frustration, Sawyer stomped up the stairs to the loft bedroom where he kept his pack and dug in the side pocket for the printed document he'd brought along in case of trouble. And she was definitely trouble, he thought to himself, in more ways than one. He'd always been a sucker for redheads, although her hair, as best he could tell when it was dripping wet, probably tended toward more of an auburn shade. Her eyes were the kind of hazel that was more green than brown, and they had tiny gold flecks…hang on, what the hell was he thinking? Maybe it was just his photographer's eye that had noticed the smaller details but that was where his interest in whoever she was began and ended.

His fingers closed around the lease agreement and he yanked it triumphantly from the pocket and marched back to the bride. She had begun to shiver, which made him feel bad, but he didn't want to invite her closer to the fire or to change her clothing. He simply wanted her out and for his isolated retreat to return to being exactly that.

"You'll find everything is in order," he said, passing her the document.

She didn't even thank him as she snatched it from his fingers and perused the legalese that gave him sole access to the property and its surroundings for the duration of his tenure.

He thought he heard her say, "Thanks a lot for keeping me in the loop, Mom," but the words were muttered so quietly that he couldn't be sure.

"Well, that's unexpected," she eventually said, passing the lease back to him. "I wasn't informed of this tenancy."

"So you agree that it *is* a tenancy?"

"I guess I have to. There's little to no reliable cell phone reception up here, so it's not as if I can check with the property manager, is it?"

"Then I'm asking you to leave, now."

"Have you seen the weather out there?"

Not really, no—he'd been lost in his thoughts before she'd arrived. But if she'd managed to get here, then it couldn't be that bad. "Not my problem. Sole and unfettered, remember."

She stared at him with those mesmerizing eyes before uttering a deep sigh. Without another word, she turned around, opened the door and lifted her bags. Outside, the rain was pelting down and even from here he could see the deep puddles forming around the midsized SUV parked outside. His conscience prodded him. He ought to offer to help her. She certainly wasn't dressed for hauling luggage. And what was up with that, anyway? It had to be unusual for a bride, without a groom, to turn up to a one-bedroom cabin miles from civilization, right?

"Need a hand?" he called into the growing darkness.

"I'm fine. No point in us both getting wet," she

shouted back as she lifted her cases into the trunk of her vehicle.

Briefly, he wondered if it was all-wheel drive or just one of those shopping carts often preferred by suburban housewives. *Not my circus, not my monkeys*, he reminded himself. She was a grown woman—she knew what she and her car could handle.

"Great, drive safe," he answered and then shut the door and, for the first time since his arrival a couple of days ago, locked it.

With every step he took toward the fireplace, he felt as though he was being tugged back toward the door. But he resisted and instead listened for the sound of her engine starting up and then diminishing as she finally drove away. The only sounds around him now were the crackling of the fire and the pounding rain on the roof shingles overhead. Bliss.

He sank into the comfortable sofa in front of the stone fireplace and watched the flames dance hypnotically over the burning logs. God, he was tired. He'd been traveling for days since he left the hospital in Estonia, but he was almost afraid to close his eyes for what his subconscious would do to him if he fell asleep. The skill that had seen him become a highly awarded international photojournalist regrettably had a side effect. It locked the pictures he took with such painstaking precision in the back of his mind. And his subconscious was always ready to haul out the most harrowing when he was at his most vulnerable.

It was easier to deal with when he kept busy. If he was fully exhausted when he fell into bed at night, he stood a decent chance of sleeping without dreaming— or at least, without remembering his dreams. Trouble was, he felt empty inside. Too empty to concentrate on anything productive.

Really, *empty* wasn't the word he was looking for, but he guessed it would do for now. This last trip had really done his head in. The senseless devastation, the lives destroyed… It had gotten to him in a way that it never had before. A shaft of grief lanced through him. Yes, that was likely the main difference, he acknowledged. He'd lost someone on this assignment. His best friend and sharpest competitor in the business had simply ceased to exist.

One second Max had been sheltering beside Sawyer as they tried to avoid a barrage of fire between opposing forces, the next he'd been gone, trying to get that all-important elusive action shot that could capture the whole story in one frame. He hadn't even known what hit him. But Sawyer had, because remnants of the same explosive device that had killed Max had hit him too and seen him carted away to emergency treatment and eventually to a hospital in another country where they fought to keep him alive.

But was this really alive?

He kept staring at the flames. He'd seen so many fires these past few years. Some, like this, passive and soothing. Others, very much not. Sawyer blinked his eyes against the grittiness that encouraged him to let go, to drift into slumber, but he knew there would be only nightmares. Coffee. He needed coffee. But he doubted even that would help him keep the demons at bay tonight. He'd stay awake as long as he could, but it was a losing battle. He knew, from watching others in the same position, that eventually the body would shut down and demand the rest it needed for survival. Until the nightmares woke him again.

Sawyer had just risen and begun to make his way across the open-plan ground floor of the cabin to the kitchen area when the front door flew open again and the crazy bride was back. She looked even worse than before. Her veil now gone completely, her hair more down than up and her gown spattered almost waist high with muck.

"I thought I made myself clear," he said, taking a step toward her and noting the key in her hand, which had made locking the door irrelevant.

"I'm sorry. I know you wanted this place to yourself, but the road's blocked by a mudslide and it's taken out the bridge. I can't get through."

A dull ache settled deep in Sawyer's stomach. He couldn't exactly cast her out to sleep in her car. Well, sure, he could, but he wasn't that much of an asshole.

"Fine, you can have the couch. But only for tonight. We'll check the road in the morning."

"Th-thank you," she said, wheeling her cases inside and securing the door behind her.

"I'll get you some towels."

"They're in the linen closet by the stairs to the bedroom," she said.

For some ridiculous reason, it irked him that she felt the need to tell him where to find the towels. He'd read the information for the cabin and he'd done a quick survey on arrival. He knew where everything could be found and every accessible exit as well. Some called it paranoia, he just called it common sense.

Sawyer grabbed some towels and brought them over to where she stood.

"Might be best if you get out of that dress first, then dry yourself."

"Y'think?" she said with a bite of spirit, then sighed heavily. "I'm sorry. Today has not been a good day."

"No kidding?"

"Look, can you unlace the ties at the back of my dress for me? I'd do it myself but now that they're wet it's harder and, to be honest, it's not something designed for the wearer to do."

He could just imagine. A gown like this was likely designed to be undone by a groom on his wedding night. Sawyer's gut twisted. He couldn't be any further from that if he'd tried. Marriage had never been in the cards for him. Not in his line of work. It was hard enough seeing the pain and fear on his parents' faces each time he left for another assignment. So much so that he'd taken a flat in London to use as his base to avoid the painful goodbyes. He could never put a wife through that.

"Look, since you're going to undress me, I think

we should introduce ourselves," the sodden bride said briskly.

"I'm Sawyer, and I'm going to undo that knot—the rest is up to you."

"It's okay, I won't bite and I'm pretty sure you won't catch any cooties if you touch me accidentally," she sniped back before sighing again. "Again, I'm sorry. I'm really not at my best today. I'm Georgia, by the way. Georgia O'Connor."

She put out a muddy hand then looked at it and swiftly withdrew it.

"O'Connor? As in, O'Connor Cabin?"

"Is that how it was listed? Anyway, yeah, my great-grandfather built this as his own retreat seventy-five years ago. Of course, it was a lot more basic then. He left it to my mother, but isolated cabins aren't really her thing, so I'd assumed it would be vacant. I didn't realize she'd started renting it out for the season, or that she'd named it." Just privately, she thought it might have been nicer to honor the man who'd built it. She shivered again and her teeth began to chatter. "I'm sorry if this crosses personal boundaries for you, but I really need to get out of this before I get hypothermia."

She turned around with her back facing him. "If you can work the tie undone on the corset back, I can probably manage the rest."

"Sure," he answered with a grunt.

He reached for the bow at the back top of the dress. She wasn't kidding that the rain had made it harder to undo. He tugged at one end but discovered it was double knotted, probably so it wouldn't come undone during the course of the wedding. Speaking of which, where was her groom, anyway? Sawyer reached for the knot with both hands and tried to work it undone, his fingers brushing the smooth skin of her back at the same time. She flinched beneath his touch.

"Sorry," he said. "It's tight back here."

"Just get a knife. I don't care about the dress anymore."

He took a step back. "Are you serious? I'm sure—"

"No. A knife is fine. Unless you're planning to stab me and throw my body under the deck outside?"

There was a thread in her voice that almost implied she didn't really care either way, but there was also no mistaking her determination to get out of that dress. Sawyer reached in his pocket for the multitool he always carried. It had survived the blast that had taken Max out, and the medical staff had kept it among the rest of Sawyer's possessions, waiting for him when he regained consciousness in the hospital.

"I've got sharp scissors on this thing," he said, reaching around her to show her the multi-tool. "And I'll be careful."

She didn't reply, but he could sense her relief when he cut through the tie and eased the lacings loose for her. The dress dropped to her waist, exposing the fact she wasn't wearing a bra. Sawyer quickly grabbed a towel and draped it over her shoulders.

"Thank you," Georgia said in a small voice.

She started to work the dress down over her hips, but the ties were still a little too tight to allow that to happen.

"Here, let me," he said.

He cut the ties again and pulled the fabric apart before yanking it down over her softly rounded hips and letting it drop to the floor. Oh man, she wore sheer white stockings and a garter belt with a cute pair of satin panties that now clung to her curves like a second skin. That spark of interest he'd felt before? It was back—and this time it carried a burn of heat that made him take several steps away and turn his back on her. Partly so she wouldn't catch his reaction if she happened to glance at his groin, but mostly so he wouldn't keep staring at her. It was unfair, especially when she was so vulnerable and at a disadvantage.

"I've turned my back, so if you want to finish drying yourself and grab some clothes from your suitcase, I promise I won't look."

"Thanks, I appreciate that."

He shoved his hands in his pockets and held himself rigidly apart as he listened to the swoosh of her kicking her dress away and the sounds of her roughly drying herself off before he heard the zipper on her bag. His rather active imagination was making his physical state very hard to control as he pictured her bending over to gather up dry clothing and putting it on. She was muttering under her breath. Something about bras and damp skin and wasn't life bad enough without that combination on top of everything else? Then she went silent.

"Can I turn around?" Sawyer asked as the silence stretched out.

"Yes, I'm decent now."

She was wearing brightly patterned capri pants with a long loose T-shirt and she'd wiped away most of the remnants of her makeup with one of the towels. Her hair was still lank and wet, dripping patches of moisture on her shirt. And while her clothing was better suited to a seaside resort in summer, he was more worried about the desolation in her posture and on her face.

"You okay?" he asked, taking a step forward before bringing himself to an abrupt halt.

What was he thinking? Was he planning to offer her comfort? A hug? Nope, not going there. Georgia wrapped her arms around her body and shivered.

"Could you grab a trash bag from under the kitchen sink for me, please?" she asked, ignoring his question.

"A trash bag?"

"Yeah, for the dress."

"You're going to throw it away?"

"Well, I'm not going to wear it again, am I?"

She shivered again and he went and got the bag and helped her stuff the sodden gown inside.

"What do you want me to do with it?"

"Maybe put it in the mudroom for now. I'll put it with the rest of the trash to remove later. Look, do you mind if I sit by the fire for a while, just to warm up?"

"Go ahead. I'll grab you a blanket."

"Thanks, I'd appreciate it. They're in the—"

"Linen closet, I know." He grabbed a blanket from the same place he'd found the towels and handed it to her before asking, "Do you want something warm to drink?"

"Cocoa would be nice," she answered as she wrapped the blanket around her and sank onto the couch in front of the fireplace.

"Right, cocoa," Sawyer said, realizing that he had never in his life made cocoa before.

How hard could it be? He could look it up online, except there was no Wi-Fi at the cabin and cell phone reception was patchy at best. Sawyer moved to the kitchen and studied the canisters on the countertop. Sure enough, one was marked "cocoa" and when he opened the tin, some kind soul had taped instructions into the lid. He grabbed the long-life milk he'd already opened from the fridge and put some in a jug in the microwave to warm through, then added cocoa powder and sugar to a mug.

From some vague memory in the back of his mind, he remembered watching his mom dissolve cocoa powder with a bit of boiling water to make a smooth paste before adding something else. He scoured his memory for what that was before remembering the enticing scent of vanilla. A quick scan of the pantry revealed a bottle of vanilla extract and he added a few drops before retrieving the milk from the microwave and blending it all in the mug.

The aroma was divine and made him crave a mug for himself, too, but first he'd give this one to the silent creature on the couch. He was pleased to see she had a little color in her cheeks now and she snaked an arm out from under the blanket to accept the cocoa.

The sensual moan of pleasure she uttered when she took her first sip almost drove him to his knees.

"Oh, wow. That's soooo good," she said. "Where did you learn to make cocoa like this?"

"Just something I picked up," he muttered as he returned to the kitchen to make another for himself.

After doing so, he joined Georgia by the fire. Her hair was starting to dry and she'd stopped shivering. All he needed now was for the weather to improve overnight and a path to clear itself for her car to leave in the morning and everything would be okay. She was staring at the flames in the fireplace, much as he'd been doing before she arrived. Which reminded him, he needed to stoke the fire again.

"I love a real wood fire, don't you?" she said as he resumed his place in the armchair he'd taken.

"When it's contained, yeah."

"So, Sawyer, what is it that you do?"

"Do?"

"Yeah, for a job. Nice that you can take a month off."

"I'm self-employed and between assignments right now."

That was a polite way of putting it. Under normal circumstances he'd have been back in the field by now, but, while his physical injuries had healed, he still couldn't get the memory of the day Max died out of his mind. Nor could he stop belaboring the question of whether he could have done anything differently to have actually saved Max's life.

"What kind of assignments?"

"I take pictures," he said flatly. "At least, I used to."

For a second she looked as though she wanted to press him for more information, but he took the reins of this uncomfortable conversation and asked her a question instead.

"What do you do?"

"I…" She bit her lush bottom lip before continuing. "I'm a wedding planner."

The irony of a wedding planner arriving here in a fairy-tale gown and without a groom was not lost on him. He gave her a hard look and noticed the tears welling in her eyes. Curiosity poked at him to ask her for more details, but he sensed that right now probably was not the best time to be doing that.

Sawyer downed the rest of his cocoa in a long swallow that seared his throat and stood up.

"I'm heading to bed. You know where everything you need for the couch is, right?"

She looked startled, but then nodded. "Sure. If you don't mind I'm going to stay up a bit longer."

"Suit yourself."

She hadn't moved by the time he'd been to the bathroom and ascended the stairs to the loft bedroom. He was nowhere near ready to sleep but being in the same space as her right now wasn't what he wanted either. Sawyer stripped off his clothes and laid them on a chair near the bed, ready to pull on in a moment's notice should he need to. Dressed only in his boxers, he turned out the lights in the loft and flung himself onto the bed. The very large and very comfortable bed. The kind of bed that was made for sharing.

Nope. Not going there either.

It must have been close to an hour later when, below, he heard Georgia get up and move around, switching off lights and humming lightly to herself. He listened as she rummaged through her suitcase and then went to the bathroom, coming out again a few minutes later. Before long, she'd turned off all the lights and the only glow in the cabin was that from the fireplace. Outside, the rain continued to pound on the roof, and inside the cabin was still. Or was it? Sawyer's finely tuned senses picked up another sound. Soft, muffled, but undeniably the sounds of a woman crying.

If he was any kind of a decent human being, he'd go down there and offer her comfort. But he wasn't that person. After all, hadn't he let his best friend die right beside him?

He huffed out a breath and rolled onto his side before forcing his eyes closed. Unbidden, the images of Max's death flared behind his eyelids. Max stepping out from behind the questionable shelter where they'd taken cover, determined to get the money shot. It had been over in seconds. Sawyer's shock and grief had been instantaneous, and it had taken seconds more before he realized that he'd been hit, too. When unconsciousness had claimed him, it had been a relief—an escape from the clawing agony that had spread through him, both physical and emotional. An agony that dwelt inside him still.

Three

The first thing Georgia realized when she woke before dawn was that the fire had gone out. The sexy satin nightgown she'd worn last night was no match for the chill that now took up residence in the cabin. She eyed the fireplace. It would take ages to build up the flames enough for the warmth to break through the frigid air, but she knew that heat pumps had been installed and if she could only find the remotes, she could get the place cozy and warm in no time. Shrugging into the matching wrap to her nightgown, Georgia made her way to the built-in sideboard near the kitchen.

"Aha!" she said softly when she found the remotes in a drawer, right where she remembered putting them the last time she'd been up here.

The air around her soon began to warm, but her feet were still frigid lumps. Georgia grabbed a pair of novelty socks decorated with pink flamingos and put them on before making her way to the kitchen. She needed to take stock of food supplies. If, as she suspected, she wouldn't be able to leave here until the road was adequately cleared and the bridge repaired, she needed to be sure they'd be able to survive on what was here. It had always been Grampy's practice to keep the cabin fully stocked at all times. Whenever guests left, it had to be inventoried and restocked in case of unexpected events stranding anyone here. As far as she knew, the property manager had kept up the practice after Grampy's death. Theoretically, there should be plenty of everything—at least enough to survive the first wave of the zombie apocalypse, Georgia thought with a grin.

But then her face froze as the reality of why she was here hit her solidly in the chest. Her breath caught and an ache dug in deep, making it a challenge to expel the air trapped there. She forced it out in a gasp, then managed to breathe in again, and again, until the ache diminished, even though it didn't quite go away.

There, everything was under control.

She grabbed a pad of paper and a pen from the sideboard and deftly drew lines on the top sheet, adding headings for product, expiration date and quantity, then opened the walk-in pantry and turned on the light.

The shelves should have been groaning they were

so packed with food. Even though, logically, she knew they had enough food to see them out for several months, she needed the calming effect of cataloging everything here. She started on the lower shelves and an hour later had worked her way up to the top section, which she'd accessed using a small stepladder, when she heard a noise behind her. She twisted around sharply and the ladder shifted beneath her.

"Whoa, there!"

Sawyer's arms wrapped around her and steadied her. Georgia's heart pounded rapidly. She couldn't tell if it was from the fright or from Sawyer's warm, strong arms banded around her torso. It had to be the fright, right?

"What the hell are you doing?" Sawyer muttered as he loosened his hold and took a step away.

"I'm sorry, did I wake you?"

Georgia closed her eyes for a second and cursed herself for the inane comment.

"No, I've been awake most of the night."

He looked it. His overlong dark blond hair was messy, his lean face drawn, and he had dark shadows under his blue-gray eyes.

"Because I'm here? If so, I apologize. I will try to get out today if I can."

Sawyer grunted. "And if you can't?"

"If I can't, at least we'll have plenty of food. Now, I was thinking, we could share duties. I'll draw up menus for the week. I'm happy to do breakfast today. How do you feel about scrambled eggs and canned mushrooms? What do you think?"

"I'm going for a walk. Don't wait for me," Sawyer answered abruptly and stalked away.

Baffled, she watched his retreating back. She'd yet to meet the man who turned down a cooked breakfast. Correction, she'd just met the man who turned down a cooked breakfast. Georgia got down from the stepladder.

"So, that's a no for breakfast?" she yelled after him as he yanked open the front door and stepped outside.

Sawyer didn't answer, just zipped up his anorak and closed the door behind him. She heard his heavy steps on the wooden porch, then nothing. Georgia rushed to the front windows in time to see him disappearing into the woods on the edge of the clearing. As far as she could tell, he hadn't taken any water or snacks with him.

"He'll be back soon," she muttered to the emptiness around her.

It shouldn't bother her. She'd been here alone before. In fact, she'd been expecting to be alone now. Yet for some reason it felt as if he'd taken something indefinable with him when he'd gone.

A cranky mood, that's all it is, she told herself as she gathered some clothes and went to the bathroom for a shower. She eyed the deep claw-foot tub and debated taking a long, luxurious soak, but her stomach chose right then to growl loudly, reminding her the last time she'd eaten was yesterday at lunchtime. Well, Mr. Grumpy-pants might like to go out without a good breakfast inside him but for Georgia that was the key to her day. She quickly showered and dressed in the capris and T-shirt she'd worn last night. The heat pumps had the cabin's interior at a tropical level of warmth, which suited her just fine given the wardrobe she had with her.

She'd poured her egg mixture into a sizzling pan when she thought of Sawyer again. She hoped he'd be okay out there. The weather still wasn't great and she had no idea how well he knew the area, or how well prepared he was. Bear incidents out here were rare, but with it being spring, the chances of a sighting were a lot higher than they'd be at other times. The cabin was stocked with bear spray, and they had a very strict refuse policy, but did Sawyer know all that?

Georgia felt her anxiety begin to tighten around her chest again and forced herself to take a moment to breathe in and out slowly, then again. It helped, but not as much as making a list would. She finished making her breakfast, grabbed a mug of fresh coffee and took it all to the dining table where she'd left the inventory list. While she ate, she started her lists. Food roster, cleaning roster, menus for breakfast, lunch and dinner. Oh, and snacks. There were plenty of prepackaged snacks, but home-baked was always best. Maybe she could do some baking this morning and fill some of the storage containers in the butler's pantry. There, she had a plan. And she could breathe.

But before she could start anything, she needed to go down the road to check whether she was still stranded here and, if so, try to call in the situation so someone could come clear the road. Georgia grabbed a jacket from the mudroom and a pair of hiking boots from the rack and, after slipping them on, went out to her SUV. The rain had stopped for now, but the sky was thick with clouds that were darkly ominous with the threat of more rain. She was grateful for the boots as she approached her vehicle. The puddles around it were deep. Soon, though, she was heading slowly down the road to check the situation near the bridge.

A man was standing there surveying the mudslide when she brought the vehicle to a halt a few minutes later. Dejection showed in every line of Sawyer's body. Georgia got out and approached him.

"No good?"

"You won't be leaving any time soon," he said gloomily.

They studied the volume of mud and trees that had come down the bank, obscuring the road. Beyond, the side of the small bridge was damaged, too. If she could get that far, she might get the SUV over it but it would be risky, and first they would have to somehow shift this debris and stabilize the bank.

"Looks like we're stuck together. Is that really such a problem?" she asked. His tone left her feeling like a pariah. "I mean, I didn't expect you to be at the cabin when I arrived, but I'm not being all morose about having to share."

He shot her a look that told her in no uncertain terms that, yes, it really was such a problem.

"I'll see to it that you're refunded for the time I'm

here," she said in a small voice before turning back to the car. "Do you want a ride back, or do you prefer to remain alone?"

There was a bite to her words that penetrated his intense frustration. He'd hurt her feelings and that bothered him more than he wanted to admit.

"Thank you, I'll take the ride, if you don't mind muddy boots in the car?"

She cast a glance at his feet. "I have a plastic sheet in the back. We can put that down for you."

He watched as she bustled round to the back of the SUV and returned with the plastic tarp she'd mentioned. She folded it to fit in the footwell and stood back holding the door for him.

"Hop in," she said.

There was still a distance in her voice. One he knew he'd put there with his surly attitude. As she did a seven-point turn to get the vehicle round and heading back toward the cabin he hunched in his seat.

"I'm sorry," he said abruptly.

"Oh?"

"The usual response is, it's okay, or something like that."

"Well, what in particular are you sorry for?" she asked pointedly. "Is it for being so tangibly horrified by my unexpected arrival? Is it for my being stranded in your less-than-illustrious company last night after what was probably the worst day in my entire existence? Is it for refusing my offer to cook you breakfast and leaving without so much as a goodbye, or a water bottle, I might add? You know you need to stay hydrated, even in this climate. Or maybe you're sorry that, due to events completely out of my control, I'm stuck here with you. And then again, perhaps it is for your very dismal attitude to the fact that I can't leave?"

He drew in a breath and let it out slowly. She sure knew how to put it to a guy. "All of the above. And I am sorry for my attitude toward you. I know you didn't ask to be stuck here with me either."

"No, I didn't, and I wouldn't have come if I'd known the cabin had been leased. It happens so rarely this time of year that I didn't think to check first." Her breath appeared to hitch and her voice wobbled a little as she continued. "I guess Mom didn't tell me because I was supposed to be somewhere else by now. I'm sorry, I wasn't thinking straight last night."

They pulled up outside the cabin and got out.

"Okay, so now we've both apologized, how are we going to do this?" he asked, wondering just how long it would be before they could expect the road to clear.

"I'll see if I can get reception on my phone and send a message to the property manager. They'll have to coordinate everything from their side."

He followed her as she walked around the back of the cabin and opened the door to the mudroom.

"You can clean your boots over there," she said, gesturing to a metal scraper at the bottom of the stairs. "Then take them off and leave them to dry in the mudroom."

By the time he joined her inside the house, she'd

hung up her jacket and swapped her boots for a pair of purple fluffy slippers. Together with her very bright clothing, for a man more used to grays and khaki, they formed a colorful assault on his eyes.

"You should warn a guy," he said, throwing his arm up to his eyes in mock horror.

"What? Why?"

"All that bright clothing."

She chuckled, and he felt something inside him warm at the sound. It was rich and deep and heartfelt, but all too brief.

"I've always loved bright colors, but for a long time I never wore them. Too busy trying to fade into the background, I guess. But then I decided I deserve to wear what I like, no matter what anyone thinks. And if they don't like it, they can just go look elsewhere."

Her words were bold, but he sensed there was some hurt lingering behind her statement.

"Aside from your slippers, you're not exactly dressed for early spring in the Pacific Northwest."

"No. I wasn't expecting to be here."

As she said the words, he saw her demeanor change.

"I'm sorry. I didn't mean to—" he started.

"It's no bother. Instead of the sunny Cook Islands, I'm here. It is what it is, right?"

"Was that where you were going for your honeymoon?" he asked before he realized this was likely a very painful topic for her.

"Not exactly. We did plan to have a honeymoon

when we first arrived, but after that, we were going to live there for five years."

Wow, that was some change in lifestyle. Sawyer didn't quite know what to say. Georgia turned toward the kitchen and grabbed her phone off the counter.

"It looks like I have a bar of reception now. I'll text the property manager and get them onto clearing the road."

It took a while for the message to go through, judging by how much muttering he heard coming from the kitchen, but eventually he heard her give a small yelp.

"Everything okay?" he asked.

"Yes, it's gone through at last. Okay, the rest is out of my hands so I'm going to do some baking."

"Baking?"

"Yes, to ensure we remain fully provisioned. You know, food?"

"Just how long do you think we're going to be stuck together like this?" Sawyer asked with a sense of growing dread.

After all, a day or two would be bearable, but more than that? Maybe she could hike out? He considered her luggage still stacked by the front door. Hiking with that lot was unlikely. For his part, he was loath to be the one to leave, considering he was already paying a princely sum for the privilege of being here. Frustration bubbled inside him. Was it too much to ask to have some time to himself? Given the size of the cabin and larger-than-life presence of his roommate, time alone would be a rare commodity.

"I really don't know, but best to be prepared in case it's a while, right?" She bustled around in the kitchen gathering supplies for baking and began measuring out ingredients.

It was all far too domestic for Sawyer.

"I think I'll go out for another walk," he said gruffly and started heading for the mudroom.

"Shouldn't you have something to eat first?" Georgia asked. "I can make you something. I don't mind taking the first day in our roster."

He stopped in his tracks. "Roster?"

"Sure, if we're going to be here a while, we need to take turns with chores, right? Here, look—"

She grabbed several sheets of paper off the dining table and waved them in front of him. Reluctantly, he took them from her and looked through them.

"You did all this?" he asked incredulously.

"It's what I do. I organize."

Organizing was one thing, but this was far more detailed than that. This was menus, ingredient lists, cooking and cleaning rosters. It boggled his mind. This wasn't what he'd come here for. He looked at the neatly ruled pages with tables and small, neat writing all over them. This was a prison.

"No," he said bluntly and put the papers down on the table before spinning on his heel and heading for the back door.

"No, you don't want anything to eat?"

"No to these lists, no to the roster, no to you being here. What is it with you and food anyway?"

As soon as the words were out of his mouth, he

wished them unsaid. He was always the epitome of calm and collected, and yet there was something about Georgia O'Connor that riled him up no end. But he'd stepped way out of line with that last remark, especially if the stunned, hurt look on her face was anything to go by.

"I'm sorry. I shouldn't have said that. I appreciate that you've gone to all this effort. Hopefully it will prove redundant when the property manager gets back to you. Like I said, I'm going for a walk. I'll take a protein bar and bottle of water, okay?"

Georgia's pretty eyes sheened over with moisture, making him feel like a class A asshole for hurting her. She hadn't asked to be stranded here with him. Given the fact that she'd obviously been in a state of distress when she got here, she'd probably been looking for a bolt-hole much the same way he had when he'd been dropped off here a few days ago.

"Suit yourself," she said with a sharp sniff, before turning her back on him.

"Georgia, I mean it—I'm sorry I was so rude."

She wheeled around, and he noted there were two spots of color on her cheeks. That warned him she was more than just upset. She was good and mad.

"Really? You think your apology means anything to me? I'm sorry I cared enough about you to want to ensure you don't starve to death out there. Okay, yes, I am overcompensating. I had a very bad day yesterday and a shitty night's sleep, and I'm not in a good mood. My Zen is organizing things. It's something I'm good at and when I do it I feel as though I have accomplished something and gotten life's twists and turns under my control. If that upsets you, too darn bad. It's how I roll. Now, go for your walk and see if you can find some manners while you're out there."

He blinked. She was right. He was being bad mannered. His mom would give him a virtual kick in the butt if she knew. Sawyer didn't know what to say, so he took the coward's way out. He said nothing. He merely returned to the mudroom, put on his boots and coat and headed out the door. He hadn't gone far when he realized he'd forgotten the protein bar and water. He squeezed his eyes shut and muttered a string of expletives. His stomach growled, but he wasn't about to turn back now. The cabin was small. That was okay if you wanted to be alone with another person, but very tight confines if you didn't. He started walking.

Georgia's temper cooled as quickly as it had risen, but the sting of his words about her and food lingered as she began to warm maple syrup and peanut butter in a saucepan and blitzed some pitted dates in the food processor for her favorite granola bar recipe. At least these would be good for Sawyer to take out on his walks.

Yes, she was bigger than a lot of women, but that didn't mean she thought about food all the time. She'd accepted long ago that this was the body she had and she had learned to love herself and dress to maximize her good points. She was happy with who she was now. Too bad for Mr. Grumpy-pants if he didn't like it.

By the time she combined the nuts, dates, toasted oats and wet mix and pressed it into a low-sided baking tray, she had regained her equilibrium. She covered the tray and popped it in the refrigerator to chill before deciding now would be a good time to check her phone. That one bar of reception was still there but no answer yet from the property manager. There was, however, a string of messages from her mom begging her to let her know she was okay. She hastened to tell her mom where she was and that she was okay in a brief message that thankfully sent just before the bar of reception disappeared again. Georgia drummed her fingers on the counter. She hated waiting. Empty time achieved nothing, so she whipped up a batch of cheese scones and popped them in the oven to bake.

Outside it had begun to rain heavily again, but she wouldn't allow herself to worry about how Sawyer was enjoying his walk. No, she wouldn't give him the real estate in her mind. He wasn't worth it. He was surly and unkind and she was just as eager to put him behind her as he was to see the back of her. Even if he was kind of good-looking in a lean, lone-wolf way. Tall and rangy, he looked as if he had barely an ounce of fat on his body. She'd bet his metabolism would normally demand a lot more fuel than she'd seen him eat thus far. In fact, she hadn't seen him eat a thing. How long had he been here anyway? She searched her memory for what she'd read last night on his lease document. As best she recalled, he was less than a week into a month-long stay.

Georgia shook her head. She'd done the inventory herself this morning and knew what the stock levels were. Unless he'd lugged in a whole lot of food with his things, she would bet he'd barely eaten enough since his arrival to keep himself upright. Not that it was her problem to worry about, but if he kept this up he'd end up positively skeletal. What was his beef anyway?

She was just taking the scones out of the oven when she heard Sawyer's boots on the back deck and listened as he came inside. He slunk into the main room of the cabin, his hair dripping and the legs of his cargo pants soaking wet. Georgia bit back the offer to get him a towel. He was a big boy, and he knew where everything was. He could get one for himself.

"Those smell good," he said, walking toward her.

Even his socks were wet, judging by the damp footprints he was leaving on the wooden plank floor. Under normal circumstances, Georgia would have hastened to offer him a scone, even plated and buttered it for him and rustled up a fresh pot of coffee to go along with it. Instead, she just looked at him from the top of his dripping head to his sodden feet.

"Okay, I'll go get cleaned up," he said, taking the hint with a rueful expression on his face. "But when I come back, may I please have a scone and a coffee?"

"Found your manners then, I see," she said, fighting to hold back a smile from her face.

"I did. They were hanging from an outcropping not far from here."

His lips twitched and that was her undoing. Her mouth split into an answering smile and a small laugh escaped her. There, that felt a whole lot better, she realized. She hated tension between people. She'd lived through enough of that when she was small and her parents were constantly fighting. It was even worse when the fighting stopped, giving way to a charged, heavy silence. Georgia wasn't an idiot. She knew her family background was a major contributor to why she always felt the need to control what was around her and why she tried her darndest to make sure that everyone was happy and had their needs met. But she was good at it and it brought her joy, so there was no harm in it, surely?

"Go get dry and changed and I'll have these ready for you in a few minutes."

"Yes, ma'am," he answered and went to the bathroom. He hesitated at the doorway and looked back at Georgia, a serious expression wreathing his face. "And I truly am sorry for what I said, Georgia. I shouldn't be taking my frustrations out on you."

"Apology accepted," she said as graciously as she could.

She busied herself measuring coffee and making a fresh pot of the life-giving elixir. The scones were cool enough to touch so she sliced and buttered half a dozen of them and arranged them on a plate. As she carried them through to the sitting room area of the cabin, she heard the bathroom door behind her open.

Instinctively, she turned and in the next moment her mouth dried and her throat froze mid-swallow.

Sawyer exited the bathroom dressed only in a towel.

"Sorry, forgot to grab clean clothes," he muttered.

"Oh, don't mind me," Georgia managed to say as her eyes roamed his body.

Yes, he had a physique that made all her reproductive organs respond instinctively, a realization that she wasn't in a state to unpack right now, but it was the clear evidence of recent injuries that had left her almost speechless. There were scars all over his chest and abdomen. The longest were clearly surgical—and recent. What on earth had he been through?

Suddenly, she had some understanding of why he wanted to be alone. He'd obviously experienced something horrific to end up with those scars. Maybe he was taking time out to fully recover. Sawyer's gaze met hers as her eyes returned to his face, and he quirked an eyebrow as if silently inquiring if she'd looked her fill.

"You need to eat more," she said. "Hurry up and get dressed so you can have some scones."

She turned away and poured herself a coffee, added a splash of milk, and wrapped her fingers tightly around the mug as she heard him ascend the stairs to the bedroom. What the hell was wrong with her? By rights, she should have been married to someone else by now. Jetting away to the South Pacific and a new life with the man she loved. And yet here she was, in a remote cabin on the outskirts of

Olympic National Park, suddenly and unequivocally turned on by a man who was a complete stranger to her. A man who had been surly and unkind. A man who'd made it patently clear that he didn't want her here under any circumstances.

And she wanted him.

Four

Georgia grabbed a buttered scone and took a bite, but suddenly she wasn't hungry anymore. Instead, she was confused. How could she feel that way about someone like Sawyer? And especially now? She'd only just met the guy last night and he'd hardly been friendly.

For her, attraction had always been a slow and gentle ride, building to desire over time and with careful courtship. Even with Cliff, as whirlwind as their relationship had been, there'd still been steps before she'd felt emotionally safe enough to allow the physical side of their relationship to blossom. But right now, she tingled in all the right places after just a glimpse of Sawyer's bare torso.

Maybe it was the bad-boy element, emphasized by the fact he wasn't friendly and that he'd obviously had a rough ride recently. Those scars intrigued her, but he definitely had a lot of barriers up, which made her think twice about asking him about them. But even with the scars, he was physically beautiful. The slope of his shoulders, well defined with lean muscle, his arms strong without being overdone. And his abdomen? Wow, just wow. The chiseled six-pack made her fingers itch to trace each of the well-defined outlines slowly and carefully.

Georgia sat back on the couch and mulled over her thoughts. Here she was, physically objectifying him, without even really trying to get to know him. She chuckled to herself. As if she'd get to do that. The man was as much of a closed book as the carved wooden bookends on Grampy's shelves—the ones that looked like great classics but which were carefully shaped lumps of wood.

Over on the other side of the room her phone let out a ping, notifying her of an incoming message. Georgia leapt to her feet and raced to the kitchen counter, the only spot in the cabin with any kind of signal right now. She opened the message, relieved to see it was from the property manager. But her delight in getting contact with the outside world was short-lived when she read the contents of the text.

Message received. Authorities notified of mudslide. Due to low traffic on your road and high demand on public areas at present, repair is low priority. Likely 2-3 weeks before they will see to bridge and clear road. Will notify updates when available.

Sawyer came down the stairs from the bedroom. "Did I hear you get a message?"

"Yeah, my text to the property manager got through, however, it's going to be two to three weeks before a crew can get to us. I'm really sorry, Sawyer. It looks like you're stuck with me."

A wave of dejection swept through her with the force of a tsunami, and she felt tears burn her eyes.

"Two to three weeks?" Sawyer was incredulous.

"If you don't believe me, read the text for yourself," she said, handing him her phone with a deep sigh.

He read the screen and passed the phone back to her. "This isn't what I signed on for."

"I'll see to it that you're fully recompensed for your entire booking."

"It's not about the money," he growled.

"Yeah, I know. It's the solitude. I think I got that memo."

He shoved a hand through his still-wet hair. His face was set in harsh lines, but that was nothing compared to the bleak expression in his eyes.

"I'll do my best to stay out of your way," Georgia added in a small voice. "The scones and coffee are on the table over there."

Sawyer couldn't believe this. He'd booked a month of alone time. Where the only sounds around him would be those of nature. Not guns and tanks. Not the chaos of a city. Not the sound of a single other person. And yet, somehow he was here with a woman who not only seemed to find a need to fill silence

with chatter, but who felt the incessant need to organize shit as well. His gaze settled on the lists she'd
obviously made this morning. Hell, even looking at
the roster made him itch.

He was the kind of guy who lived on the fly. Ate
when he was hungry, traveled on a whim, tidied up
after himself only when his living conditions got so
he couldn't find what he needed when he needed it.
She said she'd stay out of his way but in an open-plan
cabin with only one bathroom and one bedroom, that
was virtually impossible.

He'd just go out all day every day with his camera and wait for inspiration to strike. Or lightning,
whichever came first. And with the way his luck was
trending, it would probably be the latter. He hadn't
yet taken a single shot with the only camera he had
brought with him. He'd told himself it was because
it wasn't his favorite camera—that one had been destroyed in the barrage that had killed Max. He'd retrieved the memory card but hadn't gone through it
yet. Couldn't bring himself to relive the horror. The
truth was, he had no idea if he'd ever take another
photo again, and the echoing emptiness of that admission terrified him.

He'd been a photojournalist in one form or another since he'd left high school. If he couldn't frame
a single picture, where did that leave him?

"Sawyer? Are you okay?"

Georgia's tentative question pierced the fog of his
unraveling thoughts, reminding him that she'd said
something about coffee and scones. His body needed

fuel for those long hikes he was going to take, he reminded himself.

"Yeah, fine."

He strode across the room to the coffee table and helped himself to a cheese scone. Flavor burst on his tongue as he took a big bite, and he demolished the scone and quickly reached for another.

"How do you take your coffee?" Georgia asked, her hand hovering over the coffeepot.

"Black, with sugar, thanks."

He reached for a third scone and raised it to his mouth. For some reason he couldn't get enough of the things. It was as if by eating, he was trying to fill a gaping hole inside himself. There were worse things he could be eating, he reminded himself. Maybe having her here had its advantages, if her baking was this good. But then he remembered the rosters and felt the strictures of someone else's control wrap around him. Mentally, he shoved it aside. She could make all the lists she wanted, but he was his own man and no one said he had to play by her rules.

She sure could make a decent mug of coffee, though.

"What are you going to do all day?" he asked.

She flinched at his sudden question but appeared to gather herself quickly.

"Oh, I guess I'll read. I'd preloaded a ton of books for..." Her voice trailed off before she could mention the trip she wasn't on. "Anyway, I can always find something to do."

"Thanks for the scones."

"You're welcome, they were easy to make. I can show you next time."

She was as eager to please as a puppy, and it would be cruel and unnecessary to tell her he had no interest whatsoever in learning how to bake. In his line of work, you didn't have time for such niceties. You kept your eyes on the news channels and you traveled according to where the latest hotspot was. While you might check into a hotel, you rarely stayed in your room or slept in the bed. And he liked it that way. He wasn't into domesticity or putting down roots.

"Sure, if I'm around," he forced himself to say, even though he had no plan to be around much in the next few weeks.

Just how many trails could he follow? As many as he needed to, he decided, as he rose from the couch and went upstairs to the bedroom. He retrieved his computer and charging cable from his pack and went to the dining table where he set up and inserted the card from his busted camera. In the kitchen, Georgia was bustling about, cleaning what he was sure she'd cleaned already and putting the leftover scones in an airtight container. He tried to keep his eyes on the screen but struggled to focus—his gaze drifting to watch her instead.

She took something from the fridge and turned it out onto a chopping board, neatly cutting whatever it was into finger-size pieces, which she individually wrapped in grease-proof paper and put into another airtight container. As she turned from the fridge, she caught his eye on her and a flush of color stained her cheeks.

"Sorry, am I being too noisy?"

"Not at all." He forced his eyes back to the screen and to the blinking cursor that hovered over the file folder containing the photos he just couldn't bring himself to open. "What was that you put in the fridge?"

"Granola bars. D'you want to try one? I thought you could take a few when you go on your walks, to help keep your energy levels up."

"You don't have to go to any effort for me." In fact, he'd rather they barely crossed paths, if at all possible.

"It's no effort," she said as she got one out for him and put it on a plate.

She bent over the table to slide it toward him and his eyes caught on the curvaceous cleavage exposed by the deep V of her top. That telltale hit of physical interest from last night twinged again. It had been a very long time since sex was anything more than a physical release for him, and he wasn't about to embark on something as risky as acting on his body's demands now. Georgia was clearly fragile emotionally, and it would be a dirty trick to take advantage of that. That didn't stop him from appreciating the view, though.

Sawyer dragged his eyes back to his screen and forced himself to click on the folder, flinching as the photo icons marched across his view. There was one that caught his attention immediately, and he clicked on it. It was of Max as they'd transported out to the fighting zone. He'd been in a good mood, talking shit about what they'd get up to when they got back to their accommodations that night. Telling Sawyer about the contraband bottle of scotch he'd won in a card game the night before.

He hadn't realized Georgia had moved behind him until he felt her hand settle gently on his shoulder.

"He looks happy. Are you good friends?"

"We were. He's dead."

Saying the words out loud for the first time hit him with the weight of a sledgehammer. Max was dead. There. It was said and done. Even though he'd witnessed it with his own eyes, he'd never been able to articulate it before now. His friend was gone and he'd never be able to say goodbye. He'd still been laid up in hospital when Max's family had his memorial service.

"Oh, Sawyer, I'm so sorry. That must be a huge loss. Do you want to talk about him?"

"No." He reached forward and closed the laptop.

She was quick to take the hint and stepped away. The second she removed her hand from his shoulder though, he perversely wished it back. Despite everything, he craved the connection with another living being. The confirmation that even though he'd been hurt, even though he'd witnessed the obliteration of his friend, he still existed.

"I'm sorry," Sawyer said through a throat constricted with raw, aching grief. "It's still too fresh."

"That's okay. I'm here if you want to talk about him, though."

Sawyer watched her as she went through the cabin,

setting things back to rights even though nothing had really changed here in the time since she'd arrived. She was the neatest and tidiest person he'd ever come across. While he always left his clothes ready to drag on at a moment's notice, for the rest he'd always been a bit of a slob. Newspapers, books, electronics—all were usually left where he'd read or used them last. Dishes in the sink or on the countertop. Stale bread left on the chopping board. But, as he looked around him, he noticed all the little things she constantly did to keep the place immaculate. Was it that she was a neat freak or did she have some deeper reason behind her actions?

Suddenly he wanted to know more about her, but as so often had happened in his life as a youngster, he didn't know where to start with his questions. It was one of the reasons he'd turned to photojournalism as his career. Words didn't always come easily to him, but he could express a million different things in a well-executed shot.

It worried him that he hadn't been able to bring himself to lift his camera to take a single photo since Max's death. Without his craft as a photographer, he was completely and utterly adrift. He'd thought coming out here on the edge of Olympic National Park would provoke his desire to capture the world around him. Had hoped the peace of being alone would bring him some solace. But all he had was that echoing emptiness inside him. This was supposed to be a time of renewal. A chance to refill his creative well now that he was truly away from the carnage and violence of war. But it brought him nothing but a sense that he was in the wrong place and time.

Maybe he should go back. It's what Max would've done. But a big part of Sawyer's enjoyment in his work had been competing with Max for the money shot. The one the media outlets would go wild for. The photo that everyone would understand as the fullest and most honest representation of what it was really like on the ground in a modern war.

Georgia had made her way back into the kitchen and was putting the plates they'd used with the scones into the dishwasher. His grandmother would approve of those scones, he thought with a small smile. She'd been the kind of woman who was scant with her praise, which made it all the more uplifting when she gave it. She also showed love with food, and never tolerated fools. He loved her with his whole heart. After both his grandfather and his mom had died when he was twelve, his grandma had moved in with him and his dad, swiftly becoming the rock they all tethered themselves to for stability in their new shaky world. His dad had eventually remarried and moved out with his new wife, but Grandma had stayed.

She'd been the one to recognize his difficulty with expressing himself clearly with words. One day she'd given him his first camera. It was one that had belonged to his late grandfather—an Agfa Isolette 1 from the 1950s. With only twelve frames per roll of film, he soon learned to be extremely careful with what he took a picture of. But having the camera had opened up a whole new angle on the world he lived in.

Soon he'd been winning amateur photography competitions. He found a place where he fit, with people who understood how he saw things.

He owed his grandmother a lot. She'd been the one waiting at the airport when he'd been released from the hospital and returned home. As tiny as she was, her arms clasped around him had given him a deep sense of comfort. She'd seen the brokenness inside him. Had urged him to find somewhere to go and heal even when he knew she wanted nothing more than to look after him at home. She'd always understood what he needed, but maybe she'd been wrong this time because in the days he'd already been here, he'd found nothing to spark his desire.

Nothing except for a runaway bride with a penchant for neatness and baking, he admitted with a rueful shake of his head. Said bride was currently chopping vegetables and sautéing cubes of beef in a frying pan.

"More food?" he asked.

"Dinner for tonight. Just a beef stew."

She transferred the beef and vegetables into a large enamel pot, poured over some liquid and put on a lid before sliding the pot into the oven.

"Are you always this organized?" he asked.

"Always. It's what I do."

"What? Organize meals?"

"Among other things, yes. Like I said, I'm a wedding planner. It takes a lot of coordination to make sure everything runs smoothly, not to mention the preparation for just in case something goes wrong."

A vision of her arrival last night in a sodden and muddied wedding gown flashed across his memory. Suddenly he wanted to know what had brought her here.

"So what went wrong yesterday?"

"I don't want to discuss yesterday."

"Are you sure?"

She washed her hands at the sink and dried them slowly. Her shoulders were tight, drawn up around her ears, and tension held her back rigid.

"I'll give you the abridged version. I was supposed to get married yesterday. I didn't, okay?"

As far as explanations went, that was pretty scant on detail.

"Oh-kay," he said slowly.

"I'm having an existential crisis, if you must know. I'm a wedding planner who couldn't even make it to the altar at her own wedding. And that's all I'm going to say on the subject. You didn't want to talk about your friend, so I'm sure you'll respect my desire not to talk about yesterday."

"Fair point. So what do we do until dinner is ready? Play cards?"

"I don't know about you, but I have a book to read and finally have the time to read it. I'm going to make some cocoa and light the fire and then that couch is mine for the rest of the afternoon."

"Make that two cocoas and I'll bring in the firewood," Sawyer said, getting to his feet. He felt antsy and hauling in a few logs from the woodshed would at least make him feel mildly useful.

"Thank you."

The air was chilly outside and it was still rain-ing lightly. Enough light came through the thinning clouds to cast a gentle glow on the expanse of green-ery and trees that surrounded the cabin. This was an idyllic spot if you liked total isolation from the out-side world. Maybe in different circumstances, he'd be enjoying it more. To be honest, he hadn't really enjoyed his time here so far all that much, even be-fore Georgia had arrived. Sure, under normal cir-cumstances, he could be on his own for days on end without missing human interaction, but this time it had left him well and truly alone with his thoughts, and he didn't like them much at all.

Which brought him straight back to the fact that he wasn't alone now. He was stuck with a woman who intrigued him and that was a dangerous thing. Intrigue led to questions, which generally led to an-swers and sharing information. And he didn't do sharing as a rule. He loaded up several logs under one arm and carried them inside, stacking them next to the fireplace before going back for another load. By the time he'd done that a couple more times, Georgia had made the cocoa and had lit the fire.

"I've put your cocoa on the dining table next to your computer," she said, picking up her e-reader and putting a cute pair of reading glasses on the end of her pert nose.

He tried not to stare, but he was captured by the light of the fire on her skin, by the sheer abundance of life she reflected into the cabin even while reclined on the couch.

"What's wrong?" she asked. "Have I got chocolate on my face or something?"

"No, nothing's wrong," he said tightly. "Thanks for the cocoa."

He walked over to the dining table where she had left his cocoa, making it quite clear she wanted his company nearby about as much as he'd thought he wanted hers. And yet, perversely, he felt put out that she'd created this distance between them. *You're being ridiculous*, he told himself firmly. *You wanted space, you have it—metaphorically anyway.* Sawyer looked over his shoulder. Georgia was already wrapped in a blanket and absorbed in her reading. He envied her that innocence and suddenly, for the first time in weeks, his hands itched to reach for his camera so he could capture that moment.

Five

Georgia woke the next day with a distinct kink in her neck. She stretched herself out and shivered. The fire was out, and this morning felt even cooler than the previous day. She made a mental note to leave the heat pump on tonight. Sleep had been elusive. Probably because she had overcome the shock of her failed wedding and now had the mental capacity to truly process what she'd gone through. How had she not seen that Cliff was Mr. Wrong? She'd gone over and over it in her mind last night, reviewing their relationship from the first day she'd met him, as a guest at his friend's wedding that she'd organized at the resort, to the moment she'd seen the sonogram of his child on her phone. Maybe she'd ignored a few things, wanting to see the good in him, wanting to believe he genuinely loved and wanted her. Okay, more than a few things. Was she really such a terrible judge of character?

At least she'd had the courage to walk away. Well, run, to be precise. Now she needed a plan for the future. The world was her oyster, right? She had no ties holding her back, no contracts to fulfill. No house to maintain. Tears welled in her eyes and she fought to hold them back. She wanted all those things and she'd wanted them with a partner who was not only genuinely interested in her and loved her, but who would help her to be a better version of herself—the way she had wanted to do for them.

She sniffed loudly and reached for a tissue to blow her nose. The tears now coursed freely down her cheeks. She had to pull herself together. She wouldn't be a victim to Cliff's infidelity a moment longer. But no matter how sternly she tried to scold herself into a more rational mindset, the pain of the death of her dreams—the wedding, the future—inexorably scored across her heart.

"You okay?"

She jumped. She'd been so absorbed in her misery she hadn't heard Sawyer come downstairs.

"Fine. Absolutely wonderful, in fact," she stated firmly.

She rose from the couch and grabbed the wrap that matched her nightgown. Sawyer was looking at her differently than he had up until now, and Georgia was suddenly aware of the sheerness of the nightgown she'd worn to bed. It was one of several she'd bought in anticipation of her honeymoon and new life in the tropics. They'd seemed appropriate at the time, but now—not so much. Her nipples had beaded with the cold but now they tightened even more with something else. A forbidden awareness of the man standing before her threaded through her body and tightened in a coil in her lower belly.

She turned away and shrugged into the wrap, which offered another sheer layer. Hardly the coverage she really needed but better than nothing, she told herself. And what the hell was she doing having physical feelings toward Sawyer anyway? He was Mr. Grumpy-pants. Surly to the point of rudeness most of the time. Slack on his share of household duties, except for maybe getting wood for the fire. Aside from the cocoa he'd made on the first night, he hadn't so much as buttered a piece of toast for her or stacked a single dish in the dishwasher. Did he not understand the meaning of a roster?

There, that had done it. She'd successfully managed to rid herself of any sexual awareness of him. Well, mostly.

"You look like you're crying," Sawyer stated baldly.

"I might have been," she said with a large sniff. "But I'm not now. If you'll excuse me, I need the bathroom."

With all the dignity she could muster, she sailed past him and to the bathroom…kicking herself when she locked the door behind her because she hadn't remembered to grab her clothing to get changed into. She attended to her needs then swanned back out again, riffling through her suitcases to find an outfit for today. Color, she needed color, the brighter and bolder the better. She grabbed a bright green T-shirt and floral capri pants in shades of pink, green and yellow. With that gathered, together with fresh underwear, she returned to the bathroom to shower and dress.

Once dressed, she assessed herself in the full-length mirror behind the door. Well, she certainly looked bright, if not entirely inappropriate for a cool, wet Washington spring. She shivered a little with the cold, but socks, slippers and a sweatshirt would solve all that. Her tummy gave a rumble. Breakfast and coffee. That would also make a difference. The world always looked better after a good mug of coffee.

Sawyer was in the kitchen when she left the bathroom. She noticed he'd already folded up her bedding and stacked it in the corner. By the delicious aroma in the air, he'd already made coffee, too. Surprise didn't begin to cover it. He'd been long gone by this time yesterday. As she walked toward the kitchen, he turned with a mug of steaming coffee in his hand and passed it to her.

"There—milk and no sugar, right?"

"How did you know?" she asked, taking a sip of the brew and moaning in delight. "This is really good. Thank you."

"I have eyes," he said before turning back to the stove.

"You're making breakfast?"

"It's my turn, isn't it?" he said, using his fingers to create air quotes at the same time.

"Well, yes, but I didn't expect you to—"

"Look, I don't require you to wait on me and I don't plan to wait on you. I can't believe I'm saying this, but I actually think it's a good idea to have a roster of chores so we don't get under one another's feet. I came for solitude and I guess you came for the same reason. For however long we're stuck together, it's best we try and get along."

Well, that was quite a speech. She looked over his shoulder and saw the French toast he was making. The very thing she'd written on her list for breakfast this morning. A warm, fuzzy feeling bloomed inside her. Maybe this was going to work after all.

"I'll set the table," she said and turned to the drawer with the cutlery.

By the time she'd pulled the condiments from the shelf and found a bottle of maple syrup, Sawyer was plating up. He'd magicked up a dish of grilled bacon from where it had been warming in the oven and loaded each plate with a liberal helping, together with the French toast. He didn't sprinkle powdered sugar over the toast, but she could forgive him for that, and for the fact that his presentation lent more to the functional than the aesthetic. Her mouth was already watering to try it.

It might not have been the prettiest breakfast, but it certainly tasted great. Georgia felt her mood vastly improve by the time she cleared the table and loaded the dishwasher. Sawyer had put his plate on the coun-

ter, grabbed a couple of her granola bars and a water
bottle from the butler's pantry and was already pulling on his boots.

"Will you be back for lunch?" she asked as she
heard him open the back door.

"I don't know. Don't bother making anything for
me. Okay?"

"Sure, I was just going to warm over the remain-
ing beef casserole, so I wasn't going to any bother."

"Like I said, I don't know when I'll be back."

"Suit yourself," she said with a smile. "No doubt
I'll still be here."

And she would still be there. That was the whole
problem. Sawyer slung his camera around his neck
and headed for the outdoors. It was clear today but
the ground underfoot was still wet and slippery from
the previous night's rain. Even so, it was beautiful.
The sun poked through the trees and the call of bird-
song around him reminded him that life continued
regardless of what was happening in other parts of
the world. But even though everything here was pristine in its natural glory, nothing called to him to take
a picture. He felt like a writer with no words, or an
artist with no canvas or oils to paint with.

The hours passed and his legs ached with the
miles he'd hiked. He'd gone off track so many times
he began to wonder if he'd be able to find his way
back to the cabin again, but instinct won out and the
constant presence of the sun made a very welcome
change. He'd already consumed the granola bars

Georgia had made and was getting hungry again. At least that was a good sign he was returning to normal. His appetite had been near nonexistent since Max's death. He'd head back, whether he felt up to the company or not because he sure was sick to death of his own right now.

As he approached the cabin, he spied Georgia curled up on a large bench seat padded with half a dozen brightly colored cushions. The sun beamed down on her, bathing her in its warm, golden light and highlighting the range of dark reds and burnished gold in her hair. Before he even realized it, Sawyer had lifted his camera to his eye and shot off a dozen frames. She looked so relaxed as she dozed there, her e-reader discarded in her lap and one arm propped behind her head. Her skin was smooth and luscious and the curves of her body were a symphony of light and shadow, drawing him closer as he took more pictures.

He must have made a noise or stepped on something because her eyes flickered open, staring at him in surprise. He felt a pang of remorse that he'd disturbed her and regret when she shifted her position and sat up, looking at him. Her eyes were more green than hazel in the outdoor light and he itched to take a close-up, but the reserve he saw reflected there made him hesitate.

"You're taking photos of me?" she asked as he came to stand in front of her.

"Is that a problem? I can always delete them."

"I don't usually like photos of myself."

"Why's that?" he asked.

She shrugged. "Oh, a lack of confidence in my-self, I guess. I'm better than I used to be, but right now I'm feeling really vulnerable to be totally honest with you."

"Would you like to see the photos?"

She looked as if she was going to refuse but then gave a slight nod of her head and moved over on the seat so he could sit alongside her. Sawyer settled down next to her and brought the pictures up on his camera, tilting the screen so she could see them.

"You don't get a true idea of what they're like here. I can upload them onto my computer and show you there, if you'd rather."

"No, that's okay. Small is good."

There was something in the tone of her voice that unsettled him. Still vulnerable but a little bit of something else he couldn't quite put his finger on, too. He shrugged off the thought and zoomed in on the shot.

"You can see how the light dances off your skin," he said before selecting the next picture.

"If you say so," she said with a slight chuckle. "To me I simply look unbearably washed out."

"You're being too hard on yourself. Do you do that often?"

"What, be hard on myself? Yeah, I guess. A bit of a defense mechanism I learned a long time ago. I did train myself out of it, mostly."

She sighed and he heard a weight of complication in the sound. This was precisely why he'd wanted to be alone. He couldn't even cope with his own problems and insecurities. The last thing he needed was to shoulder someone else's. But still he persisted. He wanted Georgia to see herself the way he'd seen her when he'd captured her in the photos, so he selected the next shot.

"Here, look at this. See how the light plays over you. It's as if it's gilding you. And you, you look deeply relaxed and secure in yourself and your surroundings. That's a real gift, you know. A lot of people never get to let go like that."

Sawyer looked at her as she studied the small portrait on his screen. She'd caught her full lower lip between her teeth and worried at it as if she was holding back the words she wanted to say.

"And you think that's a good photo?" she eventually said carefully.

"It's a great composition and great subject matter, too," he said with a laugh.

His breath caught in his throat. He'd laughed. Where the hell had that come from? He hadn't laughed in weeks.

"You're being kind," she protested.

"I'm not a kind person," Sawyer said bluntly. "I'm a photojournalist. I shoot what I see. Look."

He scrolled through the other photos, enlarging them to show her specific highlights as he saw them. As he continued, he could feel her relaxing beside him, getting closer. The warmth of her arm against his became his sole focus.

"Oh, I like that one," she said suddenly as he brought up the last shot he'd taken before she'd woken.

"I think I can see what you mean about the light. I feel like I actually look good in it."

"Personally, I think you look stunning in all of them. Besides, you don't need to please anyone else but yourself with how you look. Feeling good is all about accepting who you are, right?"

"Are those shots really how you see me?" she asked, turning to look at him directly.

They were face-to-face. This near to her he could see the variations of color in her eyes from the golden ring around her pupil to the darker green-brown at the edge of her iris. His gaze dropped to her lips and as he did so, they parted slightly. It would be the simplest thing in the world to lean forward a few inches and kiss her. Everything inside him clamored for him to do it, but reason made him pull back slightly.

"Yes," he answered simply.

A giant grin spread across her face. "Thank you," she said before standing up. Grabbing her e-reader, she went inside the cabin.

Sawyer sat there on the seat, not entirely sure what she'd been thanking him for. He scrolled through the shots again, unwilling to delete any of them. *She hasn't asked you to.* He paused on the picture he'd taken just before she awoke. She looked so tranquil, so utterly at peace. And so incredibly beautiful that a rush of yearning surged through him. He craved that tranquility, that peace. He craved her.

He stood abruptly, uncomfortable with his thoughts and with the way his body prickled with awareness. He was angry with himself. If Georgia had any idea of how he felt, it would make things between them even more awkward than they already were. The cabin was well appointed, but compact. They were on top of one another all the time whenever they were both inside.

Sawyer drew in a sharp breath through his nostrils. He'd just have to stay out every damn day. Something other than Georgia was bound to trigger his creativity again. But why had it been her? What was it about the woman sleeping on the cushioned bench, in the lazy afternoon sunshine, that had piqued his interest enough to photograph her?

He tried to dissect the visual image of her that had imprinted on his mind. Yes, her hair was rich with color and the way it cascaded just past her shoulders was a sumptuous invitation for someone to reach out and touch it. With permission, of course. What would it be like to be that person who had her approval to do such a thing? To be that close to her that you could experience the sensation of the silky strands of burnished color as they slid through your fingers?

A burn of need glowed to life from deep inside him. He wanted that connection, that nearness. He'd avoided getting close to anyone romantically in recent years because it always ended in tears when he'd had to pull away and pursue his profession. His job had been everything, but he was wondering now if there was a lesson to be learned from Max's death and his own time in the hospital. Life was infinitely precious, and you never knew exactly when or how it might end. It was your responsibility to live your best life. To savor it and appreciate it, and the people around you.

For Sawyer, right now, the only person near him was Georgia. She'd performed acts of kindness and care the entire time she was here. All without question or expecting anything in return. Okay, he'd made a start with cooking breakfast this morning, but he knew he could do better. If he was going to rejoin the human race as a person who was worthy of good things and the gift of the life he'd been given, then he needed to make more of an effort.

She'd obviously been through some trauma—probably not in the physical sense like his own, but certainly emotionally. They were both here to heal. Maybe, just maybe, they could help each other on that journey.

Six

Sawyer didn't sleep well that night. He was plagued with reruns of Max's death. It played out dozens of different ways, but the end was always the same—and always devastating. He eventually fell into a deep, thankfully dreamless, rest somewhere close to dawn. As a result, he woke groggy and in a bad mood. He went downstairs to use the bathroom and have a shower to wash away the dregs of the bad night. Georgia was already up and dressed and busy packing what looked like lunch boxes and drink bottles into two small backpacks. He did a double take. Two backpacks?

"Good morning!" she positively trilled.

"What's good about it?" he grumbled, feeling as if he had a vicious hangover. Her chirpy attitude and bright clothing were an unnecessarily unkind assault on his senses.

"The sun is shining, and I'm going hiking today. You're welcome to join me. I've packed for both of us."

"And that's why you're in such a disgustingly happy mood?"

"Absolutely. Look…" Her expression grew more serious. "I've been struggling the past few days, but you did and said a few things yesterday that helped me realize that I don't need to be so harsh on myself. I thought I'd knocked it on the head, but with my wedding falling through, my doubts all came rushing back. Basically, what you did reminded me that I can be happy with who I am. So, are you coming with me?"

Sawyer looked at her and weighed his options. The way he saw it, he had three choices. He could go back to bed and pull the covers over his head for a few more hours, or he could let her forge out onto the trails on her own and then head in the opposite direction once he was sure he knew where she was going. Or, he could give in and go with her.

"Give me ten minutes and I'll be ready," he growled.

Even as he briskly showered, he wondered why he'd settled on option three. It wasn't as if he wanted to spend more time with her. Although, yesterday he had decided to try and be nicer about the time they had to spend together. After his shower, he wrapped himself in a towel, shot up the stairs to the bedroom and dragged on clean cargo pants, a long-sleeved

T-shirt and sweater. She said there was sunshine, but it was bound to be cold. Snow still sat high on the mountains and the wind definitely had a bite.

Georgia had pulled on a jacket in muted colors and wore sturdy hiking boots. Together with her bright green capris and patterned shirt, she presented quite a juxtaposition of styles. He assumed the jacket and boots had come from the cupboard in the mudroom because he'd seen her wear nothing approaching the jacket's camouflage tones in the time she'd been here so far.

She thrust a mug of hot coffee and a bowl filled with muesli, fruit and yogurt at him with a command to eat while she went to the bathroom. It was easier to obey than resist, he decided, and he crunched his way through the dish. Everything tasted different since she'd been here. Better, somehow. He'd bet his last dollar that she'd made the muesli herself. It didn't taste like anything out of a packet that he'd ever had before.

He was putting the mug and bowl in the dishwasher when she popped back out of the bathroom and beamed in his direction. Without thinking, he grinned back. There was something about her today, a zest for living, maybe, that was infectious. Suddenly he was looking forward to hiking with her.

"Where are we headed?" he asked as she passed him a backpack and his camera, which he'd left on the dining table the night before, and they headed out the door.

"Wherever our noses lead us. I notice you've most

often left and returned from the western side of the property, so I propose we head northeast today."

"You've been watching me return from my hikes?"

"Sure, someone had to keep an eye out. I'm the only one who would know if you didn't come back, so how could I organize a search if I had no idea which direction you'd headed?"

She had a point. "Thanks, I guess."

"You're welcome," she answered with another of those face-splitting grins.

He felt a tightening in his chest at the sight of her, all full of the joy of life and anticipation for the day ahead. He missed that feeling, he acknowledged. In fact, he didn't remember the last time he simply felt joy. Yes, he'd had deep satisfaction in his work. Had the adrenaline rush of living on the edge of danger on each assignment he took. But even on his long hikes through the area since he'd arrived here at the cabin, he had simply been driven to put one foot ahead of the other until he was so tired he could barely think. He hadn't stopped to take things in, to appreciate the view or anything around him. He had a feeling that was going to change today.

"I can lead today, if you like," Georgia offered, wondering how Sawyer would take the suggestion.

He'd struck her as the kind of guy who, if he had to have company, would prefer to be in charge. She was surprised when he gave her a sharp nod and gestured for her to go first. They'd been hiking in silence for about fifteen minutes when she found herself unable to remain quiet a moment longer.

"You know it's recommended that we be loud on the trails, so we can warn the local bear population we're out in their environment."

"I haven't seen any bears since I got here."

"That doesn't mean they're not around," she said promptly. "But we'll be fine if we do see one. Just remember we need to stay at least fifty yards distant. And the mamas will be out with their cubs, so they're more likely to be aggressive."

"Okay, message received. Watch out for black bears."

She grinned at him again. He'd been a little gruff when he'd gotten up. It must be because he hadn't slept well. She'd heard him tossing and turning up in the loft. While sleeping on the couch wasn't the most comfortable experience of her life, she was sure she was getting a better night's rest most nights than he was.

"What made you choose the cabin for your getaway?" she asked as they continued on the trail.

"Isolation."

"Sorry I messed that up for you." She looked over her shoulder and caught his shrug. "I've asked the property manager to stay in touch with the road repair people and to keep me informed of any updates. I'll be out of your hair as soon as I can. She's also reversed your payment for the lease. I thought it was only fair since I'm intruding on your plans."

"You didn't need to do that."

"I did. I feel bad I've intruded. Anyway, it is what it is. Look at us making the most of a bad situation."

They walked on a little longer and again, Georgia felt the need to find out more about him.

"Why did you need the isolation?" she asked straight out. "Forgive me for noticing, but I saw you've had some injuries recently. Was that why you wanted to get away?"

He made a sound suspiciously like a growl. She stopped in her tracks to turn and face him, and he almost barreled right into her.

"I don't want to talk about it."

"Okay, but when you're ready, I will listen. Just so you know. It helps to talk these things out. It diminishes them in your mind that way. At least, that's what I've found."

She realized she hadn't exactly been practicing what she preached and turned back to the trail, setting a faster pace than before.

"Sawyer, what are your thoughts on infidelity?" she suddenly asked him.

"Say what? Where did that come from?" He sounded startled. She wished they were walking side by side so she could see his face, but the trail didn't allow for it through here.

"Infidelity. Is it a deal breaker for you or do you think you should just let bygones be bygones and leave it behind you?"

"I haven't been in a situation where I've had to think about it."

"What? Not at all?"

She heard him sigh heavily behind her. "My relationships have mostly been brief, and it was understood that they weren't exclusive. Fidelity or otherwise never became an issue."

"Ah," she said. "So you're not into commitment?"

"I never said that, but I've never found a person yet I wanted to be committed to. And, to be honest, my line of work doesn't really lend itself to a white picket fence and two point five kids. I'm away for long stretches and when I'm back I'm usually looking for my next assignment."

"So you're a rolling stone? Gather no moss, or complications like friends and family of your own?"

He was quiet for a while. Only the sound of his footsteps and breathing alerting her to the fact that he was still there.

"I guess you could say that," he finally answered. "But I have friends. And I see my dad and grandmother when I can. But back to your question about infidelity. Is that what happened to you? Is that why you're here?"

Georgia felt the bite of betrayal anew, but for some reason the pain wasn't quite as sharp or as rending as it had been last Saturday on her aborted wedding day.

"I found out my fiancé had cheated on me."

"And I'm guessing it was a deal breaker for you?"

"Under the circumstances, yes. He and his ex are expecting a baby. One that, as I found out half an hour before our wedding, they'd conceived while he was engaged to me. He tried to convince me it didn't matter to him and it wasn't important, but I just couldn't see past the fact he'd been unfaithful." She sighed heavily. "I dunno, maybe if I'd known sooner and had time to process it, or maybe if there hadn't been a baby involved, maybe if he'd even told me himself... No, I couldn't. Infidelity is my line in the sand," she said firmly.

Her breathing was uneven, and she could feel a stitch forming in her side. It had been a while since she'd been hiking, and the terrain was getting steeper. Behind her she heard Sawyer's breath begin to labor, too.

"We need to take a break. You okay with that?"

"To be honest, I'm having trouble keeping up with you," Sawyer admitted. "I've only been out of the hospital a few weeks."

"Oh, shit. I'm so sorry. I should have—"

Sawyer put up a hand. "I'm no baby. I could've asked you to slow your pace, but you seemed to need to walk and talk it out, so I didn't want to stop you."

Georgia looked at him. He was pale and there was perspiration on his face, but even though he'd been uncomfortable he'd still given her the space she needed.

"Don't let me do that again," she said. "If you need to stop, we stop. Okay? You're probably fitter than me anyway. I'm going to pay for this tomorrow, I'm sure. But look around you. Isn't it beautiful here?"

"It's stunning."

Where they'd stopped gave them a view out over a valley. All around them were tall trees. Georgia walked over to a fallen log, inspected it for bugs and other unwelcome wildlife, then gestured for them both to sit down.

"Let's stop here," she suggested. "I need a drink and something to eat anyway."

While they sat in companionable silence, she mulled over what Sawyer had said about friends and family. Even though he said he had them, he still sounded so very solitary. Georgia struggled to imagine what that would be like. She'd always been surrounded by people. Friends from school, then college, then work. And while she and her mom were a two-person unit, her mom's friends were always over for dinner or drinks. Their home had never been empty. Maybe that was partly because her mom was still trying to fill the void that had been left when Georgia's dad had walked out on them. Had she succeeded? Georgia was beginning to wonder. Whatever her mom did, she never appeared to be fully satisfied or completely happy, and that was truly sad.

Georgia had determined that when she and Cliff moved to the Cook Islands, she'd make as many friends as she could as quickly as possible to fill their lives with company and fun, especially since she wouldn't initially have a job to fill her days. At least now she didn't need to do that, right? She mustered a skeptical grin. But then again, she didn't have a job anymore either.

"What's so funny?" Sawyer asked from beside her.

Honestly, the man had been so very still, she'd almost forgotten his presence.

"I was thinking of the good points about not being married to Cliff right now."

"That's a positive."

"Yeah."

"Are there many of them?"

She laughed. "Probably quite a few if I could be bothered to list them all. They say love is blind and I'm inclined to agree. You don't want to see the bad so you focus only on the good. He made me feel special. Right up until he didn't, I guess."

"His loss," Sawyer said brusquely.

He'd picked up his camera and Georgia could see him focusing the lens on something in the distance.

"Anything interesting?" she asked.

"I thought I caught a glimpse of a deer, but it's gone now."

"Could've been an elk."

"Shall we go again?"

"Sure."

Sawyer stood up and stretched, and Georgia found herself captured by his movements. He reminded her of a lazy mountain lion stretching out after a long nap.

"Why don't you go in front this time," she suggested. "That way you can set the pace."

"You're humoring the invalid now?" he teased.

She snorted. "Hardly an invalid." She couldn't resist an appreciative scan of his body. No, that definitely didn't look like an invalid to her.

To her relief, he merely gave her a sharp look before starting to walk again. She began to doubt the wisdom of her asking him to lead when she realized that on the incline like this, his butt was in perfect line with her vision. Not that it was a bad-looking butt, she acknowledged—quite the contrary, in fact— but looking at it constantly as he trekked up the slope was making her feel the kinds of things she shouldn't be feeling so quickly after the demise of her relationship with Cliff. And what did that say about her, she wondered as she resolutely kept her feet moving up the hill, even though her leg muscles were starting to scream in protest.

Had she really loved Cliff? Or had she simply been swept up by his attention? It had all happened so fast. They'd still been getting to know each other when he'd sprung the question, asking her not just to marry him but to move to Rarotonga with him. She'd considered it to be a wonderful adventure to embark on together. Had she loved the idea of the adventure more than she'd loved the man? The question was unsettling. She'd never traveled as so many of her friends had. Never felt the need, to be honest. She'd been happy in her life. Her work had consumed her, and leading couples through their happy ever after day had given her an incredible sense of satisfaction.

But even if she hadn't consciously realized it, maybe she had needed more adventure in her life. Maybe she'd been too ripe for the picking for someone like Cliff. What had he seen in her anyway? While she'd been at school, she learned to be suspicious of boys who showed an interest in her, especially after she'd learned that her first prom date had only asked her on a dare and had planned to stand her up all along. Most of the guys she'd dated hadn't been quite that blatantly callous, but more than a few had assumed that since she wasn't a classic beauty, she'd be so grateful for attention that she'd "thank" them by catering to their every whim and putting up with all of their bad behavior. It took her a while to realize that she didn't need the approval of some random individual to validate her as a person.

She'd lost sight of that with Cliff. She'd allowed herself to become so absorbed in him—what he wanted and what made him happy—that in the short time they'd been together she'd casually dismissed any consideration of her true self. A glimmer of joy began to unfurl inside her. This was why she'd run away. She'd needed the space to see it for herself and the time to work it out in her mind. To allow the hurt to fade. Yes, it still simmered there beneath the surface because she'd believed herself happy with the choices she'd made. The decision to walk away from her career to support him in his, in a new country so far away from her support network, had felt right at the time. But she'd never stopped to consider what would happen if Cliff's support of her wasn't there.

She didn't realize that Sawyer had stopped walking until she slammed into the back of him.

"Oof! I'm sorry. I was lost in thought."

Sawyer hooked one arm around her shoulders and turned her to face a certain direction while he pointed with his other hand. "Look over there."

Georgia did her best to ignore how it felt to have

his arm draped over her. She was close enough to smell the clean, fresh fragrance of his skin. Logically, she knew they used the same type of soap at the cabin, but on him it smelled so much better. Her nostrils flared slightly, as if by doing so she could smell him better. She was so close to him, if she turned her head ever so slightly she could nuzzle the hollow of his throat and breathe him in deep. She gave herself a mental shake. *Way to freak a guy out*, she told herself before training her eye along the line of sight he pointed out. There, about a hundred yards away were two black bear cubs.

"Oh my God, they're so cute. But we really should change direction," she suggested. "Where there are cubs, there is always a mama bear and she will be in protection mode."

Sawyer didn't say anything but dropped his arm from her shoulders and lifted his camera. He made a few adjustments to the lens and then shot off a series of pictures.

"Okay, let's go," he stated when he was done. "Where do you suggest?"

She was surprised at his instant acquiescence but grateful at the same time.

"There's a spring in the opposite direction, about forty minutes from here. It should be a nice place to stop and have lunch, if that sounds good?"

"Sure, I could eat again. There's something about being out in all this fresh air that has really worked up my appetite. You?"

Georgia gave him an ironic grin. "I have a close

relationship with food, so it doesn't really take a lot to work up my appetite."

"You're in great shape. I was struggling to keep up with you before." He gave her a smile that sent a curl of pleasure all the way down to her toes. "C'mon, you'd better lead to our lunch spot, but remember not to go too fast."

He hadn't been kidding when he'd asked her to slow her pace, and it rankled. He, who had always been the leader of the pack, the head of the line, the guy who climbed the highest peak the fastest for the best picture. He'd thought he was fully recovered, aside from the occasional physical twinge, and had accepted that his healing now was mostly emotional. But hiking with Georgia had opened his eyes up to the real state of his overall condition, and he didn't like it. He especially hadn't liked having to ask her to slow down.

Right now, though, she was walking at a gentle pace in a westerly direction. Today, he found himself enjoying her company a whole lot more than he ever anticipated. He liked the way she moved, too. Not that he could tell all that much from behind, with her in that bulky jacket she was wearing. But there was a smoothness to her actions that made her quite graceful, even on the uneven terrain they hiked over.

"Oh, look at that. Isn't nature incredible?" she said, stopping and bending down to look at something on the ground near the base of a tree.

Sawyer caught up to her and spied the fungi she

was so enraptured by. It looked like tiered layers of golden-colored leather stacked on one another up the trunk. He lifted his camera to his eye again, zooming in on the growth.

"My great-grandfather used to lead me on trails here when I was little," she said softly. "It was always a magical wonderland to me. So many treasures to find on our way. I was convinced this place was full of elves and fairies back then."

Sawyer bit back a smile at her whimsical comment. "And now?"

"Well, it's still a magical wonderland, but my belief in fairy tales is well and truly dead."

"Because of your wedding?" he asked carefully.

"Because of life, to be honest, but yeah, my wedding or lack of it, also. Anyway, let's keep going."

She carried along on the trail, pointing out various plants and more fungi as she saw them. She didn't complain every time he stopped to take more photos, which he really enjoyed—and he also enjoyed the fact that the urge to take pictures was so strong. In Georgia's company, he wanted to find things that were beautiful even among the areas of the local forest where the untrained eye could find the terrain and surrounding plant life boring.

It was actually fun getting lost in the minutiae of the forest around them. In the end it took a lot longer than forty minutes to get to their destination, and by the time they arrived, he was starving. He'd always had a big appetite and a high metabolism, but there'd been something about almost losing his life that had put a hold on that. Today, though, it seemed he was getting back to normal.

When they reached the spring, it was a relief to take a break and just sit for a while. While Georgia opened her pack and took out her lunch, Sawyer took a moment to check through the pictures he'd taken. He'd never seen himself as much of a nature photographer, but he had to admit to himself that a lot of these looked really good.

"What did you call this fungus again?" he asked Georgia as he held the camera in front of her.

"Chicken of the Woods, but it's known by other names, too. Apparently it's a good source of potassium and vitamin C, but I've never tried it myself."

"I think I'd rather eat a banana," Sawyer said.

"Me, too," she said with an answering smile, and again, Sawyer was caught by her unconscious beauty.

She didn't wear a lick of makeup, but her skin glowed with the exertion of their hike and her eyes sparkled with joy in their surroundings. He wanted to take more pictures of her, and swiftly shot off a couple of photos before her expression changed.

"Why do you do that?" she asked, a faint flush rising up her throat.

"What? Take photos of you?"

"Yeah. You just do it spontaneously. It's a bit unnerving, to be honest."

"I don't mean to make you uncomfortable. I haven't felt the urge to shoot anything in quite a while, and right now, I feel bound to capture whatever inspires me."

She looked at him incredulously. "Seriously? You're saying *I* inspire you?"

"Sure you do. You're a natural beauty and a really good person at the same time. A lot of women, facing what you did and then being stuck with me, would have been a great deal more vocal and unhappy about it."

"What would be the point of throwing a tantrum? It wouldn't change anything. I'm still a runaway bride and you're still the Mr. Grumpy-pants I blundered in on."

"Mr. Grumpy-pants?" He raised one eyebrow as he looked at her.

"Whoops, did I say that out loud?" she asked with a wicked, utterly unapologetic twinkle in her eyes. "You have to admit, you weren't the most welcoming."

"Well, it's not every recluse's dream to have a mud-spattered and soaking-wet bride arrive on his doorstep."

She sighed and the light in her eyes dimmed a little, making him regret his choice of words.

"But," he continued, "it hasn't turned out too bad, right?"

"No, it hasn't so far."

That twinkle was back, and he felt something lighten in his chest at the sight of it. They ate the packed lunches Georgia had put together and after they'd rested a while, they began to make their way back to the cabin. All the way along the trail, Sawyer felt as though there was an itch deep inside him.

Something that needed to be scratched, but he couldn't quite put a finger on it. He just knew it had to do with Georgia. It wasn't until they reached the cabin and she bent to unlace her boots that he realized what it was.

Lust. Good, honest, pure lust. He hadn't wanted anything like he wanted her right now. Maybe it had been all the fresh air, maybe it had been having her company in a stunning environment, or maybe it was just that she was one hell of a woman and he wanted to unwrap her, like a gift, from all those bright layers she was wearing and reveal the pure and essential woman she was beneath it all.

Arousal stirred as his thoughts consolidated on that one realization—but he held himself back. Only a few days ago, she'd been on the verge of marrying someone else. Someone he'd cheerfully strangle right now, he privately admitted, for what he'd done to Georgia. And what did it matter to him anyway? He was the quintessential loner, all the way through from childhood. So what was he doing now, wanting to slay dragons for her? That wasn't his style at all. But he knew somehow, being with Georgia had become important to him, as was being able to make her smile or hearing her spontaneous laughter.

The question was, what was he going to do about it?

Seven

Georgia snuggled down in the blankets on the couch in front of the fireplace. The weather, which had been relatively settled the past couple of days, was stormy tonight. Behind the safety screen, the fire still glowed with the logs she'd added before she'd curled up to sleep. A flash of lightning turned the cabin to daylight for a brief moment, followed swiftly by a crash and rumble of thunder.

She loved a good storm. Always had. She knew she was safe and secure where she was. The cabin was sound, and there were no nearby trees to fall and create havoc. Of course, the bad weather might slow the repair of the bridge and clearing of the road to the cabin, but now that she and Sawyer seemed to have come to an agreement about their time together, she didn't feel quite the same sense of urgency to vacate the area.

She thought back over the past couple of days. She'd changed the timetable to incorporate daily hikes together, and she hoped they would become a regular part of their routine over the next week. She sensed Sawyer's reserve melting by the day. He'd started to open up a little more about his childhood, mentioning that his parents had been career-driven executives who'd generally left him to the care of a sitter when he wasn't at school, at least until his mom's death, which was when his grandmother moved in.

He'd spoken of his grandfather, the man who'd shared his fascination with taking photos with him and who had shown Sawyer how to use a camera. Georgia sensed a deep love there for both the man who taught him about photography and for his grandmother, who seemed to have been more of a mother to him than his own biological mom. But overall she had the sense his growing years had been very lonely. Even though she'd grown up with a sole parent, her mom's friends had always been around and Georgia had had a close circle of friends at school.

Another brilliant flash of light illuminated the cabin, followed by another crash of thunder that seemed to roll on forever. She wondered if Sawyer had been woken by the storm as she had. Rain pounded on the roof overhead. She stiffened as she heard a new sound, and she struggled to identify it. There it was again. A sound of anger, or distress maybe?

Georgia pushed back her covers and moved closer to the stairs. It had to be Sawyer, she rationalized. After all, it wasn't her making those noises, and there certainly wasn't anyone else in here with them. A cry from the loft made her ascend the stairs as quickly as she could. As she reached the top, lightning flashed again, exposing Sawyer completely tangled up in the sheets on his bed. His body thrashed from side to side as if he was trying to break free of something she couldn't see.

"Sawyer, it's okay," she said softly as she cautiously approached the bed. "It's just the storm."

And maybe a bad dream thrown in with it, she pondered.

"Max! No!" he screamed.

Anguish contorted his features and compassion drove Georgia to the bed. She sat down on the edge of the mattress and put a tentative hand out to Sawyer's bare back.

"It's okay, Sawyer. You're having a bad dream. Everything is okay. You're safe now."

Her voice seemed to calm him, but she could feel in the tension of his body beneath her hand that he was still locked in some awful nightmare. Carefully, Georgia lay down behind him and wrapped her arms around his torso. Hopefully, if she could make him feel as if he wasn't alone, he'd realize he was only dreaming. His body was hard and hot, his muscles taut with whatever emotion was being wrung from him by the awfulness of his dream. She continued to speak gently, saying his name, telling him he was safe and that he could wake up now.

Georgia knew the moment he became aware of her presence. His mutterings stopped, and his entire body stiffened once more before relaxing. Then he turned to face her. A new shaft of lightning came through the window, not as bright as before but enough for her to see that his eyes were open now and staring straight at her.

"You're okay, Sawyer. It was only a dream," she said softly.

"I wish it had only been a dream," he rasped.

"Do you want to talk about it?" she asked him.

"No."

Georgia started to pull away. Now that he was awake, he didn't need her anymore. But for some stupid reason, she was incredibly reluctant to move. She forced herself to remove her arms from around his waist.

"Don't go," he said, still in that raspy voice.

"You want me to sleep here with you? Are you worried the dream will come back?"

"I want you here," he said bluntly. "But I don't want to sleep."

He lay next to her, his eyes boring into hers and she had no doubt about what he was asking of her. Heat poured through her veins, pooling in her lower belly and her breasts, making her skin prickle with awareness and something else far more elemental. Need, on a scale she'd never known before, filled her.

"I'll stay," she whispered.

In response, his strong, lean arms wrapped around her, pulling her closer to him. With unerring accuracy his lips found hers. The sensation of his touch was all she'd imagined it would be, and more. His lips were gentle, exploratory, then demanding as she opened her mouth to him, allowing him to sweep his tongue against hers. She leaned into it so eagerly that their teeth bumped. Under any other circumstance, she'd have felt embarrassed about her lack of finesse. But he continued to kiss her, completely unfazed by their slight awkwardness together.

"You're so soft," he murmured against her mouth. "Everything about you is warm and soft and beautiful."

He kissed her again, rolling her onto her back as he shifted over her. Her arms were still around his waist and she reveled in the wonder of him—the weight of his lower body resting against hers, the firmness of his skin and the lean muscles of his back. Beneath her fingertips she felt the ridges of the scars she'd seen that day he'd come out of the bathroom dressed in only a towel. She wished she could ask him more about them, but she knew that opening up to that extent had to happen on his own timetable, if it ever happened at all.

Sawyer was kissing a hot trail of kisses along her jaw, rendering further thought impossible as the erogenous feel of his lips and tongue on her skin enveloped her. She shuddered and uttered a sigh of delight.

"You like that?" he asked, nuzzling that spot just

under her ear that was likely the most sensitive part of her body.

"I love that. Don't stop," she commanded in a weak voice.

"But if I don't stop, how will I ever get to explore the rest of you?" he asked.

She could see the flash of his grin in the low light of the room and realized the storm must have blown past. Moonlight now bathed the room, casting a silver-blue glow over everything.

"Well, feel free to take your time, then. I'm not going anywhere," she said on a gurgle of laughter.

"You have the most amazing laugh," he said, bending his head and kissing her again. "It fills all the dark places inside me. How on earth do you do that? Never mind, don't answer. I have work to do here—don't go interrupting me."

She laughed again and was rewarded with him kissing a line down the side of her throat to her collar bone. The wet heat of his tongue on her skin made her shiver with pleasure, and she wallowed in the enchantment that suffused her body. She shifted slightly as Sawyer slid the fine straps of her nightgown from her shoulders and peppered her skin with more kisses. Then he drew the nightgown away from her breasts, his hands gently molding to their fullness as he stroked and softly squeezed them.

No one had ever been this gentle with her before, as if she was made of spun glass or the finest porcelain. As if something as slight as a breath of wind could break her. Somehow Sawyer made her feel fragile and precious at the same time. She gave herself over to his touch and moaned in pleasure as he lowered his lips to one of her nipples and rolled it with his tongue. She felt moisture dampen her inner thighs as he tugged ever so gently on the hardened nub of flesh, felt the draw that pierced right through her body from her nipple all the way to her core.

A tiny cry of protest broke from her as he lifted his head, but it was only to transfer his attention to her other breast, to lick and suck and roll her into a state of fierce need. She felt as though she was on fire, as if with the smallest amount of pressure in exactly the right spot of her body, she would combust. But despite her arching her hips against him, he managed to keep his weight frustratingly away from the part of her that craved his touch most.

"I thought you'd be more patient," he rumbled with a slight laugh as he lifted his head and looked at her.

"I am patient, but you're slowly torturing me here."

"But it's a nice torture, right? I can stop if you'd prefer."

"Good grief, no. That would be the greatest unkindness of all. I guess this is a nice torture, if you can call such a thing nice."

His face split into a grin. "I can't quite believe we're having this conversation."

She giggled in response. "Me either."

Sex had always been something conducted under cover and in the shortest time possible with her and Cliff. She'd often been left unfulfilled, but she'd figured that they'd only get better with practice. But thinking about him now, maybe that was what had been wrong between them all along. A lack of connection in the bedroom might have been what led him straight back into his ex's arms. And what the living hell was she doing thinking about him at a time like this anyway?

"Now, where was I?" Sawyer muttered to himself. "Ah yes, my voyage of discovery."

"Discovery?" she said breathless as he applied his lips to her skin once more.

"Mmm, the discovery of all your favorite places to be touched."

"Don't let me stop you."

"I won't," he promised.

"One thing, though?" she interrupted.

"What?"

"When is it my turn?"

"When I'm done."

"And when will that be?"

"I'm not working to a timetable here. Suffice it to say you'll know it."

She laughed again, loving that he could make her feel so relaxed and happy at the same time. Her breath caught in her throat as he started to move down her body. He eased her panties down over her thighs and shoved the sheer fabric of her nightgown up to her waist before stroking her belly in gentle sweeps of his fingertips that edged ever closer to the demanding bead of need at her center.

When he touched her there, she jolted with the

shock of intense physical awareness. Waves of deep pleasure began to undulate through her body. She felt tears spring to her eyes at the sheer bliss that suffused her as her climax built and built then crashed through her in a raft of sensations that left her shaking in wonder.

Sawyer lay next to her, his arms around her as she slowly recovered, pressing small kisses to her temple, her cheek, her neck.

"You okay?"

"I'm so okay I don't think I'll ever get over it," she said, turning to him and pressing her lips to his. "And I'm quite sure I never want to."

She stroked his skin, feeling every bump and nodule of scar and bone. The man was far too thin but, oh, he felt sublime beneath her fingertips. The strong, lean muscle that bunched under her touch as she skimmed his shoulders, his chest, his belly, was a reminder of his strength and determination. As she traced over the most recent injuries, the surgical scars she'd noted before, she was reminded that whatever he'd been through that had driven him to the cabin, it must have been traumatic.

He was so self-contained and she understood on a deep level that she wouldn't be able to coax or push him, but she was prepared to wait as long as he needed so he could tell her how he got his injuries. And he did need to talk it out. She knew that as well as she knew she likely needed to sort through some issues of her own. But for now, glorious now, she would revel in where she was and with whom.

Because this, this was a gift, and she wasn't going to waste one minute of it.

She felt goose bumps rise on his skin as she stroked him and felt, too, the hard evidence of his arousal pressed against her hip. She let her hand drift down, from his belly to his hip, then slide farther down to his erection. She took him in her hand and felt him shudder against her as she stroked him from base to tip and down again.

"I think you ought to stop that," he growled against her ear.

"Too much?" she asked in a voice that had suddenly grown husky.

"Not enough," he said bluntly. "But I didn't come here with protection."

"Try the bedside table, top drawer," she suggested. "We run a full-service outfit here, you know."

She felt and heard the rumble of laughter from deep in his chest. He didn't laugh often enough, she realized, but she liked the sound of it. He rolled away from her for a moment to retrieve a condom from the drawer.

"Here," she said, taking the packet from him. "Let me."

She took her time rolling the condom on him, relishing the sudden intake of breath as she sheathed him. The moment she was done, though, he was back in command and he positioned himself over her, his erection nudging the slick folds of her flesh. She ached to feel him inside her but could feel by how tensely he held himself that he was holding back.

Instinctively, she rolled her hips upward—and just like that he slid inside her. He took only a second to regain his equilibrium before pushing himself deeper into her.

Georgia moaned with pleasure. Her inner muscles clenching around his length, reluctant to let him go, but instinct overcame reason and when Sawyer slowly withdrew only to thrust within her again, she relaxed into the rhythm, letting him stoke the fire inside her and lift her to even greater heights than the orgasm he'd already coaxed from her.

Their movements became more demanding, she meeting his every thrust. She felt his back muscles bunch tightly, his buttocks clench beneath her hands, and then, just as she spiraled out into spasms of satisfaction, he reached his peak and gave himself over to his climax, his hips surging again and again.

Sawyer collapsed on top of her briefly, before rolling them both on their sides, still connected intimately. Both of them were breathless, bathed in perspiration, but neither appeared inclined to move and break the ephemeral link between them. Eventually, though, their breathing returned to normal and their skin began to cool. Sawyer shifted slightly so he was no longer inside her. Georgia felt his withdrawal physically and emotionally. He removed the condom and wrapped it in a tissue before rolling back toward her and gathering her once again in his arms. His breathing slowed and became deep and steady. Georgia realized he'd fallen straight asleep, still holding her.

She smiled to herself. She had never felt this good or this right after making love. Normally, she'd be quick to cover herself, if she'd indeed undressed fully in the first place. But here, with Sawyer, hiding behind a layer of fabric had not even crossed her mind. She wanted to relish this moment for as long as she could, but eventually deep dreamless sleep claimed her.

Sawyer woke with a sense of well-being he hadn't felt in years. Unusual, when he knew he'd had a nightmare last night. One of the worst. One where Max disintegrated into nothing right in front of him, where his own body was riddled with shrapnel and slicing, searing pain.

He stretched against the mattress, feeling the usual twinges that reminded him of his injuries and maybe a few that had come from exerting himself in a way his body hadn't experienced in a while, but today everything felt better. He felt sated and unexpectedly content. Georgia had come to him last night. When he'd first woken to find her fiercely hugging him and telling him everything was okay, that he was safe, he'd wondered if he'd merely swapped one dream for another. But the comfort of her arms, her entire body, had been very, very real.

She'd been welcoming, with no barriers or restraints between them. They had sex—no, it had been more than sex. But Sawyer wasn't prepared to label what they'd shared just yet. In fact, he almost wondered if the interlude with Georgia had been a dream after all because she wasn't there.

Footsteps on the staircase leading to the bedroom alerted him to her presence. She appeared on the landing dressed in nothing but a sheer robe. Through the flimsy material, he could see hints of every glorious inch of her, and he felt his body begin to stir again. This time when they made love it would be in daylight, and he'd be able to see her as well as feel her. But first, it appeared she had other ideas for them.

"Good morning! I hope you don't mind, I couldn't sleep any longer so I made us breakfast."

She set the tray down on his lap, and he quickly moved to steady it as she climbed in next to him. Once she was settled, she reached for one of the steaming mugs of coffee and took an appreciative sip. He watched as her throat muscles worked, swallowing the brew, but he remained still, unmoved by the delicious aromas coming from the plate piled high with bacon, pancakes and berries.

"Not hungry?" she asked, giving him a look and gesturing to the plate. "I thought we could share."

"It's not that," he said, suddenly confused.

This was all too cozy. Breakfast in bed after a sexual encounter? He'd never stayed for breakfast. Sex had been a mutually satisfying release, period. Something physical, and that was all. And here Georgia was acting like it was all so normal. As if they'd done this kind of thing together for years.

"Then what is it?" she said, reaching for a piece of bacon and taking a bite. "It's really good, I promise."

"Look, I'm sure it is, but Georgia, I'm sorry. I'm not ready for this."

"What, breakfast? Did you need to visit the bathroom first? I'm sorry, here, let me take this."

She reached for the tray on his lap, but he grabbed it before she could lift it up.

"No, look, it's not that. We had sex last night."

"Yes, we certainly did, and it was marvelous, wasn't it?"

She sounded so happy, it made him feel like an asshole to be the one to have to prick her bubble of joy.

"Yes, it was," he reluctantly admitted. "But it was just sex. I'm not into having a relationship. I know it sounds like a cliché, but truly, it's not you, it's me."

To his astonishment she laughed out loud. A hearty gut-deep gurgle of delight.

"What?" he demanded. "Why is that so funny?"

She sobered slightly but a wicked smile still played around her lush pink lips. "You sound so serious."

"I *am* serious. I'm not ready for any kind of relationship."

"Then it's just as well I'm not looking for one, isn't it?" she replied and grabbed a fork to prick a berry and take a mouthful of pancake. "Mmm, this is really good, you should try it."

"Georgia, you're not listening to me. I can't offer you love and flowers and happy ever afters. Plus, I'm a nomad. My work takes me to places that aren't the kind of spots you'd enjoy, and I can never tell when or where my next assignment will be. I just don't do attachment. People always have expectations of me that I can't fulfill. I just want to make it absolutely clear."

She looked at him and, despite the sweet smile on her lips, he could see the seriousness in her exquisite eyes.

"Sawyer, correct me if I'm wrong, but I don't recall making declarations of love and marriage here. Do you?"

"N-no."

"Then what on earth are you talking about? We're stuck here together. We're both healthy adults with healthy urges. Why shouldn't we simply enjoy each other?"

He felt stung. "Correct me if I'm wrong, but weren't you the woman who arrived here in a wedding dress? That implies some kind of expectations of a relationship."

"Or it implies I had a lucky escape and that marriage is the last thing I'm looking for right now."

"You were shattered when you arrived. I'm a rebound fling for you," he said, eyes going wide with realization.

She laughed again and patted him gently on the cheek. "For heaven's sake, Sawyer, stop being so serious. You sound like you swallowed a self-help book. Can't we just agree to enjoy each other for as long as it takes for me to get out of here?"

He turned her words over in his mind. What she was suggesting was deeply appealing.

"So you're saying you can have sex with me and not get emotionally attached?"

God, even as he said the words, he regretted how arrogant and stilted they sounded. He wasn't that kind of guy. Sure, he didn't do relationships but he wasn't averse to friends with benefits. Last night had been a benefit he certainly hadn't expected.

She loaded up the fork again and held it to his lips. He opened his mouth like an obedient child and allowed her to feed him. Flavor burst on his tongue. The woman certainly had a way around the kitchen that he would never have. It was just one of the many things he was learning to enjoy about being here with her. Topping the list was that she was damn good company. Except for the need to itemize things and schedule their days to within the last minute, she was the perfect housemate.

"There, isn't that delicious? Now, how about we eat this breakfast before it gets cold and agree not to fall madly in love with each other and complicate what is a very uncomplicated matter, okay?"

He could only agree. She made it sound simple—he could only hope she was right. He sensed that she didn't do fly by night very well, and he definitely had no wish to hurt her.

"And," she continued, "I've checked the forecast. There's another storm coming through, so we won't be hiking today. Looks like there's nothing to do but rearrange the pantry alphabetically, play Yahtzee... or stay in bed."

She said it with a slow wink that left him in no

doubt that she'd scheduled the latter. What was a man to do? Argue? Not this man and not in this life. He'd cheated death and he wanted to live. Why not have fun while he was at it?

Eight

"They're starting work on the bridge today," Georgia said, looking up from where she'd been studying her phone, which remained in its prime reception position on the kitchen counter.

"That's good news, isn't it?" Sawyer asked as he helped himself to another slice of toast and liberally covered it with honey.

"Yes, it is," she said with a forced cheerfulness.

It *was* good news, but it did mean that this idyll would have to end soon. Sure, she'd known all along it couldn't last forever, but it was kind of nice to be unplugged from the world and all its dramas, especially her own. A continual string of texts had come in from her mother over the past couple of weeks, together with several from Cliff, as well. Georgia had sent her mom brief reassurances that she was fine and that Sawyer was not a danger to her despite her mom's fears to the contrary, and had ignored Cliff completely. But she knew that eventually she'd have to face the music and make some adult decisions about her future. In the short-term, she might have to stay a few nights with her mom. But she didn't have to decide anything right now, she reminded herself.

"What's on the agenda for today?" Sawyer asked.

"I dunno. I haven't planned anything."

He stopped mid-chew and looked at her in concern. "Who are you and what have you done with Georgia?" he asked in a tone laden with mock horror.

She cracked a reluctant smile. She hadn't made plans for today because, for once, she thought it might be fun to play it by ear and let Sawyer take the lead. So far they'd hiked every nearby trail several times. She'd noticed he'd begun to take more and more photos and spent time each evening transferring them to his laptop and editing them. She'd been astonished at the time he'd put into it and the single-minded focus he displayed while he was working. And he hadn't been Mr. Grumpy-pants once in the past few days.

Maybe that had been because they'd both been enjoying their sexual encounters. She'd heard somewhere that people were generally happier and more relaxed when they had sex frequently. She'd never really considered herself a sexual being but lately, she felt as if she was primed for action all the time. Even now, watching him crack one of those silly grins at her while he finished his breakfast, her entire body went on high alert. Her veins pulsing with life and energy and the rest of her body aching to pulse with a whole lot more.

And he hadn't once said anything about her shape or size. It puzzled her in some respects. Her size was something she'd accepted long ago, but it often felt as if others had more difficulty in accepting that she was happy the way she was. Many pushed her to make small changes here and there. Nothing too overt that might be offensive, but the subtle things, like buying her a fruit basket instead of candy at Valentine's Day and saying it was healthier or better for her.

Well, it might have been better for her, but sometimes a girl needed refined sugar and if that came in Valentine candy then that's what she would have. Georgia had come to a crossroads one day when her mom had bluntly said no man would find her attractive in her current state and she really needed to do something about herself. She'd responded by asking her mother why anyone needed a man for their happiness in the first place, and, in the second, why would she want a man who only wanted her if she changed who she was?

She was a big girl. She'd always been a big girl. And it was only after Georgia realized she didn't have to please other people with how she looked that she found her internal calm. It was all about accepting that her value as a person didn't come from weight or dress size. It came from how she treated others, how she went about her every day with respect for every person who crossed her path and how she carried out her work with attention to detail, ensuring that all her brides and grooms had a wedding to look back on with joy and happy memories.

She'd found her personal acceptance of who she was to be the best thing she'd ever achieved in her life. Even so, her mom never stopped harping on her. Not even her engagement had halted her mom's calculated comments. Still, she didn't have to deal with that today, or tomorrow, or even the day after, and that thought made her happy right now.

"You look like you're going through something major in your thoughts. Everything okay?" Sawyer asked.

He picked up his plate and cutlery from the table and took them through to the kitchen where he bent and stacked them neatly in the dishwasher. Georgia couldn't avoid sneaking a peek as his worn jeans strained over his tight butt when he bent down. He straightened and caught her looking. A gleam appeared in his eyes and he took the necessary steps to close the distance between them.

"Are you thinking what I'm thinking?" he said in a low voice.

A smiled tweaked at Georgia's lips, but she refused to give in to him too easily. She'd discovered the man enjoyed the chase as much as the capture, and who was she to deny him that pleasure for however much longer they had here together.

"I haven't the faintest idea what you might be thinking," she said evasively and moved just out of reach.

But Sawyer wasn't having any of it. He moved swiftly and caught her in his arms and lowered his mouth to the curve of her neck where it met her shoulder. The spot that they'd discovered was her most erogenous zone. She felt a shiver run through her entire body as he nipped her there.

"Okay, so I have some idea," she admitted breathlessly. "But shouldn't we do something else this early in the day?"

"Who says we are limited to when we can enjoy each other?" he responded.

He started kissing a trail up her neck and to her second erogenous zone—that little hollow just behind her ear. His tongue flicked out to lick her there and the shiver turned into a deep pull through her body, from head to core. She moaned involuntarily and she heard Sawyer grunt in satisfaction as if he was proud to have elicited exactly the response he'd been looking for.

"Sawyer, we'll never get anything done if we start this now."

"Too late, I've already started," he said before capturing her lips.

She was addicted to the taste of him. Today his special flavor was enhanced with the sweetness of the honey he'd been enjoying on his toast only a few minutes ago. Georgia kissed him back with a building passion, her tongue meeting his as he licked her lips and then deepened their kiss into something that was hot and wet and demanding.

Sawyer backed her up against the table and swiped

away the fabric placemats before propping her butt up on the edge and easing her back so her legs were hanging over the side.

"I'm not sure this is a good idea," Georgia said as his hands slid under her top and he reached around to unsnap her bra.

"Why not?" he asked.

Her breath shuddered out of her as his hands moved to the front and slid under the loosened cups of her bra to caress her breasts, his fingertips unerringly finding erogenous zone number three, her tight and distended nipples.

"The table, I'm not sure it's up to what you've got planned."

She didn't want to come right out and say she might be too heavy for it because for some weird reason she thought if she didn't draw his attention to her weight, he might not notice. Yes, she knew that was a ridiculous way to think about things. He'd explored every inch of her body multiple times and brought her the kind of pleasure that she'd only ever read about. If anyone knew exactly how she was put together, it was Sawyer.

"Trust me," he said firmly.

Sawyer's hands shifted to pull her sweater up and over her head, then he tugged her bra off her shoulders and sent it flying.

"We could have fold—" She started to protest.

"Take a walk on the wild side, Georgia," he said between kisses along her jawline and down her neck. "We don't have to be tidy about this."

And then he kissed her again and she forgot all about the top and the bra and folding, and focused solely on what he was doing. Sawyer positioned himself between her legs, and she could feel the bulge of his arousal. She felt hot, so very hot, and so very hungry for him, too. She slid her hands under his long-sleeved T-shirt and dragged her nails lightly over his skin, relishing his instant reaction as his skin goose-bumped beneath her fingertips.

"Oh, the things you do to me," he murmured against her mouth before transferring his attention to her breasts.

He cupped their fullness and lifted each one for individual attention from his lips and tongue. But when he bit lightly on her nipple, she felt a jolt shoot straight to her clitoris, making that bead of nerves pulse with excitement. Her fingers tightened, digging into his skin and he flexed his hips against her.

"Sawyer, enough with the teasing. I'm ready if you are," she said.

"What, no more foreplay? I rather thought I excelled there," he said with mock regret.

"Oh, you excel, all right. I just want to get down to business this time," she said while looking up at him.

"We can do that," he answered with a slow grin that sent her heart into overtime.

He helped her up so she could shimmy out of her pants, and he dropped his jeans and briefs and yanked his shirt over his head. She stared at him while he quickly rolled on the condom that he'd taken from his pocket. She wanted to commit every inch of him to her memory, and she licked her lips as if she could taste him already.

"Uh-uh," he said. "No flirting with that sexy mouth of yours. You want it hard and fast? Then that's what we're going for...this time."

He spun her around so she was facing the table and bent her forward with her hands on the wooden surface. Georgia's legs trembled with excitement as he pushed up against her, the blunt tip of his cock nudging against her slick entrance. He entered her in one swift motion, causing her to gasp as sensation exploded pleasurably inside her. As he withdrew and slid into her again the sensation deepened and deepened until she lost track of where they were and could focus only on how she felt. The pleasure built and built until she climaxed, this time so intensely her legs all but gave out and her torso collapsed on the tabletop. The cool wood against her skin heightened her senses even more and before she knew it she was coming again, her entire body clenching and releasing in wave after wave of ecstasy.

Behind her, Sawyer gave one last thrust and with a raw cry pushed deep inside her. At that moment, it felt as if they were inextricably joined. He stroked her back slowly and gently before lowering his body over hers and hugging her tightly from behind.

"It just keeps getting better," he said on a note of wonder.

"Yeah, it does," she agreed.

Which was why she was going to make the most of every second she had with him. He might not do relationships, but Georgia knew she was developing deep feelings for this complicated man. She knew equally well that it would only end in tears. Specifically, hers. After all, he'd warned her not to get attached. She was the one who'd been foolish enough to start falling anyway. Their encounter had a time limit. The specifics of it were unknown at this time, true, but the limit was closing in nonetheless. Why shouldn't she grasp at every straw available to her and relish every moment until then? She'd had more orgasms in the past couple of weeks than she'd had in the past several years, and while she knew that wasn't the sole basis for a great human connection, it wasn't too shabby either.

If she was to sail on in her life, potentially alone for the rest of her days, at least she'd have had this incredible experience. She could hold on to that, she knew it. Sure, she'd miss Sawyer and how he made her feel, and she knew that neither her own touch nor a battery-operated boyfriend would be as effective at bringing her the pleasure he'd wrought from her. But life was about so much more than orgasms, she reminded herself—although right now it was hard to think of anything she liked better.

Sawyer shifted and pulled away.

"I'd better get rid of this," he said, removing the condom.

"And I'd better get the Yahtzee out," she said with a grin.

"You're not serious, are you?"

"Deadly," she answered with an impassive stare.

"What about strip Monopoly instead?"

She felt a smirk pull at her lips. "Seriously? We're already naked."

"We could get dressed," he suggested.

"Y'know, I don't think I'll bother. But, yeah, let's play Monopoly. I'll set it up on the coffee table in front of the fireplace."

Then, as bold as brass and feeling as though she owned the entire world, Georgia strolled casually to the shelf where the board games were stored and, after sliding out the Monopoly box, walked over to the fireplace. She turned and looked back at Sawyer who remained standing exactly where he was.

"Problem?" she asked, beginning to feel just a tiny bit self-conscious under his penetrating scrutiny.

"You have no idea how incredible you are, do you?" he said with a shake of his head. "You're absolutely mesmerizing. I'll be right back."

Georgia felt a blush overtake her entire body. No one had ever spoken to her the way Sawyer did or made her feel so desirable. It would be the benchmark for any future relationship she ever had, she decided, although she doubted anyone else would ever measure up to him.

Sawyer grabbed some more condoms from upstairs before returning to the living area. There was something about Georgia that drew him to her again and again. He wasn't entirely sure he liked that, but he certainly liked what they achieved together. Even when what they were doing wasn't going to lead to sex, she was damn fine company. With a little more confidence under her belt, she'd be unstoppable. He almost regretted that he wasn't looking for something more permanent. If he ever did, it would be with someone like her.

Why not her?

He almost missed a step on the staircase. Nope, no way. He wasn't going there. Now he was physically healed, he needed to get back to the front line of his work. He needed to expose the atrocities that were happening to decent people wanting to live their everyday lives and, with that exposure, encourage nations with the strength and the power to make a difference, to step in and help. He didn't think he was any kind of hero, but he knew what he did made a difference. Maybe not immediately, but awareness was knowledge and knowledge was everything.

Sawyer saw that Georgia had stoked up the fire and had laid out the board game on the coffee table as she'd said. While he'd been wasting time, she'd also poured them each a coffee and put a pile of home-baked cookies on a plate. He was suddenly very hungry, and he snatched up a cookie and shoved it in his mouth as he sat down opposite her on an oversize cushion that she'd tossed on the floor.

She looked comfortable perched on another over-sized cushion, her back to the fireplace and the light of the flames gilding her body. His body responded to her beauty, and he desired her more than ever. But this time they'd build up slowly with none of the frenetic pace of their last lovemaking.

"How about we make this interesting," he said as he selected the racing car as his marker.

She chose the Scottie dog and looked up at him in curiosity. "Interesting? Isn't the game enough?"

He chuckled. "Yeah, it's enough but how about the winner gets to be on top next time."

He watched as her nipples tightened at his words.

"On top? I always win. You sure you want to go there?"

For a moment he wasn't sure what she was getting at, but then it struck him. She was referring to her weight.

"You do that a lot, you know."

"What do you mean?"

"You put yourself down. You did it with the table and again now. Why? You're an incredible, sexy, attractive woman. Most of the time you act like you believe it, but now and then you say something that makes me wonder how you really see yourself."

She wouldn't meet his gaze, so he shifted around the table and tilted her chin up to get her to look straight at him.

"What? Don't you believe me?"

She bit on that deliciously full lower lip before answering.

"I believe you see me that way."

He snorted. "That's a non-answer if ever I heard one. Seriously, you dress and act like you are confident and empowered. But then you go and put yourself down. It's subtle. A lot of people wouldn't notice it. But attention to details is my jam—I notice the little things."

"And the not so little," Georgia said on a half laugh.

"That's exactly what I mean."

She sighed. "I thought I'd trained myself out of it a while back, but I guess with Cliff and the wedding and everything, the old insecurities rose to the surface again. I mean, I know I'm a curvy girl. I've always been bigger than my peers. It's just the way it has been for me. I learned very early on to poke fun at myself because it meant that others didn't do it. It's a defense mechanism. If I can laugh at myself, then if others join in, it feels like they're laughing with me instead of at me."

"I'm not laughing at you. I find you infinitely sexy. You absolutely don't need to feel defensive around me. I'll never say or do anything to hurt you. I hope you know that. You can trust me."

She didn't answer, so he leaned forward and nibbled at her earlobe.

"I'm going to play to win, and fast, because I can't wait to make love to you again," Sawyer said before scooting back to his position on the other side of the board.

"We'll see who wins," she said grimly and shook the dice.

Two sixes. She was off to a good start and a free turn. The way he saw it, there were no losers in this game. Either way he'd be happy.

It wasn't long before Georgia had the high value properties in her possession. She had become positively gleeful about collecting her dues every time he landed on one. He'd almost forgotten they were still naked because they'd grown so intently focused on the game. But eventually he ran out of money. Georgia looked across the table at him with a serious expression on her face.

"You lose," she said.

"Nah, I win," he answered with a huge grin. "Take me, woman. I'm all yours."

As he'd hoped, she laughed out loud.

"Let me tidy up the game first," she said, starting to gather up all the houses and hotels and putting them away in their designated slots.

"Leave it," he commanded. "We can do that later."

He stood up and revealed that his legs weren't the only part of his body standing to attention.

"Oh," she said in a small voice as her gaze fixed on him. "Well, I can't let that go to waste now, can I?"

It was exactly the response he'd hoped for.

"Where do you want me?" he said with a suggestive rise of his eyebrow.

"Hmm, on the couch, I think."

"As you wish."

She snorted with laughter. "I can't believe you just quoted that line."

"Oh, I'm a man of many talents. You just haven't discovered them all yet."

Sawyer settled himself on the couch and waited. He didn't have to wait long. Georgia moved over to the side of the couch and rose up on her knees.

"You have to remain utterly still," she said as she

drifted her hands across the tops of his feet and up the front of his legs.

"I will do my best," he promised and fixed his gaze on her face as she continued to stroke him.

Her hands lingered on his thighs, tracing small circles on his skin, edging closer and closer to his groin. He felt as though he was on tenterhooks, waiting for her to touch his cock, but it was soon clear that was not her immediate intention. Her fingertips traced the lines of his hips and drifted higher to his belly and then upward to his chest. He felt as though she was slowly but surely lighting him on fire, her touch leaving a scorching trail wherever she went.

From his chest she drifted her hands to his, stroking along his fingers and over his hands and wrists then up his arms to his shoulders. The featherlight touch should have been irritating. He normally preferred a far firmer stroke on his skin, but he was captivated by her delicacy.

"You have a lot of scars," she observed softly.

"I've been in a lot of scrapes."

"I'm sorry. Some of these must really have hurt."

"I've healed," he answered.

But had he? Deep down he doubted he would ever truly heal from the loss of his best friend. Learn to live with it, maybe even without the guilt that constantly plagued him, but heal? Completely? No, he didn't think so. His thoughts were stopped by the sensation of Georgia's breasts against his upper arm as she leaned forward to touch his face.

How did he get so lucky? Being stranded with her

had turned into a fantasy come true. He was about as far removed from the man who'd watched in horror as a drenched bride came in through his front door as a guy could be, he thought with a private smile. And he was relishing every second.

Her face was a picture of concentration, hidden from him only when her hair fell forward to shield her features. He lifted a hand and tucked her hair behind one ear.

"I thought I told you not to move," she admonished gently.

"I want to see your face."

Her lips curved into a smile and she leaned forward and kissed him sweetly on the lips.

"Not sick of me yet, then?"

"Oh no."

In fact, he was beginning to dread the idea of her leaving. It would also mean his own time here would be coming to an end and he'd have to make a decision about his future. But all of that could wait, he decided. For now he would take every moment with Georgia and live it to its fullest.

Georgia's touch had grown firmer as her hands backtracked on the journey of discovery she'd already taken. And she supplemented her touch with the delicious hot, wet caress of her tongue. The muscles in his belly tightened almost unbearably as her mouth got closer and closer to his groin. Her fingers curled around the base of him and stroked him in a firm, easy movement. It was all he could do to keep his hips still when every nerve in his body urged him to thrust into the sheath of her hand, to find satisfaction as hard and fast as they had earlier today. But she'd won the right to do with him what she wanted, he reminded himself. This was about her and what she desired. All he had to do was accept it.

Even so, when her mouth lowered to the head of his cock, he almost jumped off the couch. It was all he could do not to shoot off like some horny teenager, but with iron-willed control he managed to stave off his body's urge to climax and instead relaxed into the delicate sensations she wrought on him with her lips and her tongue. Eventually, though, it became too much. He knew he was close, and he wanted to be inside her when he came. Even more than that, he wanted to watch her unravel in her own orgasm. Maybe that was selfish, but right now he didn't care.

"Georgia, stop, please?"

She lifted her head. Her beautiful eyes were glazed with hunger, her lips full and moist.

"You don't like that?"

"I love that," he hastened to assure her. "But I want you to come with me. Will you do that for me?"

Those sexy lips curved into a knowing smile. "I think I can do that."

She reached across him to the side table where he'd thrown the condoms earlier and extracted one from the wrapping before slowly and carefully rolling it on his straining flesh.

"I still get to be on top, right?" she said as she stood up and straddled his hips.

"Oh yeah, definitely."

He could feel the heat from her center as she positioned herself over his erection. Again he had to hold himself back from thrusting upward. It went against every instinct to lie there, perfectly still as she ever so slowly lowered herself on him.

"Mmm," she said, rocking her hips gently. "I do like that."

So did he, too much. He watched her through slitted eyes as she undulated her lower body, pressing against his pubic bone with a firm, steady stroke, her inner muscles clenching and releasing against him. A pink flush stained her chest as she picked up momentum and her nipples drew into tight peaks. He'd been inanimate too long, he had to touch her. To cup her full breasts and tweak her nipples the way he knew would drive her about as crazy as she was driving him.

Georgia was too lost to their movements to object when his hands reached for her. When he lightly squeezed her nipples between his fingers and thumbs she groaned deeply. She had one hand on the back of the couch, steadying herself. The other had been on his hip, but she moved it now, her fingers going to her clitoris.

"So close, I'm so close," she gasped as she touched herself.

It was his undoing. His hips pushed upward and he surged deeper inside her as she tipped herself over the edge. Her body tightened around him and deep, pulsing pleasure suffused him as he finally gave himself over to his climax. It felt as though the ripples of pleasure were never-ending.

Georgia, too, was lost in the joy of her own satisfaction and now lay on him, her breathing uneven. Sawyer wrapped his arms around her and held her close. A man could get very used to this life, he thought for a moment…but then reality intruded in the back of his mind. This interlude was all very well and good, but he'd come here to heal and to work out what he was going to do next. This—whatever it was—with Georgia, had become a fine distraction from making the decisions he knew he was going to have to make sooner or later.

His arms tightened around her some more. No one said he had to make a decision right this minute.

Nine

Georgia turned the bread dough out from the bowl where it had been proving and began to knead it with intent. She couldn't help it, she was definitely falling in love with Sawyer, which meant she needed her head examined. Was it only three-and-a-half weeks ago that she was supposed to be marrying another man? A man she'd thought she loved and who she was certain loved her. Well, she knew she'd been wrong about the second part of that statement. If Cliff had truly loved her, he'd never have been unfaithful. But it was kind of shocking to realize that she can't truly have loved him either, because if she had, would she be in turmoil now, wondering how on earth she was going to overcome this crazy attraction she had to Sawyer?

The words she'd said several days ago, telling him to relax and enjoy what they had together, came back to haunt her. She was definitely enjoying the time they had together. The sex was out of this world and his company was something she'd come to cherish, as well. She treasured it all the more because she got the sense she was seeing sides of him he rarely shared with anyone else. She still didn't know the full extent of what he'd been doing before coming to the cabin or how he'd sustained the injuries that had brought him stateside, but she knew he worked internationally as a photographer, and she was pretty sure it wasn't just taking photos of historic monuments and buildings or portraits of babies.

There was still an edge to Sawyer that staying at the cabin hadn't quite softened. And she had to admit that the edge made her feel a bit off-kilter herself. It was as if he was waiting for an axe to fall, as if he couldn't quite allow himself to become fully immersed in the tranquility of the area. And it had been tranquil recently. Yes, they'd had some rain but nothing heavy enough to prevent their daily walks. For herself, Georgia had never felt so fit, and she really enjoyed having the extra energy that regular exercise had brought her. Sawyer, too, was gaining strength and stamina, and they'd both gained a light tan on the good days when it hadn't rained.

She knew the bridge repair had to be nearing completion, and a part of her was nervous about what would come next. It was all too easy to lose herself in the comfort of her days here at the cabin and the fact that they hadn't had to interact with anyone other than each other. Georgia had checked her phone at regular intervals to touch base with the property manager and reassure her mom she was still okay. She continued to ignore Cliff's repeated attempts at contact. He should be ensconced in the rental house on Rarotonga by now, she thought with a touch of envy.

Had it been the change in lifestyle that had so attracted her to him, so much so that she'd been unable or unwilling to see past the cracks that were there in their relationship? There'd been markers that she ought to have paid attention to, like the time she'd overheard one of his friends refer to them as a mixed-weight relationship. Cliff had said nothing about it at the time and had merely laughed along with his buddies, but the reference had been hurtful. Maybe not deliberately so, but the casual way it had been said and then accepted by Cliff as okay had really gotten under her skin.

Looking back, it hadn't been the only time Cliff had done nothing to stand up for her. Georgia had come to the conclusion that she'd been in love with the idea of being in love and especially the idea of going somewhere exotic to get away from the constant harping and subtle digs from her mom.

"Are you mad at the dough for some reason?" Sawyer's voice came from behind her.

She'd been so lost in her thoughts she hadn't heard him come inside. She'd opted to stay back in the cabin while he went for a hike on his own today. They'd been so deep in each other's pockets, she thought he might appreciate the time alone, and she was always happy to fill her time with baking. Kneading bread dough was one of her favorite things to do in the world, and she'd often worked through problems in her head while working the dough.

"Not at all, this is my thinking time," she said a little defensively.

"I'd offer you a penny for your thoughts but given the effort you've been putting into that, I'm not sure I want to know."

Georgia laughed, as he'd obviously intended her to. "Did you have a good hike today?" she asked.

"Yeah, but I missed your company. You could have come, y'know."

"I know, but I had a yen to bake bread and tidy up the cabin, and you'd have only gotten underfoot."

Or she'd have driven him crazy with her compulsive need to fold and put things away. Since they'd been sharing the loft bedroom, she'd noticed he was wont to leave his things lying around rather than folding anything and putting it where it belonged.

"I hope you don't mind, but I've put all your clothes away in the dresser," she said. "Didn't seem to be necessary for you to keep living out of your pack or off the bedroom chair."

"You put away my clothes?"

There was a note that underscored the incredulity in his voice that put her on alert.

"Yes. As I said, I hope you don't mind. It's just the clutter was starting to get to me."

"And if I do mind?"

She felt her breath catch in her throat. Had she angered him with what was, for her at least, a usual daily occurrence?

"Then you're welcome to scatter your things to the four corners of the bedroom again and I'll just have to suck it up, won't I?"

She fought to keep her tone reasonable. After all, it wasn't such a big deal that he was untidy. It was just that keeping things tidy was one of the things that made her feel balanced in her world.

"I guess it's okay, as long as I can find everything."

"It's pretty basic. Socks and underwear in the top drawer. T-shirts and sweaters in the middle and shorts and jeans in the bottom." She'd noticed he always set his clothes out a certain way on the chair each night and she mentioned it now. "Why do you keep your stuff out like that anyway?"

His face grew grim. "So I can be dressed and gone as quickly as possible. Some of the places I've been to in recent years haven't exactly been the safest. We'd often have to move off in the dead of night. Keeping my stuff out and in the order I dress in the morning saves valuable seconds and gives me an edge when it comes to getting out the door as quickly as I can."

"Sounds stressful. How did you ever manage to get a decent night's rest if you constantly had to be on alert like that?"

He shrugged. "It wasn't always that bad and, when it was, Max and I would take turns keeping watch.

You learn to snatch sleep where you can find it in that kind of environment."

She'd noticed he was always very quick to fall asleep, and she'd envied him that. Her brain would often head off on crazy tangents just before sleep that would stir her to wakefulness.

"Max is the guy from the picture?"

Sawyer didn't say anything straight away, but she saw the pain that shifted across his face, drawing his skin tight across his cheeks and tightening his lips into a thin line.

"Yeah."

"Oh, Sawyer, I'm sorry. I shouldn't have asked."

"No, it's okay," he said on a sharp huff of breath. "He died on our last assignment. I was standing right next to him when he bought it."

"That sounds really tough."

"It was. Hell, it still is. That's why I came here when I got out of the hospital. I needed some space away from it all, from the violence and the noise and the dark hopelessness of everything there. I still haven't been able to bring myself to go through all the photos. The window of opportunity has been lost for publishing them anyway."

Georgia bit down on her lips, unsure of what to say. Then an idea came to her. "Would you like to knead the dough with me?"

"Will it help?" he said bitterly.

"Well, it can't hurt," she said softly. "Why don't you wash your hands and then you take over from me here. I'll supervise. And once you've finished kneading, I'll show you how to roll the dough into balls for dinner rolls."

He gave her a hard look, as if she was delusional to suggest that kneading dough could chase his demons away. She met his gaze just as determinedly and nodded toward the sink. He sighed again and went to wash his hands, then dried them thoroughly before coming to stand by her.

"Now, watch me for a bit, then you try it."

He did exactly as she told him, and after a while he got into a good rhythm. He almost seemed reluctant to stop when she suggested they roll the dough into balls, but judging by the way his shoulders had dropped and how the tight lines that had bracketed his mouth had softened, kneading dough had worked its magic on him.

It didn't take long to roll the dough into the neat balls that would become dinner rolls.

"There, now we set them here in the tray on the counter and cover them and leave them to rise one more time. After that we can put them in the oven to bake."

"It's a slow process, isn't it?"

"It's methodical, and I like how the wait times can be used for other things."

"Like binge-reading romance novels?" he said with a cocked brow.

"Among other things," she conceded with a smile.

"Other things?"

"Oh, y'know, like folding laundry, straightening

the house, relabeling pantry containers," she said teasingly.

"Or, y'know, *other* things," he answered with an equally teasing smile as he held out his hand to her.

Georgia looked at him and felt her entire body respond to the clear message in his eyes. What was it about this guy that made her want him so very much? Best she didn't look into that too deeply, she decided. No, she'd just go with the flow and make the most of every minute. Georgia accepted his hand and allowed him to tug her toward him, then upstairs to the bedroom. When he kissed her it was slow and deep, and he stoked her inner fire with a deliberately measured pace.

Their lovemaking had been alternately fast and frenzied and slow and languid, but this time felt different to her. Was it because she'd finally admitted to herself that her feelings for him went as deep as love? She didn't know for sure, but she identified immediately that this was an opportunity to stow away another precious memory of her time with Sawyer. She might never say the words of love to him, but she could show him with her body how much he meant to her. And she did just that.

Later, when they were sated, they lay on their backs in the tangle of bedcoverings with their fingers clasped.

"You know we have to get the bread rolls into the oven now. It should be well and truly preheated," Georgia said in a serious tone.

Sawyer laughed out loud, and she cherished the sound. He laughed all too infrequently but when he did, oh boy, did it make her heart sing and her entire body want to join him in the humor.

When he'd stopped laughing, he said, "I can do that for you. You lie here a little longer. I'll be straight back."

She told him how long to set the oven timer for and lay back against the pillows, feeling thoroughly decadent. But inside there was an itch of restlessness. Knowing their time together was coming to an end soon made her want to stop all the clocks in the world so she could prolong this forever. But the relentless press of reality was something she was all too familiar with, and the commonsense side of her accepted that when she left, that would be it. She'd never see him again.

The thought sent a sharp pain through her chest, and she gasped in surprise at the sensation, her hand coming up to rub at her breastbone. Ironic how the thought of leaving Sawyer hurt so much more than walking out on her own wedding. If only he mirrored her feelings, maybe they could explore this further and see if, in the real world, they could be more than just stranded lovers.

Georgia rose from the bed and started to dress just as Sawyer returned to the bedroom. He didn't bother to hide the disappointment he clearly felt at seeing her out of bed.

"Going somewhere?" he asked nonchalantly as he leaned, naked, against the dresser.

"I need to do something. I can't spend all day in bed," she said a little more shortly than she ought to have.

"Georgia? Is everything all right?"

"Yes, and no."

"Tell me, what is it?"

She shrugged and blew out a breath. Should she tell him how she felt? No, that would be awkward. He'd been completely and utterly clear right from the start that he didn't do long term. To be honest, hearing about his friend's death helped her understand why he'd made that rule. She wondered if Max had left loved ones behind or if he'd lived on the edge alone, like Sawyer obviously did. She couldn't live like that, and she knew she couldn't live with someone who did. Someone who she would never be certain that they'd walk back in through the front door at the end of an assignment or if they'd come home in a box—or not come home at all.

Realizing that, she forced a smile on her face and shook her head.

"No, it's okay. I'm fine. I think I'd like to go for a walk after the dinner rolls are out of the oven."

"You want company on that walk?" Sawyer asked, a shuttered look in his eyes making her wonder if he'd sensed the direction of her thoughts just now.

"Sure, if you're up to it."

She kept her tone light and reached for a hairbrush to tidy her hair before going downstairs.

"Here, let me," Sawyer said as he took the hairbrush from her.

Georgia closed her eyes and sighed as he ran the brush through her hair with long, sure strokes. This was the kind of intimacy and closeness she'd always craved in a relationship. He might say he didn't do long-term, but he certainly knew how to do short-term very well.

"That feels great. Thank you," she murmured as he finished and put the brush back on the dresser.

"Any time," he said, and began to dress.

Yes, he said *any time*, but they both knew even that statement came with parameters. Georgia forced herself out of the bedroom and down the stairs. She wasn't usually this morose, but then again maybe she was entitled to wallow just a bit.

She busied herself in the living area, straightening cushions and floor rugs and sweeping the hearth of the ash from their fire the night before.

Sawyer thundered down the stairs with a heavy footfall, making her jerk her head up.

"Cleaning again? Didn't you just do all this yesterday?" he asked.

"It's easier for me to just do things as I go along. Saves it being a bigger job later. You know, eating your elephant one bite at a time."

"Sure, whatever floats your boat."

There was a distance between them that hadn't been there before. She'd put it there. Unconsciously perhaps, but it was her fault they'd gone from deliciously satiated to this weird stiltedness. But she didn't know how to fix it. Or even whether she should.

He didn't know what had gotten into her, but he knew he didn't like it. This wasn't the Georgia he'd come to know. Yes, her repetitive tidying up was nor-

mal, he'd grown used to it, but there was an anxious-
ness to it now that he wasn't used to. She was using
tidiness to make herself feel better, but what had happened to make her feel bad?

They'd just had sex—damn great sex. Didn't she
feel pumped and ready to go ten rounds with Mike
Tyson, like he did? Actually, no, that wasn't the right
analogy. Fighting was the last thing on his mind.
In fact, the only thing on his mind was the woman
frittering away time in front of him. He could have
sworn she'd plumped the cushions twice already
today.

Had she wearied of their routine? He wouldn't
have said so this morning when he'd gone off on
his walk alone, or when he'd come back in a bit of a
mood that she'd instinctively soothed out of him in
a way no one else had ever managed for him before.

Kneading bread, huh? Who'd have thought?

And he knew she'd been with him every step of
the way as they'd made love, the way she had been
from their very first encounter. He'd admired that
about her. That she shed all inhibitions and partici-
pated to her fullest, experiencing their pleasure together on a scale he found incredibly addictive. There
was nothing wrong that he could see, but he still
didn't know what was bugging her.

Just before he'd gone out, he'd heard her phone
ping with an incoming message. Maybe it had been
some news from the world outside their sanctuary
that had gotten under her skin. Maybe he should just
ask, and keep asking, until she gave him an hon-

est answer. But did it truly matter in the end? They weren't a couple. They were stranded housemates with benefits. Although, "stranded" didn't seem quite accurate. Technically, either of them could probably have hiked out by now if they'd really wanted to.

He sure was glad he hadn't taken that option. She was straightening books on the bookcase now, so he walked up behind her and gently caught her hands with his and crossed them in front of her body, drawing her back against him.

"What's wrong?" he asked.

"Nothing, I'm just tidying, that's all."

"Wrong answer. What. Is. Wrong?"

Her body was tense against his, but all of a sudden she softened.

"The bridge will be finished soon, and once that's done they'll be able to clear the mudslide."

That was good news, wasn't it? Oh, wait. It meant she'd be able to leave. Now he understood what was niggling at her.

"You don't want to go?"

"No. Yes. No. I don't know."

He rested his chin gently on the top of her head. "You don't have to leave straightaway."

"I need to find a job, a place to live. I can't hide out here forever. Eventually you have to leave, too."

She was right. He would have to leave. He had to pick up his next assignment and get his career back on track. This was supposed to have been a short sabbatical. A time to complete his healing and to rediscover his joy in what lay in front of his lens and, to be honest, Georgia had helped him through all that. But the idea of returning to the real world with its real world problems was as unappealing to him as leaving here obviously was to her, too.

"Let's not think about that for now."

"What? You reckon we should Scarlett O'Hara it?"

"Say, what?"

"You know, 'Tomorrow is another day'? You've seen the movie *Gone with the Wind*, right?"

"My Grandma made me watch it with her. So the idea is that we keep pushing our worries off into the future, right?"

Georgia twisted in his arms so she faced him now. "Exactly."

"If we turtled up, ignored the rest of the world… we'd run out of food eventually. And condoms," he said, smiling.

"True, there is that."

"But not right away."

"No."

"So we're okay?"

"I guess."

The oven timer *dinged*, letting them know the rolls were ready.

"How about I take care of the rolls and you go get your hiking shoes on so we can go for that walk?" Sawyer suggested, planting a kiss on her forehead.

"Yes, okay," Georgia said submissively.

That was without a doubt the least Georgia-like tone he'd ever heard from her. He needed to help pick her up emotionally to where she usually sat on the cheerfulness scale. But as she turned to the mudroom and he went through to the kitchen, it occurred to him that maybe the cheerful and positive demeanor she usually displayed was an act or some kind of shield that hid her real feelings. The thought worried him. She did have some big decisions to make, they both did, and being here had allowed both of them to ignore those decisions completely.

Maybe they could talk out their options together. Although the thought of tackling that was as unappealing to him now as it had been when he'd arrived here a month ago. And talking it out together? Well, that smacked of a relationship that went deeper than he was prepared to go. No, there'd be no heart-to-hearts, he decided as he turned off the oven, tipped the bread rolls onto an airing rack and closed the oven door.

A walk would do them both good. At least, he hoped so.

Ten

They barely spoke during their hike and, for one reason or another, Sawyer hadn't appeared to feel much like taking photos either. Georgia had kept her head down for most of the time, hardly noticing her surroundings and simply focusing on putting one foot in front of the other. An analogy for her new life going forward, she suspected.

They were approaching the cabin when they heard the sound of a vehicle coming up the road from the bridge. A muddy four-by-four pulled up outside the cabin and a guy in a Dayglo vest got out.

"You folks must be the ones who were stranded by the slip," he said jovially.

Georgia felt anything but jovial. "Yes, we are.

Since you've made it here, I'm guessing it's to tell us the bridge is all repaired now?"

"Yes, ma'am. All fixed and ready to clear out. Jeff Coltrane," he said, offering his hand. "I'm the foreman on this job. Just wanted to let you know that everything is safe for you to use the road and bridge again."

"We really appreciate it, don't we, Sawyer," she said, looking back at Sawyer, who looked anything but pleased to see the other man.

But courtesy prevailed. Sawyer stepped up and shook Jeff's hand, too. "Yeah, sure. Thanks."

"You must be about ready to head back to civilization now, I guess," Jeff commented as he turned back to the car. "Well, safe travels home."

"Thank you," Georgia said. With a wave, Jeff got in his vehicle and drove away. She turned back to Sawyer, whose expression she couldn't quite read. "Good news, huh? I can finally get out of your hair and leave you in peace. If you want to extend your lease so you can have that alone time you intended, I can have a word with the property manager for you. No fee, of course."

"No, that won't be necessary. I have a ride coming to pick me up in a couple of days. I'll stick to my schedule. It's time I got back to my world anyway."

"Yeah, both of us need to get back to our worlds. It's been nice, but…" Her voice trailed off as she realized she was desperately finding words to fill in for what she'd rather be saying. Those words remained stubbornly out of reach. "I'll go pack."

She headed for the mudroom and stowed her gear. Sawyer was still outside so Georgia went upstairs to the loft bedroom and started to pack her things back into her suitcases. Her eyes burned. She didn't want to go. If she had her way, she'd stay here forever, locked in this cocoon with Sawyer. They could make this their reality instead of what lay ahead of them when they got to the bottom of the road and back to their regular lives.

But that was just a pipe dream. She knew she had to let go of whatever it was they'd shared here. She could keep the memories locked forever in her heart. At least she had those. And being here with Sawyer had been good for her—a distraction from the shock that had sent her here in the first place. And, she truly believed, her being here had been good for him, too.

Georgia knew Sawyer still had issues regarding his friend Max, and she hoped like crazy that his opening up to her a little would help him work through his grief and see that he wasn't to blame for what had happened to Max. She stiffened as she heard Sawyer's footfall on the stairs and blinked away any vestiges of moisture left in her eyes as she neatly packed the last pair of capris in the case. She'd need to check the dryer for anything else before she closed the cases and took them down to her SUV.

"What are you doing?"

"What does it look like? I'm packing, of course." She fought to keep her voice upbeat but a tremor crept in, exposing her emotions when she was trying so hard to be brave and nonchalant about everything.

She felt Sawyer's body heat come up against her back and his arms came around her, his hands taking hers and turning her around so she faced him.

"In such an all-fired hurry to leave?" he asked, a solemn expression in his eyes.

"You heard the man, the road is open and the bridge is safe."

"That doesn't mean you have to leave right now, does it? I mean, it's not like you have anywhere else to be, right?"

"Well, thank you for reminding me. Yes, I'm well aware I'm homeless, jobless and usel—"

"Don't you dare say you're useless," he interrupted with a growl. "You are anything but that."

"Okay, maybe I'm not useless, but I am the other two. Although, I guess I'll have a place with my mom for a while at least."

"And you're in such a hurry to see her?"

Georgia caught her lower lip between her teeth. She would not lie to this man. "No, I'm not in a hurry to see her."

"Then stay with me, at least tonight."

"Are you sure? I thought you'd be grateful for some time to yourself. After all, it's what you came here for, right?"

He half smiled at her and Georgia felt something tug her heart, hard. Man, she had it bad for this guy. It would be better for her to just pick up her things and go. Why prolong the agony and indulge in a long, drawn-out farewell? It wouldn't change anything going forward. She would still be who she was, and he would still be who he was. Frankly, she couldn't see how their lives would ever have crossed paths, let alone meshed, if they hadn't been stuck together like this.

"Seems I've learned to enjoy having company," he drawled. "Particularly yours, Georgia. Don't go yet. Stay with me, tonight. Please?"

She stared into his eyes as if he might reveal some hidden aspect of himself if she could just see deep enough, but she had to admit he was still as much of an enigma now as he had been when she'd arrived. Even if he was less of a Mr. Grumpy-pants, she acceded.

"I'll cook dinner for you tonight," he coaxed and pulled her closer to him so her hips rested against his.

"What are you going to cook?"

"Well, I could check the roster and see what it is you had planned for us, or I could surprise you with my specialty."

"Which is?" she asked with a skeptically raised brow.

"If I told you, it wouldn't be a surprise, would it?"

She chuckled, and the expression on his face lightened a little.

"Does that mean you'll stay?" he pressed.

Georgia put her head on his chest and hugged him tight. "Yes."

He hugged her back even harder and pressed his lips on her hair. When he finally let her go, she saw he had a new light in his eyes.

"How about you choose a wine that goes with chicken."

"Okay, I can do that. Is there anything else you'd like me to do?"

He pretended to think about it, then one of his heart-stopping grins spread across his face.

"How about you unpack one of those sexy negligee things you have in your suitcase and put it on?"

"What, now?" she laughed.

"Why not? We're not expecting any visitors, are we?"

"Well, no, but—"

"No buts," he said, pressing a swift kiss on her lips.

"Okay, I'll put on a negligee," she agreed before looking at him with a smirk. "And what about you? What are you going to wear?"

"Hmm, good point. I can't exactly cook naked, can I? Could cause problems if I burn myself."

"An apron, then?"

"I was going to suggest boxers but, yeah, an apron works."

"They're in the—"

"Linen closet, I know," he said with another grin.

He started toward the stairs but at the top he turned back and faced her.

"Georgia?"

"Mm-hmm?" she answered absently, as she looked for the sexy emerald-green sheer nightgown and matching wrap that she hadn't worn yet. The color did amazing things for her skin and eyes, and she couldn't wait to see Sawyer's face when she wore it.

"Thank you."

"For what?"

"For staying. I know you probably just want to get on the road, but thanks for staying one more night."

She gave him a smile, and he turned and carried on downstairs. When he was out of sight, the smile on her face faded away. He'd made it clear he considered himself a loner and that his work meant he'd stay that way. But her heart ached for what they could potentially be together. She'd stay a hundred nights with him, even a thousand, if he'd only ask her to, but she wasn't about to deliberately insert herself into his life.

Georgia shook her head and pushed her thoughts in another direction. Dwelling on what couldn't be, wouldn't do her any favors, and she didn't want anything to spoil their last night together. She finally found the lingerie she'd been looking for and was about to disrobe when she had another idea. A delicious soak in rose-scented water would be perfect and would kill time while Sawyer cooked their meal. It would also be an excellent distraction to the sight of him cooking dressed in nothing but an apron.

She grabbed the froth of green fabric and went downstairs.

"I'm going to take a bath after I get that bottle of wine you wanted," she called out as she headed to the bathroom to put her things in there.

"Okay, sure."

It only took a moment to select a bottle of locally made Chardonnay from the small but well-stocked wine cellar at the back of the walk-in pantry. She headed to the kitchen and took a moment to enjoy the view of Sawyer's bare backside as he stood at the counter peeling potatoes. It was so tempting to reach out and squeeze those cute, taut buttocks but she resisted the urge, instead going to the refrigerator and putting the wine inside.

"I'll be a while," she said as she sashayed past him.

"Take all the time you need," he answered.

She hadn't been soaking all that long when there was a short rap at the bathroom door. Sawyer came through with a glass of wine in his hand.

"Did you want a drink while you bathe, madam?"

She laughed. For all his formal speech he looked a picture in his colorful apron and just enough bare skin to tempt her to quit the bath and explore his body anew.

"Thank you, that would be lovely."

He winked as he passed her the glass. "Dinner's in the oven. Do you mind if I join you?"

She was about to say something about there not being enough room, but then realized the space didn't matter. He did. And he wanted to be with her, and she definitely wanted to be with him, too.

"Of course I don't mind," she answered smoothly. "How would you like to do this?"

"I'll slip in behind you, so scooch forward for me."

He untied the apron and dropped it on the floor before stepping into the bath behind her. Georgia was grateful the tub was so deep and she hadn't completely filled it because when he got in, the water level rose alarmingly close to the edge.

"Mmm, it smells good. What is it?"

"Rose oil. Just a few drops, but it goes a long way," she said, leaning back against him and taking a sip of wine.

"It smells like you," he said, bending his head to nuzzle her neck.

Her nipples tightened immediately and a hot streak of desire licked through her body.

"Did you want some of my wine?" she asked, offering him the glass.

He took it and had a sip before handing it back to her.

"This is nice," he said. "Just lying here together."

She agreed. It was nice. It was as if they had all the time in the world to simply be. Sawyer's arms rested on the rolled edges of the bath on either side of her and she felt decadent and cherished at the same time. She'd put her hair up on top of her head with a clip, but she could feel wisps escaping and moving against her neck. The sensation heightened her sensitivity, making her all too aware of his lean, hard body cradling her back and his legs stretched out on either side of her. Her head was nestled against his shoulder, and if she turned her head slightly she could see the strong, no-nonsense line of his jaw and the stubble he never seemed to be completely without.

She'd grown used to the feel of that stubble on her body. Against her neck, her breasts, her belly, between her thighs. Looking at him now ratcheted up that flame of desire a few more notches. She reveled in her body's awareness of him, letting this moment imprint on her mind along with all the other great memories they'd created together. Georgia was glad she'd agreed to stay tonight. Even if it was only putting off the inevitable, so what? The inevitable would still be there. Tomorrow *would* come, and it would be different from all the yesterdays they'd created.

Better, worse? She wouldn't know until she took that step away from him—away from *them*.

Sawyer had shifted slightly and his hands were cupping the water and drizzling it over her breasts. Her nipples tightened even more.

"Is there any soap?" he asked softly in her ear.

"Sure, on the side there," she answered breathlessly.

He pumped a little of the liquid into one hand and transferred some to his other one before smoothing them over her breasts, gently cupping and releasing them, his thumbs stroking her nipples in firm circles that sent ripples of longing through her entire body. His hands smoothed over her belly and lower until his fingertips brushed her aching clit.

Georgia let her head drop back against his shoulder in total surrender as he stroked and soothed and stroked again until she felt a deep rolling orgasm claim her body. His hands gentled on her, and he shifted slightly just to hold her against him as her body calmed once more.

She didn't want to move or break the spell he'd cast over them. She felt so cherished in this moment. So lucky, too. She could have ended up this entire time alone, or worse, gotten through the road on her first night and had to go somewhere else—even home to her mom. No, it pierced her heart to know their time together was coming to an end, it had been an incredible gift.

Eventually the water began to cool and from the kitchen they heard a timer going off.

"That's my cue," Sawyer said, putting his hands on the edge of the bath and levering himself upright. "Take your time here. I can call you when it's almost ready."

"Okay, that sounds lovely, thanks."

She watched him as he dried himself and put his apron back on then left the bathroom. She felt so languid and calm she really didn't feel like moving, so she turned the hot faucet on again and ran a bit more water into the bath so she could linger longer. When Sawyer called out about ten minutes later, she was already out of the bath and drying herself off, before applying some of the matching rose lotion to the bath oil all over her body.

Her skin felt soft and smooth and the sensation of the long, sheer nightgown she donned, together with the matching long-sleeved wrap, made her feel decadent and wanton. When she left the bathroom she felt incredible—powerful, even—and totally secure in her sense of self.

In the living area, Sawyer had lit candles, dozens of them, in fact. Georgia mentally added new candle stocks to the inventory refill list, then concentrated on how the light cast a warm and inviting flow over the room. The dining table was set with more candles, and a casserole dish sat on a thick cork placemat at the center of the table. The aroma coming from the dish was tantalizing. Next to it stood a bowl of baby potatoes drizzled with butter and sprinkled with fresh parsley from the sheltered herb garden by the mud room door and on the other side a bowl with green beans and baby carrots.

"This looks fantastic," she exclaimed. "You're a man of many talents."

"My grandmother wouldn't let me leave home until I could cook. It's been a blessing—and in a lot of ways I find cooking cathartic."

"Well, if I'd known that, you'd have been on permanent dinner duty," Georgia said with a laugh.

Sawyer came around the table and pulled out her chair.

"Take a seat." As she settled in the chair, he leaned down to kiss the side of her neck. "You smell good enough to eat, yourself. Maybe later, hmmm?"

A shimmy of desire rippled through her at his words and again her nipples tautened into prominent peaks against the fabric of her outfit. Throughout their meal, and the dessert of apple crumble that Sawyer had created out of tinned apples with an oat-based topping, their sensual awareness of each other spun a web of insulation around them. Here, in their candlelit nest, there was no outside world to bother them.

When their meal was over, Sawyer extinguished

the candles before leading Georgia upstairs, where he peeled off the little clothing she wore and threw off his apron and they sank onto the bed together. When they made love by the growing moonlight, it was long and slow and intense. They reach their peaks together before starting all over again—as if sleep was unnecessary and they could exist only by making love to each other.

It was the wee hours of the morning before they tumbled into sleep, wrapped in each other's arms, deliberately oblivious to what the morning would bring.

Eleven

Sawyer brought her suitcases out to the car. Georgia stood stiffly to one side as he stacked them in the trunk. After he slammed the tailgate shut, she stepped up to his side and took his hands in hers.

"Thank you, Sawyer, for everything."

"No need for thanks. It all worked out in the end, right?"

She gave him a small smile totally at odds with the sensation of shattered glass that currently splintered through her body. His demeanor was so different from the man who'd made love to her with focus and passion last night. Who'd given and received with abandon. That had been his farewell. She understood that now, but she had something she needed to say before she got in the car and drove away.

"It did, but I do mean thank you for everything you've done for me. I know you don't see it that way but, honestly, you gave me exactly what I needed— the courage to be happy with who I am. I will never forget that, and I won't ever let anyone get me down about myself again."

"You always had it in you, Georgia. You just needed to believe it."

"I know, and I do. It might not always be easy, but I will believe it now. It's in me forever. I hope you find your peace, too. You're worth it, Sawyer. You're a good man and you deserve to be happy."

She leaned forward and kissed him then, pouring into that embrace all of her longing and yearning for him to reconcile with his past. Then, she abruptly pulled away and got into her SUV before she made the stupid mistake of telling him she loved him. Her throat closed up on a swell of emotion that threatened to make her cry like a baby. She might no longer be capable of speech, but she would not let his last sight of her be of her crying. She hauled back hard on the emotions that cascaded through her and pulled her door shut. She started up the car and with a short wave; she put it in motion and drove away.

Georgia told herself not to check the rearview mirror but just before she hit the corner that took the cabin out of sight, she looked. He wasn't there. Somehow that hurt more than knowing he'd remained there watching her leave. It was over now. Well and truly. She gripped the steering wheel tight and negotiated her way past where the slip had been and over the narrow one-lane bridge, then eventually onto the sealed road that would lead her to the next stage of her life.

Sawyer slammed the cabin door shut with a roar of frustration. What the hell was wrong with him? Why hadn't he asked her to stay longer? Why the hell was he so upset she'd left? He was the one who'd said no complications, no commitments. He was the one who didn't do relationships. He was left here alone, exactly as he'd wanted to be a month ago when he'd arrived, and he hated it already.

His nostrils flared on the remnants of scent Georgia had left in the air. He'd never be able to smell roses again without thinking of her. Dammit. And he was stuck here for a couple more days until his ride came to take him back to SeaTac and his flight to London. He hadn't even planned on stopping in to see his grandmother again before heading to the base of operations that masqueraded as his home.

Maybe he could change that, he thought. Stay with his grandma a few days before returning to his flat and finding his next assignment. He paced the room while he thought it out and eventually put his phone on the spot where Georgia had kept hers for the duration of her stay here—the only area of the cabin that had a patchy signal. His pulse leapt with excitement as he saw a few bars of reception kick in, and he logged into his airline booking and changed his flight to one a week from the original. Then he sent his grandma a text asking if he could visit with her.

There was no immediate reply, and he paced some more before checking his phone again, only to see that he'd lost all reception again. Outside, what had been a clear blue sky was rapidly closing over with thunder cloud as a new storm swept in. Trepidation filled him. He'd never been bothered by storms until that last assignment, but now the flashes and bangs threw him immediately back into that world—and he didn't have Georgia here to ground him.

How had he come to rely on her so much for everything that mattered to him? His grandmother had seen to it that he was self-sufficient by his mid-teens, even though she'd continued to provide him with a home and more love than anyone had a right to. She'd been his rock until she'd tipped him out of the nest to go to college and then encouraged him to follow his dreams and his need for travel. In his vulnerable state of recovery, had he merely transferred his need for an anchor to Georgia?

Sawyer shook his head. That was ridiculous. He'd known from the start that they had an expiration date. He didn't *need* her. But he sure as hell wanted her. Even now, just thinking of her—her soft skin, her burnished hair, her hazel eyes that could say so much or nothing at all with just a glance—all of her made him prickle with awareness.

Damn it, he'd go out for a hike. The storm could wait while he stomped out his frustrations with himself, with Georgia, with the whole damn world.

He yanked on his jacket and slid his feet into his boots and was lacing them tight when the rain began to fall. He didn't care. He was going out anyway. Staying in the cabin was torture. Everywhere he looked he saw Georgia, and the thought of going upstairs and stripping the bed of the sheets that he knew would smell of roses was too much right now.

He welcomed the stinging, cold lash of rain as he stepped outside and trudged through the grass to the woods. Half an hour later, he was beginning to feel the burn of his lungs. He was farther from the cabin than he probably ought to be in the storm and when the first flash of lightning appeared, he realized he'd been an idiot to forge out in this weather. The boom of thunder overhead nearly made him jump out of his skin the first time, but he resolutely turned around and headed the way he'd come. He knew there was no safe shelter out here. He needed to make it back and stay in the cabin no matter how much it drove him crazy.

As he walked, he felt as if Max was there beside him, telling him he was an idiot. Asking him what he thought Max would have done with someone like Georgia if he'd been given the chance. Sawyer shook his head and wiped the water from his eyes, realizing as he did so that it wasn't just rain on his face, but tears as well.

"Why did you do it, you idiot? Why did you have to take that photo? I couldn't stop you. I couldn't keep you safe!"

Another burst of lightning and an instant crash of thunder filled the air around him and in that flash he saw Max as he'd been just before he was killed.

He'd been alight with excitement. So certain that the photo he was risking his life for was going to be the best he'd ever taken. He knew the risks and he took them anyway, and he never knew what hit him. Even in the split second before he was hit, he'd still been living what he believed was his best life.

I did it because I had to.

Max's voice echoed in Sawyer's mind. Those seven words kept repeating as he continued to hike back to the cabin. With each step, Sawyer came closer to accepting that there had been nothing he could have done to stop Max. He'd made his own choices and died knowing he was in charge of his own destiny. By the time Sawyer reached the cabin and made it into the mudroom to take off his boots and jacket, his entire body was shaking with the effort of holding back his grief. He shucked off his gear and staggered into the living area, collapsing onto the couch and resting his head in his hands, elbows propped on his knees, as he finally gave way to the immense loss of his best mate.

He wasn't sure how much later it was when he calmed again. All he knew was that the rage against his friend's death was gone. The sorrow, yes, that was still there, but it felt like it was more manageable now. Sure, he knew that it would probably sneak up on him and whack him hard every now and then. Losing someone important did that. But he finally accepted that he had no control over what had happened. You could say they had been in the wrong place at the wrong time, but they'd both chosen to be there. Both had chosen to pursue a career that was frequently dangerous.

No one had anticipated the firestorm that had occurred. Sawyer had been lucky to survive it. Now it was up to him to make the most of his life and his opportunity to live it.

Beneath the acceptance of losing Max, though, lay another hurt. A newer and fresher one. One that had the most incredible hazel-colored eyes and deep auburn hair and skin so smooth and soft and delectable, he knew there would be no forgetting Georgia as he had so many of his previous short-lived relationships. But it wasn't just his physical attraction to her that lingered with him. It was her gentle ways, her perception of the world around her and, hell yes, even her interminable organization and tidying up of everything. He had thought he'd be so glad to see the back of her, to have these precious last days of his lease just to himself. But even though she'd only left this morning, he missed her.

Realistically he knew their lifestyles were not compatible, so he had braced himself to let her go. And he would. But for now, he'd hold those sweet memories of their time together here just a little closer.

Georgia drummed the steering wheel of her car as she waited at the Kingston ferry. She'd taken her time getting here, stopping at Port Angeles for coffee, then later in Port Gamble for lunch. All of it delaying tactics, she knew. Putting off the inevitable phone call she had to make to her mom to ask her if it would be okay to stay with her for a while. It wouldn't be a problem if she couldn't. She'd find a place for short-term rental or stay in a hotel for however long it took. She didn't feel like reaching out to any of her friends from her old job, or the few from college that she stayed in touch with. There'd be too many questions from them. Her mom, at least, would be too busy talking at her to stop and ask anything about how she was feeling or why she hadn't followed through on the wedding.

She pulled up her mom's contact number. After a couple of rings, her mom's voice filled the cabin of the car.

"Georgia? Is that you?"

Georgia quirked an ironic smile. She knew her mom's caller ID would be displaying her name across the screen.

"Yes, Mom. It's me."

"Well, thank heavens. It's about time. I don't know how you managed to stay in that awful place so far from everything for so long."

"That is the appeal of it, Mom. I needed the time away."

"How anyone would find that appealing is beyond me, nor do I understand why you had to be there, for heaven's sake. Cliff has been beside himself trying to get hold of you, the poor man. Have you even called him yet?"

Georgia closed her eyes and breathed in a deep breath through flared nostrils. She would not react, she would not take the bait. She would, however, continue with her own agenda, at the top of which was the need for somewhere to stay, at least for tonight.

"Mom, would it be okay if I came to stay with you tonight? And maybe the next few days until I decide what I'm going to do?"

"What do you mean until you decide what you're going to do? You're going to mend things with Cliff, that's what you're going to do."

Her mom's voice was emphatic on that last bit, and Georgia audibly sighed before answering.

"No, I'm not *mending* things with Cliff. Some things just can't be fixed and you're going to need to accept that. So, is it okay if I stay with you tonight?"

There was a brief silence on the other end before her mom put on what Georgia called her long-suffering voice.

"I suppose that will be okay. In fact, I insist you stay here until you get your life back on track again. Clearly, you've had some kind of breakdown and home is the best place for you right now. You shouldn't have run away like you did. It wasn't like you at all."

No, it wasn't like Georgia to have run away. Usually, she faced her issues head-on, but discovering Cliff's impending fatherhood on their wedding day had been a bridge too far. Now, Georgia felt nothing but relief that she'd had what could only be called a lucky escape from a marriage that would have been doomed to misery and failure in the long term.

Her mom lived in Mill Creek, which was an easy forty- to fifty-minute drive from the Edmonds ferry terminal this time of day. Georgia knew she'd spend that time shoring up her mental defenses against her mom's onslaught of opinions on all the things she figured Georgia had done wrong. She loved her mom, really she did, but just once she'd like to have her wholehearted support without the litany of things she needed to change to do better. She knew her mom thought her "advice" and "corrections" came from a place of love, but sometimes it was hard to see that.

"I'm waiting for the ferry to Edmonds now. I can be at your place in about an hour and a half. Do you need me to stop and pick anything up for you from the store?"

"Salad greens" came the predictable reply. "And fresh tomatoes. I'll make us a nice salad for dinner."

"I'll grab some wine while I'm at it. Talk soon!" Georgia said, disconnecting the call before her mom could complain about the caloric content of wine.

She might be prepared to accept a bed from her mom for now, but she wasn't going back to her old ways and her old life again. Her time with Sawyer had shown her who she could be if she really wanted to. A woman who was sexy, confident, self-aware and, most of all, happy. And she *had* been happy these past few weeks at the cabin, most of the time anyway. Certainly once she and Sawyer had begun sleeping together.

She'd never considered herself a sensual being before but now she most definitely was. She could feel it in her bearing and in her heart, that she had found the person she'd always wished she could be. And who knew that it had been inside her all along?

By the time she pulled in at her mom's, she knew that no matter what her mom said, she would be okay. Lonely, possibly, but okay. Her mom was waiting at the front door as Georgia got out of the car and grabbed the grocery bag from the passenger seat. The smile on her face was genuine as she walked toward the woman who'd raised her with very little input from Georgia's dad.

"Have you lost weight?" her mom said as she accepted Georgia's one-armed hug. "There's something different about you."

"Mom, it's great to see you," Georgia answered. "Here's the groceries you asked for and a bottle of wine for us. I'll go get my suitcases."

By the time Georgia got her cases in the front door, her mom had opened the wine and poured them each a glass.

"Leave your bags there, Georgia. We can take them through to your room after dinner."

"Sure, thanks for pouring the wine."

Georgia accepted a glass from her mom and sat down on one of her small sofas with a sigh of relief. She felt shattered—emotionally and physically. Leaving Sawyer had been tougher than she'd expected, but she knew she couldn't have continued to stay at the cabin, especially since it was only a matter of days before he'd be leaving there, too. In fact, it would have crushed her to watch him drive away from her. At least it had been her choice to leave when she did. Sawyer had been all about consent and choice. He'd never taken anything about her for granted, and he'd enabled her to heal from her wrecked wedding day and come out stronger at the end of it. She owed him a massive debt for that, although she doubted he'd see it that way at all.

"Tell me, what have you been doing these past weeks since you got stranded?" her mom prompted.

Georgia took a big sip of her wine and looked across to where her mom sat perched on the edge of her matching sofa. Looking at her mom, she saw an air of tension about her that Georgia now realized never really left her. Two questions struck her. Did her mom ever truly relax, and how had she never noticed that before?

"A lot of hiking, reading, baking and relaxing, to be honest."

"Relaxing? Seriously? While you were stranded with a stranger? What if he'd been an axe murderer?"

Georgia let a smile pull at her lips. "Mom, Sawyer wasn't an axe murderer, and if he was I wouldn't be here now, would I? Seriously, he's a really nice guy who was extremely accommodating in the circumstances. Why didn't you tell me the cabin had been leased, anyway? I wouldn't have gone there if I'd known."

"It shouldn't have mattered to you, remember? You were supposed to be in the Cook Islands with Cliff. How was I to know you'd run out on all of us and head into the wilderness?"

Her mom looked seriously put out, as if Georgia's actions had caused her extreme difficulty. And, Georgia realized, they probably had. She'd left her mom to try to explain the situation to all the guests, not to mention the groom, alone.

"I'm sorry I put you through that, Mom. I did speak to Cliff briefly from the car."

"He told me you wouldn't listen," her mom said with a sniff of disdain. "Honestly, Georgia, hearing him out was the least you could do after crushing that poor man's heart the way you did."

Georgia bit back the urge to snap back at her mom. After all, she wasn't the one who'd been caught cheating, was she?

"He kinda crushed mine first, though, didn't he? Don't you think I deserved to have some space away from that?"

"But you ran away from me, too," her mom said in a voice that betrayed how hurt Georgia's fleeing had left her.

"I'm so sorry you feel that way, Mom. But I really needed the space. After seeing what Dad did to you when I was little, I had very-well-defined expectations of what I would accept in my own marriage, if I was lucky enough to find someone I wanted to marry. Faithfulness has always been one of my top priorities. Right up there with unconditional love."

"It wasn't my fault your father was unfaithful," her mom said defensively.

"I know that, Mom. Just like it wasn't mine that Cliff cheated on me."

"But maybe if you'd made more effort to lose a

few pounds, it wouldn't have happened. I hear his ex is very beautiful, and slender."

"Mom! Can you hear yourself? A few pounds here and there wouldn't have made any difference if Cliff had meant it when he said he'd fallen in love with me." She waved her hands wide, spilling a little of her wine. "I had no reason to believe any different until I saw her social media post. Happiness isn't confined to size, Mom. After all, you have an amazing figure and can you honestly say you're happy?"

"I wasn't always this way. I gained weight when I was pregnant with you, and I couldn't get it to come off again. Your father didn't like it. That's when the affairs started."

"Then that's on him, don't you think? Not on you." Georgia tried to assure her mom, finally understanding what drove her mom's insecurities. "And it's not on me either. I am who I am and I'm happy this way. I'm in shape, I'm healthy and I'm confident with myself and my body. You should be, too. For both our sakes."

"We will have to agree to disagree on that, Georgia."

Georgia sighed inwardly. She worried that her mom would never truly understand and likely never truly accept her the way she was. But she also had to accept that that was the way her mom had conditioned herself to be and if she was ever to change, it would take time and love.

"We can do that, Mom. Shall we have dinner? I'm really beat and I'd love an early night."

"Sure, let's go through to the kitchen."

Angela had set the small dining table in the kitchen with flowers and matching placemats, and Georgia exclaimed over the prettiness of the table setting, knowing it was important to her mom.

"When you said you were coming back, I wanted to make it a bit of a celebration," her mom said softly, showing a hint of the love that she obviously did feel for Georgia, even if that love was tempered with criticisms.

"It feels like it. It's lovely to be here. I'm so grateful to you for having me."

"You're my daughter. Where else would you go?"

Where else, indeed? She'd need to find her own place again and look for work soon, but she wasn't particularly worried in the short-term. She had quite a bit of money saved, so she knew she'd be okay financially, and she'd pay her way here at her mom's. She focused on the meal her mom set before her. Poached fish with salad, no dressing. It was her mom's way of trying to control what Georgia ate, and she had to laugh a little inside. She ate the meal without complaint but made a mental note to take over the cooking while she was here. She might even be able to coax her mom into gaining a pound or two to soften her hard edges.

Georgia talked a little about the hiking she'd done during her time at the cabin, trying to tell her mom about the beauty she'd encountered while she was there. Each word she chose brought back more memories of the time with Sawyer. Of his keen interest in the plant life she'd pointed out on their walks and the insects and animals they'd seen. Angela feigned interest, but Georgia understood it really wasn't her mom's thing. More surprising was that she had shown little curiosity about Sawyer and what he was like. Georgia was fine with that. It actually hurt to talk about him.

"Well, all that walking has done you a world of good," her mom said as they cleared the table after their meal. "You might be needing some new clothes. Shall we go to the mall tomorrow?"

"Sure, Mom. We can go shopping together if that's what you'd like."

Her mom brightened visibly. Shopping at the mall had always been her answer to everything, and she was happiest in a new outfit or buying something new for her home. The local thrift stores benefited greatly from her need to cycle things through her wardrobe and her house with great regularity.

"Great, it's a date. Now you head on off to bed. I'll take care of all this. I'll see you in the morning."

Georgia kissed her mom on the cheek and went to take her cases through to her room. She showered and got ready for bed in a haze of weariness, but when she lay in her old bed she found herself staring at the ceiling, missing Sawyer's company. Missing everything about him, from the sounds he made when he slept to the feel of his hands and mouth on her body. She'd get through this, she told herself. She'd gotten through worse, right? Because running away from your own wedding was right up there in the traumatic experiences department.

Speaking of traumatic experiences, Sawyer never had told her the full story behind his injuries, only that he'd been hurt in the line of his work. Suddenly curious to know more, she got out of bed for a second to grab her laptop, then turned it on. She typed his name in the search bar. She got a lot of hits, several citing awards he'd won for his work, but what struck her the hardest was the type of photos he was renowned for—usually wartime conflict and its effect on the people in the countries in turmoil. His portfolio of work depicted those who were wrenched from their homes with only what they could carry. Oftentimes that was solely their children, nothing else. It was heart-rending stuff.

She found a translation of a short article in an overseas newspaper that talked about two photojournalists who'd been caught in crossfire between warring factions—one dying and the other seriously wounded. Her eyes filled with tears as she researched further and discovered more information about Sawyer's journey back to health and how close he'd come to dying himself. No wonder he had nightmares. He'd lived them, over and over, in every country he'd gone to. And still he kept going back, kept bringing the world the photographic proof of the atrocities, of the sorrow and, yes, even the lighter moments to be found among the rubble. Above all, he showcased the strength of the men and women who had to pick up their lives and rebuild all over again—the tenacity of the human spirit.

By the time she shut her laptop, she felt she understood him a little better but realized that the time she'd spent with him, as intense as it had been, had only scratched the surface of the complexity of the man he truly was. And it only made her want to know him better, to be there for him when the nightmares struck, to soothe away the sorrow that she'd caught in his eyes in an unguarded moment.

She understood that sex had been an escape for him, and possibly an affirmation of the fact he had survived a particularly harrowing assignment. No wonder he didn't do relationships. It was as if he felt his own life was insignificant in the face of what was happening in other parts of the world. He was an artist and a storyteller. A survivor. A loner.

And she wanted him more than she'd ever wanted another human being, ever. She missed him desperately. Georgia put her laptop away and crawled back into bed, but as she lay there staring at the ceiling all she could think about was Sawyer. Who would hold him through his next nightmare? She wished with all her heart that it could be her. But if it was, if she could be with him despite his resolve to avoid relationships, wouldn't she just be pinning her happiness on him and how he made her feel rather than learning to find happiness within herself?

Twelve

There was an unfamiliar car waiting in the driveway when Georgia and her mom returned home from their shopping trip. For a brief second, Georgia hoped against hope that it was Sawyer, but the man alighting from the vehicle was, although familiar to her, not the man she most wanted to see. She got out of her SUV and walked toward him.

"Cliff—" she acknowledged her former fiancé "—what are you doing here?"

"Your mom told me you were home. I had to see you."

Her mom? Seriously? She turned and gave her mom a questioning frown, but Angela was busy taking shopping bags out of the back of the car. Georgia turned back to Cliff.

"But aren't you supposed to be in the Cook Islands?"

"Yes, of course. This is just a quick trip home to tie up a few loose ends with resort designers and take a meeting with the board of directors. Besides, I couldn't come back and not try and see you, Georgia."

Angela brushed alongside them, heading to her front door. "Perhaps you two would like to come inside for your chat?"

"That would be great, Ang, thanks," Cliff said with an expression not unlike a puppy who just received high praise.

Georgia followed him into the house, where he made himself at home on one of the living room sofas and looked at her expectantly. Georgia sat opposite him and decided silence was the best way to approach this unexpected meeting. It didn't take long for Cliff to start talking.

"Look, I'm sorry about that business with Shanna. I specifically told her not to post anything until after the wedding. But that aside, I still want to marry you, Georgia. I still need you to come with me to the Cook Islands."

Georgia waited for the declaration of love everlasting, but unsurprisingly it didn't come. She remained silent and kept her face blank as she stared back at Cliff. He shifted uncomfortably under her scrutiny. As she looked at him, she tried to study him objectively. Yes, he was good-looking. Yes, he kept himself fit and healthy and had a great job with wonderful future prospects. He was a catch for anyone for whom fidelity wasn't important. He was not, however, a catch for her. Eventually, she spoke.

"Why?"

"What do you mean, why? Georgia, we were about to get married and you walked out on us. I know you were upset about Shanna being pregnant but, hey, we can have a baby as soon as you want."

She blinked in shock. Seriously? "Cliff, I don't want a baby with you."

"Well, that's okay. We can share custody of—"

"No. Cliff, you don't get it, do you? I told you about my father and how he cheated on Mom. I told you about how that messed us both up and made us very careful about who we chose to let into our lives. I swore from childhood that if I ever married, it would be to a man who could commit to me and our children wholeheartedly. Not just when he was at home. Not just when it suited him. All. The. Time."

"I can do that, Georgia," he protested.

"No, Cliff, you can't. You already proved that by cheating on me with Shanna. We were already engaged when your child was conceived. What were you thinking?"

"I don't know." He hung his head in shame. "I was out with some friends for a drink and saw Shanna and it kind of went from there."

"Did it not occur to you that your actions might hurt me?"

"I didn't expect you to find out. When we woke up the next morning, we both knew we'd made a mistake and that what we'd done was stupid. Neither of us expected her to get pregnant."

Georgia studied his face carefully. It was blatantly apparent that if Shanna hadn't become pregnant, Cliff would never have told her about his lapse with his ex. In fact, he obviously hadn't intended for her to know until after they were married, if even then. And how often would that have happened once they were married, she wondered. If she'd allowed their wedding to go ahead, she would never feel secure or safe in their marriage. She'd have doubted Cliff whenever they weren't in the same room together.

"I'm sure you didn't, but that doesn't change anything as far as I'm concerned," Georgia said firmly. "I loved you, Cliff. I trusted you with my heart and my future and, basically, you stomped all over that when you chose to sleep with Shanna while we were engaged."

"But we had a future together!" he protested.

"*Had* being the operative word here," she said dryly. "I can't be with someone who thinks sleeping with another person while they're with me is okay. And I told you that, Cliff. You knew right from the start of our relationship how I felt about it."

"I guess," he admitted. "But won't you reconsider? I promise I'll be faithful from now on."

She raised one eyebrow. "You say that, but I'm not sure that even you believe it. I know I don't. Besides, you still haven't answered my earlier question. Why did you want to marry me so much?"

"It makes sense, doesn't it? I'm overseeing the

project for the newest resort in the Cook Islands. You'll be my right-hand person. You're an adept organizer, not just of weddings. You'll be able to see issues before they arise, and I'll be able to present a great end product to the board of directors. We'll work in tandem, Georgia, can't you see? And when the resort is done, you will be a shoo-in for the senior event organizer role because you'll already know the place inside and out." He beamed at her as if what he'd just said would make all the difference.

Georgia shook her head. "So, let's get this clear here. You basically wanted me to be an unpaid support assistant for your role as project manager there?"

Color suffused his face. "You don't have to be so blunt, Georgia."

"Yes, I do. I thought you were marrying me because you loved me." She fought to keep her voice emotionless because if she let the burning anger that was building inside her now creep out, she'd likely say something she'd regret later.

"Well, that too, of course. Does that really need saying?" he blustered.

Yeah, it really did need saying. It actually needed observing as well, because to Georgia, when love entered the equation, you didn't risk it on a one-night stand with an ex. You committed to it and the object of your affection wholly and with a full heart.

"You need to leave." Georgia rose from her seat and walked toward the hall leading to the front door. "I'll see you out."

Cliff followed her, gesticulating wildly with his

hands. "But you haven't said yes. We haven't set a new date. We can keep it simple. I'm sure you could pull something together with all your experience."

"I will not be saying yes, there will be no new date set and, simple or not, I will absolutely not be pulling anything together with you. And, Cliff, you're going to be a father, so you're really going to have to step up your game. Be someone your son or daughter can be proud of."

She opened the front door and stared at him with a withering glare. Finally, he took the hint. As soon as he was over the threshold, she closed the door firmly behind him. When she turned around, her mom was hovering in the hallway.

"Is everything okay?" Angela asked. "I know you're probably mad at me for letting him know you were here but, seriously, Georgia. It was silly of you to let him go the first time. He's quite the catch, and opportunities like that don't just come along every day for girls like you."

"Girls like me?" Georgia asked, pinning her mom with a hard stare.

"Y'know, big girls."

"Mom, not everyone has your fixation on weight. I'd be grateful if you'd keep my shape and size out of our conversations from now on. As I've told you before, I'm happy with the person I am today. So can we please just leave it at that? I love you, Mom, but you need to let go and just love me for me as well."

Tears filled her mom's eyes. "But I do love you,

honey. So very much. I just want the best for you in every way."

"I know you do, Mom," Georgia said on a sigh. "But Cliff was definitely not the best for me. Look, can we talk about this without any accusations or finger-pointing? How about I pour us each a glass of wine and we sit down and clear the air."

"I'd like that," Angela said.

They sat together on one of the sofas, and Georgia took the lead. For once and for all, this would be sorted, and if her mom didn't like it she'd move out.

"Mom, have you ever wondered why you're so hell-bent on making me lose weight?"

"Well, darling, it stems from my own experience, of course. I don't want you to go through what I did."

"Tell me about what happened to you."

"Your father left me because of my weight," Angela said on a hiccup of emotion. "He told me all through my pregnancy that I was packing on the beef, and afterward he was disgusted when I couldn't immediately shed my pregnancy weight. He went looking elsewhere because I wasn't what I used to be before I had you. If I'd only snapped back into shape, he would never have strayed. If he could see me now he'd—"

"Seriously? You really believe that? Mom, he was a serial philanderer. He cheated on the woman he left you for and no doubt he cheated on the next woman, too. He left you emotionally long before he left our house. You raised me on your own. He never supported us. You did everything. You held down a full-time job, you made us a beautiful home, you supported me through college so I wouldn't need any loans. You did all that by yourself, and you think the most important thing about you is your size? Take it from me, size has nothing to do with who you are. What matters is your heart and your determination and your intelligence."

"You think so?"

"I know so. Look, I love you, Mom, but you really need to learn to love yourself, too, and you need to stop punishing yourself for Dad leaving all those years ago. *He* was the problem. Never you. Now come here and give me a hug."

Georgia put her glass down and held her arms open to her mom, who was freely crying now. Georgia couldn't remember a single time in her life when she'd seen her mom cry. She'd always been stoic and focused, but never truly happy either. Hopefully that could change going forward. For herself, she was glad they'd cleared the air. She knew change wouldn't happen overnight. You didn't change a pattern of behavior or a mode of thinking that you'd lived with for thirty years without a lot of hard work, and that applied equally to both her mom and herself. But she knew she was ready for change, and they could help each other through this. After all, neither of them had anyone else right now, did they?

Sawyer watched as his grandmother slid cookies off the baking sheet and onto an airing rack, and he immediately reached to grab one, only to earn a slap on the back of his hand.

"Wait for them to cool, Sawyer. Honestly, you never change, do you? Always in a hurry. You know the flavor is best when they're cooler."

"Yes, Grandma," he said with a quick grin, then as soon as her back was turned, grabbed a cookie.

"I can see you, y'know."

His mouth was too full of hot cookie goodness to reply. He hadn't tasted anything this good since— hell, since Georgia had baked at the cabin. And there it was again. This powerful sense that he was missing something very important. He'd been here with his grandma for a couple of days now and he knew he was going to have to leave soon. Why had leaving all of a sudden become so hard? Was it because his grandmother was showing signs of her age more clearly than ever this visit—moving just that little bit slower, her hands a little less deft when it came to decorating her famous cakes for the local church bake sale?

"I can hear you thinking, young man. C'mon, give it up. What's bothering you?"

His grandmother poured them each a cup of coffee and they sat at the kitchen table, where he'd sat with her for so many meals together after his mom died. She'd been a stickler for family time at meals with no TV, radio or other devices. He appreciated that now more than he ever did back then.

"I met a girl," he stated simply.

"She must be pretty special if she's still on your mind."

"Yeah, she's special. But I don't want to hurt her."

"Why would you hurt her?"

He took a sip of his coffee, savoring the dark brew and relishing the heat on his tongue. "Because when I leave to do a job, I don't always know when I'll be back." *Or if I'll be back.*

The words hung silently in the air between them. His grandmother sighed.

"That's a tough choice, Sawyer. Do you continue to isolate yourself from friendships and potential relationships for the rest of your life because of what might happen, or do you entrust it to the universe and see what happens?"

"We both know what might happen, though, right?"

She nodded quietly and sighed again. "Sawyer, you never chose your profession, it definitely chose you. I could see it the day your grandfather showed you how to use a camera. Do you remember that?"

He smiled and nodded.

She continued. "And I understand your compulsion to expose the atrocities in our world. It's all too easy for us to simply live our lives in our neat little corners and have no depth of understanding of what is happening. You bring the truth to people, and you've done that for a long time now."

He could see where she was heading with this. "You think it's time I gave up?"

She shook her head. "No, I never said that. I know you've always felt like you had a strong purpose, and you've shown incredible empathy and talent while you've worked. I've always been proud of you, Sawyer, and your dad is, too, although I know he hasn't always shown it."

No, his dad had pretty much never shown it. Ever since remarrying, his dad had made it clear that he had little time for Sawyer in his life—but the truth was, even prior to that, he'd never felt like a priority. His parents had both been focused on their careers first. Their relationship with each other came second, and their relationship with their son was a distant third.

"I know, Grandma," he lied, not wanting to upset her by sharing his real opinion. "And I appreciate it."

"But as proud as I am, I still worry about you," she continued. "Are you content?"

"Is anyone, ever?" he hedged. "I've seen so much and I can't say at any time that the people around me have been content. Determined and focused as they fought for their lives or their livelihood, yes. Committed to defending their country and everything it stands for. But content?" He shook his head. "I'm not sure I know what that feels like, or even looks like."

But as he said the words, he thought back to his time with Georgia. To the evenings when they'd sat together on the couch while she read and he watched the flames in the fireplace and played with her hair. Or the mornings when they'd wake and not move and just be still, in the moment together. It had felt different from anything he'd known before. Would it be the same for them out in the real world? Or was their time together merely an aberration? A contrast to the world he'd worked in for so long?

Was he burned out? The thought terrified him. If he wasn't representing the people affected by atrocities across the world, who and what was he? His entire identity was wrapped up in what he did. Something heavy and unpleasant settled in his stomach as he realized how much that sounded like his father.

"Tell me about this girl you met," his grandmother prompted him. "What's she like?"

"She's…" Sawyer let his voice drift off, suddenly reluctant to talk about Georgia because doing so might dissolve the carefully stored memories he had locked deep inside him.

He went on to describe her physical appearance, earning a snort of disdain from his grandmother.

"I asked you what she's like, not what she looks like, Sawyer. How did you meet her?"

He laughed. "She turned up at the cabin in a rain-soaked wedding dress and ended up stranded there."

"And you were friendly and accommodating to this damsel in distress?"

He had the grace to look shamefaced.

His grandmother snorted again. "I might have known you'd have been unwelcoming. But she stayed."

"Pretty much for my whole time there. You'd like her. She bakes her bread from scratch like you do— taught me how to do it, too."

"Takes more than that to win me over, but I can see she made an impact on you. Tell me more."

Sawyer described how the first time he felt like

taking a picture again had come when he'd caught her sleeping outside in the sunshine and how she'd gone on hikes with him, introducing him to a whole new world out there. Showing him things he hadn't noticed on his earlier solo treks in the area.

"Sounds like she made you stop and look around. That's a good thing. And she got you baking bread, you say?"

"She did. I get it now, why you enjoy it so much. It's cathartic."

"Show me some of the photos you took," his grandmother said.

Sawyer got his laptop and set it up on the table, flicking through the pictures of the mushrooms and the creeks and rivers and some of the animals and insects he'd photographed. Then the screen filled with a picture of Georgia. It was the first one he'd taken of her while she slept. His heart leapt at the sight of her.

It had been less than a week since they'd parted and he missed her with a physical ache—a hollowness that had taken up residence deep in his chest.

"She's beautiful. How lucky were you that she happened upon you. And she'd run away from her wedding, you say? Brave girl."

"She's incredibly brave, and strong and gentle. I'll admit I was none too pleased to have company at the beginning. But I got over that."

He explained about Georgia's lists and rosters, earning a blast of laughter from his grandma.

"I'd have loved to meet her," his grandma said before stiffly getting up from the table and making up two plates of the cookies she'd baked. "So, Sawyer, what are you going to do? Head back to Europe or somewhere else this time? Africa maybe?"

The thought of going to either of those places held little appeal. Maybe it was losing Max, maybe it was the severity of the injuries he'd received, but the thrill of the job had dulled for him. Sure, he could forge out there again, take on a new assignment and see what came next, but he suddenly realized his heart wasn't in that anymore. In fact, his heart was somewhere north of Seattle with a certain redhead.

"I think I love her, Grandma."

"I think so, too," she said softly as she passed him one of the plates of cookies before covering the other and picking it up. "I'm off to my card game. Looks like you have some thinking to do."

After she'd gone, Sawyer sat at the table, staring at the photo of Georgia on his computer screen and mindlessly working his way through the cookies on the plate. He hated this sense of uncertainty in his life. He'd never been that guy who hesitated over anything. He saw what he wanted and he went for it, whether it was an assignment or a casual fling. It kept life simple—but if there was one thing about Georgia, it was that she wasn't simple at all. No, she was complex and nuanced in the extreme. And that was one of the things he really liked about her. Ha, who was he kidding, he *loved* that about her.

But he wasn't prepared to make any promises of forever, to anyone, and Georgia had "forever" written over every line of her delectable body. His line of work didn't allow for that.

What if he didn't return to his regular line of work? Sure, he'd made great money and earned several prestigious awards, but that had never been what was important to him. Somewhere, deep inside, he'd always craved more, had never felt entirely fulfilled no matter how hard or how long he pushed himself. And, thinking about it, the only time he'd found that elusive contentment his grandmother had spoken about had been during his time with Georgia.

He had to see her—to talk with her and see where this could go. Finally, he was prepared to walk away from what had been the major focus of his life. It was past time to invest himself in something new. Almost losing his life had been a serious wake-up call. One he'd probably needed for a long time, as his assignments had become more and more dangerous. He'd gotten into such a rut that he hadn't realized how necessary a change was for him. But now he knew that it was time to look to his future, rather than just tomorrow. And maybe, just maybe, that new future could be with Georgia.

He had to track her down somehow. How hard could it be? After all, how many wedding planners were runaway brides? There had to be something online about her. And if worse came to worst, he'd appeal to the sensibilities of the cabin's property manager, or say Georgia had left something behind that he wanted, no *needed*, to personally return to her.

Feeling better than he had since he'd watched

her drive away, Sawyer started making a list, stopping for a moment to laugh at himself for doing the very thing that Georgia had always done that had driven him crazy those first few days she was at the cabin. Seems she'd rubbed off on him more than he thought—and he didn't mind it one bit.

Thirteen

Georgia set down her phone and thought about what she'd just been offered.

"They want you back, don't they?" her mom asked from the kitchen where she was trying out a new sauce recipe to go with poached fish.

Adding a sauce was a small step toward not caring so much about every calorie that went into her body, and Georgia was pleased and relieved to see it. She appreciated that it was going to take her mom a while to relax the stringent controls she'd kept on herself for so long, but they'd found a counselor her mom was comfortable with and even attended a few sessions together already, which was a great leap in the right direction as far as Georgia was concerned— for them both. They'd come a long way in the two weeks since she'd returned home. She looked up at her mom with a smile.

"Yes, they do," she said.

"Are you going to take it?" Angela asked, turning off the burner and taking the pot off the stove before grabbing a teaspoon to taste the sauce with. "Oh, this is heavenly. Grab a spoon and try it," she urged.

Georgia did as she was told and agreed, yes, the flavor was definitely wonderful. Somehow, she'd managed to imbue in her mom her own love of cooking. Or maybe it had been there all along, just latently sitting beneath the surface of her mom's insecurities.

"No, I'm not," she said firmly.

"Not even tempted?"

"No. It's not really where I see myself. I think I want to travel a bit before I fix on one thing again."

"That's good. Travel broadens the mind, or so they say. I wouldn't know. Aside from the occasional break in Hawaii, I've never really been anywhere," Angela said ruefully.

"Maybe we should plan a trip together. Somewhere exotic, like Cambodia, or even somewhere steeped in history, like Italy. Maybe we could do a cooking tour."

"That sounds like fun. Let's think about it and do some research," Angela said brightly.

"Excellent. That'll be fun to do together."

Her mom patted her on the hand and said, "I'm off to the store. Is there anything you need?"

"No, I'm all good for now."

"I'll see you later then."

Georgia smiled. It was cool to think she and her

mom could plan a big trip together. They'd have a ball, she was sure, wherever they decided to go. But thinking about travel made her wonder anew about Sawyer. She missed him more every single day they were apart. She kept telling herself she wasn't ready to let herself go into something new with someone. She was still recovering from her failed attempt at getting married, and she didn't have the head or heart space to devote to getting to know someone and seeing how their lives could mesh. It would take time before she was ready to trust anyone again, too.

She sighed heavily. Oh, who the hell did she think she was fooling? Certainly not herself. She hadn't been ready for someone new, but it hadn't stopped her from falling for Sawyer, had it? She cared for him, deep down to her soul. It was the greatest pity that they'd met each other when neither of them was up for a commitment. They'd been incredible together. His company had been easy and fun, once he'd gotten over his initial irritation at having to share the cabin, and the sex had been out of this world.

Georgia went up to her room and stood in front of her full-length mirror. It was something she'd always avoided, but now she felt comfortable looking at herself and she could admire how she looked. Yes, she'd always preferred strong colors that highlighted her skin and hair, but in the past the necklines were high and the hemlines low, and heaven forbid she show her upper arms. But she'd bought some new things recently, having donated a lot of what she'd bought for her new life in Rarotonga to a nearby thrift store, and when she wore her new things, she felt fantastic. She was present and proud of herself. No more hiding, no more compromising. Georgia O'Connor had arrived.

She giggled. She'd never felt this good about herself, ever. And while this journey was her own, she knew deep down that Sawyer's utter acceptance of who she was and how she looked had been an important part of that. She had a lot to be grateful to him for, and she only hoped that her being with him had helped him in some ways, too.

Georgia stepped back from the mirror with a quiet nod to herself for being all right. Actually, better than all right. The distant sound of the doorbell came unexpectedly. She and her mom weren't expecting visitors or any deliveries. She hurried down to the front door and peeked through the peephole.

Sawyer stood on her front doorstep. Her heart immediately kicked up double time and her legs turned to jelly. What on earth was he doing here? The logical side of her brain told her to open the door and find out, but the frightened Georgia, the one she thought she'd banished, poked her hard in the chest and reminded her how difficult it had been to say goodbye to him last time. Could she do it again?

Sawyer shifted and stared at the front door, oblivious to the battle going on in Georgia's mind. If she opened the door, how would she greet him? Would she invite him in? Would they kiss, shake hands, do neither of those things? She was in an agony of indecision until she saw Sawyer's expression change and he turned to walk away. In that brief moment, she'd seen his face go from expectant to regretful.

Before she had time to outthink herself again, she reached for the doorknob and opened the door wide.

"Sawyer!"

"You're home," he said, turning back to her, that expectant light back in his eyes.

"I'm sorry I took so long."

"I was beginning to wonder if you didn't want to see me or if you just weren't there."

"Please, come in," Georgia said, avoiding explaining her delay.

He stepped over the threshold and she was hard-pressed not to lean in and just smell him. He hadn't worn cologne at the cabin and they'd used the same soaps and shampoos, but there'd been something about his intrinsic scent that fired all her receptors. He stood awkwardly in front of her as she stood, equally awkwardly, still holding the door open.

Georgia forced herself to move and closed the door before gesturing to him to precede her into the living room.

"Can I get you a drink or anything?"

"Sure, a glass of water would be good, or a cold soda."

"I'll be right back. Take a seat."

She hurried into the kitchen, where she forced herself to take three long, deep breaths before she did anything else. He was here. In her house. Waiting in her living room. And here she was about as nervous as a naive girl waiting to go to her first prom. But she wasn't naive, she told herself. She knew this man intimately, even though, on balance, she didn't really know many of the facts about him and his life. But she knew his heart, she reminded herself. She knew the kind of man he was deep down. *Get the darn drinks*, her logical mind told her, so she aimed to do just that.

As she carried to the living room the tray with their glasses, two cans of soda and a plate of sliced brownies that she'd baked this morning, she forced a smile on her face.

"I wasn't expecting to see you again. What brings you here, Sawyer?" she asked as she set the tray down on the table.

"You," he said bluntly.

He looked up at her, ignoring the glass she offered and the plate with fresh, gooey, chocolatey brownies.

"Me? Seriously? Did I leave something behind at the cabin?"

"You could say that," he said with that captivating, crooked smile of his.

"I haven't missed anything," she said, furrowing her brow as she tried to imagine what she could have forgotten.

"Not even me?" he asked.

Her body tightened on a rush of awareness. She took another one of those deep breaths before answering.

"Yes, I have missed you." *More than you will ever know.* "But we agreed, didn't we? No long-term commitments and all that."

There, she'd handled that beautifully, and she silently congratulated herself on it. Her heart might have leapt at his arrival, but she wasn't going to make a fool of herself or rush into making the same types of mistakes she'd always made with men by being too eager and, yes, sometimes pathetically grateful for the attention they offered her. She still wanted to be proud of herself every day, without relying on someone else to make her feel that way.

"I missed you, too. From the moment you closed your car door and drove away, to be honest."

She blinked and blinked again. Was she imagining what he'd just said? Had he been suffering as much as she had? Had his body ached at night for her touch the way hers had for his? Did he ache to touch her now?

Sawyer watched her face for any clue as to how she was feeling but, for once, Georgia was a closed book. Had he misread what they'd had? Was she happily moving on from their stay in the cabin? The only thing he could be certain of was that he'd never find out any of that without laying his cards on the table. All of them, including why he'd been at the cabin in the first place.

"I didn't want you to go, Georgia. If we could have stayed there together, forever, that would have been fine with me," he said quietly.

Her eyes flicked to his, before darting away. "That would have been hiding, though. For both of us."

"Yeah, it would have. I was never reluctant to be an active participant in the outside world, whatever it held, but I do know that I don't want to go back to what I was doing before."

"What do you mean? No more photography?"

She looked worried, so he hastened to put her mind at rest. "Not that. I don't think I could ever give up my cameras. But no more covering violent conflicts. It's important, valuable work—but I've put in my time, and it's not what's right for me anymore. I was lucky to get out alive the last time. I'm not tempting fate again."

"That's a big decision to make, Sawyer. I looked you up on the internet. You're a big deal out there."

"You're only a big deal for as long as you deliver. I don't want to deliver that stuff anymore. I'm ready for a change."

Georgia nodded. "I can understand that. I read a little online about you being injured. There wasn't a lot of detail, but I'm not blind, I've seen your scars."

And traced them with her fingertips and tongue, silently willing him to heal both physically and emotionally from what he'd been through.

"Yeah, about that. I need to tell you what happened. All of it." He paused and rubbed his eyes with one hand.

"Go ahead. I'm listening."

"Do you remember when you saw that picture of my friend on my computer?"

"Of course. You said his name was Max, right? You worked together, didn't you?"

"Not exactly. He and I were fiercely competitive and generally took assignments for rival news agencies when we weren't freelancing. That particular trip, we'd been more competitive than usual. Taking more risks to get that money shot. We'd both lost sight of why we were bringing those photos to the world. It had become a game instead, to keep cheating death, I guess."

"You do what you have to do to get through these situations, I'm sure," Georgia said softly.

"That's kind of you, and I can't say you're wrong— when you see that much death and destruction, you have to find coping mechanisms to get you through the day. But we picked the wrong one. In truth, it made us careless. That particular day we'd been playing our usual games of one-upmanship, even though we knew the area we were in was dangerous. Both of us were high on adrenaline. We'd taken shelter in a bombed-out home. There were no windows left, no doors. We were tucked inside, against an outer wall, when the shooting started. Max knew that was his moment. He was closer to where the front door had been than I was and he stepped toward it, giving me a grin as he did so, letting me know in no uncertain terms that this was going to be the picture that beat everything we'd done in that shitty war until that moment.

"He was still grinning at me when he got hit by an RPG. He never knew what struck him. One second he was there, the next he wasn't. I was injured in the explosion. I was lucky to be shipped out quickly to a hospital on the border, away from the fighting. There, I was patched together and transferred to another hospital in Germany. Eventually I caught a plane home to see my grandma. She was waiting for me at the airport. I'll never forget the look on her face when she saw me come through from the arrivals gate. I'd never considered the toll my job was taking on her until that moment. It was a harsh wake-up call."

"But she never asked you to stop, right?"

"And she never would. To tell you the truth, I had never stopped to consider the toll it was taking on me, as well. I think I knew then and there that I couldn't go back. Coming to terms with it was entirely another thing." He laughed and it was a dry, rusty sound. "You helped me with that."

"I did?" Georgia looked startled.

"Yeah, you made me see that there's so much more to life and living it, really living it and sharing it with another person."

"Well, glad to be of help," she said with an attempt at humor that didn't quite make the mark.

A silence fell between them, but it wasn't like the comfortable companionable silences they'd shared at the cabin. This one was different, fraught with all the things he hadn't said yet because he was afraid of what her answer would be. He might not be staring down the muzzle of a grenade launcher right now, but he was just as apprehensive.

Georgia began to speak before he could continue. "Sawyer, you helped me, too. You made me see myself through your eyes, and y'know, I really like what I saw. I still do. I know I'll never settle for anything less than the best for me now. I thought that I was confident in myself and what I had to offer, but after Cliff and what he did, well, it brought back a lot of old fears. My dad was unfaithful to my mom, and it's a real trigger for me. I never imagined that I would face the same thing and especially not on my wedding day. It rocked my confidence big time. Being with you at the cabin was probably the best thing that's ever happened to me. We were stuck there, but I never felt so free in my whole life."

"You're beautiful, you know that?" Sawyer said softly. He ached to reach out and touch her but he didn't know if he had the right anymore. Still, he consoled himself, she wasn't kicking him out the door so there was hope. "I know what you mean about the freedom. It was great, wasn't it?"

"Yeah, but it had to come to an end."

And here was his opportunity. Sawyer grabbed it with both hands.

"It doesn't have to if we don't want it to. I know I don't, do you?"

He heard her sharply drawn in breath and waited for her to respond.

"Sawyer, I'm not sure what you mean. We couldn't stay at the cabin forever. That was just a moment in time."

His heart almost shuddered to a halt in his chest, but he wasn't going to give up. They were worth fighting for.

"No, I don't just mean at the cabin. I mean us. Together. A couple."

She didn't look appalled at the idea, but she didn't

look convinced either. Mostly, she looked confused. "But how would that work? You spend more than half your life overseas. I'm here." She shook her head. "I won't settle for half a relationship."

He was proud of her for sticking to her guns and frustrated all at the same time.

"Like I said, I'm not going back to the work I did before. I can't. I'm done. I wanted my work to mean something, and it did. But I know I can still do great work and have it mean something to people without risking my life for it. And I don't want to risk my life anymore. I want to spend my life with you, if you'll have me.

"We would be incredible together, Georgia. I wouldn't stop you in your career. I know you're great at it—I did a little online snooping as well and your online reviews are all five star—it's clearly something you love to do. But why confine yourself to just one venue? Why not broker your services on a global level? Create signature weddings for brides and grooms anywhere in the world they want to be married. Hell, we could be a package deal, planner and photographer. What do you say?"

He could tell she was intrigued and excited by the suggestion by the way she was leaning forward as he spoke and from the light of interest in her beautiful eyes, but she wasn't rushing into accepting his suggestion.

"It would be a huge change for you. Tame by comparison to what you've done. I'm worried you'd get bored. Are you really ready to give up the danger and the thrill of what you used to do?"

He reached for her hands and held them as he looked deep into her eyes. "I am. I'd begun to lose my taste for it before the incident that took Max. Losing him cemented it for me. I don't want to go back to being callous and taking stupid risks anymore. I want to return to taking pictures I care about, and I don't think I can still do that in war zones. I'm not that man anymore and I'm good with that. In fact, I'm better than good with it, because letting it go means opening up my life to the idea of having something more—the kind of life I never let myself have before. I love you and I want a future with you. I reckon that you and me together will create more than enough adventure for both of us."

He leaned forward then and kissed her, hoping that it might help him seal the deal. Her lips were as soft and lush as he remembered and the taste of her as exquisite. When they broke apart there was a bittersweet feeling about it, and Sawyer began to worry that things weren't going to turn out the way he'd hoped for after all.

At the cabin he'd always been able to read her like an open book, but right now, her expression was closed. He didn't like it, but he respected her enough not to push. If she didn't want to enter into this with him, heart and soul, then he certainly wasn't going to force her even though he was already formulating arguments in his head about why this would be an excellent move for them both.

"I can see you need time. I threw a lot on the table here, didn't I? Look, I'll leave you my number and you can call me when you're ready to talk about it, okay? I'm not going anywhere." *For now, at least.*

Sawyer rose and made his way to the front door. He'd done his best. Now it was up to him to wait and see if Georgia was willing to take that next step with him. He had the door open and was ready to head out when he heard her behind him.

"Sawyer, wait."

He turned to face her.

"I wanted to say thank you for coming."

She stopped abruptly, and he waited for what felt like an eternity before she spoke again.

"Not just that, but I need to tell you something. That new confidence in myself I was telling you about earlier…it comes from not letting other people affect my choices or my happiness. If I'm to live my best life, I know I need to be prepared to take risks… and if loving you is a risk, then that's one I'm prepared to take. I've thought about what you said just now and I love your idea. Even more, I love you, too, so very much. You're right—together we can have the best adventure. A future together."

At first Sawyer couldn't quite believe her words. They were everything he'd been hoping to hear, and it seemed too good to be true. But it only took a second before he closed the distance between them and wrapped her in his arms.

"I promise you will never regret it," he said before tilting her face up to his and kissing her soundly.

A sound behind them made them spring apart. Angela stood in the doorway with grocery bags.

"So this is Sawyer, I take it?"

"I am, ma'am. Can I take those bags for you?"

Angela handed them over to him wordlessly and looked at Georgia with a wry expression.

"I guess this means no cooking lessons in Italy or Cambodia?"

Georgia laughed. "I don't see why not."

"I'm not going to be a third wheel," Angela said with a big grin. "So, this is it? The real thing this time?"

"Yeah, Mom, this is the real thing."

"Then be happy, my darling. I love you."

"I love you, too."

Sawyer watched from behind them as the women embraced. His heart was full. He knew things had been tough sometimes between Georgia and her mom and it was great to see that they'd resolved that between them, due in no small part, he was sure, to Georgia's newly claimed confidence.

"So, when do we start planning the wedding?" Angela asked, arching a brow at Sawyer.

"Mom, we haven't even discussed going that far!" Georgia exclaimed in shock.

"I was thinking a quick elopement with a honeymoon at the cabin," Sawyer suggested.

"Are you asking me to marry you?" Georgia asked, her cheeks flushing with joy.

"I believe I am." Sawyer set down the grocery bags and reached for Georgia's hands once more. "Would you do me the honor of being my wife?"

"I most definitely will," she answered without hesitation.

"Good," said Angela, brushing past them. "Now let's go make dinner, I'm starving."

Sawyer laughed as he picked up the groceries again and followed mother and daughter to the kitchen. Everything was going to be all right and for the first time that he could remember, he was completely and truly happy.

* * * * *

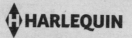

HARLEQUIN

Dear Readers,

From the 1982 launch of *Silhouette Desire* to this month's final lineup, readers have turned to *Harlequin Desire*, where our sexy and successful alpha heroes have had hearts of gold, and our strong, independent heroines have been their equals. Now, after thousands of romances that have made us laugh, cry and swoon, Harlequin Desire's story is coming to an end.

We thank you, readers, for coming back to Desire month after month. For choosing your favorite authors and asking for more of their novels. If you're a fan of Brenda Jackson, you can look for her upcoming Harlequin books in the *Canary Street Press* imprint and in *Harlequin Special Edition*. If it's Maisey Yates's Western romances you crave, her books will also be available in *Harlequin Special Edition*. You can find backlist and new releases from all of Desire's talented authors by visiting their author pages on Harlequin.com.

And, if like most romance readers I know, you're always wanting more great reads, we'd like to introduce *Afterglow Books by Harlequin*, which launches at the end of January 2024 with stories from some of your favorite Desire authors as well as exciting new voices. These sexy, sizzling romances follow characters from all walks of life as they chase their dreams and discover that love is only the beginning. In early 2024, *Afterglow Books by Harlequin* will be available at a retailer near you.

Our readers and authors are at the heart of what we do, and we so appreciate your decades of support for Desire. We hope you'll join us as we begin a new chapter with *Afterglow Books by Harlequin*.

Sincerely,

Stacy Boyd
Senior Editor
Harlequin Desire